The Jewel of Medina

◆

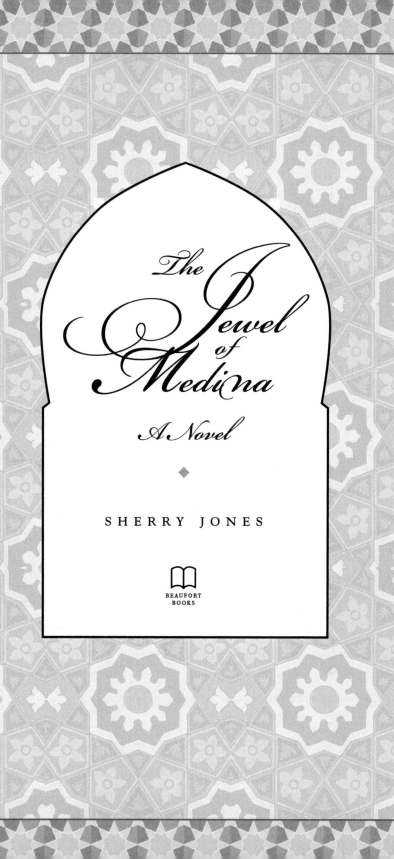

The Jewel of Medina

A Novel

◆

S H E R R Y   J O N E S

BEAUFORT
BOOKS

COVER IMAGE: The Queen of the Harem (oil on canvas) by Max Ferdinand Bredt (1868–1921) used with permission of the Bridgeman Art Library

MAP: Kat Bennett, 360Geographics
Library of Congress Cataloging-in-Publication Data

Jones, Sherry, 1961–
   The jewel of Medina : a novel / Sherry Jones.
      p. cm.
   ISBN-13: 978-0-8253-0518-4 (alk. paper)
   ISBN-10: 0-8253-0518-7 (alk. paper)
   1. 'A'ishah, ca. 614-678—Fiction. 2. Muhammad, Prophet, d.
632—Marriage—Fiction. 3. Muhammad, Prophet, d. 632—Relations
with women—Fiction. 4. Muslims—History—Fiction. 5. Islam—
History—Fiction. I. Title.
   PS3610.O6285J48 2008
   813'.6—dc22   2008039823

Published in the United States by Beaufort Books, New York
www.beaufortbooks.com

Distributed by Midpoint Trade Books, New York
www.midpointtrade.com

Printed in the United States of America

10 9 8 7 6 5 4 3 2 1

For my mother,
who taught me to reach for the stars,
and for Mariah,
the brightest star in my sky.

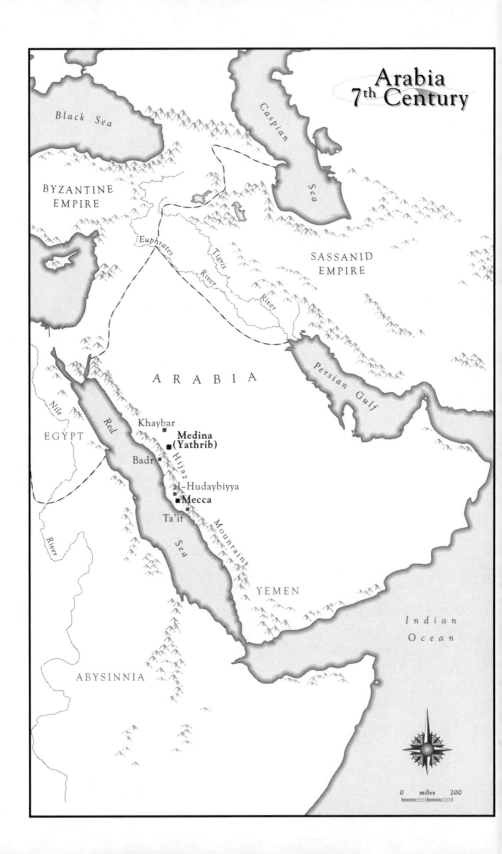

Arabia
7th Century

Black Sea

Caspian
Sea

BYZANTINE
EMPIRE

SASSANID
EMPIRE

Euphrates

Tigris

River

River

ARABIA

Persian Gulf

Nile

Red

EGYPT

Khaybar

Medina
(Yathrib)

Badr

Hijaz

al-Hudaybiyya

Mecca

Ta'if

Sea

Mountains

YEMEN

Indian
Ocean

River

ABYSINNIA

0   miles   200

Author's Note

◆

*J*oin me on a journey to another time and place, to a harsh, exotic world of saffron and sword fights, of desert nomads living in camel's-hair tents, of caravans laden with Persian carpets and frankincense, of flowing colorful robes and kohl-darkened eyes and perfumed arms filigreed with henna. We are in seventh-century Hijaz, in western Saudi Arabia, not far from the coast of the Red Sea, a vast desert dotted with lush oases where bedouin raiders fight for survival and women have few rights, and a religion destined to be one of the greatest in the world has sprung from the lips of a man regarded, until he reached the age of forty, as unremarkable.

This was A'isha bint Abi Bakr's world. When she was born, in 613 A.D., women were regarded as chattel, the property of men, so worthless they might be buried alive at birth if there were too many girls born that year. When A'isha became engaged, at age six, she was confined to her parents' home, forbidden to run and play outside or to even speak to boys. Yet she grew up to be a strong, powerful woman: an outspoken, red-haired beauty with a quick wit and a shrewd mind; an influential political advisor; a warrior; a religious scholar; and, in one of the most touching love stories ever recorded, the favorite wife of the Prophet Muhammad.

According to numerous accounts, A'isha married Muhammad, the revealer of Islam, when she was nine years old. They consummated the marriage later, when she had begin her menstrual cycle. Although her tender age may seem shocking to us now, scholars generally agree that the marriage was motivated by politics. A'isha's father, Abu Bakr, supposedly hurried the wedding to establish his position as chief Companion to the Prophet. As for Muhammad, he doted on A'isha, playing dolls with her when she was young, and, as she matured, turning to her for political advice.

Yet their marriage had its difficulties. Wife and husband were both willful, dynamic, complex individuals. Having known Muhammad all her life, A'isha was extremely jealous of the other wives and concubines—a total of twelve—whom he brought into the harem. A consummate mischief-maker, A'isha played pranks on her sister-wives and on Muhammad, hoping to thwart romance between him and any of them. At times, her ploys succeeded—splendidly and to her husband's great displeasure.

Outside stress took its toll on their marriage, as well. As the leader of a growing community of Believers, Muhammad had to contend with a steady stream of rumors regarding his wives. (At fourteen, A'isha was embroiled in a devastating scandal that nearly ended her marriage.) But there were other problems, too. The powerful Meccan tribe of Quraysh— Muhammad's kinsmen—hated Muhammad's message of one God, and attacked him and his followers viciously and relentlessly. There was no quelching the Prophet of God, though. The angel Gabriel had told him to "Recite!" and Muhammad was bound to obey.

Islam came to Muhammad in a vision on Mecca's Mount Hira around 610. His family members, including his wife, Khadija, with whom he had a monogamous marriage for twenty-five years, and his cousin, Ali, whom he raised, were the first to believe in Muhammad's message of one God. Others were less enthusiastic. Mecca was the idol-worshipping capital of the Arab world. Hundreds of gods filled the Ka'ba, the cube-shaped shrine in the city's center, and they attracted caravans coming from near and far to worship and trade. In the eyes of the Qurayshi merchants, this new religion meant economic disaster. It—and its prophet—had to go.

After years of persecuting the Muslims, Mecca's leaders finally sent their sons to assassinate Muhammad. He escaped, with the help of Ali and Abu Bakr, and joined the rest of the *umma* (the community of Believers) in Medina, an oasis town some 250 miles to the north. There, members of the city's Arabic tribes, the Aws and Khazraj, had offered to house and protect the Muslims. Yet life was dangerous in Medina, too. The Quraysh continued to attack, enlisting the help of the *umma's* new neighbors. Particularly threatening were three Jewish tribes, the Kaynuqah, Bani Nadr, and Qurayzah. The fact that Muhammad worshipped their God wasn't enough to win their loyalty. Not only did they mock his claim to be a prophet foretold in their religious texts—would God choose an Arab for that honor?—but these tribes were trading partners with the Meccan Quraysh.

Against this backdrop of scandal, danger, and oppression, A'isha grew up with, married, and loved Muhammad. According to most sources, he adored her, indulging her outspokenness and soliciting her advice on various matters. Her role in the *umma's* battles seems to have been limited to carrying water and bandaging wounds, but other women, such as Umm 'Umara, did fight alongside the men in Islam's early years.

So little is known about Muhammad's wives, and even that is disputed. History, like genealogies and poetry, was transmitted by word of mouth, not written down until hundreds of years after Muhammad died. Almost everything is open to debate, it seems, from A'isha's age at consummation to Muhammad's attitude toward her. Was she his favorite wife, as the Sunnis claim, or did he dislike her because of her disobedience, as one Shiite man insisted to me?

Whatever your opinion of A'isha, she remains larger than life, an unforgettable heroine who spoke her mind, followed her heart, loved her God, and won a place in her community and in history as the Mother of the Believers. For me, she is a role model, a consummate survivor who overcame enormous cultural and personal obstacles to make her mark on the world.

Muhammad died at age sixty-two with his head upon A'isha's breast (Shiite accounts say he died in Ali's arms). At nineteen, A'isha was just beginning her life and her work. A champion of her family's interests as well as Muhammad's legacy, A'isha went on to advise the next three caliphs succeeding the Prophet and, ultimately, to lead troops against Ali in the Battle of the Camel, the first Islamic civil war. But that's another story . . .

The Jewel of Medina
of

Prologue

◆

A SINGLE POINTING FINGER

*S*candal blew in on the errant wind when I rode into Medina clutching Safwan's waist. My neighbors rushed into the street like storm waters flooding a *wadi*. Children stood in clusters to point and gawk. Their mothers snatched them to their skirts and pretended to avert their eyes. Men spat in the dust and muttered, judging. My father's mouth trembled like a tear on the brink.

What they saw: my wrapper fallen to my shoulders, unheeded. Loose hair lashing my face. The wife of God's Prophet entwined around another man. What they couldn't see: my girlhood dreams shattered at my feet, trampled by a truth as hard and blunt as horses' hooves.

I let my eyelids fall shut, avoiding my reflection in the stares of my *umma*, my community. I licked my cracked lips, tasting salt and the tang of my wretchedness. Pain wrung my stomach like strong hands squeezing water from laundry, only I was already dry. My tongue lolled like a sun-baked lizard. I rested my cheek against Safwan's shoulder, but the horse's trot struck bone against bone.

"*Al-zaniya!*" someone cried. "Adulteress!"

I made slits with my eyes. Members of our *umma* either pointed fingers and shouted at me or spread their arms in welcome. I saw others, Hypocrites, jeering and showing their dirty teeth. The *ansari*, our Helpers, stood silent and wary. Thousands lined the street, sucking in our dust with their sharp breaths. Staring as though I were a caravan glittering with treasure instead of a sunburned fourteen-year-old girl.

The horse stopped, but I continued—over its flank, headfirst and into the arms of Muhammad. Into my husband's control once more and sighing with relief. Trying to forge my own destiny had nearly destroyed me, but his love held the power to heal. His thick beard cushioned my cheek, caressed me with sandalwood. *Miswak* unfurled from his breath, clean and sharp as a kiss.

"Thank al-Lah you have made it home safely, my A'isha," he murmured.

The gathering crowd rumbled, prickling my spine. I lifted my heavy head to see. Umar rolled in, thunder and scowl. He was Muhammad's advisor and friend, but no friend to women.

"Where, by al-Lah, have you been? Why were you alone with a man who is not your husband?"

His accusations whipped like the wind through the crowd, fanning sparks into flames.

"*Al-zaniya!*" someone cried again. I ducked as if the word were a hurled stone.

"It is no wonder that A'isha rhymes with *fahisha*—whore!" People laughed, and soon they began to chant: "A'isha—*fahisha!* A'isha—*fahisha!*" Muhammad steered me through the crush toward the mosque entrance. As if in a mosaic their faces swirled before me: the jowly Hamal and his pale wife Fazia-turned-Jamila, screaming and plum-colored; the town gossip, Umm Ayman, pursing her wrinkled lips; Abu Ramzi, the jeweler, flashing golden rings on his waving fists. I'd expected murmurs when I returned, and lifted eyebrows—but this? People who had known me all my life now wanted to tear me apart. And Safwan—I turned my head to look for him, but he had disappeared. As always.

Rude fingers yanked my hair. I cried out and slapped them away, and a stream of spittle landed on my arm. Muhammad set me on my feet and faced the mob, then raised his hands into the air. Silence fell like a shroud, muffling even the glares.

"A'isha needs to rest," Muhammad said. His voice sounded as weary as I felt. "Please return to your homes."

He curled his arm around me and we ducked into the mosque. My sister-wives stood near the courtyard entrance, two and two. Sawdah rushed forward, ululating, enfolding me in her plumpness. She praised al-Lah for my safe return, then kissed her amulet to ward off the Evil Eye. Next came Hafsa, weeping, kissing my hands and face. She whispered, "I thought you were lost forever." I didn't tell her that she was nearly right. Umm Salama nodded, unsmiling, as if she feared her head might topple off her long stem of a neck. Zaynab slanted lusty eyes at Muhammad as though she and he were alone in the room.

But my husband's concerns were only for me. When my stomach clenched again, slumping me in pain, he caught me and lifted me up as though I were filled with air. And in truth, I had little else left inside me. I floated in his arms to my apartment. He kicked open the door and carried me inside, then placed me on my feet again while he unrolled my bed. I leaned against the wall, grateful for the quiet—until Umar's shout barged into the room, followed by the man himself.

"See how she shames al-Lah's holy Prophet!" he cried. "Galloping through the center of town with her hands on another man and her hair waving like a harlot's dress."

"A harlot with vomit-stinking breath and hair like a bird's nest?" I blurted.

"Please, Umar," said Muhammad. "Can you not see that she is ill?"

"You indulge her."

"I am happy to see her alive, praise al-Lah." The love in my husband's gaze made me blush. How close I'd come to betraying him with that trickster! Safwan had lured me with freedom, then tied my destiny to his desires. No different from any other man. Except, perhaps, Muhammad.

"*Yaa habibati*, what reward should I offer Safwan ibn al-Mu'attal for bringing you home safely to me?"

"One hundred lashes would be fitting," Umar grumbled.

"But Safwan saved her life."

"Apparently, Umar thinks I should have been left at the mercy of the jackals—or the Bedouins," I said.

"At least you would die with your honor intact."

"Nothing has happened to A'isha's honor," Muhammad said.

"Tell that to Hassan ibn Thabit," Umar said. "I heard him moments ago reciting a damning poem about your wife and that womanizing soldier."

A poem. No wonder the *umma* had snapped at my heels like a pack of dogs when I'd ridden into town. Hassan's words could incite a crowd into frenzy nearly as quickly as Muhammad's raised hand could quell it.

But I refused to let Umar see me tremble. "Me, with Safwan? That's ridiculous," I said. "I'm the wife of al-Lah's holy Prophet. Would I want a nobody like him?"

I felt Muhammad's eyes watching me. Heat spread like flame under my skin. Had he heard the lie beneath my laughter?

Clipped steps rapped on the courtyard stones. A man's hand flung open the door to my apartment. His silver ring flashed like a sword's blade: Ali, related to Muhammad in three ways—cousin, foster-son, and son-in-law—yet bitterly jealous of his love for me. Stabs of pain pierced my stomach. I leaned my head against Muhammad's shoulder.

"Here she is!" Ali extended his arm to point at me. "Medina churns with sickness over your ruin, A'isha. Men are fighting in the streets over your guilt or innocence. Our own people have turned against one another. The unity of the *umma* is threatened because of you."

"Did you defend me?" Even as I challenged him, I knew the answer.

He turned to Muhammad. "How can I defend her when Safwan himself will not speak on her behalf?"

Of course. Not only had Safwan disappeared when the crowd grew menacing, but when my father and Ali went to question him, he'd hidden inside his parents' home. Some rescuer. I felt tears burn my eyes, but I willed them away. The only one who could save me, it seemed, was me.

"Safwan doesn't need to defend me," I said, although my voice quavered and I still leaned on Muhammad for support. "I can speak for myself."

"Let her rest," Muhammad said. He helped me walk to my bed, but before I could lie down Ali was insisting I tell my story. The *umma* could not wait to know the truth, he said. Another crowd was forming outside the mosque at this very moment, demanding answers.

I closed my eyes, recalling the tale I and Safwan had fashioned on the ride home, during my lucid moments. "I was looking for my agate necklace," I said, fingering the smooth stones. "My father gave it to me on my wedding day. Remember?" I looked at Muhammad. "It means as much to me as the necklaces you've given your *other* wives."

His expression didn't change. I pressed on, spinning a tale that began with me slipping behind the sand dunes to relieve myself, then returning to my *hawdaj*. As I waited to be lifted onto the camel's back I felt for my necklace—but my throat was bare.

"I searched my clothing, the floorboards of my *hawdaj*, the ground. I wanted to ask the driver to help me, but he was watering the camels." My voice stumbled like tender feet on rocky ground. I took a ragged breath, trying to hold steady. "I followed my path back to the dunes. I sifted the sands with my fingers. Then, when I was about to give up, I found it. I ran back to the caravan—but you were far away." *Like ants crawling single-file into tomorrow*, I'd thought at the time. "I knew I could never catch you. So I sat down to wait for someone to come back for me."

"Someone?" Ali pointed his sharp nose at me, sniffing for lies. "You mean Safwan."

"*Yaa* Ali, let her tell her tale," Muhammad said.

"In truth, it is a tale, and nothing more." Ali spat on the dirt floor and wiped his mouth with the back of his hand, glaring. "You waste our time with this fantasy, while we all know the real story."

"Ali, please," Muhammad said, more sternly. Ali folded his arms across his chest and curled his lips. My courage wavered under his scrutiny. Did he truly know the reason I had lost the caravan? Maybe it would be better for me to tell the truth—but a glance at my husband's concerned face changed my mind. Even Muhammad, who knew me as if our souls were one, wouldn't understand why I'd risked so much for so little—and he might not believe me when I told him I was still pure.

"You sat down to wait," Umar said. "What occurs next in this unlikely tale?"

I closed my eyes, feeling faint. What was the story? I and Safwan had rehearsed it during our ride. I let out a long sigh, calming my frantic pulse. This next part was true.

"As the sun rose, I found shade under a grove of date-palm trees," I said. "I lay down, keeping cool. Then I must have slept, because the next thing I remember is Safwan's hand on my shoulder."

Umar grunted. "Did you hear that, Prophet? Safwan ibn al-Mu'attal is now touching your wife. We all know where that leads."

"Why didn't you both ride home right away?" Ali barked.

"Something happened to me." This part was also true. "I felt a sharp cramp, like a knife in my stomach." Muhammad's eyes seemed to soften— a good sign, meaning he must believe me at least a little.

"I couldn't travel, not while I was doubled over with pain. So Safwan pitched his tent for me to rest in, out of the sun."

Ali guffawed. "And where was Safwan while you were lying in his tent?" I ignored him, wanting only to finish this interrogation and go to sleep.

"I retched for hours. Safwan tried to help me. He gave me water and fanned me with a date-palm frond. Finally he became frightened, and we came back for help." I didn't tell how he'd nearly made me scream with his hand wringing. *Al-Lah is punishing us,* he'd moaned, over and over again. Along with the water, I began to spit up bile and remorse. *Take me to Medina,* I said sourly. *Before al-Lah kills us both.*

When I finished my tale, Ali was scowling. "This is not the full story," he said. "Why was Safwan lagging so far behind the caravan? Was it because he knew you would be waiting for him under the date palms?"

"I asked Safwan to remain behind," Muhammad said. "To watch for the return of the Mustaliq to their camp."

"She has been flirting with him for years!"

I snorted, as if his words amused me instead of chilling my blood. He spoke the truth—but who else knew?

"Where is your proof, Ali?" I said, meeting his angry gaze for a moment, then dropping it for fear he'd see the panic in my eyes. "A single pointing finger makes an insignificant mark."

◆

Then, with Muhammad's help, I lay down on my bed and turned my back to them all: the ever-suspicious Umar; Ali, so eager to think the worst of

me; and my husband, who could quiet an angry mob with a raised hand
but who had allowed these men to slander me. Why had I returned? I
closed my eyes and dreamt, again, of escape. This time, though, I knew it
was only a dream. There would be no escaping my fate. At best, al-Lah
willing, I might shape my destiny—but I couldn't run from it. This much
I had learned from my mistakes these past few days.

I slept lightly, tossed by fever and regret, until whispers whipped about
my head like stinging sand, jolting me back to consciousness. Muhammad
and Ali were sitting on the cushions near my bed, arguing—about me.

"I cannot believe A'isha would do such a thing," Muhammad said. His
voice was a broken shell, fragile and jagged. "I have loved her since she
sprang from her mother's womb. I have played dolls with her and her
friends. I have drunk from the same bowl with her."

"She is fourteen years old," Ali said, his voice rising. "Not a little girl
anymore, although she is many years younger than you. Safwan is much
closer to her age."

"Shh, Ali! Do not disturb A'isha's rest."

"Then let us find a more suitable place to talk." I heard the rustle of
cloth. *Don't go*, I wanted to beg, but I was too weak. So I moaned, instead.
Muhammad laid his hand on my forehead.

"Her skin is hot," he said. "I cannot leave her alone."

"Then I must speak here."

"Please, cousin. I value your counsel."

I held my breath, dreading Ali's next words. What kind of punishment
would he suggest for me and Safwan? A whipping? Banishment from the
umma? Death?

"Divorce her," Ali said.

"No!" I sat up, ready to throw my arms around my husband's neck and
hold on with all my strength. Muhammad stroked my damp brow, his
smile shifting like a shadow under a changing sun.

"Don't leave me," I said, forgetting about Ali, the last person I would
have wanted to hear me beg.

"I am not leaving you, *habibati*. But I have decided to send you to your
parents' house for a while. Abu Bakr and Umm Ruman will nurse you
back to health, al-Lah willing, away from all these wagging tongues."

"Don't divorce me." Weeks later, as I waited in my parents' house for

Muhammad's verdict, I'd wince to recall how I'd clung to his hand and cried in front of Ali: "I love you, *habibi*."

I meant those words as I'd never meant them before. I'd learned much during those hours in the desert with Safwan. Safwan, who'd promised one thing and delivered another, the same as when we were children.

"I love you, too, my sweet." But his voice sounded far away, and his eyes looked troubled. I lay down and clutched his hand as though it were a doll, then drifted slowly back toward sleep.

As I slipped away again I heard Ali's voice, urgent and low.

"Think of the *umma*, how delicate its weave," he said. "A scandal like this could tear it apart. You must act now, cousin. Send her back to Abu Bakr for good."

"Divorce my A'isha?" Muhammad's laugh sounded nervous and faint. "I would rather cut out my own heart."

"She's tainted," Ali said—increasing my hatred for him with each word. "You must put her away from you before this scandal marks you, also. Many men in this town would love to see you fall."

Muhammad slowly pulled his hand from my grasp, leaving me to drift alone on my sea of fears.

"Can't you see it?" Ali pressed. "I know you can. Then why do you look so worried? Wives are easily acquired. You will find another child-bride."

◆

Centuries later, scandal still haunts my name. But those who scorned me, who called me "al-zaniya" and "fahisha," they didn't know me. They never knew the truth—about me, about Muhammad, about how I saved his life and he saved mine. About how I saved all their lives. If they knew, would they have mocked me then?

Of course, they know now. Where we are now, all truth is known. But it still eludes your world. Where you are, men still want to hide the women away. You, in the now, they cover with shrouds or with lies about being inferior. We, in the past, they erase from their stories of Muhammad, or alter with false tales that burn our ears and the backs of our eyes. Where you are, mothers chastise their daughters with a single name. "You A'isha!" they cry, and the girls turn away in shame. We cannot escape our destinies, even in death. But we can claim them, and give them shape.

The girls turn away because they don't know the truth: That Muhammad wanted to give us freedom, but that the other men took it away. That none of us is ever alive until we can shape our own destinies. Until we can choose.

So many misunderstandings. Here where we are, we cup the truth in our hands like water, trying to contain it, watching it slip away. Truth is too slippery to hold. It must be passed on, or it slides like rain into the earth, to disappear.

Before it disappears, I will pass my story on to you. My truth. My struggle. And then, who knows what will happen? Al-lah willing, my name will regain its meaning. No longer, then, a word synonymous with treachery and shame. Al-Lah willing, when my story is known, my name will evoke once more that most precious of possessions. Which I claimed for myself and for which I fought until, at last, I won it from the Prophet of God—not only for myself, but for all my sisters also.

My name: "A'isha." Its meaning: "life." May it be so again, and forevermore.

Bedouins in the wild

Mecca, 619
Six years old

*I*t was my last day of freedom. Yet it began like one thousand and one days before it: the wink of the sun and my cry of alarm, *late again*, the spring from my bed and the flight through the windowless rooms of my father's house, my wooden play-sword in my hand, my bare feet slapping the cool stone floor, *I'm late I'm late I'm late*.

Oil lamps flickered dimly against the walls, their feeble light a poor substitute for the sun I loved. As I passed the cooking room the tangy fermented smell of barley mush made me gag. *Faster, faster.* The Prophet would be here soon. If he saw me, he would want to play, and I would miss Safwan.

Yet I should have known my mother would find me: She was more vigilant than the Evil Eye. "Where do you think you are going?" she cried as I hit the solid wall she made standing in my path with her hands on her hips.

I would have reeled back, caught my breath, and run around her but she seized me with hands made strong from years of bread making. Her fingers gripped my shoulders like the talons of a hawk. She ran her gaze like rough hands over my sleep-tossed hair, my sand-colored shift marked like a map of yesterday's play: Roundish smudges where I'd knelt in the dirt, hiding from Bedouin enemies. A rip in the sleeve from my struggle against my captors, Safwan and our friend Nadida. Red flecks of pomegranate juice from yesterday's meal. Streaks of gray from the giant rock Safwan and I had quietly rolled beneath the bedroom window of our neighbor Hamal, Mecca's newest bridegroom.

My mother said, "You are filthy. You will not leave the house like that."

"Please, *ummi*, I'm late!" I said, but she called for my sister.

"No child of mine is going anywhere looking like a wild animal," she said. "Go change into clean clothes and meet Asma in the courtyard. She will need to tame that tangled mane of yours today, while I fetch water to wash the Queen of Sheba's hair."

She was talking about her sister-wife, Qutailah. My father's *hatun*, the "Great Lady," or first-wife, Qutailah assigned all the tasks in the *harim*. Tall, dark-skinned, and increasingly plump, Qutailah envied my mother's fair skin and wild rays of red hair and feared her fiery temper, so she reminded her always who was first in the household by calling my mother *durra*, or "parrot," the name for second-wife. And she assigned my *ummi* the jobs usually given to servants, such as lugging huge skins of water from Mecca's well. It was a humiliating task, for the well of Zamzam was in the center of town and everyone could see my mother huffing home with the sloshing skins slung on a pole across her small shoulders. Facing this chore always put *ummi* in a bad mood. This wasn't the time to argue with her.

"Hearing and obeying," I said, but when *ummi* disappeared into the darkness I slipped into the kitchen. Our neighbor Raha sat in a shady corner fanning herself with a date-palm leaf. She dimpled when she saw me and pulled from her sack a pomegranate as shiny and red as her cheeks.

"No, you have to give me a kiss first," she teased when I tried to snatch the fruit from her hand. I settled in her lap for just a moment, long enough to press my face to hers and breathe in the lavender she wore tucked in her braided hair. She rubbed the tips of our noses together, making me giggle, making me forget my hurry until Asma walked in. I tore the pomegranate in half, heedless of seeds falling in wet plops on the floor as I raced out the door, dodging my sister's grasping hands.

"*Yaa* A'isha, where are you going?" I heard Asma call, as if she didn't know. She and Qutailah, who was her mother, were always scolding me about my "obsession" with Safwan. *He will only cause you trouble. Playing with your future husband will invite the Evil Eye.*

Away I ran, ignoring my sister's shouts, waving my pretend sword and kicking up soft hot sand as I passed the jumble of tall terrace-roofed houses of dark stone with their arched doorways and sun-bleached palm-frond roofs, homes crowded together and watching me like gossiping, gap-toothed old men. Beyond them, Mecca's caravan of rock-strewn mountains pulled in their shadows under the relentless eye of the sun.

I found Safwan huddled with Nadida inside her play tent, whispering.

"*Marhaba*, lovebirds," I said. Nadida's long, narrow face blushed a deep red. I started to laugh, but Safwan leaped up and pulled me into the tent.

"Hush!" he rasped. "Do you want them to hear us?" He nodded toward the bridegroom Hamal's window and, beneath it, the rock that we'd rolled there last night.

"They're in there now," Nadida said. "You should see her. She's the same age as me, and married to that old goat." She touched the small red figure dangling from a string around her neck. "May Hubal protect me from that fate." Her parents still worshipped idols in those days, not the real God as I and Safwan did.

Safwan placed a finger to his lips and tugged at one of his big ears, listening. A sharp, keening cry, like the wails of Medina's mourning women, made me shiver. Then we heard a man's growl, and his laugh as rough as scraped skin.

"By al-Lah, is he killing her?" I said.

Safwan and Nadida snickered. "She probably wishes she were dead," Nadida said.

Safwan moved to the tent entrance and beckoned me to follow him. Crouching, we tiptoed over to the great rock. Safwan lifted his foot to climb it and a loud groan from inside shook me to my senses: That Hamal was a giant. If he caught us peeking in his window, he could crush us both with one hand. I tugged at Safwan's sleeve, but he pulled himself up and peered over the edge of the window, then smirked at me.

"Come on," he whispered. "Don't be a baby." He reached out a hand to boost me up, but I scampered to the top of that rock like a lizard, ignoring my pounding heart, which I was certain Hamal would hear. As my eyes adjusted to the shadowy light inside, I could see only scattered clothing at first, strewn across the floor, then trays of half-eaten food and dirty dishes and a water-pipe tipped over on its side. The odors of barley and decaying meat and rotting apple mingled with the damp smell of sweat.

A low, steady grunting pulled my gaze to the bed. A trickle of sweat crawled down Hamal's broad, naked back as he lifted his body off the bed then slammed it down again and again. I stared at his behind, as big as my goat's-bladder ball and covered with hair, as it clenched and relaxed with each thrust. Beneath him, skinny arms and legs stuck out like the limbs of a scarab beetle under a sandal, flailing and clutching at him. A girl's voice seemed to sob, and her heels pounded against his hips. I gasped and grabbed Safwan's arm: He *was* killing her!

But when I looked at Safwan he was grinning, and as Hamal's voice grew louder and his body-slams faster, Safwan pulled me down beneath the window. Hidden from their view we heard Hamal shout, "Hi! Hi! Hi!" like a hyena. I covered my mouth with my hand and stared at Safwan, but he was snickering. I pretended to laugh, also, not wanting him to see my horror, while the image of the girl's squashed body under that hairy beast replayed itself in my mind.

I leaned against the house, trying to keep my breath even, praying Safwan couldn't hear the churn of my stomach. Someday I'd marry him— and we would do *that?* His smile was fierce; his eyes seemed to mock me as if he were having the same thoughts. But, unlike me, he seemed to relish the idea. Of course, he would be the one who crushed, while I'd be the poor girl underneath, sobbing and flailing my arms and legs. "That's marriage, A'isha," he whispered, making me want to run away. I thought of my mother: No wonder she frowned so much.

And then, as though I'd conjured her, my *ummi* came flying around the corner, her dark robe flapping like the wings of an agitated crow.

"What are you doing here?" she yelled. Shouts from inside the room made her glance up at the window, and she shrieked as if she'd been burned. I looked over at Safwan, but his place on the rock was empty. He'd vanished like a *djinni,* leaving me alone to face my mother's wild shrieks and slaps. Not only had I disobeyed her by leaving home without cleaning up, but she'd caught me outside Hamal ibn

Affan's bedroom window with bewilderment and fear groping like hands across my face.

I smiled at her—the very image of innocence, I hoped. Her face looked pulled apart and pinched back together, like scraps of bread dough.

Then Hamal filled the window. I felt his knuckle rap my crown and I shrieked, then scampered down from the rock and ran toward *ummi*. A part of me wanted to hide in her skirts from him—but I knew better than to place myself within my mother's grasp. Once she got hold of me, she wouldn't let go until she'd left the imprint of her hand on my cheeks and backside.

"One thousand apologies, Umm Ruman," Hamal said, tucking his hair behind an ear. He'd pulled on a faded blue robe and tied it about his broad girth. His face was very mottled and beaded with wetness. "I thought I had closed this curtain."

"I am certain you did." My mother eyed me. "But someone else opened it."

"No," I said, "it was already open."

Ai! What had I just said? Now they knew I had been watching. I wished the noontime heat would make me faint, or that I could disappear like Safwan in a blink. Hamal's great roar made me leap to my mother's skirts, more afraid of him than of her.

"If you are going to spy, little girl, you had better learn how to lie," he said with a scowl. My mother apologized, but he told her not to worry: He had children of his own. "I married off my girls as soon as their monthly bleeding started. It is the only way to avoid trouble."

Had I come to see his new bride? he asked me. Her beauty was the talk of Mecca. "*Yaa* Jamila," he said, without turning around. Her real name was Fazia, meaning "victorious," but Hamal had changed it, he told us, so no one could say, "Hamal's wife is victorious." A pale, frail-looking girl appeared in the window next to Hamal. She clutched a bed sheet to her chest and kept her eyes lowered. With swollen lips she shyly smiled to reveal large front teeth that stuck out, and her nose was so big it covered half her face. A real beauty! A part of me wanted to laugh, but the other part noticed the shadows under her eyes and the trembling of her hand as it held the sheet.

She really was just a girl, not even as old as my sister, and married to a man my father's age. She looked so timid and afraid that I wanted to reach out and stroke her forehead, the way Asma sometimes did to me when I'd had a nightmare. But this was no nightmare: For Fazia-turned-Jamila, this was a woman's life, to be endured with downcast eyes and nary a whimper of complaint. *Not for me,* I vowed. If any man ever tried to hurt me, I'd fight back. And when I had something to say, I wouldn't say it with my head down, as if I were ashamed. If my husband didn't like it, he could divorce me and I wouldn't care. I'd rather be a lone lioness, roaring and free, than a caged bird without even a name to call my own.

"*Ahlan,* Fazia," I said, giving her name back to her. She raised her head to look at me with a smile that had reached her eyes.

My mother said a hasty farewell then yanked me home, panting as if I were as large and heavy as Hamal. With those fierce strong fingers she clamped my hand in hers so tightly I thought my bones would break. I'd be whipped for sure, but I wasn't thinking about that. Instead, I replayed the images I had just seen, of Hamal on top of the frail girl. That would be me someday—but not, thank al-Lah, with a man so much older than I. The girl must have been in pain, judging from the way she'd been crying out and clutching so helplessly at Hamal's back. No man or woman would ever hold that kind of power over me. Except, for now, my mother.

Inside the house, *ummi* let go of my throbbing hand and I massaged it, but I refused to wince in front of her.

"What were you doing under that window?" she said.

"Sitting in the shade."

"Sitting in the shade." She folded her arms. "On a rock that just happened to be under Hamal ibn Affan's bedroom window? And how did that rock get there? Hamal said it was not there yesterday."

I opened my eyes as wide as they would go. "Maybe he never noticed it before."

"You were spying!" she cried. "And you brought Safwan along to spy with you." Her glare was pointed, as though it were she, and not Qutailah, who had warned me away from Safwan. As though she hadn't scoffed at her sister-wife's Evil-Eye superstitions. *The known is better than the unknown,* my mother would say, and send me off to play with him.

"We were sitting, that's all. We didn't know they were in there."

"Enough!" She raised her hand high above me. "I should beat those lies out of you right now." Her fire-red hair seemed to flame about her head.

Unflinching, I waited for the blow. How proud Safwan would be to see me face my doom without any sign of fear! When he left Mecca to join the Bedouins, I'd be ready to go with him.

Instead of striking me, though, *ummi's* hand lowered slowly down to smooth the hair back from my forehead. I searched her eyes: What would she do to me? Her lips twitched at the corners, holding something back.

"I almost forgot the reason I came to find you today," she said. "You are to remain indoors, A'isha. It is forbidden for boys or men to see you unless they are relatives."

"Stay inside?" I frowned. "But I and Safwan are going to the market to see the caravan from Abyssinia."

"You won't be going to the market anymore, or going anywhere else without me or your father," she said in the clipped voice she used for rule making. "Starting today, you are in *purdah.*"

"*Purdah?*" I felt all my senses sharpen. "That's for Asma, not me."

"It is for you, too, from now on."

"What?" I gaped at her like a fish pulled from the water, trying to breathe. "For how long?"

"Until your husband says otherwise."

"My husband?" For the first time in my life, I raised my voice to my mother. I knew she'd beat me for my shrill, whining tone, but I also knew I had to convince her to change her mind now, before she pressed her lips together and refused to speak—a sign that her mind was set and that no argument would change it.

"Safwan wouldn't want you to hide me away," I begged. "Go ask him, *ummi*. He'll tell you."

"Safwan has nothing to do with this," my mother said. From the court-yard came Qutailah's call: "*Yaa durra!* Parrot! Where is my meal?"

Ummi's sigh scraped like a blade on a stone as she turned away from me. "When you marry, daughter, make certain you are the first-wife in your household. Make certain you control your destiny, or it will control you."

The pounding of my heart, like the hooves of panicked horses, sent me running to her, dizzy with the need to stop this imprisonment before it started. In *purdah* I wouldn't be allowed to step outside my parents' house until my wedding day. I'd be stuck in this cold, dreary tomb until the day my blood flow started, six years away or maybe even longer, with no Safwan to play with, no boys at all, just the silly girls who came with their mothers to visit.

"It's not fair to lock me up!" I threw my arms around my mother's waist and held on as she tried to move away. "You're punishing me, aren't you? I embarrassed you at Hamal's house, and now you want to take revenge."

"Let me go!"

"Not until you change your mind. I want to go outside, *ummi*." I tightened my grip, holding on to the notion that this was just a cruel joke—and fearing that if I let her go, I might crumple to the floor.

Years of hauling water and making bread had made my tiny mother an amazingly strong woman. She reached behind her and gripped my forearms so tightly I thought she would snap them in two. Yet I clung to her until she pried me loose, then pushed me backward onto the floor.

"You will do as I say, unless you want to be whipped," she snapped. "This confinement is not a punishment."

Sprawled at her feet, I looked up into her flushed face and realized she wasn't going to change her mind. I felt as though hands were closing around my throat, squeezing tears from my eyes, making me gasp for breath.

"I don't want to stay inside!" I wailed. "I'll die in this stuffy old cave."

"Al-Lah has blessed this family today." My mother's voice was as hard and cold as the stones under my bottom. "But a girl's honor can easily be stolen. If you lose it, you might as well be dead."

Qutailah called for her again, this time in a sharper tone. "By al-Lah, you will be shoveling out the toilet if I have to ask for my meal again!" My *ummi* turned and walked with brisk steps—and slumped shoulders—to the courtyard entrance.

"When I marry Safwan, we're going to run away to the desert!" I cried after her. "You'll never see me again. You'll be sorry then!"

She stopped and turned to give me a long, last look. "Do not think you know what al-Lah has planned for you, A'isha." She pressed her lips together, turned away from me again, and walked out of the house.

I scrambled to my feet and ran after her, but stopped at the arched passageway to the courtyard. Outside, our ghaza'a tree drooped its lacy leaves as if in sorrow. Beneath it, my grim-lipped mother served a heaping portion of barley to Qutailah, who scolded her for cooking it too long.

"After all these years, have you still not learned how to cook, Umm Ruman?" she said with a sneer. "A toothless infant could eat this soggy mush. Did I ask you to make baby food?"

The women visiting Qutailah began to snicker, but my mother kept ladling the barley, her eyes lowered although I could see her face redden. I felt my cheeks stiffen where my tears had dried. I crouched, ready to race into the courtyard and defend my *ummi*, but I knew it would only make things worse for her—and for me. Instead I ran to my bedroom, where I flung my toys against the walls and screamed and punched my bed with my fists.

Buried alive in this house for the rest of my days.

I'd known it would happen someday, but not when I was six. Only a very few girls were engaged at birth, as I had been, but they were never confined until they began their monthly bleeding. To begin *purdah* at my age was unheard of.

Someday, I and Safwan would ride far away from Mecca and all its foolish traditions. We had already taken the blood-oath, had pricked our fingers and smeared them together and sworn to leave the city behind, once we were married, and become Bedouins in the wild. Nothing could break that vow. If they tried to lock me away forever, I would escape. With the Bedouins, I'd be free to live my life the way I wanted, to run and yell and fight in battles and make my own choices. Because, in the desert, it didn't matter whether you were a woman or a man. In the desert, there were no walls. *Control your destiny, or it will control you.*

With those thoughts, my hands clutching my pillow, my body as rigid and straight as an arrow, I fell out of my unhappy world and into deep, thrilling dreams of riding on horseback with the wind in my hair and a sword in my hand, free at last.

Shifting Sands

Mecca, 622
Nine years old

*G*limpses of his face and bright shards of his laughter kept Safwan alive for me over the years. From behind my bedroom curtain I watched him scamper, strong and free, over rocks and sand, chasing his friends with stick-sword brandishing, curdling wild Bedouin yells in his exuberant throat. I peeked through the cloth like a shy moon veiled by clouds, longing to be seen yet fearing it. My parents had drummed the dangers into my very bones until I dreaded the gaze of any man not in my family. One illicit glance, it seemed, could pierce the veil of my virginity. So I watched life outside go on without me as though I had died, shrouded by my curtain.

Restless, I learned every stone in the floor, every crack in every wall of our Meccan home during my years in *purdah*. Fortunately, our house was large—but plain, not showy on the outside like some of the newer homes Mecca's fat merchants were building. And it was comfortably cool, thanks to the thick stone walls and dearth of windows in all the rooms except mine, which I'd chosen for the light, and the kitchen, which needed the extra ventilation. As in most homes, ours separated the *harim*, the women's quarters, from that of the men, which included my father's *majlis*, a rectangular room whose walls were hung with tapestries of red and gold and whose floor was plump with cushions. The *harim* consisted of the women's bedrooms, the kitchen and sitting area, a store room, and, outside, a private bath enclosed by high stone walls. A spacious courtyard separated the men's and women's living areas; this held a few thorn trees for shade, from which hung swings for my friends and me to play on, and a see-saw of acacia wood. The *harim* was connected to the front of the house, which included the living room and a stairway leading to a balcony where my father sat most nights with his wives. Date-palm fronds criss-crossed the ceilings throughout, letting in fresh air but blocking out most of the heat. How I longed to climb the walls and wiggle through, then fly up and away!

"Why so sad, donkey-face?" my father would ask. I'd sigh loudly and droop my head, hoping for his embrace. He might pull me down into his lap and tickle my chin, making me giggle, coaxing laughter into that house whose windowless walls blocked out the sun I craved. I breathed in my father with my eyes closed, smelled his deliciousness, honey and garlic with a hint of sweet cardamom. I pressed my face into his beard, gray and wiry as a *shaykh's* on a face as smooth as a young man's. My pleasure, however, was always short-lived. In a moment he would nudge me away, telling me he had work to do.

In truth, *abi's* support for his friend Muhammad brought him as much grief and worry as delight during those years. Not everyone in Mecca believed Muhammad was a prophet, or that there was only one God. The city's merchants, in particular those of the ruling Qurayshi tribe—Muhammad's tribe, and my *abi's*—scorned his beautiful, poetic revelations from al-Lah. *He is only a djinni-possessed* kahin, they'd scoff, likening him to the hooded "oracles" who wandered through the public market spouting gibberish.

Yet Muhammad's words weren't nonsense. His *qur'an*, or recitations, not only proclaimed the oneness of al-Lah, but revealed the other gods in the Ka'ba, Mecca's holy shrine, to be false. They were only chunks of wood or stone, he contended, angering the merchants who depended upon those idols to bring worshippers—and their gold—into the city. Quraysh's leaders, including Muhammad's cousin Abu Sufyan, vowed to stop him any way they could.

Yet who would dare to harm him as long as the mighty Mu'tim was his protector? The Qurayshi merchants jeered when Muhammad recited his verses and struck him with a sheep's uterus when he prayed in public, but their fear of his protector was too great for them to do him harm. It was unfortunate, *abi* said, that Mu'tim couldn't spread his tent of protection over all the Believers.

My father's protector kept him from harm, also, but only barely. *Abi's* clan, the Taym, had turned its back on him, as he realized one day when Abu Sufyan and a friend of his tied my father and my cousin Talha back to back and left them in the desert to broil. When the Bedouin chief Ibn Dughumma discovered them there, he took them to his tent and slathered their burnt skin with *khatmi*, then offered himself as my father's protector. Quraysh agreed to respect the arrangement, but only if my father stopped reciting the *qur'an* and praying in public. The merchants were afraid of the sweet, tearful expression on my father's face when he prayed: *That face will seduce our wives into following Muhammad!* My father built a mosque beside our house, which became a gathering place for Believers—irritating Quraysh even more.

Meanwhile, my days in *purdah* stretched and thinned, past into present into future, like a slow-moving caravan whose beginning and end had disappeared from sight. During the day I listlessly kneaded bread dough, spun wool, and wove cloth, dreaming of the time I would be free, unbridled by *purdah* or my neighbors' tongues. I loathed the women's chores, dull and repetitive, and lived for the evenings I would spend with my *abi*.

We'd sit together for hours, I and *abi*. At first, he taught me the Prophet's recitations, which I lovingly memorized, each word as sweet as honey on my lips. He read to me the poetry of the *jahiliyya*, the time of ignorance before *islam* was revealed to Muhammad, and when I begged for more verses he taught me how to read them for myself. Noting the pallor in my skin, he chose a horse from his stable for me—a sleek, night-black mare that I named Scimitar—and took me riding in the desert on cool evenings. These were the nights I cherished most in all my years in my parents' home: the quickening of my pulse as we galloped over the soft red earth; the ripple of the horse's flank under my hand; the rush of the fresh breeze over my skin and through my hair.

I lived for the nights, but the days offered one highlight, also: the

visits to our home by the Prophet of al-Lah. In the early years, especially, Muhammad came every day to pray in the mosque, then to sit in
my father's *majlis* and sip coffee and discuss the day's affairs. Afterwards,
he'd present me with a toy hidden in his robe and laugh and tease while
I tried to find it, then he'd sit on the floor with me to play. I never wondered why he was allowed to do so when no other man was permitted
even to look at me. Muhammad had been a part of my life since I'd
been born, and it seemed natural to clash toy horses with his and
scream, "Die, Bedouin cur!"

But in my ninth year, a series of events changed the way I viewed
Muhammad.

He arrived in our doorway one morning with a face as unsettled and
dark as a storm cloud. He murmured something to my mother. She cried,
"By al-Lah!" and sagged against the door like a deflated ball. I ran to her
side, my heart nearly bursting to see her so upset, but she waved me back.
I turned to Muhammad for an explanation, but he was striding toward the
majlis with my father—followed, in the next instant, by me.

"Mu'tim is dead," Muhammad said as I listened outside the door. "He
was found in his bed with his throat slit. Some are blaming Abu Sufyan."

"I would not be surprised if Abu Sufyan had arranged it," my father
said. "Mu'tim has prevented him from assassinating you more than once,
I have heard."

"Mu'tim protected me from death," Muhammad said in a strange,
choked voice, "but in doing so he lost his own life. *Yaa* Abu Bakr, this cannot continue. We must leave Mecca before any others die on my behalf."

I gasped and pressed my palms to my hot cheeks. Leave Mecca? How
could we? No man ever moved away from his tribe, and women did so
only to marry. Our ancestors had settled this land. Our families were all
related to one another. Yes, Safwan and I had plotted to run away and join
the Bedouins, but that was different: We'd be moving for adventure, not
out of shame. We could always return. But those of us who ran from
Quraysh now would never be allowed in Mecca again, except as slaves.

For days I walked with trembling steps as if the earth shook under my
feet. *We must leave Mecca*, I kept hearing Muhammad say, and I'd feel my
heart flutter as if it might run away from me and hide, refusing to let me
leave Nadida, my cousins, Safwan, and the market and the mountains I

loved. My father was as tense as I. As he visited with Muhammad one day, I entered the *majlis* to pour their coffee and, distracted by their talk, spilled some of the hot liquid on my father's arm. He raised a hand to strike me, but, to my amazement, Muhammad grabbed his arm to stop him. "Be gentle with her, friend," he said. "For my sake."

A look passed between them as I watched, stunned by what I'd just witnessed. For a man to interfere in another's home life was unheard of. Men had fought and killed each other over these very acts. But my father was nodding, as if Muhammad had every right.

"Forgive me," *abi* said—to Muhammad, not me.

Later, as he was leaving, Muhammad patted my cheek in farewell. "After today, A'isha, you will not need to worry about being treated harshly again." His golden eyes softened, like honey in the sun. "That much, at least, I can do for you now."

Later, in my room, I pondered Muhammad's words. How audacious of him to tell my father how to discipline me, as if I belonged to him!

Maybe I do.

The thought hit me like a slap, making me sit up straight and sending all worries about leaving Mecca flying from my mind. Was I—could I be— I could barely bring myself even to form the thought—might I be engaged to Muhammad instead of Safwan?

Do not think you know what al-Lah has planned for you. I remembered my *ummi's* words, spoken on that dreadful day I'd started *purdah*, when I'd told her that Safwan and I would be fleeing to the desert once we were married. I'd shrugged her warning away, knowing that, as Safwan's wife, I'd never have to take orders from anyone but him. Even al-Lah couldn't change that, for it was written in our laws and traditions like the etchings of the wind in the rocks of Mount Hira.

Now, though, I wondered: Had al-Lah changed my destiny for me already, by switching my engagement from Safwan to Muhammad? My *purdah* would make sense then. If I were the future wife of God's Prophet, I would be much more valuable, and more vulnerable—especially with men like Abu Sufyan skulking around, looking for every opportunity to hurt Muhammad. If I lost my virginity, even to rape, not only would I be sullied but Muhammad would be, also.

I slumped onto my bed, feeling as though stones filled my body.

Married to Muhammad! It couldn't be. He was older than my father, much older than Hamal in comparison to Fazia-turned-Jamila. But then, why was he allowed to visit me during my *purdah,* when all other men were forbidden? Suspicion was a heavy hand squeezing my chest, stealing my breath.

"Safwan," I whispered. "Come and rescue me. Hurry, before it's too late"

♦

After the death of Mu'tim, I noticed changes in the shifting sands of my father's face, in the set of his mouth. At night he would sit in the court-yard with my mother and Qutailah and talk while I, long banished to bed, hovered in the shadows and sifted the menacing words from their susurrant tones.

"Torture," my father would murmur. "Assassination." And my mother and Qutailah would exclaim, then cry when he spoke of leaving Mecca.

"Al-Lah will take care of us," my father would say. "There is nothing to cry about. Nothing to fear."

One night, as I lay in bed under the weight of their words, a woman's shriek pulled me to my window. In the thin light cast by the crescent moon I spied four men dragging my beloved neighbor Raha, she of the pomegranates and twinkling eyes, out of her house, slapping and punch-ing her as she struggled.

"Where is your precious Prophet now, you Muslim whore?" a man said with a coarse laugh. In the starlight I could just see the face of Abu Sufyan, whose sweat glistened like beads of grease in every fold and crease of fat, and of his companion Umar, whose pocked face seemed to writhe with hatred as he pressed his hand to Raha's mouth. I jumped up and down and pounded the wall with my fist, spurred by my speeding pulse.

"Raha!" I shrieked. "Let her go, you Qurayshi dogs!" I ran to the kitchen, Raha's shrieks ringing in my ears, and grabbed a knife, then flung open the front door—but my mother caught my wrist and held me there.

"Where do you think you are going?" she cried.

"Raha!" I said, trying to yank myself free. "Abu Sufyan is beating her up."

My father grabbed his robe and raced out the door, grappling with his sword as he went. My mother slammed the door behind him, then turned to me with flaring nostrils.

"And what did you plan to do once you got there? Let those men look at you, or worse?" she demanded.

"I wanted to rescue Raha—"

"With what? A kitchen knife? Those men have swords, A'isha. Swords! They could cut you into pieces, or worse."

"*Yaa ummi,* I can fight. Safwan taught me how. See?" I swished my knife—impressively, I thought. "Let me go to her, *ummi.* They'll kill her if we don't save her."

"Sword-fighting in the streets? Do not be ridiculous. You are a girl, not a boy. You cannot save anyone. That is the task of men."

"But what about Raha? What about *abi?* I saw four men, and there's only one of him."

"Your father would lose his life before he would accept your help," she said. Her eyes were fierce, like a wild animal's. "You know what those men would do to you. Then your family would be disgraced. Is that what you want?"

"But Abu Sufyan—"

"Abu Sufyan is the reason you are in *purdah* now!" she shouted. Her face had turned as red as if she were strangling. "He was bragging to everyone in Mecca that he was going to deflower you. He said you had teased him with your red hair."

The thought of that greasy-bearded goat touching me made me feel as if rats were scuttling all over my skin. I ran to my bedroom window to urge my father on in his fight for Raha, hoping to see him knock Abu Sufyan to the dust. What I found made me scream: my father on his back and Abu Sufyan standing over him, pressing the point of his sword into my father's cheek. Blood oozed around the blade. In the background I saw Umar tying a gag across Raha's mouth and shoving her into a wagon.

Abu Sufyan looked up and saw me in my window, shrieking and jumping up and down. He leered and licked his thick lips. "*Yaa* Abu Bakr, your lovely little fire-haired daughter has come to say good-bye."

"*Yaa abi,* let me come out!" I cried, glaring at Abu Sufyan. "I'll save you and Raha."

"Yes, let her come out," Abu Sufyan said, baring his teeth. "I will warm myself in those flames of hers, and your life will be spared."

His foe distracted, my father rolled away from Abu Sufyan and leapt to his feet, snatching up his sword. Abu Sufyan lunged at him with his blade but my father stepped nimbly to the side before striking back at him. They exchanged blows until Abu Sufyan slashed my father's forehead, sending blood gushing into his eyes. As he wiped it away Abu Sufyan climbed onto his horse, and he and Umar rode away with Raha in their possession and my screams pelting their ears.

My mother ran outside carrying a strip of cloth to bandage my father's head. "I am unharmed, A'isha," *abi* called. He and my mother approached Raha's house, its broken door agape like a crying mouth, and tended to her husband who lay in the front yard, bleeding in the dirt, his sword in his hand.

"Raha," I moaned. "I could have saved you, I know I could. Oh, Raha, I'm so sorry."

My stomach clenched like a fist, folding me in half. I dropped to my bed, curled like a question around myself, soaking my pillow with great, hot sobs. Poor Raha, always so jolly and as gentle as a lamb, filled with love for everyone. What would become of her? I'd heard my father talk about Believers getting whipped—women, feeble *shaykhs*—their lives seeping away through their wounds. I pictured Raha's dimpling cheeks, the spark in her eyes as she'd slipped me forbidden sticks of honey and adorned my hair with blossoms. What were they doing to her now? Her cries echoed in my head. I pulled my pillow over my ears, but nothing helped.

I could have stopped those men if my mother hadn't interfered. Fighting with a real blade couldn't be much different from fighting with a wooden sword, as I'd done so many times with Safwan. I would have sent that dung-breathed Abu Sufyan's head rolling in the dirt, and the mean-faced Umar would have run whimpering home like a whipped dog.

Why, al-Lah? Why would He let this happen to Raha, who loved Him so much? Wasn't He supposed to protect us? Maybe He was so busy, he hadn't noticed Raha's cries.

My arms and legs still hummed with the longing to run to Raha and free her. That energy was God's; I felt it in the blood that sang though my veins. He had heard Raha's cries, and He'd called me to fight for her. But I couldn't.

You cannot save anyone. That is the task of men.

My mother's rebuke stung me more sharply than it had the first time. In my mother's world, being female meant being helpless. Powerless. Because what else was a sword but power? In her world, women weren't supposed to fight, only to submit. They weren't supposed to plan, but to let others plan for them. They weren't supposed to live, only to serve.

I pulled myself up to my windowsill and peered into the stars, imagining they were the one thousand and one eyes of al-Lah. When He looked at me, what did He see? Inferiority, a shrunken soul, a light that shone more feebly than that of a man? Or did He see what I felt—a bright burning, like the bush He'd inhabited the day He'd revealed Himself to Moses? Muhammad, who knew the stories of the People of the Book, had told me the tale, how the bush had burned but never expired, with a fire that breathed and spoke and lived, like the fire that burned in my breast right now.

Raha was gone, to be rescued not by me, but by men. Her husband had lain on the ground but he was standing now, leaning on my father, alive and not taken, his sword in his hand. Raha had neither the sword nor the skills with which to defend herself. Now she was a prisoner of Quraysh, completely vulnerable to their will, while her husband, who could fight back, remained free.

"Raha," I whispered. "If only I could save you now." Tears filled my eyes again, but I blinked them away. As a warrior would have done.

Imprisoned in my room, I could save no one. My mother had spoken the truth in that respect. But I wouldn't be trapped here forever. Someday I'd get married, either to Safwan, who would be my side-by-side warrior in the desert, or to Muhammad, who would teach me to use a sword if I asked him. I'd make it seem like a game, and he'd play it with me in his courtyard.

Either way, I was not going to live my life in fear and submission to the whims of men like Abu Sufyan. Not to be able to fight for myself, or the people I loved, would be the worst kind of slavery. Never again would I watch, helpless, while those Qurayshi bullies threatened my people. I'd become the best fighter, male or female, Mecca had ever seen. If Abu Sufyan attacked us then, he'd have to defeat A'isha first. And that he would never do.

HE WAITS FOR YOU

uhammad's adopted son, Zayd, found Raha the next day tied to a tree and bleeding all over.

"They tried to force me to denounce the Prophet," she told my mother on our balcony a few nights later, her soft voice quavering, as I listened from the ladder below. "I wanted to curse them, but my mouth would not form the words."

Umar and Abu Sufyan had taken turns at the whip, threatening to kill her if she wouldn't obey them. When she'd passed out, unable to bear the pain anymore, they'd left her, assuming she was dead or would be soon.

Ummi sucked in her breath, then spoke in a hushed, urgent voice. "Did they—are you—"

"My honor is intact, thank al-Lah," Raha said. She paused. When she spoke again, she sounded tiny and far away. "But to my shame, I had to be examined by a midwife before I could return home. My husband's family demanded it. If I had been raped, they would have insisted he divorce me."

I gasped in outrage at her words—why should she be punished for others' evil deeds?—then clamped my hand over my mouth. But it was too late: My mother's head snapped around before I could duck out of sight and in a moment she was leaping up from her seat and shooing me down the ladder, following close behind.

"You are supposed to be in bed, not listening to tales for adult ears," she muttered as she pushed me along to my bedroom. "But I am glad you heard Raha's story. Maybe now you will be thankful that we keep you inside. Raha is fortunate, but those men would have ruined you."

Like the lavender plant she loved so much, the delicate Raha was a hardy survivor. One week after her abduction she loaded up all her household goods and led her husband to Yathrib, the Jewish city to the north where Muhammad's distant relations had agreed to harbor him and his followers. As I watched their slow retreat from my window I swallowed my sorrow by the mouthful, reminding myself that I was a warrior now. Yet as her little caravan moved away from me, diminishing with each step, my chest tightened as though my heart were shrinking also. May al-Lah curse that villain Abu Sufyan for chasing my Raha away! Yet, as it turned out, we would join her very soon.

The next evening Ali pounded on our door, yelling for Muhammad. When I arrived at the entryway, my mother was holding the door open and pressing a hand to her throat. Ali burst past her with eyes like shooting stars, waving his arms at Muhammad, who had just come in from my father's mosque.

"*Yaa* cousin, Abu Sufyan and his friends are sending their sons to murder you tonight," he said between gasps. "One youth from each tribe in Mecca, so no tribe will bear the blame for your death."

My mother cried out, causing my heart to miss a beat. I ran to her side, but she shook her head and told me to go to my room. Instead I turned to Muhammad, whose face was as pale as if he were already dead, but he only nodded to Ali and headed with the men toward the *majlis*. I made sure my mother wasn't watching me, then followed them. After more than two years' *purdah*, I knew no one would bother to tell me what was happening. But I had become a very stealthy spy.

I listened in silence, crouching outside the *majlis* curtain, while the men devised their plan. Since the assassins would strike tonight, they'd have to work quickly. Muhammad needed to get out of Mecca as soon as possible, and he'd have to stay away a long time—forever, perhaps.

"Al-Lah has made His intentions clear," Muhammad said to *abi*. "I will leave for Yathrib as soon as it is safe."

"And I will escort you," my father said. "Not a single hair on your head will be harmed, al-Lah willing."

"*Yaa* Abu Bakr, I am more capable of protecting him than you are," Ali said. "Wouldn't it be better, cousin, if I escorted you to Yathrib?"

"God has other work in mind for you, Ali," Muhammad said.

My father borrowed some clothing from one of his servants and cloaked Muhammad in it, disguising him, then hurried him away to a cave outside town. Meanwhile, Ali wrapped himself in Muhammad's red robe and lay on his bed, pretending to sleep. I, Asma, and my mother and her sister-wives went to Muhammad's home—me bouncing in my saddle all the way across town, thrilling at the adventure and the fresh air. We climbed the stairs to a bedroom and watched from the windows as a gang of men crept toward the house. When they banged on the door, we stuck our heads outside as Muhammad had told us to.

"Come back tomorrow," Muhammad's wife Sawdah called in a calm voice, although she gripped her Evil-Eye amulet as though it held her rooted to the earth. "The Prophet is sleeping. He will be ready enough to see you in the morning."

Unwilling to force their way inside and kill Muhammad while women were in the house, they waited outside the door, murmuring and watching him sleep—or so they thought. In the morning, when *abi* and Muhammad had had plenty of time to get away, Ali stepped outside, dropped the robe, and whipped out his sword, scattering the sons of Quraysh like so many flies. When the assassins were gone, we women went home and packed our belongings. The time had come for us to leave Mecca.

We fled on a moonless night, cloaked by a darkness as close as the grave. Tears choked our whispered good-byes to our motherland, the city of our ancestors, the home of our births and our blessed temple, the Ka'ba. We carried almost nothing with us, just food and water and a few clothes. Leaving our dirty dishes behind. Tossing our family histories into the fire. What good had our relatives done for us? We had the *umma*—the Believers—and Muhammad. Our caravan included me; Muhammad's daughters Fatima and Umm Kulthum; his wife, Sawdah; my mother and Qutailah; my brother Abd al-Rahman, and my sister. We left behind my father's wife Alia, who refused our God. She pressed her idol Manat between her palms as she watched us slip away. She would pray for us, she said, that we would realize our error before it was too late.

"You'd better pray for yourself," I muttered, but my mother wept and clung to her until Qutailah pulled them apart.

I would have cried, also, except for my resolve to become a warrior. Mecca was the only home I had ever known, and even in my *purdah* I'd dreamt of her colorful market, her craggy mountains, her enormous, cube-shaped Ka'ba crowded inside and out with scary, beautiful carved gods. Would I ever see my beloved city again? Would I ever see my friend Nadida, who could turn her long face and wide mouth into likenesses of the Ka'ba's idols, making us laugh so hard our sides ached? Would Safwan's family join us, or would they remain in Mecca and marry him to someone else? I looked back at the city as we rode away, yearning for a glimpse of my friends, but it was late and the houses of Mecca slept as if assassins had never roamed her streets.

We rode north to Yathrib, the Jewish town, where the Arabic tribes living there—Aws and Khazraj—had agreed to offer refuge to Muhammad and his followers. The journey was long, through desert sands so deep we had to place blankets before our camels' feet so they wouldn't sink to their knees. Over vast, desolate plains of jagged black rock and desert wilderness where a single misstep could break a bone. Through forests of palms so dense we had to shout to keep from losing one another. Beside the foreboding ridge of Mount Subh rising like a massive *djinni* between us and the Red Sea. Onward we pressed, to our Prophet and my father and a new life, free, we hoped, of fear.

At the break of our twelfth day we arrived, me weeping and rubbing my eyes against the onslaught of green. Green glowed in bawdy profusion over the daisy-strewn fields, the hills blaring with lushness and lavender, the promenade of grasses and shrubs and trees. It dripped from delicate green limbs dangling unripe pomegranates, from gnarled and woody acacias, and, in whispers, from pale-leafed olives dappling the terrain with dabs of blue and gray like shade, relieving the eyes from the emerald glare. Against the ring of rust-red hills surrounding the town on three sides, green leapt up as if alive. From my camel's hump I could feel the leaf-kissed air moving like a cool moist cloth across my brow as I inhaled the fresh clean scents of petal and blade and springs gilding the morning.

This was Yathrib. Or, as Muhammad called it, al-Medina, "The City." Some city! As we entered the humble arched gate of stone and mud, a different aroma greeted us along with the bleats and moans of sheep and cattle. I gasped and covered my nose against the tang of manure, sharp as a slap, rank enough to sting my eyes. Flies whirled like sandstorms in constant frenzy, clustering in the corners of our eyes, blocking my view of the homes in all their mud-bricked squalor and the rotted grins of farmers in grimy clothes. My *ummi's* eyes brimmed with tears as we rode down the single, sorry street.

In only a few days my mother was fretting: Why had we ever moved? Mecca had its problems these days, but compared to Medina it was Paradise. Where, in this town, was the bustling market offering everything we could ever want? Where were the shops and the colorful caravans? Where were the crowds of people from faraway lands in their strange costumes, speaking in tongues like music? We missed our majestic Mount Hira, stony and black as a thunderhead, and our families and friends.

We didn't, however, miss Abu Sufyan. He made sure of that.

We'd ridden eleven days to get to Medina, but it wasn't far enough. The Quraysh threatened us still. For them, idol worshipping and money were as tightly intertwined an orb weaver's web. To disrupt one, they thought, would destroy the other. So they tried to destroy our *umma* instead. Every week we heard about another assassin sent by Abu Sufyan to kill Muhammad. Fear filled our mouths like the Meccan dust in our new oasis home. Muhammad urged us to enjoy the moist green grass and shade here, but his worry showed in the constant click of his prayer beads through his fingers. Alone in our new home, I played with my stick-sword in the courtyard, pretending I fought off murderers, protecting our Prophet. In all the excitement, I almost forgot about the engagement announcement that my parents were too busy to make. But I didn't forget to watch for Safwan.

His family would have to make the *hijra* to Medina soon. We heard more terrible stories every day. Abu Sufyan was enraged over Muhammad's escape. His men had begun snatching Believers in the daylight and cutting their throats in Mecca's streets. Ali and Zayd helped hundreds flee. No Believer could remain in Mecca and hope to live.

When Safwan arrived, would he be able to find me? The houses stood apart from one another here. The people of Medina made their living growing crops, mostly date-palm trees and barley, and raising animals. I could see more sheep and goats from my window than people. Not that I looked out my window all that often: The stink of manure blew into my room with the slightest breeze. So I played instead on the long swing my father hung for me under the sheltering date-palm tree in our courtyard. I learned to swing so high and so far, I could see over the edge of the house and into the valley below. Every time I glimpsed the rolling land and horizon, I looked for Safwan.

Perhaps his parents had delayed their emigration because of the troubles we'd suffered here. Many of us caught a horrible fever, from the flies and mosquitoes, my mother said. My father almost died from it. I lay in bed for days, delirious. My hair snarled on my pillow in a web of tangles my *ummi* had to chop out with a knife. When she finished, I looked more like a son than a daughter.

"It will grow back," she said. I looked in the mirror and saw my boyish self, hair splayed like an open hand and eyes gleaming, and hoped she was wrong.

When I'd fully recovered from my illness, my father invited me into the courtyard for a cup of galangal water and a "talk." In my room, my hand jittered as I combed my hair for the event, and I had to force my breath to slow down. My parents had never made this kind of invitation to me before. I could easily imagine what they wanted to discuss.

Please, al-Lah, oh please let them say my husband will be Safwan. Don't let them marry me to Muhammad. I know he's Your Messenger, but he's an old man—and I want to ride free with the Bedouins.

But al-Lah didn't hear my prayer. As I sat across from my beaming parents and sipped the delicate spicy water, their words clashed with my desires like metal bars against the whirring wings of a bird.

Muhammad, they said, was to be my husband. It had all been arranged on the day I began my *purdah*.

I set down my drink so violently it sloshed over the lip of the bowl. "But what about Safwan?"

My mother *hmphed*. "That boy? He will never be more than a foot soldier in the *umma's* army. But you, my daughter, will be married to the
Supreme Commander."

"*Yaa* A'isha, Muhammad is very fond of you," my father said. "We have
planned a wedding for next week."

Next week? The wings in my chest flapped wildly. My parents' faces
seemed to spin before me. "But I'm not a woman yet," I squeaked. Our tradition was to wait until a girl's menarche occurred before wedding her to
a man.

"That is what I said." My mother turned sharp eyes on my father. "But
your father wants to have the ceremony now, before Ali marries the
Prophet's daughter Fatima."

"Ali thinks we are in a contest for Muhammad's love," *abi* said, shrugging. "I only want to make certain Muhammad does not forget which of
us is his closest Companion."

As they spoke, the wings in that cage drowned out their voices, beating harder and harder like the slap of the fat Hamal against his frail young
wife. In only one week, I would lie under Muhammad while he pinned me
down with his body, imprisoning me, hurting me. Would he hear my cries
of pain? Or would he only pound into me harder and faster, as Hamal had
done to Fazia-turned-Jamila?

"A'isha. *Yaa* A'isha!" My mother's shout startled me out of my terrible
vision. I stared at her, wondering how she could let this happen. Was she
my mother, with a woman's heart and a woman's knowledge of the marriage bed?

"What is wrong with you?" *ummi* said, narrowing her eyes. "Those do
not look like tears of happiness."

"I—," I hesitated, fearing her tongue as sharp as any sword. But then I
thought again of marrying Muhammad and sharing his bed, and my mother's
fury seemed less forbidding. "I want to marry Safwan," I said in a tiny voice.

My father wrinkled his forehead and stroked his beard, as if puzzling out
a problem. My mother, on the other hand, exploded in a high, harsh
laugh.

"Did you think your father invited you out here to ask what you want?"
she said, piercing me with her eyes. "You foolish girl. When are you ever
going to learn?"

◆

Marriage was a charging horse, bearing down on me fast. My days in my parents' home, always excruciatingly slow, now sped past in a blur of tears. I forgot my vow to become a warrior, but dreamt instead of Safwan's rescue. Disappointment tinged each sunrise as I awakened to another day of dread. My mother tried to cheer me by showing me the wedding gown she'd bought for me—*Red and white silk, A'isha, all the way from Yemen!*—but I burst into sobs at the sight of it, making her *tsk* with annoyance. Tears filled my mouth, my nose, my stomach, churning with the food I managed to choke down and bringing it back up again.

All around me the household bustled in preparation for the wedding while I hid in my room, waiting for a miracle. My mother came to my bedroom curtain every day, hissing that Muhammad was here and wanted to see me, but I sat silent, with my back to her. *She is suddenly shy since we told her the news,* I heard her say to him. In truth, the idea of seeing Muhammad made my stomach lurch like the hump of a moving camel, and I knew if he looked on my face he would see my revulsion. I couldn't help the way I felt, but I didn't want to cause him pain. Muhammad had always been kind to me.

What would marriage to him be like? Would he forbid me to play with my dolls and toy horses, as Qutailah had done to Asma when she'd begun her menarche? *You are a woman now, with no time for childishness.* Would he change my name? Would he lock me away as Umar did his wives and daughters? I couldn't be his *hatun,* since he already had a first-wife in Sawdah; I'd be the *durra,* the parrot, serving her every whim. Would Sawdah make me her slave, giving me the basest of chores? My head ached more with each question, as if my worries were fists pounding against my skull.

The day I'd dreaded arrived all too soon. *Ummi* swept into my room and flung open the curtains, spilling the sun's harsh light like water over my face.

"This is one day you will not be hiding in your room," she said. "Arise and dress yourself, A'isha. The wedding guests will arrive in one hour."

I lay in bed for as long as I could, until the need to relieve myself at last tugged me upward like an insistent hand. I pulled on a clean chemise and skirt and tramped barefoot into the courtyard, barely feeling the cool grass under my feet. In a few hours, the sun would blast us with its fiery breath, and Muhammad would take me home with him to recline in our marriage bed. My breath came in short gasps at the thought, as though he were already lying on top of me, and I ran in circles around the yard until all I could hear was the *thrum* of my pulse in my ears and all I could feel was the pounding of my feet on the ground.

When the guests began arriving, my mother called me indoors to greet them. The smell of roasting meat drifted in from the cooking pit beside our house, but for once my mouth did not water with anticipation. *Ummi* smiled to see my skin all glowing and pink from running.

"I knew you would be excited when the Great Day arrived," she said.

I said nothing, not to her; not to Umm Ayman, Sawdah's friend and Zayd's wife, who crinkled her old face at me and told me how fortunate I was; not to Muhammad's daughter Fatima, who hissed that I'd never replace her mother in Muhammad's heart; not to his *hatun*, Sawdah, who pinched my cheek and said what a good time we'd have together as sister-wives. And, when all the women had gathered in our living room and I found myself forgotten, I sneaked outside to play—for the first time in years—with the children filling the courtyard.

Children—lots of children! My body felt as light as air as I bounded out to join them: cousins, children of my parents' friends, little girls, older girls, girls I'd never seen before and girls who often came to play with me, and, praise al-Lah! boys, rambunctious, boisterous, gleeful boys, boys with big ears like jug handles, boys with voices that cracked, boys who chased each other with stick-swords and captured girls as their hostages, making the girls shriek with delight. Children kicked a goat's-bladder ball across the grass, shouting and squealing. They pushed each other daringly high on the swing, then leapt into the air to land on the ground. They pushed and tugged and growled at one another on the teeter-totter, struggling for the seat at the very top.

Within moments I'd not only joined them but I stood at the pinnacle, ruling the seesaw like a queen. Nadida clambered up toward me, and I waved my stick-sword, thinking she would try to push me off.

Then she said "Safwan," and I stopped.

"He arrived in Medina last night," she said.

I almost fell off the teeter-totter. Boys circled below me like upside-down vultures, touching my bare feet with their sticks. I kicked them away with a mighty roar. Was Safwan here now?

I snarled and pushed Nadida to the ground, showing off for a Safwan who might or might not be watching. When my *ummi* came out to call me indoors, I growled at her, too.

"Can't you see I'm playing?" The children around me gasped, thinking I'd be whipped—but I wasn't worried. Since Muhammad had asked my parents to "be gentle" with me, they'd treated me like a princess.

Now, though, my mother's eyes glittered, as hard and black as onyx.

"A'isha, this is no time for games. He waits for you inside. Everyone waits!" She grasped my ankle and yanked me to the soft dirt. My playmates cheered and screamed.

"Go to your husband!" Nadida cried, carried away as usual. "He waits for you in bed."

My mother gasped, glaring at her, and yanked me to my feet. Stomping toward the *harim* she dragged me behind her, nearly pulling my arm from its socket.

"Look at you," she scolded as she jerked me along, to a cacophony of hoots from my delighted playmates. "Breaking your *purdah*, risking our good name, and rolling in the dirt on your wedding day. Are you the daughter of Abu Bakr, or a wild animal?"

Inside the house, the smell of cardamom sweetened the air from the *majlis*, where my father sat with the men and drank fragrant coffee. I craned my neck as we passed, searching for Safwan. I tried to dig in my heels as *ummi* pulled me along, but my feet only bumped along the stone-and-clay floor.

In the living room the women fanned themselves with date-palm fronds and smiled as *ummi* pulled me past them to the walled-in area behind the house where our family bathed. A large pot of water steamed over a bed of black coals, which gave off an acrid odor. Asma dipped a rag into the pot and began to scrub my face.

"Soiled and spoiled," she said. Her eyes danced under heavy eyebrows. "Some wife you are going to make."

My mother raised my shirt over my head, ignoring my protests. I felt my face flame to be so exposed, and I covered my budding breasts with my arms, which made Asma laugh.

"You won't keep those date-seeds hidden much longer," she teased.

"Starting tonight, you'll have to share them with your husband." She winked at me. "Just hope he doesn't nibble too hard."

I felt a creeping over my skin as if I'd rolled in a nest of scorpions, and I shivered even as my sister poured hot water over my back.

"Do not be a fool, Asma," snapped my mother. "This is only the marriage, not the consummation. A'isha has not begun her blood flow yet."

No consummation! I didn't know what the word meant, but it had something to do with blood. I pressed my hands harder against my chest so my heart wouldn't burst through.

"Why marry her to him now, when she is so young?" Asma said.

"Blame your father, not me," *ummi* said, and poured a cup of water over my head. "This rivalry with Ali has affected his reason."

"But whoever heard of a nine-year-old getting married?"

"That is what I asked Abu Bakr." My mother hurled the cup into the pot, splashing water over the edge and onto the hard-packed dirt, where it scattered like marbles. "But you know how he is. Stubborn, like his youngest daughter." She gave me a pointed look, then continued her conversation with my sister.

"'These are new times,' your father said. 'We have a new home in a new city, with a new God. Why should tradition still rule when it comes to marriage?' As for me, I prefer to wait. But your father makes the decisions and I obey. Tradition still rules in that respect, it seems."

From a camel's-hair bag she pulled out my wedding gown and held it up to me. Once again, I nearly burst into tears at the sight of it. But then I reminded myself to pretend I was happy. That way, everyone would be caught off guard when I and Safwan ran away.

"This is too large for you," *ummi* said. She slipped the gown over my head, covering my eyes and binding my arms while I fantasized about escape. "We did not expect a wedding so soon."

The silk felt cool and soft against my skin, like water. The neck of the gown scooped slightly, baring the hollow pressed like a thumbprint into my throat. The white sleeves rippled loose at the shoulders, then tapered to encircle my wrists like a father's hand. For a moment, I felt beautiful—until my mother offered me my reflection in a piece of polished brass and I noted my hair's garish color, like a flag, and the muddy green tint of my eyes. Why couldn't I have lovely dark features like the beauties the poets wrote about?

I asked for a scarf or wrapper, but my mother shook her head. "The Prophet loves your red hair. You know that."

Another devil-wind began deep in my stomach, then whirled wider and higher until I thought it would consume me completely. By al-Lah, it was already beginning! The marriage hadn't even happened yet, and already Muhammad—or, at least, the idea of him—was determining how I should dress.

I saw my dreams of freedom fade like the light from my grandmother's eyes as she'd lain on her deathbed. Dizziness staggered me. This was not my life! I, A'isha, was supposed to wield a sword and race camels in the desert. Instead I was about to march under my *ummi's* glaring eye to a life of servitude with a *shaykh*—an old man—and the toothless, grinning Sawdah as my only companions.

But the promise of a rescue brightened my mood like a shimmering oasis on the desert horizon. By the time Sawdah poked her jowly face into the room and announced that "he" was ready, I'd talked a smile onto my lips. My mother must have noticed the change because she squeezed my shoulder in a rare sign of affection.

"Such pride you bring to our family today," she said in a choked voice. I turned away from her, ready to bolt, but she stopped me with a hand on my arm.

"Walk slowly, with your head high, for everyone will be watching," my mother said. "A bride carries herself with dignity."

But how, with legs that trembled as if they had no bones? I wobbled as I walked, my legs growing heavier with each step and my pulse thudding in my ears, into the dim *harim*, the women's living area, where women rattled tambourines and lamp flames flung dancing shadows on the walls. Raha floated like a cloud to me, her eyes shining, and handed me a fragrant bouquet of lavender.

"Be strong, Little Red," she whispered as she pressed her cheek to mine. "Al-Lah will reward you for it." Then she turned to the other women and lifted her hands into the air. "Our A'isha, exalted above all women!" she cried.

Ululations filled the room like the warbles of a thousand and one birds. Shining, smiling faces swirled before me like colors through a prism. Sawdah, grinning and showing her black teeth and blacker holes where teeth used to be, strew rose petals at my feet. Their fragrance softened the faint unctuous tinge of burning lamp oil before getting lost among the perfumes the women wore. Muhammad's daughters from his marriage to Khadija, who had died years ago, stood in a cluster and watched the procession: Ruqayyah, pale as the belly of a pigeon and smiling wanly; Umm Kulthum, broad-waisted and robust; and bland, bowl-faced Fatima, whose polite smile didn't reach her eyes. Where was Safwan's mother? I glanced past the faces before me, into the corners, into the hallway beyond. Hadn't she made the journey from Mecca with her son?

"Keep going," my mother whispered. "To mine and your father's bedroom. The Prophet waits for you there."

I stepped into the dark hallway, my legs still shaking. No one had to tell me to walk slowly now. My pulse charged my legs with blood, urging them to run—but in the opposite direction. Just beyond the curtain to my parents' bedroom, I could hear the laughter and shouts of men. Men! I had been cut off from them for so many years—and now I was going to have to walk into a room full of them.

One by one Muhammad's daughters disappeared through the curtain, then the neighbors, still ululating and rattling their tambourines, followed by Sawdah with her rose petals. Next it was my turn. I stopped, staring at the saffron silk curtain, which had once been my mother's wedding gown. *Where is Safwan?*

"Go, A'isha!" My mother's voice jolted me back to the moment. I told my right foot to step forward. Nothing happened. I closed my eyes and took a deep breath. My future awaited on the other side—a fate chosen by others, as though I were a sheep or a goat fatted for this day. I began to tremble like the branch of a tree.

"What are you waiting for? Ramadan?" My mother's voice rasped in my ear. Her hand reached forward to pull the curtain aside. Light poured like honey over my skin, light from myriad lamps and candles warming me. The thick aroma of—what? A fragrance so rare, so intoxicating— frankincense—prodded my nose and mouth, gagging me. Song trilled from the throats of the women who lined the room, while the men who'd crowded at the front craned their necks to see me: the wealthy Uthman, twirling his mustache with ringed fingers; the narrow-eyed Umar, now a convert to *islam*, licking his thick lips and appraising me with cold eyes.

Hamal, the man whose hairy backside had haunted my days and nights for years, winked at me, and I shivered.

My father towered over them all, as tall and imposing as the angel Gabriel himself, his beard burnished with henna, his bearing proud, his eyes radiating love for me, drawing me into the room at last. He greeted me with a kiss on the cheek, as soft as an oasis breeze, then draped a beautiful necklace of milky-white agate stones about my neck.

"Do not be afraid," he whispered. "Summon your courage and make us all proud of you."

I faltered ahead, step by agonizing step. Ali, with his bad-smell sneer, stood in front of me, blocking my view of everyone behind him. I twisted my neck to see around him, wishing he would disappear. Back in the front of the room, my father now held a silver bowl of milk in both hands, like an offering. Gazing soft-eyed at me. Blinking wetly. *Abi*, crying! I wanted to run to him, to curl against him and forget all the knowing eyes in the room. After only two steps, I stopped again, glaring at Ali. Then my sister's hands were on my back, shoving me forward. Soft laughter broke up the singing as I stumbled ahead, tripping on the hem of my gown. Ali stepped aside just in time to avoid the stomp of my sandal on his foot. I looked up from the floor to the end of the pathway now cleared for me— and I cried out in alarm. Muhammad sat just a few steps away on my parents' bed, holding his hand out to me, his eyes as soft as cloud-misted moons.

I reeled, unsteady, as if the earth were buckling under my feet. I stared at Muhammad, face to face with my future, and swallowed the bile that rose in my throat. He offered me his beautiful smile with those flawless teeth as bright as the sun.

"A'isha," he said, his deep voice meant to comfort, but jolting me like an earthquake. "My delightful child-bride. *Yaa* Little Red, there is nothing to worry about. It is only me."

His face looked so kind—and so old. His hand nearly touched me. I drew back, eliciting gasps from the crowd. The shock on his face brought tears flowing like rivers down my cheeks.

Sobbing, I turned away from Muhammad, the friend I'd hurt, and my *abi*, whom I'd betrayed, and ran—once again, into the formidable wall that was my mother.

She grabbed me by the shoulders and jerked me back, snapping my neck. Her eyes stabbed me with their murderous glare. I wanted to keep running but she held me tight, so I let my knees collapse, trying to sink to the floor—anything to escape my mother's look of utter disgust.

"What are you doing?" she said in a hissing voice, shaking me and making my head loll. "Are you trying to ruin us?"

"By al-Lah, what is going on?" Umar's gruff voice silenced all the murmurs in the room. "Is there going to be a marriage today, or not?"

"Do not scold her, Umar." Muhammad spoke gently. "She is still young. Perhaps this ceremony is too much—" My hopes lifted at his words, but my father dashed them again.

"No!" At the sound of *abi's* shout I turned to look at him. His eyes had lost their softness, and seemed to bulge from their sockets. He gestured toward my mother. "Umm Ruman, help your daughter."

"What is done is done, *yaa* A'isha. You must go," my mother said.

I shook so hard my bones would have clattered if not for the cushion of my skin. I looked wildly around me, at my *abi's* panicked eyes. Fretting over his future. I looked at Muhammad—and, for a moment, his steady gaze calmed me. Would marriage to him be so awful? I'd be queen of Medina—one of them, at least. I would always be loved in Muhammad's home. But—never allowed to charge through the desert, wild and free, or fight with a sword.

I might as well die now.

And with that thought, my legs collapsed, and I crumpled in a soggy, quivering heap to the floor, tucking my head under my arm like a sleeping bird to avoid the smirks and stares of the people in the room.

I heard my mother groan, and I sneaked a glance at her. She spread her hands in the air, looking up at the ceiling as if to say, *Must I do everything?*

Then in a single, swift movement she snatched me up in her arms, and I was in the air, being carried like an infant against her breast. It was the first time in years I had been so close to her. As she strode across the floor I inhaled her spicy perfume and brushed my cheek against hers. *Ummi.* Before I could kiss her, though, she was dumping me into Muhammad's lap. The onlookers cheered, and I cried even harder.

"See how she honors her mother with her tears," I heard Qutailah say.

"Praise al-Lah for those tears," Sawdah said. "A happy bride attracts the Evil Eye."

Muhammad's arms closed softly around me, and, though I wanted to shrug off his embrace, I didn't. I tipped my streaming eyes toward my mother's hard face, pleading, but she didn't look at me. She brushed her palms together as if she'd gotten flour on her hands.

"May you have a long and prosperous life together," she said. She turned and glared at my father, then stomped out of the room.

The Scorpion's Tail

Medina, 623–625
Ten to twelve years old

At least I'll be free from this prison. So I consoled myself on the day I married Muhammad. Although my body tensed at the thought of sharing his bed, my heart leapt to think of leaving my parents' home at last. But then, at the door, he kissed the crown of my head and said "good-bye," and I felt as though my heart were a little bird and a hand had closed around it and begun to squeeze.

"You cannot come with me, Little Red—not yet," he said. "It would not be proper. You must remain with your parents until you grow up. But I will visit you every day."

I watched through my tears as he mounted his camel, but before I could call out to him my mother had pulled me inside and slammed the door.

"I told you, this is the marriage, not the consummation," she said.

"But I want to go with Muhammad. I'm tired of living in this cave."

My mother *tsked*. "Go with Muhammad? And then what? Everyone would cluck their tongues and talk about poor A'isha, being taken so young by that cruel lecherous Muhammad."

Qutailah, standing beside her, nodded. "The *umma* is already buzzing like a beehive over the Prophet's marriage to a nine-year-old."

"Why can't I just move in with him, then?" I asked. "If everybody is already talking."

"*Yaa* Umm Ruman," Qutailah said, "you need to teach this child a few things." She arched her eyebrows at my mother, then looked at me. "Men marry women for two reasons, A'isha. To give them pleasure in bed, and to bear their children. You cannot do either for the Prophet now, not until you begin your blood flow." She wagged a finger. "Save your tears for that day."

My mother cried out and pulled me to my bedroom, where she told me to forget Qutailah's foolishness and get some sleep.

"Forget your silly notions about Safwan, also," she said. "You are the wife of Muhammad now, for which you should be thankful, not crying."

What mother ever truly knows her daughter? A stranger to my desires, my *ummi* could not begin to fathom my misery at being locked indoors or my longing for the mystery of womanhood to pin me with its red badge. For other girls, the marriage ceremony opened the doors of *purdah* and out they flew, transformed like butterflies by the wedding night. Only my blood—and my body—would win my emancipation.

I spent many hours swinging in the courtyard, searching over the rooftop for Muhammad now, the only one who could free me—even as I dreaded the price of that freedom. For nearly three years I arced toward womanhood, then swooped back to girlhood, wavering between daughter and wife, between yearning for my new life and dreading it. Inside, I bumped against the walls in my father's dark home, hidden from view like the holiest idols in the Ka'ba, my breasts now as sacred as Mecca's twin hills, my virginity a temple to be guarded against marauders and Hypocrites like the would-be king of Medina, Ibn Ubayy.

A man with a stout body and eyes like dark pebbles, Ibn Ubayy had been Medina's leader before we arrived. Yet his hard swagger could never compete with Muhammad's sweet smiles. His followers flocked to *islam*, discarding Ibn Ubayy as if he were a stale crust of bread. Jealous, he complained to anyone who would listen: Couldn't people see how soft and weak Muhammad was?

Desperate to discredit Muhammad, Ibn Ubayy began to insult Sawdah and Fatima in public. Whenever they went to market, Ibn Ubayy or one of his grunting friends would snuffle up and try to touch them. *How much for an hour in bed, habibati? I'd pay in gold for a feel of those glorious breasts.* Listening to these tales, I shuddered. How much to let a man sweat and grunt all over me like that? There weren't enough *dinars* in all of Hijaz.

After our marriage, as promised, I saw Muhammad more than ever. Not only did he visit me every day, but now he spent hours with me in the courtyard, stick-sword fighting with me and playing dolls with me and my friends. My pulse had fluttered strangely in his presence at first and I shrank from his touch, fearing the marriage bed and his new power over me as my husband. But his laughter and kindnesses soon put me at ease.

I'd known Muhammad all my life. He'd held me in his arms just moments after I was born, blessing me with a special prayer as I'd flailed and rooted against his chest in search of a nipple, hungry from the start. He'd saved my life, my parents told me, by convincing my father to break the Meccan law. Too few boys were being born that year, so the Qurayshi leaders had decided that all newborn girls should be buried alive in the desert. *Are not girls also the creation of al-Lah?* Muhammad had said to my father, who wept with relief.

In Muhammad's eyes, girls and women were more than just chattel for men to own and disown depending on their whims. They were valuable in God's eyes, and in his own. As his wife, unlike so many other women, I would have a voice that my husband would listen to. I'd have Muhammad's respect.

And, *ummi* said, I would also be revered by the Believers, whose number had grown since God's first revelations to Muhammad ten years ago. One taste of al-Lah's poetry, pouring like sweet rain from Muhammad's lips, could transform the hardest of hearts. Even Umar, sent by Abu Sufyan to assassinate Muhammad in Mecca, had left the Prophet's house a Believer, changed by his recitations. I had heard many such stories, told to me by my mother in breathy, awestruck tones.

Now, away from the clutches of Quraysh, our *umma* stood to become a powerful force in Hijaz, and those closest to Muhammad would gain the most.

"You will hold the highest status among women in Medina—and, someday, in all of Hijaz," my mother said, her gaze as misty as if she longed to wed Muhammad herself.

When my menarche began, I would move to Muhammad's home to become his wife "in every way," my mother said, making me gasp as if a great weight lay on top of me. *What prestige you will enjoy as the daughter of Abu Bakr!* she added. And with the lumpish, motherly Sawdah as my only sister-wife, I would hold Muhammad's heart in my hand.

"Sawdah is no *hatun*, but only a housekeeper for him," my mother said. "Earn her trust, and she will give the position to you. Because of your age, you may have to fight to keep it if he marries again—unless you bear his heir. Then you will rule the *harim*, if that is your desire."

I clenched my jaw, holding in my bitter words. Being the *hatun* was more than a desire for me now. After watching my mother scrub Qutailah's clothes, struggle to carry Qutailah's water, and endure Qutailah's snide insults, I'd made it my goal to become Muhammad's first-wife. Then, one day, that goal became a burning necessity.

"Trim a fingertip's length off my hair," Qutailah ordered my mother that hot afternoon.

"I am not experienced at hair-trimming," my mother said. "You will do best to ask Barirah." A new servant from Abyssinia, Barirah had aston-ished us all with her skills as a hair stylist.

"I sent Barirah to the market more than one hour ago. She has not returned," Qutailah said, handing my mother the scissors.

Her mouth set grimly, *ummi* began to trim the ends of Qutailah's hair. But, unlike Barirah, she didn't cut in a straight, even line. The edge she made zigged slightly upward to the center of Qutailah's back, then down-ward again. I felt my chest swell with dread as I watched her work, her eyes narrowed in concentration, her skin beginning to flush as she realized how badly her "trim" was turning out.

"By al-Lah, are you planning to spend all day on this?" Qutailah snapped.

"Your hair is drying so quickly, it is difficult for me to cut it evenly," *ummi* said. "Let me cut a little more."

Qutailah *hmphed*. "I should have known better than to entrust a woman with six thumbs to perform even this simple task."

In truth, she should have known better. Hadn't *ummi* warned her? When Qutailah looked down and saw all that hair spread like a carpet around her, she leapt to her feet and grabbed my mother by the shoulders.

"You idiot!" she screamed. "Look what you have done to me!" She raised her hand high above her head and brought it down on my mother's face.

The sight of *ummi's* tears, as rare as rain, and the flurry of her hands to cradle her burning cheek made my blood turn cold. A gleam of metal in the blazing sun caught my lowering glance as the scissors fell from my mother's hand. I pounced on them, then pointed them at Qutailah. The fear in her eyes made me laugh, which caught my mother's attention.

"A'isha, no!" *ummi* cried. "Drop those scissors at once."

"Don't ever touch my mother again," I snarled, advancing on Qutailah. "If you do, I'll cut you to pieces." Her eyes grew as large as bowls.

But before I could get any closer to her my mother reached out and snatched the scissors from my hand. "Go to your room," she said. "And wait for me there."

I waited for what seemed like an hour, walking circles and fuming over that slap. How viciously Qutailah treated my mother, as if *ummi* were no better than a dog! And how doglike my mother had responded, whimpering and holding her paw to her face.

I would never, ever live the way my mother did. If Sawdah tried to order me around in Muhammad's *harim*, I'd show her with one sharp sentence who was quicker of tongue. If she hit me, I'd either kill her or make her wish for death. I was A'isha bint Abi Bakr, beloved of the Prophet of al-Lah, slave to no one.

When my mother finally came to my room, her mouth trembled and her face was colorless except for the red welt on her cheek.

"I was defending you," I said to her. Her laughter mocked me. She lifted her hand and slapped my face so hard my ears rang. I crouched over to comfort myself and also to hide from her, but when I glanced up she was crying softly.

"You defended nothing," she said. "You have enraged Qutailah. Now she will punish me for your attack."

"Punish you? Why? I'm the one who threatened her, not you."

"*Yaa* A'isha, do you know nothing after all this time sequestered here?" She wiped her tears with her sleeve and sighed. "Qutailah has hated me since the day I arrived in this *harim*. She hates me because your father loves me. Her only desire is to cause me misery." Her shoulders sagged as she turned to leave.

"*Yaa ummi*," I said weakly. "Isn't there anything I can do for you?"

Her smile hung crooked, like a broken wing. "The best thing you can do, A'isha, is remember what you saw today—and to make certain you never let it happen to you."

◆

Outside our home the *umma* grew, but our food supplies did not. People came to Medina to escape the Qurayshi, yet they soon began to ask one another if this new religion was worth starvation. In my father's *majlis* Muhammad and his Companions wondered how to feed all the converts, while I hid outside the arched entryway and listened, as still and quiet as a lizard on a rock.

Spellbound, I listened to Ali propose caravan raids as a way to enrich the *umma*. My father spoke against it, saying we were merchants, not Bedouins.

"We are not farmers, either, yet Medina has nothing but crops and live-stock," Umar said. "With whom will we trade in this backward town? The sheep?"

"*Yaa* cousin, Quraysh forced us to leave our homes and our livelihoods," Ali said. "Should we not demand payment from them, at least?"

Muhammad laughed. "Abu Sufyan, willingly parting with a single *dirham*? Even after his death he would come back to guard his loot."

"Then we must force him to pay," Umar said. "All of Hijaz will scorn us for our weakness if we do not."

Ali and Umar's arguments were irresistible. Muhammad ordered his mighty uncle, Hamza, to organize a raid on the next Qurayshi caravan that passed our way. A few weeks later, a furious Abu Sufyan vowed to retaliate for his lost goods by killing every Believer in Hijaz.

"Let them try to fight against us," Ali boasted, brandishing his sword and flexing his arms. "Those soft-bellied merchants will faint at the sight of their own blood."

In my twelfth year, our scouts warned Muhammad that Abu Sufyan was on his way to Medina with an army of nine hundred men.

Uthman's voice shook as he repeated the news. "How can we defeat so many men, when we have so few?"

"With Ali on your side?" I heard the *swish* of Ali's blade. "Do not fear, old man. I and Hamza will kill them all."

Umar grunted in response. No one else spoke for a long moment. Then I heard my father speak words as calming as a cool breeze.

"*Yaa* Muhammad, I am grateful to have Ali on my side, and also Hamza. But most of all, I am glad that al-Lah fights on our behalf. I agree with Ali. Let us go to meet Abu Sufyan and show him whose god is to be feared."

The day our tiny army left Medina, Qutailah clung to my father, weeping, while my mother stood stolidly beside him, not blinking or speaking a word. Asma, also, cried until her eyes looked like raw meat, but I grasped *abi's* beard and kissed his cheek and told him I would pray for his safe return. I stood at my window and watched, my heart a brimming vessel, as he mounted his horse and rode away, the picture of valor in his chain-mail vest and leather helmet and shield. How I longed for the day I could go along to provide water on the battlefield, as women did in those times! I'd bring my sword and join the fight at the first opportunity.

In only a few days, our scouts returned to Medina with the news: The *umma's* army had won the battle at Badr! Not only that, but they had slaughtered so many Qurayshi men that the Red Sea's color had deepened with their blood.

Inside our house, Qutailah and my mother actually hugged each other, and Asma and I danced in the courtyard, giddy with laughter. Outside, the men who had not gone to Badr filled the streets with shouts as jubilant as if they had played a part in the victory. We ululated with pride for our army and in thanksgiving to al-Lah. Some shed tears over their Qurayshi kin who had died in the battle, but not me. I rejoiced to be free from the fear Abu Sufyan had caused us for so long. After such a defeat, he would surely leave us alone from now on.

A few months later, when my blood began to flow, I felt light enough to dance again. At last Muhammad would come for me, and I'd be able to leave this tomb! Yet as my mother washed my legs and fastened a cloth between them, I stared without blinking to force the water to my eyes. According to custom, I was supposed to cry when I left my parents' home.

"By al-Lah, what are you sniffling about?" my mother said, waving her hands as if to sweep away my tears. "You are a woman now, A'isha. You should be rejoicing, not acting like a child."

Yet, what woman played with toys? My wooden horses still gave me hours of pleasure. My soft dolls and cloth animals knew all my secrets. But *ummi* shook her head when she saw me pulling them off my bedroom shelves and placing them in a goatskin bag.

"Leave those here," she said. "You will be busy at the mosque. Muhammad does not keep slaves or hire servants. Sawdah does the work, and you will help her." I shrugged and continued packing my dolls, but she snatched the bag out of my hand. "No daughter of Abu Bakr's will enter her bridal chamber with arms full of toys! You are the Prophet's wife—not his daughter."

When I had finished packing, she turned to leave the room. I grabbed my favorite doll, Layla, from my bed and stuffed her inside my robe. Then I followed my *ummi* into the living room, where Muhammad greeted me with a smile as warm and bright as the sun. He looked much younger than his fifty-five years that day, standing in my parents' cool, whitewashed room with legs apart and his hands planted on his hips. His white tunic and skirt hung loose over his compact body, and his dark curls sprang, unruly, from beneath his white turban.

His eyes like honey flowed sweet glances over my face and body, lingering appreciation over my red-and-white striped wedding gown as though he'd never seen it before.

"Today," he said, "I am the most fortunate man in all Hijaz."

"Today and every day, from now on," I flirted back.

"Yes, very fortunate," he said, nodding, "to be married to such a modest young woman."

"If it's modesty you treasure, you should have married al-Qaswa. I have never heard that camel brag about anything."

Muhammad's laugh was like a lion's roar. My father laughed, too, and even my mother, whose eyes seemed to dance like candlelight whenever she looked at Muhammad. "You see what you are contending with, Prophet," she said. "I hope you will not change your mind."

"And forgo the opportunity to wake up laughing every morning?" Muhammad said.

The image of us in bed together flashed like a bolt of lightning through my mind, and I heard nothing else anyone said. I don't remember whether my mother kissed me good-bye or cried a single tear; I don't know what my father murmured as he pressed into my hand a leather pouch containing five silver *dirhams*. All I could think about was that old, hairy-bottomed Hamal astride his small young wife. Fazia-turned-Jamila had been only a year or two older that day than I was now.

Red tinged the morning sky as Muhammad and I rode together on al-Qaswa, his pure white camel, away from my parents' house and across the meadow separating us from the city proper. Clouds shifted uneasily before the sun. Palm fronds waved as if welcoming us. Purple lavender flecked the pale, scrubby grass, scenting the breeze. Sheep billowed past, bleating like crying babies. I gripped the bridle in my hands and wondered if I would ever visit my father's house again.

Then we were in the shit-stinking city. I never saw more flies anywhere than in Medina in those days. They feasted on the manure that sheep, goats, and dogs dropped in the streets, then came to sip from the corners of our eyes. I forgot, for a moment, about the marriage bed as I flailed my arms to shoo them away.

"The flies love whatever is sweet," Muhammad teased. "See how they are leaving me alone?"

Their attack subsided as we neared the mosque. I blinked and beheld the city for the first time since I'd entered it two years ago. Straight-backed women walked to and from the pond where water was collected, balancing clay jugs or laundry baskets on their heads. Men in coarse, pale clothing led donkeys with their carts past rude houses of dried mud and grass. Al-Qaswa stopped, halted by a tall, thin man with a wandering eye and a shorter man with a long, drooping mustache. Both of them bowed to Muhammad and ogled me. I pulled my wrapper about my neck.

"*Yaa* Muhammad, is your young bride ripe at last?" the shorter man said with a dirty grin. "I hope you will not scream too loudly tonight, little girl. It would be cruel to torment those of us who sleep alone."

My face filled with heat. Behind me, Muhammad's body stiffened.

"Do you sleep by yourself? You poor, lonely man," I said, and wrinkled my nose. "But, by al-Lah, from the smell of you I can guess why." The man's face reddened as the people around him—including his tall friend—filled the street with laughter.

"Well spoken, Little Red," Muhammad said as we continued our ride. "Those are Ibn Ubayy's men. A few more embarrassments like that one, and they may learn their manners."

"I've never known an ass to learn anything," I said.

He laughed and squeezed my arm. "I'm going to have to practice my retorts to keep up with you." But he didn't remark on the wedding night, or what it held for me. I recalled the whisperings of Asma, who was married now and lived with her husband. *Hands like scorpions scuttling across your skin,* she'd breathed in my ear last night as she brushed my hair. *And then—the sting of his tail between your legs!*

My jaw dropped when Muhammad pointed out the mosque. This hovel was the home of God's Messenger? I had expected a palace, not this low, squat building of mud bricks. It didn't even have a door! Al-Qaswa kneeled at the entryway and Muhammad stepped down from her hump, then helped me to the ground. A man with a black face as shiny as his bald head stood before us: Bilal. He, too, wore a white tunic and skirt, but with a necklace of pale shells and dark bone plus pieces of ivory in his ears. This was the man whose voice I had heard gonging from atop the mosque five times a day, summoning the Believers to prayer: *Al-Lahu akbar!* Even at a normal volume, his voice seemed to chime. His smile was generous, full of teeth as white as bleached bones. His kind gaze calmed my churning stomach. If he was imagining my upcoming night with Muhammad— as everyone else seemed to be—he did not reveal it.

Muhammad held my hand and led me into the mosque, a large, plain, oblong room colored in varying shades of brown from the floor strewn with pebbles and sand to the dried mud walls. Date-palm fronds slanted across the ceiling, forming a loosely woven roof that allowed the sun to filter through in tiny pinpoints, as though it were raining light. In each stream of diaphanous gold, fine dust swirled as he walked me around with his arm about my shoulder, pointing out the date-palm trunks he and his helpers had cut with long knives and placed through the room as columns to support the roof—"a design of my own devising."

He boosted me up to stand on a tree stump so large it could hold my entire family. Here was where he led the Friday afternoon prayer services.

He cupped his hands to catch the water trickling from the sacred spout on the room's north end, then offered me a drink. As I sipped, he told how he and Umar had built the spout from copper tubes to extend through the wall from a nearby well, bringing in water for cleansing the hands and feet before worship. I marveled at the humble contrast this building made to my parents' home, and decided to talk to Sawdah about adding furniture and colorful cushions to this dreary room.

We walked through another arched doorway on the east side of the mosque and into the courtyard, a large, circular area tufted with long strands of gray-green grass and shaded by a variety of trees: scrubby acacias; a date-palm rising as if to touch the heavens, its leaves shooting outward from its crown like the rays of a green sun; ghaza'a trees with their feather-leafed branches bending as if in prayer. A hut of unbaked brick huddled on the north side of the courtyard, next to a huge tent covered with long camel's hair, which served as insulation against the heat. Muhammad led me around the corner of the mosque where, outside the northern wall, a well-trodden path led to a stone well and, beside it, a garden flourished in glittering display: pomegranate trees bearing orange, bell-shaped blossoms; elegant lime trees; indigo plants flowering the deepest blue; lacy flax plants not yet in flower. This was his daughter Fatima's garden, Muhammad told me. She still tended it daily, but being married to Ali now she had outgrown the swing hanging from a thorn-tree.

"I hope to see you enjoying it, Little Red," he said. I slanted my eyes at him. Wasn't I also a married woman?

Back in the courtyard, Muhammad pointed to the little hut I'd pitied and told me it belonged to Sawdah. If I needed anything and Muhammad was busy, I could usually find her there or in the cooking tent.

"She took care of my daughters after their mother died, and I am certain she will take good care of you." Again, I nearly protested. Did he think I was a child? Did I want him to? I stilled my tongue.

Inside the tent, a black kettle of barley bubbled over an enormous fire pit, and discs of bread puffed on flat stones. A flap in the tent sucked the smoke upward into the tender morning air, but the tent retained the smells of bread and grain and burning coal. Openings at either end of the long, wide tent and a main entrance in the center of the west wall, facing the mosque, provided the only other natural light, but oil lamps hanging from carved date-palm stands illuminated the room so that it was nearly as bright as the outdoors. The fire pit, a large, deep bowl lined with rocks along the long eastern wall, served as the room's centerpiece. At the south end, under one flap, a small boy squatted on his heels and played with toy soldiers on a faded red carpet. Behind him, marbles, dolls, shells, and colorful sticks told me this was a play area for the household's children—most of whom, as Muhammad had said, were grown. The north end of the tent held a second carpet, also faded to a bare blush, scattered with plump tan and brown pillows. This was where Sawdah and I would dine during the hottest part of the day, sheltered from the sun and insulated from the heat.

Directly across from the pit, beside the main entrance, large wooden boxes held more knives plus bowls and plates of fired clay, red and gray, brown and dark green, many of them chipped. These boxes sat on the floor, next to a large slab of white marble streaked with gray, where food was prepared. On it sat a great gray mortar and a pestle as big as a club, a basket of pale ground barley, and a bowl of clarified butter. A tall wooden barrel beside this food-preparation area held dates and the sticky-sweet nectar they seeped, used as a sweetener or, best of all, mixed with water for a refreshing drink.

Near the fire pit a red-faced Sawdah squatted beside a stone slab, grinding barley with a rock. Muhammad greeted her with a smile. She lifted a hand to the windowsill and, with a grunt, hoisted herself up to stand. She waddled across the room wearing a grin riddled with gaps on her broad, round face, and folded me into her body in a doughy embrace. Her musky, unperfumed odor took my breath away.

"Tut, what a tiny thing!" she said. "I had better get busy cooking. You need some padding on those hips!" She nudged me with her elbow. "A man needs something to hold on to, as you will find out soon enough."

A telltale heat crept up my neck to my cheeks. By al-Lah, was the bedroom all anyone could think about today? I lowered my eyes so she couldn't see my irritation.

"*Yaa* Sawdah, see how red my bride's face has become!" Muhammad chided her gently. "You embarrass us both."

But she only laughed and hugged me again, then turned to embrace Muhammad. She called her son from her previous marriage to meet us— just six years old, the pudgy-cheeked Abdal already showed signs of inheriting his mother's shape—then nudged us toward the courtyard, say-ing she needed to finish preparing the daily meal.

"Go! Enjoy these days and nights alone together," she said. "They are the most memorable times for any bride." Her eyes danced. "Savor them, A'isha. You will be working with me in the cooking tent soon enough."

Days and nights. Alone together. What would I and Muhammad do? Many things, according to Asma. Unspeakable things. *When she bleeds, she's ready to breed.* Me, bear a child? I could not imagine revealing my body to any man. *Close your eyes and it will be over quickly.* Muhammad led me across the courtyard to another, newer hut, attached to the mosque and fronted with a small, plain door of green wood.

"This is where you will live, and where I will sleep on my nights with you," he said. My wedding gown dragged like chains around my feet as he led me into the mosque to wash our hands at the spout. The water trick-led cool across my trembling fingers, calming my clamoring heart.

"Let us ask al-Lah to bless our marriage," he said. He reached for a pair of date-fiber mats leaning against the wall and unrolled them to face south, toward Mecca. Together we performed two *raka'at*, bowing at the waist, then lowering ourselves to our knees and pressing our foreheads to the ground.

"Oh God, nurture my love and affection for her and nurture hers for me," Muhammad prayed as we bowed and prostrated ourselves. "Inspire us with love for each other."

Give me courage, I prayed. *And please don't let it hurt too much.*

We rolled up our mats and replaced them. He took my hand and led me outside again. Dizziness muddled my vision as if I had sunstroke. At the door of my hut, we stopped. Muhammad stepped behind me and placed his hands over my eyes.

I stifled a cry and clung to my doll, which was still hidden beneath my robe. I felt his body radiating heat just inches away.

"Enter, and let us express our love," he said.

I walked with faltering steps into the hut. The dirt floor crunched beneath my sandals. The dark smell of mud mingled with the sweet aroma of straw. Muhammad pulled his hands away from my face, and I opened my eyes.

"By al-Lah!" I cried. "Have you brought me to Paradise?"

Wooden soldiers, an entire army of them, filled the shelves and win-dowsills of my bedroom, as well as miniature horses with real horsehair manes, two girl dolls with dark hair and a boy doll wearing a turban, a rope for skipping, a ball—and, leaning beneath a window, a real sword with a curved blade and a hammered brass handle, small and light enough for me to lift easily.

"No more fighting with sticks," Muhammad said. "I will teach you how to use the real thing."

I tucked my doll inside my shirt, then slashed the blade through the air. "Now?"

He laughed and shook his head. His eyes glinted as he stepped toward me. He said: "I had another game in mind for today."

The sword fell from my hand and thudded on the earthen floor.

I held my breath as he reached his fingers toward me. I watched his eyes change, as if catching flame, and I waited for the scuttling hands, the stinging tail. This was the beginning of something new, something terri-ble. Soon I would be lying on my bed beneath him, squashed like a scarab beetle, flailing and sobbing while he slammed himself against me. He would not want to hurt me, but how could he help it? *It's always painful the first time. Just close your eyes and pray he will finish soon.*

"Wait," I said. My voice shook. I grabbed my doll, Layla, and thrust her in front of me. My hands trembled, making my doll quiver, also.

"*Yaa* Muhammad, what do you want to play?" Layla said, shaking her hair at him. "Hide and seek? Horses and soldiers? Or maybe you want to push us on the swing."

His eyes gazed deeply into mine. "This is a solemn occasion, A'isha. The time for children's games is later."

He took a few steps closer, and reached out one hand to tug my wrap-per away from my head. It slipped over my shoulders and onto the floor with a *whoosh.*

"Such lovely red hair, like liquid fire," he murmured. I closed my eyes and tried to savor the caress of his fingers against my cheek, the slide of his palm across my scalp, but all I could think about was the next piece of clothing to fall.

He kissed the crown of my head. He slid his fingers down my arm. He pulled gently at my robe until it slipped off my shoulders and slumped, also, to the floor. I wanted to cover my bare arms with my hair, or with my hands, but I clutched my doll instead and prayed he would finish with me soon. His fingers lightly swirled the skin on my arms, causing chill-bumps. Even in the sultry air of this small, stuffy room, I felt cold.

"A'isha," he said. "Look at me."

I opened my eyes and looked up into his. They were soft and fierce at once, and coming closer as he dipped his head down to kiss my lips. I closed my eyes again and tried to make my body relax, but the feel of his breath on my skin and his mouth against mine only made me grip my doll more tightly. He slipped his tongue inside my mouth. He moved his hands to my waist, and then slowly up my ribcage, toward my breasts. I twisted my doll frantically, willing my hands not to push him away. Then I heard a ripping sound that made me gasp.

I looked down at my hands. Poor Layla lay limp, her eyes vacant, her head torn almost completely off her body.

"Oh, no!" I cried. "I've killed her." Bits of sheep's wool trickled out of her neck and fell across my hand. Her pretty head dangled at an odd angle. I began to sob as if she were a real, flesh-and-blood child instead of an old rag doll.

Tenderly Muhammad took her from my hands and examined the tear.

"She is not dead, only injured," he said. "Fortunately, Sawdah is very adept with a needle. She will mend your dolly without leaving a scar."

"No!" I cried harder. "She'll ruin her. I've seen your sandals—"

Muhammad's laughter boomed, startling me out of my tears. "*Yaa* Little Red, Sawdah works hard enough minding the household. I mend my own clothing—including my sandals."

I laughed, too, through the tears, and put Layla down. How foolish of me to cry over a doll! Many husbands might shout or even slap me, but not Muhammad. I stepped up to him and wrapped my arms around him like a necklace. He folded his arms around me and held me close against him. His body felt as warm as if he'd been out in the sun all day. He smelled sweet and clean, of cardamom and *miswak*. His heart skipped against my ear like a child's feet. His hand stroked my long hair—but differently now, with his whole hand rather than just his fingertips.

"My Little Red," he said. "Your body may be ready for me, but I am afraid your heart is not."

I looked up into his face, expecting to see desire kindling again—but amusement twitched his lips.

"Do you think I don't love you?" I said.

"I know you do, *habibati*. But it is not the same love that I have for you. Yours is a young girl's love, not a woman's." He sighed. "It is the risk I accepted when I married a child-bride."

I sucked in my breath. A child! Children lived with their parents. Would he send me back to that prison?

"I am a child, in some ways," I said. "But I've been trapped inside my father's house for five years. How could anyone grow up without adventures, or at least experiences? If you sent me back there today, I would be the same in five more years."

He grinned. "Send you back? Why would I want to do that? Already you have brought laughter to this lonely place. Little Red, you will not reside in your parents' home again. You and I will stay together for as long as we live—and afterward, in Paradise."

"But—what about the consummation? We're not truly married without it."

"A wedding takes place in the heart, not in the bedroom." He pulled me close and kissed my forehead. "Although, I like the bedroom part. And so will you—when you are ready. In the meantime, we have other, very important, things to do."

He loosened his hold. I stepped back from him and looked up at his face—but he had already moved past me to the sword I'd dropped on the floor. He picked it up and held it to the light, turned it this way and that, flashing the sun against his face. He turned to me with a fierce grin.

"Lesson number one," he said. "How to disarm your opponent."

TROUBLEMAKER

MEDINA, MARCH 625

The sun was a white hot sword, striking feeble *shaykhs* and panting dogs to the parched ground. Its relentless blows sent the wilting Fatima to seek refuge in her room, where she hung dark cloths on the windows and lay with a dampened rag over her face. As for me, I was no cringer from the heat, especially not today.

During those years in my father's house I'd had to miss the sights, sounds, and flavors of Medina's big yearly market, whose festivities brought traders from all over Hijaz and beyond to the Kaynuqah neighborhood on the city's edge. Now, in spite of Ali's protests, I was finally going. Nothing would keep me away: not the heat, nor Ali's surly glares, nor even the danger of attack by our Kaynuqah neighbors.

As we saddled our horses and Sawdah's camel, Ali glowered and complained about the heat—but I knew it was the errand he resented. I'd seen the sullen droop of his eyelids when Muhammad had asked him to escort us. It was clear that he considered the task beneath him. Resentment, and not the weather, was why he slumped against the mosque wall, in the shade, and watched poor Sawdah struggle to heave her bulk over her camel's hump.

"Everyone with a brain is at home today, keeping cool," he said loudly, as if he were speaking to al-Lah Himself. His face was taut, all angles and planes and sharp points.

"*Yaa* Ali, the heat keeps only the lazy from an event like this one," I said, glaring at him from my horse. "Of course, no one needs to tell *you* about laziness."

As slowly as a snake wriggling out of its skin, he peeled himself from the wall to amble over to Sawdah's side.

"What am I supposed to do?" he drawled. "It is forbidden for any man to touch the Prophet's wives. But little girls might not know that." He draped the edge of his robe over his hand, then used it to hoist Sawdah over the camel's hump until she'd finally settled in her saddle. She mopped her sweating face as he commanded the camel to stand. I cringed to hear her thank Ali profusely for his help.

"I know you did not want to come with us," she told Ali. "But I swear by al-Lah, I did not ask the Prophet to send you. In truth, I tried to talk him out of it."

Sawdah just wanted to sell her saddlebags; she didn't want to bother anyone. That was what she had told Muhammad this morning, when she'd asked for permission to go to the Kaynuqah market.

From the tilt of his head and the set of his jaw when she'd come to my apartment to ask, I could see that Muhammad wanted to say "no." But how could he? The Kaynuqah *suq* was the only worthwhile market of the year in Medina. There, Sawdah's lovely leather work would sell for a good price. Yet something worried him: The Kaynuqah had traded for many years with our enemy Abu Sufyan. Their alliance with the Quraysh was strong, and driven by something Muhammad didn't possess: money. Because of money, our raids on Qurayshi caravans were causing resentment from our Kaynuqah neighbors—that, and Muhammad's claim that he was the Prophet their holy Book foretold. Their leaders had mocked him for it, saying their God would never send an Arab to minister to Jews.

"I am sorry, Sawdah, but I cannot allow you to go," Muhammad had said. "There is much tension between us and the Kaynuqah. Their market is too dangerous for you." Sawdah looked as if she might crumple into a heap. She'd been working for months on her saddlebags, tanning the pieces of leather to a butter-soft consistency, tooling moons and stars into them, stitching them together with a needle of bone, adding fringe as thick and wavy as camel's hair. Now that they were complete, who could blame her for wanting the best price?

I spoke out on her behalf. "*Yaa* Muhammad, are we training our army to fight our enemies or to run away from them? Warriors don't cower in their homes, afraid of the next battle. I will be Sawdah's guard. Anyone who touches her will lose his hand."

Muhammad's lips twitched, holding back a smile. "You want to go to the market, Little Red? Will you prevent trouble there, or cause it?"

I lifted my chin. "I'll stop whatever trouble there is to stop, and cause whatever trouble needs to be caused."

Eventually, he did let us go—with Ali, who urged him to change his mind about me. "I am no baby-sitter," he said. "I think you should follow Abu Bakr's example and keep A'isha at home, to avoid trouble."

Keep me at home! My chest tightened as though a harness had been attached to me. Yet I knew my sense of humor could win Muhammad's favor, so I forced a laugh. He looked at me with raised eyebrows.

"Have I missed a joke, A'isha?" he said. "Please share it with me."

"Nothing, husband," I said, then gave him a wink. "Only that, from Ali's words, I see that he knows nothing about my abilities. If there's a fight, he'll need my help!"

Muhammad chuckled, but he shook his head. "You may speak the truth, A'isha, but Ali is also convincing. Yet, since we have heard no reports of conflict at this market, I will allow you to go."

"By al-Lah, cousin, you are making a mistake," Ali said, glaring at me. "Will you at least make her leave that sword at home? You see how eager she is to use it."

"Leave it at home?" My pulse skittered. "But what if I'm attacked? How will I defend myself?" Without my sword, I'd be just a helpless female in need of male protection.

"I will let you to carry it to the market," Muhammad said. "But you must promise not to use it unless you are attacked. Even then, you must first ask for Ali's help. I am sending him to protect you and Sawdah. It is better if you allow him to do so."

I ran to him and flung my arms around his waist. I was going to the market! It would be my first excursion in six years.

"Watch A'isha closely, cousin," Muhammad said with a grin. "She bested me last night with that sword of hers. If there is a fight, observe her. You may learn something." Ali didn't smile, having the humor of a rock.

"Silly fools, going out while Medina blazes like the fires of Hell," Ali grumped as we rode. Sawdah turned fretful eyes to me; she hated to displease any man. I had no such problem. "Don't worry, Sawdah," I said— loudly, so Ali could hear. "Wait until you've sold your saddlebags. When Ali sees your purse bulging with gold coins, he'll be nice. He'll probably carry you home to the mosque on his own back."

Ali *hmphed*, and then we were all quiet as heat covered our noses and mouths with its smothering hand. The tang of manure stung my nostrils. Flies whirled in frenzied clouds, aiming for my eyes. The sun flashed, dazzling us. Somewhere in the city, wailing women screeched over a dead body. I pulled my wrapper close around my face. Through the narrow opening I peered at the city of Medina. Carefully I breathed through my mouth, trying to avoid the stench. Just ahead, Sawdah huffed and prayed, drawing disgusted looks from Ali.

"Oh God, why did you choose this day of all days to blow Your hottest breath on us?" she moaned. Then, so He wouldn't feel criticized, she quickly added, "But You know best."

Soon we passed through the shade of date palms, where a few women strolled to the market in twos and threes, mopping their faces and carrying empty baskets on their heads. Their colorful garments added greens, reds, and blues to the drab streets lined with mud-brick houses. Children laughed and ran among their legs, oblivious to the sun. I delighted in their freedom, remembering how I'd kicked up the sands in Mecca with strong leaping feet and shouted until my lungs felt sore. Coming the other way, men trudged behind their donkeys, spurring them on with whips and sun-sparked curses. The bedraggled animals pulled wooden carts laden with wine, honey, and rice—rare goods, from faraway lands—purchased in the Kaynuqah market. My pulse quickened as I remembered the exotic aromas, bright colors, and strange, musical tongues that had made the market in Mecca so exciting. Would we see a similar scene in the Kaynuqah neighborhood today?

A few Believers passed us as we lumbered along. They grinned and made comic faces at Ali, teasing him for riding with two women.

"Someone alert the Prophet!" cried a lean man with ears that stuck out from his head like open doors. "Ali is stealing his wives!"

"One wife is not enough for a man with two blades," called another, and everyone laughed. Ali's eyes narrowed as he brandished Zulfikar, his double-bladed sword. I'd heard him brag that he'd split the blades by yanking the sword from a scabbard that had been nailed shut—quite a feat of strength, if it were the truth. But I knew that Muhammad had given the sword to him, twin points and all, after the battle at Badr. The men cheered to see its blades reflecting the sun. Some of them chanted a name—Ali's or al-Lah's, I couldn't tell which.

After a short time we reached the far edge of Medina, and it seemed as if we'd entered another world. The farm-town, with its streets full of sheep and goats, had faded away. The Kaynuqah neighborhood was dark and full of shadows. Shops lined the edges of the cobbled, canopy-filled street, the tall stone buildings blocking out the sun and casting a menacing pall. Men stood in the shaded doorways of their stores and watched us from the corners of their eyes. The aromas of roasting lamb and mint made my mouth water, but I clenched my stomach against the leers of the venders. From the tents, men and women announced their wares, filling the air with their cries—until we passed, and the exuberant shouts faded to suspicious murmurs.

I tensed every muscle in my body as if to cover myself with armor, and kept my gaze on the colorful beads dangling from racks alongside copper bracelets and bolts of dyed cloth. A grinning bald man with a gold tooth and a booth filled with jewelry held up a long knife as we passed, turning it this way and that as if to see his reflection, then gave me a pointed look. A goat-faced vendor darted out his tongue, lizard-like, then laughed when I hid my face in my wrapper. A chill seemed to drip down my spine as I remembered Muhammad's warnings about the Kaynuqah. I turned to Sawdah, intending to suggest we return to the mosque, but the smirk on Ali's face stopped me. He'd tell Muhammad I'd been afraid, and that would be the end of my excursions. I touched my sword, reminding myself that I was a good fighter, and I felt my heartbeat and my breathing become slower and more steady.

Our little caravan stopped. I hopped down from Scimitar and tied her to a post, trying not to think of the eyes watching me. Ali helped Sawdah dismount her camel and the two of them walked away, leaving me behind to calm my skittish horse. I scouted the crowd for hostile faces. Now it seemed everyone was too busy buying and selling to notice the presence of a few Muslims in the crowd, and I gave myself a shake for letting my imagination get the best of me. For the first time in years I was free to wander about, and I wasn't going to let my childish fears ruin my pleasure. As for Sawdah, Ali would take care of her. All I needed to do was avoid trouble so Muhammad wouldn't stop me from going out like this again.

I wandered among the stalls, forgetting about danger in the thrill of being surrounded by beautiful things: ornate *kohl* pots and perfume bottles of silver and colored glass; fragrant myrrh and frankincense; rubies like blood-drops on a gold necklace. I lifted the jewelry toward the sky, trying to see the color of the light in the stone. A hand snatched it away. I stared at the twisted face of a woman with eyes like hot coals.

"Muslim thief!" she snarled. "Is it not enough that you steal our goods from Quraysh's caravans? Keep your fingers away from my merchandise." I stepped back onto someone's foot.

"By al-Lah! Forgive my clumsiness." My skin began to flood with heat even before I looked up into the smooth, sculpted face of Safwan. He had grown nearly as tall as my father since I'd last seen him, and his ears no longer jugged out from his head. The strong line of his jaw, the slant of his dark eyes and the long hair hanging like a mane down his back made me think of an Arabian steed. The curl of his lips reminded me of the nights, long ago, when he'd filled my dreams. I lowered my gaze, too flustered to speak.

"My feet are honored to carry such a pretty load." His voice was as soft as the purr of a cat. My pulse fluttered and I pressed a hand against a stall for support. "Are you going to faint?" Safwan said. "It must be the heat. You need a cool breeze."

He plucked a fan made of date-palm leaves from a nearby pile and held it out to me. I stood there as if my body had turned to wood. It wasn't proper for me to accept a gift from any man except Muhammad or my father— but that wasn't why I froze. I worried that his fingers might brush mine, or that I would feel the heat from his hands on the fan as I touched it. Surely al-Lah would strike me dead for betraying His Prophet! Safwan watched me standing like a statue, struggling to breathe, and his eyes glinted.

"We of the *umma* must relieve one another's sufferings as we can." He

waved the fan over my head and face as if he were my servant—but no
servant would have moved so close to me, or caressed me with his eyes as
the palm fronds tickled my nose and cheeks. My pulse raced like that galloping horse I'd dreamt so often of riding on with him.

"By al-Lah, that smile is worth the pain in my toes!" he murmured. "I
wish for a camel to trod on my feet next. Then I might have a thousand
of your smiles to console me."

I couldn't help laughing, he was so audacious, but when I glanced up at
him the expression on his face told me clearly that he was not joking. And
I wondered: Was this the danger I'd sensed when I'd approached the
market?

"*Yaa* A'isha," he said. "I miss our times together."

A shriek shattered our moment, drawing our attention to the goldsmith's stall. There a group of women pointed to Sawdah and cawed with
laughter. Oblivious, she fingered a new piece of leather and waddled
toward the outdoor cafe where Ali drank coffee with his friends. As she
walked, her thighs jiggled like dancers, bared to the world. Someone had
pinned the back of her skirt up to her belt.

The baldheaded goldsmith doubled over and grabbed his sides in
laughter. Other merchants slapped him on the back, congratulating him
for his trick.

"The true face of the Muslim is revealed!" he shouted.

Ali continued to talk, unaware. I cried out and would have run to her,
but Safwan grabbed the sleeve of my robe. "No, A'isha, it's too dangerous
for you," he said. I jerked myself out of his reach and fled through the
stalls, ignoring his shouts, toppling baskets of fruit and scattering jewelry
with my feet.

I ran straight to Sawdah and stopped behind her with my arms spread,
blocking her backside. "Don't move, Sawdah," I said. "Your skirt is pinned
up in back."

Sawdah cried out and waved her hands across her rear, felt her bare
legs. "Move out of the way!" someone yelled. "We can't see her." The
goldsmith took a step toward me, flashing his gold tooth.

"I dare anyone else to come near the wives of the Prophet
Muhammad," I shouted, hoping no one could hear the tremor in my
voice.

After only a few weeks' lessons from Muhammad, I wasn't skilled enough to fight a donkey, let alone a man. But someone had to defend Sawdah, and Ali was occupied. Besides, I could afford to be brave: No man would confront a twelve-year-old girl. Or so I thought.

"Look, another Muslim whore who wants her skirt pinned up," the goldsmith jeered. "Come here, darling, and I'll do your front." He lunged for me, his hands grasping like a scorpion's pincers. I whipped my sword from its sheath and slashed the back of his hand with the tip of my blade. He cried out and pressed the wound to his mouth. The taste of his blood filled his eyes with hatred. He drew a dagger from his belt and raised it, popping his eyes at me.

"Sawdah, move away!" I cried. She ran to the stone wall and pressed her back against it. I turned to face my attacker. The goldsmith advanced, grinning, but he wasn't careful, probably because he was fighting a girl. I raised my child's sword and lunged, using a trick Muhammad had taught me to knock his knife out of his hand. He stared at me, confused, as his blade thudded to the ground. Some of the men around him laughed, but others grabbed their blades and moved slowly toward me. I looked around for Ali, but before I could call for his help Safwan leapt into the fray with a snarl, flashing his sword.

"Any coward can fight a girl," he said. "Let's see you Kaynuqah pigs best a Muslim warrior."

The men clashed their blades with ours, and for a few short moments everything was just the way I'd imagined: Safwan and me fighting side-by-side. I cut the arm of one man, making him fall back. Safwan took a slice off his opponent's nose, but the man continued to attack.

"You must leave here at once, A'isha!" he cried. "This is no place for you."

Still bristling from his "any coward can fight a girl" remark, I turned and knocked the dagger from his opponent's hand.

"Maybe it's no place for *you*, Safwan," I retorted, and took satisfaction from the way his eyes widened when he glanced over at me. But in the next instant, an arm closed around my neck and yanked me backward against a man's hard chest, choking me as it pressed into my throat. Breath blew hot against my ear, and a bleeding hand smeared my lips.

"Lap it up, dear," the goldsmith snarled. "Never again will you be so close to Kaynuqah blood."

I jabbed him with my elbow, and brought my sword down on his leg. He let me go and I whirled around to fight, but Ali and his friends leapt into the crowd with their swords already in the air.

"You have done more than enough, you troublemaker," Ali snarled at me as his friend with the big ears skewered the goldsmith through the belly. I watched, shaken, as the goldsmith fell to the ground, writhing and gurgling blood.

"We need to remove ourselves. Now!" Ali shouted.

He ran to collect Sawdah and led her to her kneeling camel. I leapt up onto Scimitar and wiped my blade with the cloth on my saddle, but kept my sword in hand in case anyone else tried to attack.

Sawdah wept, red-faced, as her camel stood. "I have never been so ashamed," she said. "Those people saw everything."

I tried to slide my sword into its sheath, but my hand trembled so badly I missed. A man had been killed, and I could have been also, but over what? A senseless prank! My nights of mock sword-fights and pretend battles had been games—but this was life. And death. I took a deep, shuddering breath.

"Don't worry, Sawdah," I said, keeping my voice as steady as I could. "When Muhammad hears about this, he'll make the whole Kaynuqah tribe pay—with their blood."

A scream curdled the thick, hot air, and I looked toward the roiling crowd of men with swords and sticks and pounding fists. Safwan was nowhere to be seen; apparently, he hadn't forgotten how to vanish like a *djinni*. Ali's friend with the big ears slumped on the ground, and a Kaynuqah man stood over him with a sword dripping red.

Ali glared at me as he took the reins of Sawdah's camel. "See what you have caused?"

"I protected Sawdah while you loitered on cushions with your friends," I said.

"Yes, A'isha, you did," Sawdah said. She wiped her wet cheeks and gave me the tenderest of smiles. "You risked your life for me. Thanks be to al-Lah for a sister-wife like you!"

"You started a bloody fight with your eagerness to show off," Ali said. He shook his head. "Maybe now Muhammad will listen to me and Umar. Wherever women go, trouble follows. The best place for you is at home."

A Bad Idea

THAT SAME DAY

*A*s I'd expected, Ali went straight to Muhammad when we returned from the market and told him all about the fight. And, as I'd expected, he portrayed himself as the valiant warrior coming to my rescue and me as the reckless child who'd caused all the trouble.

I'd made haste, with Sawdah huffing along behind me, to approach Muhammad myself. When I arrived at the *majlis*, Ali was already there, boasting and thumping his chest as he described in vivid detail the death blows he and his friends had dealt to the men who'd pinned up Sawdah's skirt. One thing he didn't mention was how he'd shrugged off his duties at first to gossip and drink coffee.

"I would like to hear those Kaynuqah cowards laugh at us now, cousin," he said with a laugh of his own. "With these two blades I pierced both eyes of every man who approached me. Now their refusal to see the truth of *islam* has made them truly blind!"

Listening to Ali boast, I resisted the urge to jump in with tales of my own exploits. I wasn't proud of the bloodbath that had resulted from something as trivial as a prank. And besides, Muhammad knew I wasn't capable of holding off experienced fighters for long, not by myself. If I told him about my part in the ugly scene, I'd have to tell about Safwan. Still in a daze from meeting him again, I was far from ready to discuss him with Muhammad.

As I and Sawdah stepped through the doorway, Ali pointed his long finger at me.

"Here is the one who started it all," he said. "*Yaa* cousin, you should have seen her. A girl, and, worse, your wife, shouting out a challenge to the entire market! She broke her agreement with you at the first opportunity."

I felt my ears burn as if his lies were candle-flames licking at their edges. Yet I held my retort because I dreaded any mention of Safwan—while, at the same time, I hungered for news of him. What had happened to him? Had he been wounded in the fighting, or killed? I tried to remember seeing him in the fray after I'd mounted my horse. Of course, Safwan had always been good at vanishing.

Fortunately, Sawdah had no such qualms about speaking.

"*Yaa* Prophet, you should have seen A'isha," she said. "A little thing like her holding off three big men! She threatened to kill them all if they didn't leave us alone. She would have done it, too."

Ali folded his arms. "Truly, they would have died—of laughter. She was quite a vision, lunging around with that child's sword you gave her. She was more dangerous to herself than to anyone else. I told you, cousin, she should be kept at home."

"By al-Lah, she stood up for me!" Sawdah glared at Ali. "When nobody else would."

Muhammad frowned at me. "I only used the disarming trick you taught me," I said. "It was enough to slow them down, at least. And besides—" To my chagrin I felt myself blush, which made me redden more—"I wasn't fighting alone, not the whole time."

"That is right, you had that boy jump in to help," Sawdah said. "He was no better fighter than you, though."

"Safwan ibn al-Mu'attal," Ali said. He folded his arms and narrowed his eyes, as if he'd caught me in a lie. "What was he doing at the market, A'isha?"

"How would I know?" I said, more sharply than I'd intended. What was Ali accusing me of? He smirked and nodded as though I'd just confirmed his suspicions.

Safwan's handsome face as he'd fanned me with the palm frond flashed before my mind's eye, and I began to perspire. Ali was watching me so intently, I wondered if he could read my thoughts. Had he seen me and Safwan talking together? Had he noticed how close Safwan had stood to me, and how I hadn't moved away?

"*Yaa* A'isha, weren't you told to summon me if there was trouble?" Ali said. "Yet you jumped in and started a fight without even calling my name."

Muhammad's eyes snapped when he looked into mine, and the tiny vein between his eyes bulged—always a sign of his anger.

"You behaved impulsively today, A'isha," he said. "You could have been killed. Perhaps I would be wise to limit your freedom for a while, until you can restrain your actions."

"By al-Lah, don't do that!" I blurted. I pressed my hand to my chest and felt a frantic thumping, like the foot of a frightened rabbit. "I promise you, nothing like this will happen again."

"But you have already broken a promise to me. You said if there was trouble, you would go to Ali."

I looked down at the floor, avoiding the disappointment in his eyes. I'd been so eager to show off with my sword, I'd forgotten my promise to call Ali. And I'd acted on impulse, as Muhammad had said.

"I meant to keep my word to you," I said. "But everything happened so fast, and I wanted to protect Sawdah—"

"A'isha is quick-spirited," Sawdah said. "She did not mean any harm."

"She needs a firm hand," Ali said. "Sawdah's care has always been lenient. Of course, cousin, your daughters were all well-behaved." His eyes gleamed like daggers at me. "If you do not wish to restrict your child bride, perhaps your bride-to-be will do it for you. Hafsa bint Umar could be a true *hatun*, the Great Lady of your *harim*, and prevent this kind of disaster from happening again."

◆

"New wife?" I asked Muhammad later, when he visited me in my room. "But why? I just moved in. Are you already bored with me?"

"Of course not, A'isha," Muhammad said. He reached out and pulled me onto his lap. "But Umar wants to establish a bond with me, so he has offered his daughter Hafsa. Her husband died fighting for me. She has no one to care for her."

"Does that mean you're going to marry all the widows from Badr?" I slanted sly eyes at him, hiding my dismay. "Where will they all live?"

Of course, I knew he had no plans to marry every widow in the *umma*. Umar was a special case. Once a bitter enemy of *islam*, he'd become an important member of Muhammad's circle of Companions. "I must marry his daughter," Muhammad told me. "There is no other way."

Umar had already suffered humiliation enough, Muhammad said. First he'd asked their Companion Uthman to marry her. But Uthman, a plump, wealthy man with a mustache as long as a pump handle, had just married Muhammad's daughter Umm Kulthum. "I cannot take another wife so soon," he'd said.

"Having deep respect for Uthman, Umar said nothing," Muhammad told me. "Then he approached Abu Bakr."

Wouldn't my father like to marry the beautiful Hafsa? Umar had asked. *Abi* bowed his head and stared at his hands, wondering what to do. If he said yes, he'd be saddled with a hot-tempered wife who would forever disrupt the peace in his home. If he said no, he would insult Umar. So he said nothing. Watching my father stand still and silent, Umar turned red, then gray, like a spent coal, before rushing away to find Muhammad.

"These so-called friends mock me with their indifference to my daughter," he ranted.

"Uthman and Abu Bakr declined her hand, but only because I asked them to," Muhammad said to him. "I want to marry Hafsa myself."

As he finished his tale, I pressed my hand to my twisting stomach. Hafsa bint Umar was known to be a spoiled, self-centered woman whose screams at her husband had awakened her neighbors many times.

"If you have to marry someone," I said, "can't you find a wife who's nicer? Hafsa will make me her *durra*, and I'll be miserable."

Muhammad chuckled. "You, the second-wife? After seeing you stand up to Ali today, I doubt it."

I hoped he spoke the truth—yet hadn't my mother once been strong also? Seeing the amused glimmer in his eyes, I decided to try another approach.

"Umar is a new convert to *islam*, and he was a close friend of Abu

Sufyan's before the *hijra* to Medina," I said. "How do you know he's not a spy? If you marry his daughter, you might put us all in danger."

Muhammad shook his head. Our army had crushed the Qurayshi fighters at Badr, he pointed out. Not only did the victory unify the *umma*, but it demonstrated to Abu Sufyan—and all of Hijaz—that we were to be feared and respected.

"This marriage is for the good of the *umma*," he said. "We are a brand-new community, doing something no group of Arabs has ever done: leaving our homeland to form a family outside the bonds of kinship. Hafsa's widowhood has created a rift among my closest Companions. If marrying her will mend that tear, then naturally I will do so."

◆

After that awful day in the market Muhammad tried to make peace with the Kaynuqah, but they jeered and threw rocks, telling him to send real men to fight next time instead of an old woman and a little girl. Worried about the threat they posed to us, Muhammad sent the men of the *umma* to drive the entire tribe out of the city. Then, with that concern out of the way, he made preparations to marry Hafsa bint Umar.

I understood why Muhammad had to marry again. Yet how I dragged my feet across the courtyard on the day of the wedding! Sawdah was all smiles and congratulations, but welcoming a hateful new sister-wife into the *harim* was far from my pleasure. Especially when that wife shimmered with beauty, and with the haughtiness of a peacock in her expensive gown of the most vivid blue.

I forced my legs to carry me past the looming date palm, through the wizened acacias, across the long, gray grass and the blood-red sands to where she stood under the weeping ghaza'a tree. My eyes returned again and again to her garments, as if she were a flower and my gaze a desperate bee: to the gloss of the brilliantine under-gown, more deeply azure than the midday sky; to the rich sheen of her brocaded purple silk shift, slit in the hem and plunging in the front to display the luscious blue beneath; to the girdle of fine blue lace encircling her waist; to the silken wrapper, also a rich, heady blue, sliding down the wave of ink-black hair I was certain she dyed with indigo. My precious red-and-white gown seemed shabby, all of a sudden, and my rust-colored hair more garish than ever.

As I approached, Ali stepped up with smiling eyes and murmured to her. She laughed, darting her glance as she made a reply so low he had to bend his ear to hear. He laughed, also, and their eyes exchanged a sly glance before he moved to Muhammad.

As I stood before Muhammad and Hafsa and mouthed blessings on their marriage—tripping like a clumsy child over the hated words—Ali watched with his tongue pressed smugly against his cheek. Hafsa regarded me with her nose so high in the air she might have been offering it to the birds to perch upon. In fact, her finely plucked eyebrows reminded me of birds in flight as she raised and lowered them over eyes like toasted almonds in burnt-butter skin.

"What a lovely dress," she said, raising them at my gown. I bit back a taste as bitter as grape seeds. Her tone made me want to rip out that shiny hair she kept flicking off her shoulders. Beside us, Sawdah fingered her amulet against the Evil Eye and wished Muhammad happiness with his new wife.

"You must be A'isha, the child-bride," Hafsa said. Her question dripped like venom from her pointed smile.

"Muhammad's favorite bride," I said, glaring at her so she would know I planned to stay that way.

She raised a dainty hand to her prettily yawning mouth. "How nice for you." She reached out and patted my head. I resisted the urge to slap her arm. "I hope you have enjoyed his attentions while they lasted." She shifted her glance to Ali, who watched us with a cunning smile, and then back to me. "After he's spent his seven nights with me, you may find his heart has changed."

"Yes, after seven nights alone with you, my husband will be more in love with me than ever," I said. I thought her eyebrows would fly away completely.

If Muhammad loved me more the next day—or at all—I couldn't tell it. As I laid out their meal in Hafsa's new hut, the pair settled themselves on a single cushion, so close she might as well have been sitting in his lap. And such an appetite Muhammad displayed! He and the ravenous Hafsa devoured a pile of dates nearly as big as her head.

She was resplendent. Her thick hair spilled like a river of ink over her shoulders. Her blue silk trousers embroidered with yellow birds narrowed at her waist, then billowed over her hips, accentuating their fullness. Already she had lined her eyes thickly with *kohl*, which dramatized their erotic dance. Her gazes at Muhammad invited, then rebuffed, then teased, then laughed. Around her neck she wore a necklace of lapis lazuli flecked with golden glints like stars on a slender bronze rope.

They cooed and preened like two nightingales in a nest. I thought of the night they had just spent, of her body under Muhammad's, and my stomach churned. The tip of her breast brushed his arm as she leaned across him for another piece of fruit. He made a sound in his throat and looked at her with a hunger all the dates in Hijaz could not satisfy.

"By al-Lah! Marriage has made you both so eager for food," I said. Forcing a laugh. Vying for my husband's attention. Yet he seemed oblivious to my presence.

"Yes, we are insatiable." Hafsa pushed a date slowly between Muhammad's lips, then pulled her fingers just as slowly from his mouth. Giving him a long, sultry gaze. "*Yaa habib,* what's this I hear about a disturbance in the Kaynuqah market? Did your child bride really start a fight? If I were the *hatun,* it wouldn't have happened."

A force gathered in my belly. The hair on my neck stood up. She arched her eyebrows up at me.

"Are you still here? Eyeing my new necklace, I see. It's a gift from Muhammad. A token of his love. I'm sure you have one just as nice."

"A token?" I said. "Who needs a token, when I have the real thing?"

But—did I have Muhammad's love? Had he looked at me a single time this morning, as I'd served him and his new bride? As I walked across the courtyard with my empty dish in hand, I wondered if my fears were coming true. Would Hafsa win his heart and make herself the *hatun? Please, al-Lah, haven't I suffered enough?* I had to find a way to knock her off that throne. But how? She had six more days alone with Muhammad and two ample breasts with which to enchant him. Still as virginal as an infant fresh from the womb, I couldn't hope to compete with her. In the cooking tent, I set down the platter so hard it broke in two.

"By al-Lah, what is the matter, Little Red?" Sawdah clucked, taking my face in both hands and peering down at me. "You look like you want to cry."

"Cry? What do I have to cry about? Because my husband is in love with another woman, and has forgotten all about me?"

Sawdah's grin was lusty. "You remember those first nights. Like a pair of rutting goats, eh? The man and the woman cannot keep their hands off each other. But it does not last."

I frowned at her. Being grunted and sweated on was supposed to feel good? That wasn't my impression that day at Hamal's window. But— Jamila hadn't pushed him away. Her arms and legs had clung to him and her body had moved with his, as if she were riding a horse. I felt Sawdah watching me; she was probably wondering why I didn't agree with her. In a moment, she would guess that my marriage hadn't been consummated. I picked up the pieces of the plate I had broken and threw them into the fire to scatter her thoughts.

"She'll be the *hatun* soon," I muttered. "And you and I might as well kill ourselves."

"*Hatun?*" Sawdah frowned. "That is supposed to be my position, I guess. But I do not want it, A'isha. I raised Muhammad's girls from his first wife, and I have my own boy from my previous marriage. I have spent enough time giving orders."

I felt my hopes lift. "Why don't you appoint me?"

She shook her head. "You are awfully young to be in charge of a household."

"But not too young to fight for you," I pointed out.

Sawdah cocked her head, pondering, then broke into a laugh. "By al-Lah, you speak as truly as Gabriel himself. All right, A'isha, I will make you the *hatun* of this *harim.*"

I would have flung my arms around her in glee, but she stopped me with a lifted hand. "Do not get excited yet," she said. "Not until Hafsa bint Umar agrees."

I kicked at the dirt floor. "She'll never respect my authority, and Muhammad will be too dazzled to make her do so."

"Not for long." Sawdah chuckled. "That Hafsa has got an awful temper. Worse than her father's, I hear. Have you heard the saying? 'A nail that has a blunted point brings shame upon itself.' We will not wait long before her first outburst, you will see. The clouds will part from the Prophet's eyes then."

An idea flew into my head. A good idea—but also a bad one. I talked myself out of it, but when Hafsa called me *durra* three times the next day—and suggested to Muhammad that I should be kept at home—I began to change my mind. Something had to be done about her, and quickly. Clearly she was in league with Ali. I hoped Muhammad wouldn't let slip that we weren't consummated or Hafsa would seize the first-wife position without a thought.

She needed to be humbled. If I told her what I knew, she'd never look down her nose at me again. How could any woman preen like a peacock when so many men had rejected her?

But Muhammad had sworn me to secrecy. To diminish Hafsa, I would have to betray him. I convinced Sawdah to deliver their meals, afraid of what I might say to her. But on Friday, five days after the wedding, she sauntered into the cooking-tent and demanded some date juice—then stood idle and watched me and Sawdah clean the dishes from her meal with Muhammad.

"I said I wanted date juice," she demanded. "Are you two deaf, or ignoring me?"

Only the first-wife in the *harim* was entitled to give orders to the others. "Did you hear something, Sawdah?" I asked.

"I am claiming for myself the role of *hatun*," Hafsa said. She folded her arms and drummed her purple-hennaed fingertips against one of her forearms. "I'm certain you know what that means. My desires are to be fulfilled."

"Oh, but we all have desires, don't we, Sawdah?" I said. "As for me, I desire help with these dishes."

"I desire to leave this tent before I say something unholy," Sawdah said, and hurried out to collect water for the dishes.

"I know what your desires are, A'isha." Hafsa lifted her long, elegant nose. "How sad for you that your husband doesn't return them."

For a long while I stood without moving, blinking at her smirking face and wondering how much she knew about me and Muhammad. Had he told her that our marriage wasn't consummated?

"How strange to hear you speak of Muhammad's feelings," I said. "Since he's never had feelings for you."

"No? Then why did he ask to marry me?" Her eyebrows swung upward. The half-smile remained on her lips. The bad idea bounced around in my head, confounding my good intentions with evil wishes—wishes to see

Hafsa reduced, and to raise myself above her. Then, almost before I knew it, that bad idea flew right out of my mouth.

"Muhammad didn't ask to marry you," I said. "Your father was the one who made the request. Muhammad obliged him as a favor." Hafsa rolled her eyes and gave a short laugh. Seeing her disbelief, I plunged into the tale of how Umar had gone from man to man in search of a husband for her—adding my own details here and there.

As I spoke, I watched her superior smile fade to a trembling frown. The triumph in her eyes turned to indignant sparks. Here were the first signs of the terrible temper I had heard so much about! But then my words began to stumble from my lips, as I saw her proud expression crumple. At the end of the story, a single dark tear rolled down her cheek, trailing *kohl*.

Yet it was too late for me to turn back now. "Your father had to beg Muhammad to marry you," I said.

"Where did you hear these tales?" Her voice rose. "Don't you know better than to repeat such hurtful rumors? Wait until Muhammad hears about this. He'll beat you until your back is as red as your hair!"

"I was there when your father implored Muhammad to take you," I lied.

"You she-dog!" she cried. "I'll beat you for those sorry tales." And in the next moment we writhed in a flurry of fists and kicks, teeth and hair—until Sawdah yanked us apart with arms as beefy and muscular as the legs of an ox.

"Tut! What shame! The Prophet's wives fighting like a couple of Bedouins," Sawdah huffed. "What would he say if he saw you?"

"He'd say she deserves to be beaten for her stupid lies!" Hafsa was screeching and pointing her index finger at me.

"Hush! You will deafen me," Sawdah complained. "What tales, A'isha?"

"I only told her the real reason Muhammad married her," I said. "But the truth is painful to hear."

Sawdah grabbed her amulet. "A'isha, you did not."

"That story is a lie!" Hafsa continued to scream. "My father told me what happened. Every man in the *umma* wanted me, but Muhammad won. He's the one who begged, not my father. Sawdah knows the truth! *Yaa* Sawdah, tell her how Muhammad asked my father for my hand."

Sweat popped out like blisters on Sawdah's forehead and upper lip. She knelt to pick up the dishes I had stacked, then stood with them in her arms. "By al-Lah, it does not matter who asked whom," she said. "You are married to the Prophet of God. Forget the rest."

Hafsa stamped her foot. "You're on her side, I knew it! By al-Lah, I know where to find the truth." She stormed past us, knocking the dishes out of Sawdah's arms. The crash must have drowned out my warning not to disturb Muhammad while he was preparing for the prayer service. In a whirl of dust and angry oaths Hafsa was gone, leaving me and Sawdah to pick up the broken platters and bowls. As I fumbled with the pieces, my hands trembling, I wondered how Muhammad would feel when he found out I'd betrayed his confidence. Would he ever trust me again?

Sawdah shook her head at me. "You are a good girl, A'isha, but you have made a big mistake."

"She goaded me," I said. Sawdah grunted. As if in a dream, we moved to the entrance of the cooking tent, neither of us daring to say more.

From the mosque we heard shouts, another crash. We heard Hafsa's sobs like the wailing of one in mourning, and Muhammad's low voice coming closer. My pulse rippled and I leaned against Sawdah, slightly dizzy. Would he divorce Hafsa for this outburst? That would be a disaster for her, and my fault. But no, his friendship with Umar was too important. At least, though, he wouldn't allow Hafsa to be *hatun*. But would he let me fill that role?

From behind the tent flap we watched Muhammad stomp through the courtyard, his face as hard as stone. His red ceremonial robe was streaked with *kohl*, and his turban sat askew and unraveling on his head. He strode across the grass to Hafsa's hut. She burst from the mosque screeching his name.

"Am I less than an ass, who at least is sold to the highest bidder?" she cried, then tripped and fell to her knees.

I would have run to help her up, but Sawdah grabbed my arm. "You have done enough."

In truth I had—and alas! None of it could be undone. *Forgive me for this pain I've caused*, I prayed. Hafsa pulled herself up off the ground and ran to the hut, threw open the door, and flung herself inside. From there, I and Sawdah could hear her screams. Probably all of Medina could hear them.

In a while the noise subsided. Sawdah and I stood in the strange, sharp silence, watching and waiting. The door to the hut opened and Muhammad stepped out. He had rewound his turban, but the black stains remained on his robe. As he walked past the cooking tent, he jerked his head around to look at me.

In his eyes: Betrayal. Anger. Disbelief.

"May al-Lah forgive you, A'isha." His calm voice cracked, and tears welled in his eyes. I opened my hands to him, wishing I could carry his sorrow, but he bared his teeth.

"May He give me the strength to forgive you, also," he said. "With your cruel words you meant to break only one heart, I know. But, by al-Lah! By betraying my trust, you have broken two."

Muhammad Is Dead

Uhud, April 625

For weeks after that terrible night when I'd humiliated Hafsa, Muhammad chose his words carefully when he spoke to me. His guarded demeanor made me want to cry, but I couldn't blame him. I didn't deserve his trust.

That would change at Uhud, I vowed.

Abu Sufyan was bringing an army to attack Medina. Our scout's report surprised no one: We knew he'd been recruiting warriors. After Quraysh's humiliating loss at the battle of Badr, he needed to salvage his reputation. Since Badr, poets had been spouting satirical verses throughout Hijaz, making fun of the Meccans. *Lazy merchants with soft hands and softer heads*, our own city's poet Hassan ibn Thabit had famously quipped.

Losing that battle had cost Abu Sufyan many Bedouin allies—tribes he'd relied on to protect his precious trade caravans—because Bedouins liked to fight on the side of winners. Loyalty meant nothing to some of these tribes, who wanted only more loot and female captives. Abu Sufyan could promise neither until he defeated our army.

So when our scouts reported that he was approaching our city with five hundred men, we were ready to meet him. Our army had been training for months.

"Let them come to us," Muhammad said, standing on his tree stump in the mosque and announcing the invasion to the *umma*. "We will defeat them easily on our own ground."

But he was outnumbered. The men who'd fought at Badr were heroes in the *umma*, and those who'd missed that battle wanted their chance at glory. Hurling arrows from behind the city's walls wasn't nearly as exciting as chopping off heads in hand-to-hand combat. *We must go out to meet them,* these hotheads argued. *Give us the chance, also, to be martyrs for al-Lah.*

At last Muhammad relented. "If they want to fight, can I say no?" he said when I protested. He and his warriors donned what little armor they had, gathered the women who'd volunteered to help, rode a full *barid* to Mount Uhud, and waited, as they had done at Badr.

To my delight, Muhammad had allowed me to come along—as a helper, but secretly I hoped for a chance to do battle against Quraysh. I remembered clearly the ugliness on Abu Sufyan's face as he'd slapped and dragged away poor Raha in Medina. Since that night, I'd tended a flame of resentment in my breast, waiting for the day I could repay that overfed swine for his cruelty. At the same time, I yearned to redeem myself in Muhammad's eyes for showing off in the Kaynuqah market and starting a fight, then betraying his confidence in order to humble Hafsa.

A mere girl, I wasn't allowed to join the army, even though I knew I could outfight half our men. A few women had taken sword in hand at Badr, but for the most part our task was to carry water and tend our wounded. No matter: Whatever Muhammad asked of me I'd perform so well that he would know I was worthy of him, and of *islam*.

At Uhud, I could tell from the frown creasing Muhammad's face that I was far from his mind. He was worried that, by agreeing to meet the Qurayshi here, he'd made the wrong choice. The desolate landscape, all dirt and sand and burnt-black rock, offered little protection. And our army was pitifully small. We'd started out with one thousand men, but then our scouts reported seeing three times that many warriors and camels on the Qurayshi side, plus two hundred on horseback. After that news, the leader of the Hypocrites, Ibn Ubayy, ran away with three hundred of our warriors.

Midmorning, I and dozens of other women from our camp watched, stunned, as the Qurayshi army came spilling down the distant hills, pouring like a silver flood over the colorless sand. Their chain-mail and painted shields flashed the sun into our eyes and filled me with dread. Just below us, Muhammad arranged our troops in a broad swath, with their backs to the jutting mountain of black rock. After being awake all night planning strategy and praying, he looked haggard, bleary-eyed and pale.

"If Quraysh reaches the higher ground, we will be lost," he said. He placed fifty archers on the rock-strewn pass. "Guard the mountain as if it were your mother," he commanded. "Do not leave her side no matter what happens, do you understand? Remain on that pass even if you see birds picking the flesh from our bones."

His ominous words filled me with dread, and I realized for the first time the horror of war. My heart began to pound violently and would not stop, even as Muhammad led our troops in prayer. We women on the hill joined the prostrations, murmuring praise to al-Lah and asking Him in our hearts for an easy victory.

"Their numbers may be large, but we have al-Lah on our side!" Muhammad shouted. The roar of our men rose like a whirlwind, lifting my hopes and soaring my spirits. Compared to the armored troops kicking up dust in the distance, our fighters made a sorry sight, most of them in flimsy robes without even a shield to protect them, and a cavalry of only two horses. Yet what Muhammad had said was true: We had defeated Quraysh at Badr with fewer men—and less training—and, al-Lah willing, we would best them again.

Caught up in the excitement, I ran down the hill toward Muhammad, through the men who milled about in readiness for the battle. I wanted so badly to fight. Muhammad knew I was skilled with sword and dagger. If I asked him again to let me join the battle, would he relent? As I scanned the crowd in search of him, I heard a voice that made my heart seem to turn over.

"I should have known you would be here."

I looked around: Safwan stood behind me, tall and lean, chain-mail fitted like a skin over his broad shoulders and chest. His tilted eyes smoldered. His thin mouth curved slightly.

Locked in his gaze, I flinched. What if someone should see us exchanging glances? I lowered my eyes.

"Good luck today."

"*Yaa* A'isha, you know it takes skill to win a battle. Fortune only helps in matters of love. And my luck in that area is pitifully poor."

"May you fare better with the Qurayshi, then, than you do with women," I said in a ragged voice, glancing around for fear someone might be watching us. Everyone else, though, seemed too intent on preparing for battle to take notice of a warrior and a battlefield nurse.

"I aim to kill the Meccans, not kiss them," Safwan said. I could feel his eyes pulling at me. Almost against my will I looked up at him again. His gaze was so deep I thought I might fall into it and never return. "And there is only one woman for me."

A cry arose from the pass. *Quraysh is arriving! Prepare to kill or be killed in the name of al-Lah!* I turned with my heart in my throat to see our enemies charging in a rush like a wind storm with swords in their hands and death in their eyes. I cried out, terrified, and clutched Safwan's arm.

"The battle begins!" I choked, and turned to run up the hill, but Safwan patted my hand.

"They're only trying to frighten us," he said. "We still have the formalities to go through. You'll see: They'll stop when they draw near and start boasting about how they're going to slaughter us all. Then they'll send their best warriors forward and we'll send ours, and those men will fight to the death. *Then* the battle will start."

Umar marched past, looking like a peacock with feathers waving from atop his helmet. He stopped when he saw me standing in the ranks, and shouted at me to retreat and join the women at the camp. With a burning face I glanced at Safwan, but he had gone.

Umar eyed my sword dangling on my belt, and held out his hand for it. "We will not have children fighting on the battlefield, especially females."

Give up my sword? I'd have rather handed him my arm. But the men around us were watching. Defying one of Muhammad's commanders would be an ill-omened start for the battle. So I pulled my child's sword from its sheath and handed it to Umar, then trudged up the hill to the tents.

Hafsa came over to join me. Since our fight I'd worked hard to gain her forgiveness, and she finally seemed to be warming to me.

"Did you think my father was going to let you join the battle? He didn't want any women here."

"He's afraid I'll outfight him," I grumbled.

The Qurayshi army spread like a swarm of locusts over the sand, dwarfing us. The drum of my pulse filled my ears, and sweat trickled down my back. By al-Lah, how would our puny army escape annihilation? In the front and center of their force stood Abu Sufyan, fat as ever, moistening his lips with his thick tongue and showing his yellow teeth in a grin. Bile rose in my throat and I glanced wildly around for a sword to replace the one Umar had taken away. *Please, al-Lah, give me the chance to kill him today.*

On Abu Sufyan's right a young fighter threw hostile glares over a beard that reached almost to his navel. On his left, Khalid ibn al-Walid, the famous Qurayshi fighter, sat astride a dark horse, his back as straight as a standard and the scar on his cheek livid.

Abu Sufyan stepped forward and raised his hands to silence his troops. Gradually, the din of their murmurs and clanking armor faded. Our army stood in perfect formation, not even twitching an eye.

"Men of Medina!" Abu Sufyan called. "Members of the Aws and Khazraj tribes. We have no quarrel with you. You are not the ones who raid our caravans and steal our gold and silver. You are not the ones trying to destroy our city by demeaning our gods. We have come to fight Muhammad, son of Abdallah ibn al-Muttalib, and the men of Mecca who follow him.

"You see the size of our army. We have many Bedouin fighters with us, bloodthirsty warriors. You have a puny handful of ragtag soldiers without armor or horses. Is this man Muhammad worth losing your lives for? Because we will kill you all, if that is what it takes to reach him. *Yaa* Khazraj, go home! Go home, Aws! It is not your blood—"

Before he could finish his speech, the *ansari*, or "Helpers," as we called the Aws and Khazraj, began to shout back at him.

"We will never leave our Prophet!" some cried.

"Long live Muhammad, Messenger of al-Lah!" others said. Pride swelled my chest. Sawdah, who had joined Hafsa and me, sniffled and wiped a tear from her cheek.

"Al-Lah bless the Helpers," she said. "They love us more than our own relatives do."

The fight began, and we raced onto the field, tying our bandage-cloths about our waists and toting water skins. At first we stood idle, for our warriors proved impenetrable, clustered on the field as they had at Badr, keeping the Qurayshi army from bursting through to the mountain. The Qurayshi hurled themselves at us in great waves, but our unity was a cliff they couldn't scale. We women cheered as they fell back again and again—with fewer numbers each time. We had good reason to exult: If Quraysh succeeded in destroying our army here, they'd push on to Medina and kill the men who remained, then make slaves of us women and children. Their goal was to rid Hijaz of Muhammad, the *umma*, and *islam*. Our goal was to survive. And so far, it looked as though we might prevail.

On the sidelines, Abu Sufyan's shrewd-eyed wife Hind rattled her tambourine and urged her side to keep fighting. She and three or four other women wearing silk and lace—a mark of their high status in Mecca—ululated and sang: *If you advance we hug you, spread soft rugs beneath you. If you retreat we leave you, never more to love you.*

The pounding of drums joined the rattle and song—or so it seemed at first. Then we realized the noise we heard was the Qurayshi cavalry. Warriors on horseback thundered up, intending to trample our men. I clutched Hafsa's arm, my every muscle tensed, my eyes bulging with fright. They were coming directly toward us, and, unlike the infantry, their horses wouldn't distinguish between warriors and nurses as they ran us down. The whiz of arrows over our heads made us duck and I shrieked, trembling, as I waited to be struck from behind or crushed by hooves. But our archers on the pass above us hurled their arrows across impossibly long distances to pierce the eyes of the Qurayshi horses. The riders tumbled down with their screaming animals. Relief flooded our limbs and we cried and laughed and called out thanks to al-Lah. Soon the corpses of Qurayshi, Bedouins, and beasts littered the sand, filling the air with the smell of blood, and the Qurayshi army was running away across the desert, abandoning their camels. I jumped around, hugging Hafsa and Sawdah and weeping with joy. Praise be to al-Lah! We had won.

Cheers filled the battlefield. Our men raised their swords and ran after the Meccans, cocky, laughing and calling out insults. When they reached the Qurayshi camels, though, they abandoned the chase and began stripping the animals of their goods. They tore open saddlebags and spilled rice on the ground. They broke the necks off wine bottles and guzzled the contents. They seized daggers and swords and stuffed their mouths with fruit and dried meat. And then, with exuberant shouts, the archers spilled down from the pass to share in the booty.

"Watch your backs!" I shouted, waving my hands in the air. "What are you doing, you greedy fools?" My elation turned to panic and I began to scream Muhammad's name, but he was nowhere in sight.

The Qurayshi army had not retreated. The clamor of hoof beats shook the earth behind me and with a flailing pulse I watched Khalid ibn al-Walid lead his cavalry around the back of the mountain and up to the abandoned pass. I and Hafsa yelled until our throats were raw, but no one on the battlefield could hear us—and then the Qurayshi had outflanked our men. Our fighters turned with full mouths to see the Meccan troops rushing down Mount Uhud like an avalanche, headed directly toward them. Before they could lift their swords they were falling, spilling wine and blood on the desert floor. Clutching my bag of salves I ran toward them, not letting myself think of the arrows raining to the ground about me. My heart skittered as I dodged the angry-eyed men raising daggers and swords, knowing they would not harm me purposefully but also knowing that, in the rage of war, accidents could happen.

In less than the time it takes to tell the tale, the stars had realigned themselves. Victorious only a moment earlier, every Muslim on the field now battled for his life. While bandaging the head wound of my groaning neighbor Hamal, I saw the mighty general Hamza fall, and heard the delighted scream of Hind, whose father and brother he had killed at Badr. Crossing the field in search of Hafsa, I saw Muhammad's milk-brother, Abdallah, stumble to his knees with an arrow in his shoulder. His wife Umm Salama ran past us and caught him in her arms—and then we were all running, looking for our loved ones, our husbands and brothers and sons, with prayers in our hearts. I scanned the field for Muhammad. *Oh please let him be alive.* I saw Safwan slashing his way through a tangle of Qurayshi, his sword work sloppy, impulsive and angry. Muhammad had taught me to ignore emotions when I fought. *Think only, and cast aside your feelings,* he would say.

But where was Muhammad? His horse ran untethered, its eyes rolling, away from the carnage. I ran to Abdallah, who had been fighting alongside him. His wife, Umm Salama was tearing her gown and tying the cloth around his gushing arm.

"We were fighting below the pass when Quraysh attacked," he said. "They threw rocks and slung arrows at us, aiming at Muhammad. I would have battled on, but the arrow paralyzed my arm. Talha sent me to the well for water. Then I grew dizzy."

My heart clamoring, I ran across the empty sands to the well in the shadow of the great, foreboding Uhud. There the skinny, pointy-nosed Hind, who had forsworn her tambourine, held the water pail in her hands and refused it to our women.

"You prevented kept our men from quenching their thirsts at Badr, but now we are in control," she said with a cackle. Her narrow face and cunning eyes reminded me of a jackal's. I wished for my sword, then: I would have loved to cut off her hands.

"Hand me that bucket," I snarled, "or I'll take it from you."

Her laugh was like a shriek, high-pitched and harsh. "You are Muhammad's little whore, are you not?" she said. "I don't know why you are in a hurry. Your husband is dead."

"Liar!" I lunged forward and grabbed the bucket, then slammed it into her with all my might. The force knocked her to the ground, where she gasped for air. The women of the *umma* crowded around me, ladling water into their skins. After I'd filled mine, I lifted the bucket to drop it back into the hole. But as Hind's cronies aided her to her feet, I turned the pail on its side and jerked it toward her, splashing the remaining water in her face and on her clothes. The women around me laughed, and we scurried back toward the field to help our men.

"Laugh while you can!" Hind shrieked after us. "Soon Quraysh will be howling with laughter as we devour the livers of your pitiful fighters— including your precious Prophet!"

Panic gripped me with cold hands as I careened about the field, looking for Muhammad. Was he truly dead? Yet, if he had been killed, wouldn't we hear the Qurayshi shouting in victory? As if in response, the jubilant cries of our enemies echoed off the rocks. On the field, the Meccans cheered and raised their flag, and seized one another's beards.

"It is done!" Abu Sufyan bellowed from atop the pass. "Muhammad is dead! Praise Hubal! We have vanquished the traitors forever!"

The shouts of the Qurayshi pounded like fists against my ears, but I refused to listen. He couldn't be dead! Al-Lah wouldn't let it happen. Ali was protecting him, and also my cousin Talha. *Please, al-Lah, guard him from harm.* Holding the water skin in my hands, I ran, dodging men and rocks and wiry brush clinging to the dry hills. Crying Muhammad's name, seeking him in the roil of dust and flailing horses' hooves. Imagining him broken and bleeding on the ground. Gagging at the metallic stench of hot blood, the acrid odor of vomit, the tang of shit. I wiped my tears with the backs of my hands so I could see. One of the *ansari* motioned to me for water—before a dagger pierced his throat. His eyes bulged, and blood bubbled from his mouth. I watched, paralyzed, as he fell. I looked up to see his attacker running toward me, grinning. He was a Bedouin, judging from his long headdress, with a nose as big as a fist. I grabbed the dead man's sword and raised it, snarling—and the Bedouin retreated.

I climbed the hill and scanned the writhe and thrust of bodies, alert for Muhammad's profile, his double chain-mail suit, the gleam of his helmet. A horse reared next to me but, alerted by God, I ducked my head and narrowly missed the splitting of my scalp by sharp hooves. I climbed, and spotted Ali's double-bladed sword flashing in the sun. For once in my life, I thrilled to see him. Muhammad could not be far away.

Then I spotted him on the ground, at Ali's feet. Blood spattered his face, and his eyes were closed. I cried out, but no one heard me. Qurayshi attackers flung themselves with growls and snarls against the group defending Muhammad: Ali, Talha, Umar, my father, and—I caught my breath—Umm 'Umara, an *ansari* woman I knew from the public baths, running her sword through the belly of one attacker and yanking it free to fling blood into the eyes of the man behind him. Her dark hair flew; her eyes blazed; her mouth was a rictus of ferocity. My heart sang at the sight of her, fearsome and snarling and covered in dirt and blood, as glorious a sight as I'd ever seen.

Emboldened by her courage, I thrust myself through the melee, unnoticed by the fighters, glad for once to be small, needing to reach Muhammad. As much as I longed to be in Umm 'Umara's place someday, my thoughts were for him only at that moment. I dropped to his side and ripped a strip of cloth from my robe, wet it with the water in my water skin, and, with trembling hands, dabbed the blood from his face.

"Open your eyes," I begged. "Look at me, *habib*. Please be alive! *Yaa* al-Lah, let him live, I beg you!"

Muhammad lay still. His eyes remained shut. I heard a cry and looked up to see Talha drop his sword, clutching his hand, and fall into the pit our men had built to trap Qurayshi fighters. I wanted to leap up and help him, but how could I leave Muhammad? I crouched beside my husband with my sword drawn, daring anyone to approach him.

But no one remained to fight us. Above us on the pass, Abu Sufyan announced the death of Muhammad and the victory of the Quraysh.

"Al-Lah is dead!" he cried. "Long live Hubal! Long live Quraysh!"

I clutched my sword. Ali waved his in the air. "Let me go and silence that loudmouth once and for all," he said, but my father shook his head.

"You know what the Prophet says: We fight only when we are attacked. This battle is finished."

I heard a moan, and looked down to see Muhammad's eyes slowly open. Relief washed over me like a rain-soaked breeze.

"Praise al-Lah, he lives!" I called.

My face was the first sight he saw, my hand the first he squeezed. "My angel of mercy," he said. "Am I in Paradise?"

I laughed through my tears. "You won't get away from us that easily," I said. "Al-Lah still has work for you to do."

He raised his fingers to feel the bandage I had wrapped around his head, and, wincing, touched the links of chain-mail embedded in his cheek.

"*Yaa* Prophet, please allow me to remove those," an *ansari* man said. "I promise you will not feel pain."

He lowered his mouth to Muhammad's cheek and began to suck. Soon he had pulled out first one of the rings, then the second.

"He has tasted your blood, cousin." Ali glared at the Helper.

Muhammad smiled. "So he has," he said. "*Yaa* Ubaydah, you have guaranteed yourself a place in heaven. No one who has tasted the Prophet's blood can be touched by Hell-fire."

"Some people will do anything to get close to him," Ali grumbled as we all headed down the mountain. "I could have removed those rings with my fingers."

The *ansari* man heard him and frowned. "Don't listen to him," I said. "Ali hates to see Muhammad favor anyone besides him."

"Why are you here, A'isha?" Ali said. "Didn't Umar tell you to remain at the camp?"

"She does not obey her own husband," Umar said. "Why would she listen to me?"

Safwan caught up to us then. "*Yaa* A'isha, I saw you frighten off that Bedouin," he said. "I was ready to save you."

I didn't return his gaze, but heat flooded my face. What if Umar or Ali noticed the familiar way he looked at me?

"I can save myself," I said, keeping my eyes lowered.

Ululations pierced the air like daggers. On the battlefield below us, a bedraggled Hind stood amid the steaming carnage, her eyes bulging as if they might burst from their sockets, her graying hair frizzing about her head, her deep-blue robe—the color of mourning—billowing outward as she thrust her arms upward. One hand clutched something dark.

"*Yaa* Muhammad, we've now repaid you for the battle of Badr!" she screeched. "Your uncle Hamza, the so-called 'Lion of al-Lah,' murderer of my father and my brother, is dead!" We watched as she lowered the dark thing, purple and dripping, to her lips.

"By al-Lah, is she possessed by a *djinni?* What is she doing?" I whispered.

"Hind vowed to eat Hamza's liver in revenge for Badr." Muhammad's voice was calm, but his eyes filled with tears for his beloved uncle. "Apparently she has not forgotten that promise."

As she bit into the wiggling liver, I fought the urge to retch. Then, when she doubled over and vomited into the dust I had to look away, fearing I might do the same.

"Let me kill her." Ali pulled his sword out of his sheath. "Al-Lah would rejoice to send her to Hell."

"Put away your sword, Ali. Do you never tire of fighting? The battle has ended." Muhammad spoke in a pale, weak voice. "If al-Lah wants Hind to die, He will kill her Himself."

To Make a Man Wild

Medina, April 625

*T*he journey from Uhud to Medina isn't a long one—only half a day by caravan—but our return home in defeat seemed to drag like the tail of a whipped dog through the sand. The deaths of sixty-five men weighted our steps and our tongues, stifling our talk.

We'd buried the fallen warriors at the base of Uhud the night before—while I sneaked glances at the glorious Umm 'Umara, noting her simple dress, the strong, sure way she carried herself, her long stride. Muhammad had declared the dead to be heroes, martyrs for *islam* who would find great rewards in Paradise. Yet the ceremony was anything but jubilant. We knew many had died ingloriously, the victims of greed and wine and impulsive behavior. Muhammad's response to the battle at Uhud was to forbid his followers to drink wine. Mine was to examine my own behavior, particularly where Safwan was concerned.

Ever since the incident in the market, Ali had been watching me closely, looking for some way to discredit me in Muhammad's eyes. In that way, he might step into my father's place as chief Companion to the Prophet of God.

As a married woman—and a prominent one—I was extremely vulnerable to gossip, especially concerning Safwan. Talking with another man even in the most casual way could cause speculation about me. *"Why does she not walk away?"* people would say. *"A woman's lowered eyes and murmured responses only encourage a man."*

I returned to the mosque with a vow in my heart: I'd forget about Safwan, who was nothing to me now, and focus on Muhammad, my husband and friend. After this defeat, he'd need me now more than ever.

But when Muhammad married again just a couple of days later, I found it hard to worry about him or anyone else but myself.

Zainab bint Khuzainah was no great beauty, but she was no donkey, either. She possessed some promising features: hair the color of burnt honey, a deep dimple in her chin, and a complexion as clear as the first light of day, although as pale and fragile-looking as an egg. As Hafsa and I agreed, she could have been quite lovely—with a little effort.

"By al-Lah, hasn't she ever heard of rouge? Or *kohl?*" Hafsa said as we watched the wedding guests greeting Muhammad and his bride, who was better known as Umm al-Masakin, the "Mother of the Poor."

"Those little rabbit-eyes of hers really need help," Hafsa went on. "And look at that wedding gown! She must have borrowed it from one of her tent-dwellers."

Indeed, Umm al-Masakin's gown was a drab and shabby garment. Yet her smile was as warm and rich as gold. When she turned it on Muhammad, he beamed back at her with eyes full of wonder, as if he couldn't believe he had captured such a prize. I felt my blood simmer. Wasn't that the look he'd given Hafsa before she'd almost taken his love—and my position—away from me?

But Umm al-Masakin was as far from Hafsa as anyone could be. Instead of looking down her nose at me as Hafsa had done on her wedding day, she greeted me as lovingly as if we'd known each other all our lives. Looking into her eyes, I saw sincerity. I didn't see beauty, which made me wonder: What had inspired Muhammad to marry her? Yes, she was another Badr widow, but as I'd already pointed out, there were plenty of those.

"It is my duty to care for her, and also to help her care for the poor," Muhammad had told me last night. But I'd seen no duty today in that lust-bitten gaze of his.

That look haunted me for the next three days, as I waited for Muhammad to emerge from his seclusion with her.

"She could have had seven nights, but she wanted only three," Sawdah told us. "She said she could not let the poor tent folks go without her for so long."

"I hear she gives enormous sacks of barley and dates to those tent people every week," Hafsa said.

"While we in the mosque waste away," I said. "It's been difficult enough for us already, with Muhammad sending off all his booty from the raids. Now that *she's* here, what's going to happen to the small amounts of grain and fruit he puts aside for us?"

"No one can touch those," Sawdah said. "I hide them away. In a secret place." She gave Hafsa and me a long look, waiting for us to ask her where she kept them. Neither of us said anything, so she finally burst out, "In the Prophet's attic apartment. Bilal climbs the tree to get another bag for me whenever I run out."

Hafsa nudged me with her elbow as she and I headed to our huts to prepare for Muhammad's visit. "Take my advice: Don't tell Sawdah anything you don't want the whole *umma* to know," she said. "That woman is such a tale-teller, she can't even keep her own secrets."

I barely heard her words. I was still haunted by the desire in Muhammad's eyes as he'd gazed at the Mother of the Poor on his marriage day. Even with her so-so looks and lack of style, could Umm al-Masakin steal Muhammad's love from me?

Yet what was I willing to do to keep Muhammad's favor? Umm al-Masakin was a widow. The marriage bed would be familiar to her, while the very thought of the scorpion's tail still made me tremble. Hafsa reassured me when I told her about my fears—after she'd gotten over her shock at learning that our marriage wasn't consummated.

"The pain only lasts for an instant before turning to pleasure," she said. "And Muhammad would not be rough with you."

Pain or not, I determined to do whatever was necessary to turn his attentions back to me. When his ardor for Hafsa had faded, as Sawdah had predicted it would, he'd plunged into his preparations first for the battle at Uhud and then for the wedding. Now, during this lull in marriages and military action, was the best time for me to win Muhammad's heart again. Now—tonight—was the time to shrug off my fears and become a real wife to him, the way my mother was to my father, inspiring in *abi* a love that made him look at *ummi* as if she carried a precious treasure in the folds of her dress. I'd begun seeing affection in Muhammad's eyes again since the battle at Uhud, where I had run to his side when he'd needed me. Tonight, with the help of my sister and my sister-wife, I hoped to light the fire of love in his heart.

In my room, I bathed myself thoroughly and rubbed my skin with dried lavender blossoms. To lighten my complexion, I smoothed a lotion made with gypsum on my face, and I lined my eyelids with collyrium, using a lavender stem to spread the dark paste. Somehow I managed to keep my hands steady although I trembled inside. I slipped on my red-and-white-striped gown and brushed my hair until it threw sparks. I lit candles and incense to give my room a soft, romantic atmosphere. Then I picked up my tambourine and practiced the dance my sister had taught me. *It's a dance to make a man wild*, she'd said with a sly smile.

The jingle of the tambourine bells must have prevented my hearing his knock. I spun across the floor, my hands clapping the instrument high over my head and sliding my bare feet across the hard-packed earth, when I glimpsed him standing in the room, smiling. I rattled my tambourine and tossed my hair. I teased him with my eyes, the way I'd seen Hafsa do. I danced up to him and whisked his turban from his head. As I whirled it to the windowsill, I recited verses from a love poem.

As I moved in the soft light, I sneaked glances at him, hoping to see the fire that had sparked his eyes that first day I'd come to the mosque. I spun over to him, untying the belt of my gown with trembling fingers, but when I looked into his eyes I saw only bemusement.

"*Yaa* husband," I said. Feeling vulnerable, I reached out so he could see the elaborate henna patterns Hafsa had painted on my hands and fore-arms, and gestured for him to step farther inside my room. "What do you think of my dance? I've been practicing it just for you."

"It is very nice," he said. His tone was warm, like a hug. "I did not know you were a dancer. I am beginning to think you can do anything."

"That's right." I slipped my arms around his waist. I tilted my face upward to gaze into his eyes.

"I can do anything you want, *habib*. Anything you desire." I pressed my chest against him, but he looked down at me with furrowed brows. Before he could speak, though, someone pounded on my door.

With a sigh of frustration I yanked it open. Umar stormed past as though he hadn't seen me. My spirits drooped, and also my body, like an early spring flower wilted by a nighttime frost. The distress in Umar's eyes told me my evening of love with Muhammad would have to wait.

"*Yaa* Prophet, forgive me for intruding," he said as he and Muhammad greeted each other in the traditional manner—grasping each other's right hands, placing their left hands on each other's shoulders, and kissing each other's cheeks. "Something terrible is happening, and I thought you would want to know right away."

"He may forgive you, but I don't," I said, only half-joking. Umar flung a glance at me as if I were a dog begging for treats, then began to pace the room, pulling his beard with frantic hands and glancing at me as if deciding whether it were safe to speak in front of me. I moved to a cushion in the corner and folded my hands in my lap, lowering my gaze so he couldn't see how I longed for him to leave. Yet I also hungered to hear his news.

At last he turned to Muhammad, ignoring me. "Ibn Ubayy has gone too far. I have come from the market, where I heard him laughing with his friends at a slanderous poem about you!"

Muhammad's face pinkened. He was especially sensitive to the verses of the public poets. Poets could destroy a man with a single turn of phrase. It had happened to Ibn Ubayy, when Muhammad arrived in Medina. *Here*, cried the old *shaykh* Hassan ibn Thabit, *is the man sent to unite our divided city.* In the span of a few breaths, thanks to some well-placed words, people's allegiances changed. They'd lined the street to cheer for the Prophet of God on his spotless white camel and pushed Ibn Ubayy to the back of the crowd.

Umar's news was disturbing—but I scowled at him. Why couldn't his "urgent business" have waited for another time? The excitement Muhammad had felt at my dance was gone, obscured by Umar's warnings. *Get out!* I wanted to scream. But to do so would upset Muhammad even more, so I fumed silently.

"Prophet, this poet is saying you caused the defeat at Uhud," Umar said. "I heard his verses myself. He said you were the first to loot the Qurayshi camels. He said your greed cost the *umma* a great victory, and lost many lives."

The vein on Muhammad's brow was throbbing. "Who is telling these lies?" he growled. He seized Umar's beard with both hands. "Who is it, Umar? I will have him silenced for good."

"Ibn Ubayy is paying him," Umar said. "Ibn Ubayy is the one you need to silence. Let me take care of him for you, Prophet. You will be avenged by nightfall."

Muhammad dropped his hands. "You know we cannot kill Ibn Ubayy. He would gain more followers dead than alive."

"He has already deceived quite a few into joining him. The leaders of the Nadr clan have reneged on their treaty with us and pledged their allegiance to him, instead. Some of the Bedouin tribes are supporting Ibn Ubayy, also. They want to make him the ruler of Medina."

Muhammad chuckled and said he'd like to see whom the Bedouins favored next week. "They shift their loyalties as the wind changes direction," he said. But after Umar had left us alone again, he slumped on a cushion near me and brooded over what he'd heard.

"Why worry?" I patted his hand. "You don't want to be ruler of Medina, anyway, do you? Let them crown Ibn Ubayy king. If he gets what he wants, maybe he'll leave us alone."

Muhammad frowned harder than ever. I stared at him. The Muhammad I knew lived for Paradise, and the rewards that waited there. Since when had he concerned himself with earthly power? "You don't agree," I said.

"When we first arrived in Medina, I did not think about ruling anyone." He grimaced. "I was embarrassed by Hassan ibn Thabit's poem praising me. It was not my intention, then, to take anything from Ibn Ubayy. But things have changed, A'isha."

His fingers, which had held mine so softly, now clenched my hand. His eyes turned as fierce as a lion's. "If we give up our power, Quraysh will devour us," he said. "The *umma* will scatter like sands in the wind. The name of al-Lah, which we now shout from the rooftops, will become a whimper."

And Muhammad would lose everything he had fought for all these years. The realization sent a rush of sympathy sweeping over me, and I blinked back the tears of disappointment forming in the corners of my eyes. There would be no consummation tonight. Instead, Muhammad needed my consolation.

"Enemies are nothing new to you," I said, stroking his fingers with my own. "But you also have more followers than ever—even among the Bedouins! One lost battle means nothing. People soon forget." He frowned and shook his head, gazing far away. I moved my hand to his cheek, pulling his eyes to meet mine. His tortured expression filled me with tenderness. "All you have to do is raid a few Qurayshi caravans, and everyone will exclaim, *How fierce is Muhammad's army!*"

Softness spread like warm cream through his eyes, smoothing his face, melting his features into a look of pure love. Love! The husband I'd worked so hard to regain was mine once more. I felt a soaring in my breast, lifting me to my feet, and I twirled over to my screen. Perhaps I could remove some of his sadness. I knew how it felt to have enemies. Thanks to Ali, I knew the helplessness and sorrow of being mocked and lied about, and the fear of losing everything that means anything.

Behind the screen, I slipped off my gown. Under it I wore a dancer's costume Asma had loaned to me, a form-fitting skirt and a gauzy short blouse over a chemise, red, *to inflame his passions*, my sister had said. I emerged in a frenzied display of music and dance, shaking my body like a flower in the wind and darting my eyes away from him, then back to his troubled face, feeling my heart fill to brimming with sympathy. He watched me with a vague smile, but his eyes never locked with mine. He wandered in his thoughts like a man lost in the trees.

I finished my dance with a bow. As I dipped down, I lifted my hand to stroke his cheek and gave him a soft smile.

"What will worrying change, my love?" I said, and knelt before him. "Place it in al-Lah's hands, and trust Him to solve your problem. In the meantime, there is here, and now, and there is us, alone together for the first time in many nights."

To my delight his smile widened, and his eyes seemed to spark to life.

"*Yaa* A'isha, you speak truly," he said. "We have each other, do we not? And that was a wonderful dance. Let me thank you properly, *habibati.*"

It was what I had wanted, yet I trembled as he pulled me into his lap.

"You have given me my answer, Little Red," he said, caressing my hair with his fingers. I shivered with pleasure and leaned my body against his.

"I do have more followers than ever—and friends, too," he murmured.

"My marriage to Umm al-Masakin has been very fortunate in that respect. Her father is a Bedouin chief, did you know that? His tribe will come to our aid whenever we ask."

Heat stung my cheeks as though I'd been slapped. How could Muhammad speak of his new wife with me sitting in his lap? Torn between the urge to leap up and run from him and my desire to consummate our marriage, I lost control of my tongue.

"So that's why you married that dull little dough-face," I blurted, forgetting to fight with my wits instead of my feelings, as he'd taught me. "I wondered how you could be attracted to someone so . . ." His face clouded, but it was too late for me to stop. "Unremarkable."

"Your jealousy is very unbecoming, A'isha," he said, his body stiffening. "I cannot understand it, given my attentions to you. Umm al-Masakin is quite remarkable. You can learn much from her."

"I would like her better if you hadn't married her," I said, blinking rapidly to hold back my tears. A frown covered his face, but I ignored it. Had he considered *my* feelings before taking another wife?

"Umm al-Masakin's husband was killed at Badr, and there is no one to care for her." Muhammad raised his voice slightly. "Without my help she would have starved, and so would the tent people she has provisioned since coming to Medina."

"While you're busy taking care of her, who will take care of me?" I said. His wince was barely visible but I, ever vigilant to his moods, noticed it as if he'd scowled in disgust.

I lowered my eyes, ashamed. What a selfish thing to say—and stupid, also, if I wanted him to stop thinking of me as a child. Would I ever learn to think before I spoke, to hold my feelings on my tongue? Now my chance to win Muhammad's heart was lost. Tears welled up in my eyes again, but this time I couldn't stop them from spilling onto my cheeks. "Please forget I said that," I said.

"Now you are the one who needs cheering, *habibati.*" Muhammad held up an arm, dangling the sleeve of his robe before me. I understood: We had played this game for years. "Look inside," he said. "There is something for you in there."

My pulse leaped. I'd seen the Mother of the Poor's lovely new necklace of rubies—"for virtue," Muhammad had said. Sawdah owned a necklace from him, also, one made of shells from the Red Sea, but she preferred to keep it in her room. "Wearing it might attract the Evil Eye," she'd said.

I wiped my tears and slipped my hand inside his sleeve. I felt for smooth stones or beads—and, in one last effort at seduction, I caressed the tender skin on the inside of his arm. I wanted to make him sigh with pleasure, but he chuckled instead.

"Keep looking," he said. My fingers closed around something hard. I pulled it out to see an exquisite horse carved from ebony wood, muscular and lifelike, with a real leather saddle.

"It is Scimitar, your mount," Muhammad said. "My son Zayd carved it for you, and Sawdah made the saddle. It is for your collection, Little Red."

I turned it over in my hands. It was, indeed, a work of beauty. Yet it was a child's toy. For all my efforts today, I was still Muhammad's child bride. Probably he expected me to bury this horse in his beard, or make it whinny, then invite him to play. And, in truth, a part of me wanted to. But another part of me wanted to carry his gift to the cooking tent and hurl it into the fire.

"I think Scimitar would like to meet her new companions," Muhammad said. "May I retrieve your other horses?"

I stared at the toy in my hands, wondering what to say. Muhammad placed a finger on my cheek. "Are these tears? Forgive me, Little Red. I have offended you with my gift."

Regret rilled through the lines in his forehead, at the corners of his eyes, deepening them. Warmth filled my body like light from a soft-burning lamp. How could I complain to Muhammad about anything? So many worries plagued him already.

"I—I love your gift," I managed to choke. "It's very beautiful. These are tears of joy!" I forced a smile. "*Yaa* Muhammad, what are you waiting for? Gather the other horses, and let's play."

Mother of the Poor

I'd tried pleading, sulking, and cajoling, but Muhammad had insisted: Not only must I walk to the tent city with his timid bride, but I'd also have to spend the morning there with her. *You will learn what it means to be truly poor, and you will gain respect for your new sister-wife,* he'd said.

Umm al-Masakin's face shone when we told her the news. "What an honor," she gushed. An honor! By al-Lah, was I the angel Gabriel? But then she turned and bowed to me, warming me to her.

Muhammad might consider me a child, as our ill-fated evening of "romance" had shown, but that didn't have to be my downfall, I'd realized. Lying in his arms that night as he drank deep draughts of sleep, I'd blinked against the dark and my tears and asked al-Lah why I had to fight for all I wanted. Yet as I listed my opponents, I saw that they weren't so formidable. Ali was a vexation, not a danger. Umar was all bluster. Hafsa had become my ally, no longer interested in being *hatun*.

Nor, apparently, was Mother of the Poor a threat to my status. I'd feel more secure once I and Muhammad had consummated our marriage, but in the meantime I could hold my ground against the new wife. She was quiet and shy—pure weakness, while I was strong. Yet Muhammad was stronger—which meant that, no matter how I resisted, I had to spend a day with Umm al-Masakin, Mother of the Poor, in the stinking, flea-infested tent city.

I dawdled as I got ready for the journey, hoping Umm al-Masakin would leave without me. She liked to depart after the early morning prayer, but how could I go until the bread was baked? I thought Sawdah would topple over when I offered to mix the dough. Then she spied Mother of the Poor waiting for me in the corner, clicking her prayer beads like nervous teeth, and she shooed me away.

I fed my runt lamb and changed clothes, and still she waited. At last I ran out of excuses to delay, and we said *ma' salaama* to our sister-wives. How they clucked over me—as if I were going far away, instead of to the edge of Medina! Sawdah handed me her cowrie-shell necklace to wear as protection against the Evil Eye, and Hafsa whispered a warning not to get too close to anyone. "You don't want to catch any strange illnesses," she said.

Of course, Umm al-Masakin fed and nursed the poor every day, and she seemed healthy enough, if a bit pale. As we walked through Medina together—her with her heavy bag of medicines and a sack of barley and me with a sack of dates—I asked her how she kept from getting sick.

"By the grace of al-Lah," she said, and nothing more.

"What about me? How do I protect myself? Is there a medicine in your bag for that?" I asked.

She cut me a mischievous look from the corner of her eye. "Would al-Lah allow anything to happen to His Prophet's favorite wife?"

"How do you know I'm Muhammad's favorite? Did he tell you?" Pleasure, like the morning sunshine, spilled warmth over my face.

"He does not need to say so. I must only look at his eyes when he looks at you. Even the mention of your name causes him to glow."

"Sometimes I wonder." I paused, pondering how much to tell. "He treats me like a child—in every way." She blushed and pulled her wrapper about her face, and I wondered if I'd revealed too much.

We walked through town, brushing away the flies rising like steam from the scattered piles of manure, keeping our eyes down so we wouldn't draw attention from Ibn Ubayy and his men. At this early hour, though, the flies and the men were scarce. Umm al-Masakin moved her feet at a pace so quick I had to trot to keep up with her.

Then a baby's cry pierced the air. I raised my eyes to see the infamous "tent city" littering the desert like dirty laundry scattered by the wind. Puzzled, I searched for tents, but I saw only tattered pieces of dingy gray cloth spread across acacia branches stuck into the sand. These "poles" leaned at haphazard angles, threatening to collapse if anyone breathed on them. Some tents didn't even have poles. Their owners sat with pieces of cloth over their heads, or draped between their heads and those of their family members.

The stench here was much worse than anything in Medina. Urine, feces, the rotting carcass of a fly-blown dog, and unwashed bodies made a sickening stew of odors, nearly gagging me. A man hunching on the rust-red sand noticed my discomfort and laughed, baring bright, swollen gums and green-black teeth.

"*Yaa* Mother of the Poor, who is your helper?" the man asked. "I do not think she will be much help today."

"Abu Shams! Where is your tent?" Umm al-Masakin said.

"My son found a goat, and the goat ate it," the *shaykh* said. "My son is going to butcher the goat and give some of the meat to me, though, so I will be eating my own tent for supper!" He laughed at his ridiculous tale, and Umm al-Masakin laughed with him. I smiled politely, wondering how he could chew anything with those teeth.

"If your son will give me the skin of that goat, I can have a goatskin shelter fashioned for you in two days." Already she had recruited Sawdah to tan and stretch animal hides for this purpose.

Umm al-Masakin motioned to me for the sack of dates, opened it, and pulled out a handful of fruit.

"These will satisfy your hunger until mealtime," she said to the old man. I stared as she put the dates in her mouth, chewed them, and spat them into the wooden bowl he held out. He dipped his fingers into the concoction and slurped it down.

He lifted his eyes to catch me watching him. I quickly looked away, but he laughed again. "Never seen a starving man before, sister?" he said.

"*Yaa* Abu Shams, please speak to A'isha with respect," Umm al-Masakin said. "She is the favored wife of the Messenger of God. She honors us with her visit today. You should honor to her as you honor the Prophet."

He raised his eyes to me—hungry eyes, filled with pain. "The Prophet is the greatest of all men," he said. "Without him, none of us here would even have tents. But it is the Mother of the Poor who feeds us and tends to our health every day. She is the woman I honor." He folded his arms and glared at me as if I had asked him to bow down before me.

Umm al-Masakin thanked him and led me away. "Pay no attention to Abu Shams," she murmured, lowering her eyes in embarrassment. "The more he ages, the more eccentric he becomes."

Abu Shams had spoken truly about one thing: I wasn't much help to the Mother of the Poor that day. I knew nothing of the bundles of herbs, plant extracts, and incenses she carried in her bag, so I could only watch as she ground mixtures together with her mortar and pestle and gave them to a man to apply to the sores on his arms and legs, or spread them on the chest of a coughing baby, or fed them to a boy whose guts contorted with pain from the spoiled meat pies his mother had "found" at the Medina market the day before. (Just as the old *shaykh's* son had "found" the goat, I assumed.)

In the corner of the tent, the boy's mother moaned and clutched her stomach. "Mix that barley you cooked with some vinegar and give it to her," Umm al-Masakin told me. "It will cleanse the bad meat from her system."

I carried the bowl of food to the poor woman, and she clasped my hand with rough fingers, as my beloved grandmother had done when I'd visited her deathbed as a child. Now, as then, I could see the bones of her face as plainly as if she had no skin at all—but instead of staring at her in disgust, as I had the rotten-toothed old *shaykh*, I squeezed her hand in return.

"In the future, if you need food, tell Umm al-Masakin," I said to the mother.

"Can Mother of the Poor keep the stomachs of my babies full?" She peered up at me with knowing eyes. "Their father never could. From the looks of you two, your husband struggles, also."

"Al-Lah provides for me, and He helps me provide for you," Umm al-Masakin said. She came over and knelt beside me. "I have only barley, not meat, but it will not make you ill."

She pulled out a folded handkerchief from her medicine pouch, and opened it to reveal several silver *dirhams*. The woman's eyes tracked Umm al-Masakin's fingers, watching the coins as if they were fish in the water and she a bird of prey. Yet she offered a feeble protest.

"God bless you, Mother of the Poor. You feed my children while your own flesh wastes away and your skin turns pale from hunger. How can I accept yet another gift from you?"

"Do not worry about me, Umm Abraha. I am provided for." Umm al-Masakin pressed the money into the mother's palm. "Everything my husband left behind when he died went to his brother, including my children." Sorrow crossed her face like a shadow. "But I had some clothing I could sell, thank al-Lah. I thought I would use the money to buy food, but the Prophet was kind enough to marry me. He feeds me, so now I can feed you."

"But what would the Prophet say—"

I leaned forward to touch her arm. In that touch, I felt a warm rush from my heart through my arm and into my fingertips, as if I were pouring pure love into her skin. "The Prophet would bless Mother of the Poor for following his example and sharing with those less fortunate."

"Take the money, Umm Abraha," Mother of the Poor said. "It may prevent you from stealing tomorrow. Thievery is a great risk for a widowed mother. If you lose your hands, who will care for your babies?"

Bilal's voice tolled, summoning Believers to Friday prayer services. The clamor of voices and tramp of feet past the tent almost drowned out Umm Abraha's tearful thanks and our good-byes to her and her son. Mother of the Poor ducked out of the tent, and I followed, stopping first at the entryway to bid Umm Abraha farewell once more. Our gazes met, and I saw, beneath the gratitude in her eyes, a look of determination so fierce it took me aback.

"Tell the Mother of the Poor that I will repay her," she said. A smile passed over her lips like a shadow. "And not by thieving. When I have recovered from this illness, I will find work, by al-Lah!"

I returned her smile, although I doubted her words. What kind of work could she do in Medina? For an unmarried woman with no family to support her and no skills, two prospects were available: begging and prostitution. From what I'd seen, Umm Abraha was too proud to beg, and too devout to sell her body.

Guilt panged me as I joined Mother of the Poor outdoors and we began to walk through the tent city back toward the mosque. How selfish I'd been these years in the mosque with Muhammad, moping about my own hunger while others in my backyard faced starvation every day! My struggles for power and freedom seemed petty compared with the tent-dwellers' constant struggle for food and shelter. I would never complain again. And from now on, when I heard others denigrate the tent people as I'd once done, I'd make sure to tell them of the pride and dignity I'd witnessed today.

As we wound our way among the small lean-tos and rude tents, men and women shouted their blessings to Umm al-Masakin. She nodded to them, calling out that she would see them all tomorrow. I said nothing, for who knew when I would return to this place?

A shirtless girl ran up and tugged at Umm al-Masakin's robe. She was six or seven years old and she wore a skirt full of rips and holes. Her hair was cut short, reminding me of myself on my wedding day.

"*Yaa* Mother of the Poor, will you give me some barley?" the girl said, her dark eyes bold.

"*Ahlan*, Bisar, what happened to all your hair?" Umm al-Masakin said.

"Lice," the girl said. "But I don't care. I like my hair better this way." I laughed, remembering how I'd wished my cropped hair would never grow long again. "Can I have some barley?" she said. "I'm hungry."

"I'm sorry, I gave the last of my barley to Umm Abraha," Umm al-Masakin said. "Go and see her. She has enough to share. Tomorrow I will come back with more—and with some clothing for you, little one."

The child began to run toward the tent, but I called out to her and she returned. "No girl should be without a wrapper," I said—and, with a heart so full I thought it might burst, removed my wrapper and draped it around her shoulders and head. "You don't want the sun to burn your tender skin."

"*Yaa* Bisar, take good care of that garment," Umm al-Masakin said. "I will bring you clothes that fit you tomorrow, and you can return it to me then."

"No, I will come back for it," I said. Mother of the Poor turned her eyes to me, questioning, and I dipped my head. "If you'll allow me to accompany you here again, Umm al-Masakin." Her delighted smile was my answer.

When the girl had run gleefully away, billowing my wrapper behind her, my sister-wife shook her head at me.

"I am afraid you are too generous," she said. "Without a head covering, how will you attend prayer service?"

"Al-Lah will provide," I said. "If we return to the mosque in time, I can borrow something from Hafsa."

As we walked through the Medina streets again, however, I began to regret my impulsiveness. My bright hair hadn't been all that unusual in Mecca, where various kinds of people walked the streets. But in Medina, even Muhammad's pale skin stood out amid the uniform dark hair and eyes and skin the color of toast. Hurrying through the market with Mother of the Poor, I attracted stares from everyone we met. I felt my face burn, and knew it must be as red as my hair—but, as I'd told Umm al-Masakin, it was better for me to bare my head than for a young girl to have to run around with naked shoulders.

As we hurried, with our eyes downcast, toward the mosque, I asked Umm al-Masakin why her husband's brother hadn't married her when she'd been widowed, as was the custom.

"I had been married to him already," she said, "before Ubaydah made me his wife. My first husband divorced me years ago because I refused to stay at home instead of tending the poor. Ubaydah married me to save his family's honor."

"But did you love him?" I said.

She smiled as though she held a secret in her lips. "What is love, A'isha? Is it something you feel, or something you do? If it is something you do, then I loved both my husbands."

"But not enough to submit to their wishes."

"Al-Lah is greater than any man. He called me long ago to do this work. How could I abandon it because of a jealous husband?"

"Some husbands would insist."

"If you mean using force, yes. Al-Tufayl, my first husband, tried that. But I could fight back, to his great astonishment." Her eyes glinted. "I'd learned much about self-defense on my walks to the poor neighborhoods."

As if she'd conjured them, six filthy men approached us from an alleyway. My blood ran cold as I looked into the leering faces of Ibn Ubayy and his friends—two of whom I recognized from the day I'd moved in with Muhammad.

"*Marhaba, habibati,*" the short man with big ears said. "Remember me?

You're a tiny thing, but you've filled out nicely. Are you still the Prophet's toy, or are you looking for a real man?"

"Do you still sleep alone, or have you found a dog to meet your needs?" I retorted, but Umm al-Masakin's voice cut in as sharp as a whetted blade.

"Step aside," she said in a stern tone. The men nudged each other and grinned.

"I'll take her," Ibn Ubayy said. "I prefer grown women to redheaded brats."

I glanced about the street, searching for help, but Medina was deserted. Everyone, except these Hypocrites, was at the mosque. I would have to fight them myself. My pulse reared like a spooked horse. I reached for my sword, but the big-eared man yanked me into his arms before I could draw it out.

"Don't even think about fighting me," he said. His breath smelled like meat left in the sun too long, and wine. "You're right, you know: I do sleep alone. But not tonight."

Then he groaned and clutched the back of his head, releasing me, and slumped to the ground. Umm al-Masakin stood over him with a crazed expression in her eyes and her medicine bag dangling from one hand. Ibn Ubayy stepped toward her, but she whirled around, swinging the bag again, and hit him in the face. Blood gushed from his nose, which he tried to stem with his fingers. She turned to his tall companion, her eyes flashing.

"Approach either of us, and you will be next," she said.

What she didn't realize, though, was that her bag had spilled its contents all over the ground. Now she had no way to defend herself—but I had my sword. The tall man laughed and lunged toward her with his arms outstretched. Blood surging through my limbs, I yanked my blade from its sheath, making it *zing*.

"Touch the wife of the Prophet of God if you dare," I snarled, dancing about to hide the trembling in my legs. He pulled out a dagger and turned to me with his teeth bared, but I used my favorite trick of knocking his blade to the ground.

I waved my sword, all bluff and bluster, fending him off while I snatched up his dagger. "Leave my sight!" I shouted. "All of you. Or prepare to burn in Hell this very day." The tall man turned and ran, leaving his friends behind. Ibn Ubayy eyed my sword, but apparently he decided not to fight. He and the short man limped away from us holding their wounds.

I slipped my sword back into its sheath, took a few deep breaths, and knelt down to help Umm al-Masakin gather her medicines. She frowned to see how my hands shook.

"Are you unhurt?" she asked.

"Thanks to you, sister-wife," I said between gasps. "And you?"

"Untouched, praise al-Lah," she said, as unruffled as ever.

I laughed—at myself, for getting so agitated, and at her composure. "*Yaa* Umm al-Masakin, such a fierce fighter you are!"

"You would not believe the threats I have encountered over the years. That medicine bag has saved me many times."

We finished stuffing her mortar, pestle, and incense burner into her pouch, then hurried to the mosque. Alas, we were late. Inside, worshippers crouched on their mats, crowding the floor like gulls on the sand, murmuring praises to al-Lah as they stood in unison behind the red-robed Muhammad. I didn't dare enter with my head bare. So I climbed the wall to the courtyard and helped Mother of the Poor over. Together we slipped into my apartment to wash and pray there.

When we were finished, she hugged me and thanked me for my help in the tent city. Tears pricked my eyes as I returned her embrace. I'd had such evil thoughts about her—all of them untrue. She was no docile, mindless sheep but a real warrior, fighting husbands, disease, and would-be attackers to defend the lives of the poor.

"I should be thanking you," I said. "Muhammad told me I could learn from you, and I have. Never again will I resent his generosity to the tent people."

"A'isha, you have always been compassionate. Look at how lovingly you tend to the runt goats and lambs! No wonder the Prophet esteems you above other women."

I sighed. "I'm afraid you're mistaken about the 'woman' part. In Muhammad's eyes, I'm still a child. I've never minded that before, but lately . . ."

Umm al-Masakin opened her medicine bag. "Take this," she said, and pressed a small pouch into my hand. Inside, a fine yellow powder wafted sesame.

"*Wars,*" she said. "Mix it with some of your face lotion and wear it on the Prophet's next night with you. It is an aphrodisiac."

"What does that mean?" I frowned.

Umm al-Masakin's smile showed her beautiful, straight, white teeth. "It means," she said, "that the Prophet will never think of you as a child again."

The Wrong Prayer

*O*n the anniversary of our defeat at Uhud, it was time for us to reclaim our dignity. Not content with winning one battle, Abu Sufyan challenged us to meet again at Badr, hoping to firmly establish that his army was superior—and to kill Muhammad and put an end to *islam*. But we knew he wouldn't succeed. Our men had been training doubly hard since Uhud.

We prepared to meet the Quraysh again with fifteen hundred warriors, five times the number who'd fought with us at Badr eighteen months ago. With such a strong army and al-Lah leading the charge, we hoped to win so decisively that Quraysh would leave us in peace, at last, to worship as we wished. With victory in their hearts our men sang as they packed their camels and dreamed of glory on the battlefield or in the afterlife.

Given the festive mood surrounding our caravan, an outsider might have thought we prepared for a wedding instead of a battle. Ali hummed as he loaded his donkey with swords and arrows and thick leather shields. Even seeing me walk by didn't alter his song. Lavender, daisies, and roses scented the air, clustered in garlands about the shaggy camels' necks. My cousin Talha, tall and strong as a ben-tree, smiled as I hand-ed him a pile of blankets. Women flung their arms around their hus-bands' necks and kissed them, forgetting all modesty, and pinched the cheeks of their sons and grandsons with proud grins. Even the camels, usually so calm, stepped and shifted in their long parade, sloshing the water in the buffalo skins weighting their sides, clanking the bells on their ankles, and snorting as though they were restless to begin moving. Every last member of the *umma* was eager to kick those Qurayshi dogs into the Red Sea.

As for me, I was determined that no one, not even Umar, would stop me from fighting for my people and my God. Al-Lah had called me to action that night as I'd watched Raha's abduction. But He wasn't going to make it easy for me to fulfill my role. At Uhud my challenge became clear: I would have to fight for the opportunity, and the right, to defend my *umma*. For this battle, I had a plan. And I had the sword I'd taken from the fallen warrior at Uhud.

How I'd love to sink my blade into the massive gut of Abu Sufyan him-self! At Uhud, he'd increased my hatred with his exultant lies about Muhammad's death. And then, as we'd straggled in defeat to our camp, he'd mocked us with his reminder: *I will see you at Badr, mighty Prophet! If you dare to fight us again.* If we dared? Our men couldn't wait to erase the memory of Uhud from people's minds. And I, who had been practicing my swordplay for more than a year, couldn't wait to free my *umma* from the ever-present fear of Quraysh, whose leaders had bragged they would kill every man among us.

Abu Sufyan wasn't the only rival we needed to silence. Ibn Ubayy had increased his attacks on Muhammad, calling him a "lion with no teeth" to everyone who would listen. After that unpleasant encounter with me and Mother of the Poor that day, Ibn Ubayy left us alone. But, in his never-ending effort to make Muhammad look weak, he continued to harass poor Sawdah and Hafsa whenever they went out.

"Muhammad is afraid to confront me, no matter what I do," he boasted.

By insulting Muhammad's wives, Ibn Ubayy proved himself the real coward. Others in our city weren't so timid. The Nadr clan had grown more aggressive every day. Like their kinsmen the Kaynuqah, they traded with Quraysh, and they resented Muhammad's claims that he was the Prophet their Jewish Book had foretold.

One night, as Muhammad stood outside their walls conferring with my father and Umar, a group of Nadr leaders tried to drop a huge rock on Muhammad's head. Ali urged him to execute the entire clan, as a lesson to his other enemies. But Muhammad chose mercy. Instead of killing the Nadr, he directed our warriors to escort them out of town as they had done the Kaynuqah. Their long, slow, caravan trudged past the mosque while crowds of Believers pressed into the street to spit and jeer at them. I stood in the doorway of the mosque with Hafsa, Sawdah, and Umm al-Masakin to watch the sorry show, but I shed no tears for the traitors. Thick carpets, sun-glimmering candlesticks, and enormous sacks of food sagged on their animals' haunches, leaving no room for anyone to sit but forcing all— women, children, men—to walk beside their beasts. Tears streaked Nadr faces, making me wonder if exile was really preferable to death. But Muhammad could not bear to kill the People of the Book.

"They worship the same God as we do," he'd told me.

Later we heard how the Nadr had fled directly to the bosom of Quraysh—and laughed at us for letting them go. "The sight of blood makes the mighty Muhammad squeamish," they were saying. We hoped to see them at Badr, where they'd quickly find out how squeamish we were.

As I walked along the assembling caravan, looking for Muhammad, men in tattered clothing from the tent city greeted me with smiles and nods as they loaded the camels they'd been given for the journey. They were among the first to volunteer for this fight, Umm al-Masakin had told me. "They want to repay the Prophet for his goodness to them," she'd said.

I stopped to speak with them, but it was Umm al-Masakin they wanted to see. On my visits to the tent city with her, the residents had treated me deferentially, while they greeted Umm al-Masakin with warm embraces. Although I struggled to remember names and still cringed at the infections and sores and foul smells their poverty created, Umm al-Masakin seemed to feel more at home with her tent-dwellers than she did in the *harim* with her sister-wives. Of course, she'd grown up helping the needy. Her mother had been the daughter of a midwife and a poor Bedouin; a great beauty, she'd married an affluent husband but never forgot her beginnings. She and her daughter spent their days among the poor, delivering their babies and tending to the sick.

"I always feel closest to al-Lah when I am helping others," Umm al-Masakin said.

Helping the tent dwellers made me feel close to God, also. Working side-by-side with Mother of the Poor brought me an inner peace I'd never imagined possible. And I developed such affection for the sweet, gracious Umm al-Masakin that I wondered how I could have ever distrusted her.

She and I would care for the wounded at Badr, but I had another goal, as well. I wanted to fight, to prove myself a true warrior to Muhammad. If anyone besides lovely widows could catch his glance these days.

For several months Muhammad had been visiting the home of Umm Salama, one of Medina's most beautiful women. At first, he'd kept company with her injured husband, his milk-brother and friend Abdallah. When Abdallah died of the wound he'd received at Uhud, Muhammad continued to visit his widow, consoling her in her grief. Or so I'd thought. Months later, he was still going to see her, causing whispers in the *umma*.

"Umar and Abu Bakr asked to marry the widow Umm Salama and she refused them both, can you believe it?" Sawdah said, cackling over this rumor. "She is preserving herself for the best, by al-Lah! I, for one, will not be surprised when the Prophet brings her home for himself."

Scanning the caravan for Muhammad now, I found him holding Mother of the Poor awkwardly against his chain-mail suit. I scowled. How disrespectful to the rest of us in his *harim!* But as I drew nearer, I saw that theirs was no passionate clutch. Worry shadowed Muhammad's eyes like a hood.

"Help her, A'isha. I fear I am not much comfort in these chains," he said.

That's when I heard her sobbing. I pulled her close and asked what was wrong.

"Bisar died," Umm al-Masakin said in a choked voice. "That poor little girl! It was smallpox, A'isha. She was too weak to fight it." Tears welled in my eyes, also, for the child of the tent city we'd both grown to love. "I remained with her all night, grasping for remedies and fumbling for cures. But I neglected to pray. I thought I could save her, by al-Lah! Now she is lost because of my vanity."

I *tsked*. "Al-Lah alone decides whether we live or die. That's what Muhammad says." I pulled back to give her a stern look. "Giving up your sleep to help another isn't vanity, Mother of the Poor. Vanity is blaming yourself for her death, as if you had the power to stop it."

My words rang harsh even to my own ears, but they seemed to work: Umm al-Masakin's sobs became a sniffle. I helped her onto her camel, but the slump of her shoulders told me she was too exhausted to travel. Although I knew I couldn't treat the wounded alone, I asked Muhammad if she shouldn't remain in Medina. I'd find another way to get onto the battlefield.

He stroked his beard, frowning. "The tent-dwellers have asked that Umm al-Masakin accompany us. They think she will bring them luck. They will not fight at Badr without her."

"Tell them she has sent me in her place." I drew my sword with a flourish. "I'll bring not only luck, but skill to the battlefield!"

He laughed and gave me a look so warm I thought I would melt. He reached out to brush my cheek with his thumb.

"My little warrior-bride."

"Not so little," I said. "I'm thirteen."

"Yes, and I see your sword has gotten bigger, as well." He eyed the blade with its nicks and dents. Umar had never given my child's sword back to me. *Weapons are not for little girls*, he'd scolded when I'd asked him for it. "I have forgotten to ask Umar to return the one I gave you."

"I don't need it anymore," I said. "This one was clumsy at first, but now I like it better." I gave him a meaningful smile. "I'm growing up."

"But you are still too young to fight, Little Red. We do not even allow boys on the battlefield until their fifteenth year."

"I know I can't fight." I gave him my best wide-eyed look. "I only have my sword in case I need it. To protect Umm al-Masakin as she treats the wounded."

Muhammad grinned. I grinned back. We both knew better.

We rode for four nights to Badr, not bothering to hurry this time. Who cared if the Qurayshi arrived first and blocked the wells from us, as our army did to them last year? We carried extra water skins—and with al-Lah's power we'd defeat them no matter what tricks they tried.

I worried, though, about Umm al-Masakin. The first morning I helped her down from her camel she stumbled against me and then staggered to her tent.

"My energy will improve when I have had some rest," she said.

But she didn't improve. Her pale skin pinkened with fever, and her breathing labored as if a heavy stone crushed her chest. I urged Muhammad to send her home, but she convinced him that she was only exhausted from caring for the tent people.

"Take care of her, Little Red," he said. "Make certain that she does not exert herself."

I tried, but she insisted on visiting the men from the tent city before we rode each night. The effort it took to drag herself to the back of the caravan, to speak to them in lively tones, and then, leaning on my arm, to walk back to her camel, sapped her energy before our night's journey even began. After the second day we had passed the midway point between Badr and Medina. Sending her home no longer made sense.

"In you, A'isha, I have the very best caretaker," she said.

Through the vast, friendless desert we marched, lighted by the glow of torches so brilliant they illumined our way like the sun. Our scouts watched not only for shadows of Bedouin raiders and Qurayshi spies but also for signs of sand storms, especially the dreaded *samoom*, the hot wind of Hell, known to devour entire armies as if the desert were a beast that needed feeding. If Muhammad thought about such dangers, he never let his worries show.

"Would al-Lah desert His faithful as we defend His name?" he said.

As if aided by God's hand, we passed easily through the cruel desert to the cool well at al-Rawha—forgetting Sawdah's warnings against *djann* who lurked in its crevices—to al-Safra, with its elegant sun-bleached buildings topped with belvederes, and palm gardens redolent with the sweet scent of glossy-leafed privets.

One *barid* from al-Safra, we passed through a series of palm groves, relishing the shade, to the hills of Badr between which a spring-fed river flowed like the silvered tresses of a moonlit maiden. The vast, sand-swept field on the edge of the little town was devoid of Qurayshi when we arrived, to the delight of our men. They immediately began digging sand to pour into the wells as they had done at the first Badr fight, but Muhammad stopped them.

"We do not want Quraysh to brag that we needed trickery to defeat them this time," he said.

The rising sun spilled light the color of blood into our eyes as Muhammad led the morning prayer. Umm al-Masakin, her face as pale as the waning moon, prayed next to me, but I barely noticed her. In my prayers I asked al-Lah for the courage to fight bravely that day, while in my heart I hoped for the chance to show Muhammad that I was as capable a warrior as Umm 'Umara. And as much a woman as any of my sister-wives.

After nearly two years in his *harim*, I knew too well the folly of not consummating our marriage. Eyebrows would lift across the *umma* if the news were to spread. Seeking advice, I'd already confided in Hafsa and my sister, Asma, and I'd turned for consolation to Mother of the Poor. With each new confidante I risked exposure, and for what? Asma's dance had failed me. Hafsa's henna had gone unnoticed. And *wars*, the aphrodisiac Umm al-Masakin had given me, had only drawn anxious glances from Muhammad, who'd stared at the weird yellow lotion on my face and asked if I were sick. Impatient with the subtle approach, I tried bluntness.

"It's supposed to heighten your desire," I said. He ruffled my hair.

"*Yaa* Little Red, do not be in such a hurry to grow up," he said. "Enjoy your childhood while you can." That's when I knew Sawdah's stories were true: Muhammad's interests had turned elsewhere.

After we finished our prayers, I tucked Umm al-Masakin into her bed, then ventured over to Muhammad's tent—an enormous shelter covered in long, shaggy camels' hair of rust-red, like my own hair. A cool, moist breeze stroked my skin. I breathed in fresh water and almond flowers. The stoop-shouldered old poet Hassan ibn Thabit strode past, his hands careening as he shouted verses commemorating the first Badr fight:

Would that the people of Mecca knew how we destroyed the unbelievers in their hour of reckoning,
We killed their leaders on our battlefield and when they retired their backs were broken,
We killed Abu Jahl and 'Utba before him, along with Shayba falling with hands outstretched for sacrifice.
We killed Suwayd, then 'Utba after him, and Tu'ma too as the dust flew,

How many men we killed of nobility, leadership, respect and good repute among
their people.
We left them for yelping animals to attend, later to cook in the hot depths of Hell-fire.

Men cheered and thrust daggers and swords through phantom enemies
as Hassan passed. I ducked into Muhammad's tent. It was too vast for two,
set up on tall poles, but it would also serve as his *majlis*, for meetings with
his advisers out of the sun and away from the ears of spies. I rolled out a
blanket to keep the sand out of our hair and our bed, spread our sheepskin
on top of it, and lay down to sleep so soundly I didn't notice when
Muhammad slipped into bed beside me, or when Barirah, the servant girl
my parents had sent with me, called my name from outside the tent.

"Mother of the Poor calls for you. Hurry," she said, awakening us both.

Clutching our robes about us, Muhammad and I ran to Umm al-
Masakin's tent.

"Her skin heats more every hour," Barirah said to me. "She calls your
name."

Inside, I found Mother of the Poor lying on her back and tossing her
damp head from side to side. A smell like sour milk pervaded the tent. I
sent Barirah for a wet cloth to dampen her fevered forehead and cheeks.
Umm al-Masakin stared at me with eyes like obsidian, shiny and opaque.

"I fear it is the smallpox. Please give me some *khatmi*," she gasped.

I rummaged through her bundle of clothing and pulled out her medicine bag. Barirah slipped in holding several damp cloths. Muhammad
mopped Umm al-Masakin's face while I pounded the *khatmi* paste, made
from the mallow plant, in the mortar with a little vinegar and helped her
drink the concoction. I forced a smile, hoping she wouldn't see my fear.
Khatmi and vinegar worked wonders for ordinary fevers, but for smallpox
it had accomplished few, if any, cures.

Carefully I tipped a ladle of water between her cracked lips. She
grabbed my hand and squeezed it hard.

"This sickness is very contagious," she said.

I ordered Barirah outside. "Don't let anyone come in. Tell them the
Prophet has forbidden it."

Then I turned to Muhammad. "You should leave, also. You can't risk
this illness. You have an army to lead."

"A'isha." Umm al-Masakin squeezed my hand again. "You, also. Go."

"Never." I lowered my voice. "*Yaa* Muhammad, are there no other healers in our caravan? I'm so inexperienced."

"I will find whom I can," he said. "Will you remain here?"

Shouts clamored outside the tent. Muhammad stood. I heard Barirah shrilling in her native tongue before Umar stormed in with her clinging to his arm. He knocked her aside as if she were a fly, sprawling her to the floor. I leapt to my feet.

"This tent is off-limits!" I cried.

"More than a skinny female is needed to keep out Umar ibn al-Khattab," he growled. He apologized to Muhammad for intruding, taking no notice of Mother of the Poor sweating at his feet.

Our scouts had seen a small group of Qurayshi approaching on horseback, he said. "They bring a message from Abu Sufyan."

Muhammad excused himself to prepare for their visit—after asking Umar to find a healer for Mother of the Poor. I followed my husband to the tent flap.

"I'll send Barirah with you for my sword," I told him. "Just in case we need them."

He clasped my hands in his. "Forget the battle," he said. "Umm al-Masakin must not be alone now. I fear she is not far from the grave. Promise me you will remain with her, no matter what happens."

Not fight! I felt as if I were a goat's-bladder ball losing its air. Not help the *umma* defeat Abu Sufyan? Not see the regard and respect—and maybe, desire—in Muhammad's eyes after we'd won the battle? Umm al-Masakin had been sick before, but she'd always recovered. Nursing the poor had given her the strength to resist disease.

"What if Umar finds a healer?" I said. "Why do I need to be here then? There's nothing I can do for her, but I could help the *umma* on the battlefield."

"She loves you, A'isha. You will be a comfort to her." He kissed my forehead. "Stay."

After he'd ducked out, I blinked back my tears, telling myself not to be selfish. Helping Umm al-Masakin was more important than fighting a thousand battles. I knelt beside her and smoothed her hair off her face, and soon those familiar feelings of peace enveloped me. I sang to her and sponged her forehead, oblivious to everything outside the tent, until she drifted off to sleep. Then, from outside I heard more shouts. I moved to the tent flap, where Barirah stood with me and watched as four of our warriors raced past waving their swords, headed for Muhammad's tent. I heard Ali's cry and saw his warriors begin to move into battle formation. My fingers itched for my sword.

"I feel vulnerable without a weapon, and an army on its way," I said to Barirah. "But I told Muhammad I'd stay here with Mother of the Poor. Will you bring it to me? Don't let anyone see you." Soon Barirah was slipping, unseen, into mine and Muhammad's tent.

Back inside I found Umm al-Masakin still sleeping, her lips moving and her face bathed in cold sweat. *Where is that healer?* I wiped the water from her skin, searching her face with my eyes for some sign of improvement, but finding none. Yet she didn't appear to be worsening. She'd been more ill a few months ago when I'd cried for her, certain her end was at hand. Consoled, I moved again to the tent entrance to see the lines of our men lengthening and Ali strutting among them, barking orders.

"The Quraysh are coming!" someone cried, running past me.

Camels snorted. Armor clanked. Swords sang and clashed. Where was Barirah? I paced the tent, stepped outside, then returned inside to check on Umm al-Masakin, who slept. After what felt like an eternity, Barirah ducked into the tent, opened her wrapper, and pulled out my worn blade with its old tarnished handle.

She watched, curious, as I practiced my swordplay, but she frowned when I bragged about all the Qurayshi I planned to kill in the battle. "I heard you tell your sister-wife you will not leave her," she said.

By al-Lah! Was Barirah my conscience? I shoved my sword back into its sheath.

"When she wakes up, we'll see."

Five men rode past on frothing horses. They wore chain mail and helmets, and their horses wore leather armor. Their accoutrements gleamed like scrubbed teeth, bright and new, not like the dented, beat-up armor our men wore, salvaged from dead soldiers. In the front of the group I recognized the hard, cold eyes of the Qurayshi warrior Khalid ibn al-Walid. He turned those eyes on me, and I gasped, gripped so tightly by fear that my breath ran away. Mesmerized, I stared at the long scar twitching on his left cheek like a man writhing in pain. I'd heard how his face had bled in the first battle of Badr.

"He's come back for another scar to match," I boasted in a voice that shook.

How I longed to sneak away and listen to the men's discussion! But I *had* promised not to leave Umm al-Masakin, so I sent Barirah instead with an admonition not to be seen.

Meanwhile, Umm al-Masakin slept. *Look at her, so peaceful—definitely recovering.* I kicked at the dirt floor, sending little puffs of dust into the air. Apparently, no healer had been found. Yet if she was seriously ill—and I couldn't believe this fever was as dangerous as Muhammad feared—I lacked the skills or the knowledge to help her. Barirah could nurse her just as competently while I joined the men outside.

But if Muhammad saw me on the battlefield, he'd turn red with rage. He might lose his trust in me again. Staying in the tent, though, meant missing my chance—again—to help my *umma*.

I had done everything I could to answer God's call to arms: I'd trained, I'd acquired weapons, I'd found ways to accompany our troops to every major battle. I was ready to help liberate my community from the threat of Quraysh, yet I seemed destined to fail. *Why, al-Lah?* First at Uhud, when Umar had taken my sword, and now at Badr, confined to the camp with Umm al-Masakin and her sickness while she slept, oblivious to me beside her.

Her limp hand lay in mine like a wet rag. I searched for a pulse, and my own heart fluttered when, at first, I felt nothing. At last I pressed my fingers to her throat and found a faint beat, as erratic as a drunkard's stumbling. And her skin had turned from rosy and hot to pale and cold.

My scalp tingled, and the hair stood on my neck, as if a chilly wind had blown through the tent. "Umm al-Masakin!" I whispered, half-hoping she'd wake up and smile at me, showing me that all was not as bad as it seemed.

The thunder of hoof beats shook the tent. I leapt up and ran to the flap to see the Qurayshi messengers ride past, heading out of camp. Khalid ibn al-Walid, in the lead, nurtured a twisted smile that filled me with dread. Our archers stood in formation and practiced shooting their arrows in unison. I struggled against the longing in my heart to join them. Umm al-Masakin and I would have been on the battlefield now, with her medicine bag and my sword. We'd be wishing the fighters good fortune and dispensing herbs to increase their energy. We'd move about in the thick of the excitement, and Umar wouldn't complain because we were healers and he might need our help himself today. Instead, Umm al-Masakin lay sick on the ground, unable to help herself, and her assistant paced the tent and prayed for a chance to fight.

"Can't You do something?" I prayed out loud, looking toward Paradise. "*Yaa* al-Lah, I beg You to free me from this tent. I can't breathe!" Feelings of entrapment and helplessness—the same as I'd experienced in *purdah*—overcame my love for my sister-wife.

Barirah slipped in like a whisper. "The army is not coming to Badr."

"That's impossible!" I snorted. "Abu Sufyan challenged us himself!"

"He tricks the Prophet into coming here today, while he leads a great caravan around Medina," she said. "His messengers laugh when they tell the Prophet. Umar wants to kill them, but the Prophet says no."

Relief swept over me like a sudden wind. Not coming! There would be no fight. I wouldn't have to miss the battle, after all. And now we could start for home this evening. We needed to get Umm al-Masakin back to Medina as soon as possible. There, more skilled hands than mine could nurse her back to health.

A moan drifted to our ears. I stepped inside the tent with a smile, hoping to see Umm al-Masakin much improved after her long sleep. Instead, her eyes bulged with panic.

"*Yaa* A'isha!" she cried. "Help me!"

I ran to her and pulled her into my arms. She trembled all over; her skin felt cold, as if she'd fallen into a well.

"My children," she said. "I should never have left them. I want to see them, A'isha! Take me to them, please." She was delirious, I realized. She'd left her children years ago with her first husband, in Mecca.

"There will be no fight, Umm al-Masakin. We're going home. You'll see your boys very soon." I stroked her hair and murmured calming words, but my heart pounded. *Stay with me, Mother of the Poor. Just for a few days more, until we can get help for you.*

"The fight, canceled?" She smiled. "Praise al-Lah. Brothers will not kill brothers this day."

"Yes, praise al-Lah," I said woodenly, as shame flooded my skin. I'd rejoiced at the news, but for selfish reasons. I'd never even thought about the bloodshed, or about the lives of the warriors on either side. But now I realized that Umm al-Masakin spoke the truth: These battles with Quraysh did pit brother against brother, father against son, cousin against cousin. I still carried the stench and horror of death in my memory from the battle at Uhud. I hadn't let myself think about it before, when I was preparing to fight, but now I uttered a prayer of thanks for a respite from that nightmare.

"My babies," Umm al-Masakin moaned again, tossing her damp head on her pillow. "My husband took them from me. Why did I let him, A'isha? My little boys." Tears streaked her face.

"*Yaa* Mother of the Poor, save your strength. You'll see your boys," I said. "And all your tent people, also. They're your children, aren't they? That's why your name is 'Mother of the Poor.'"

"The tent-dwellers—who will provide for them?" she gasped.

No, please, I prayed silently. *Please don't take her.* Why had I asked God to free me from Umm al-Masakin's care? I'd promised Muhammad I would remain with her, and now al-Lah would end her life so I could join a battle that would not be fought.

"Call the Prophet," she said. "I need Muhammad!"

I summoned Barirah, and sent her to find him. "He's coming," I said to Umm al-Masakin.

"Promise me you will take care of the tent-dwellers," she rasped, clutching my arm so hard I winced in pain. "They have no one else."

I gulped. Me, care for them? How could I ever take Umm al-Masakin's place in their hearts, she who had given all of herself, who had risked her life, and now stood to lose it for their sakes?

Yet her grip on my arm and the panic in her eyes forced me to say what she needed to hear. "I—I promise," I said. "Don't worry about your tent people, Mother of the Poor. I'll take care of them, if needed."

Her trembling stopped. She lay back in my arms, suddenly calm.

"But it's not going to be needed, sister-wife." I swallowed the tears filling my throat, hiding my sorrow. "As soon as we take you back to Medina, you'll get better."

She gazed up into my eyes. "How loving you are, A'isha."

I began to cry. She was wrong about me. A loving person wouldn't have paced the tent floor and clutched her sword while her sister-wife lay dying. A loving person wouldn't have prayed for release so she could strut on the battlefield. If I'd been sick, Umm al-Masakin wouldn't have left my side for even the flickering of an eye.

"You're the loving one," I said, but her eyes had gone blank.

"Umm al-Masakin," I choked. "Umm al-Masakin!" I shook her. Her head lolled.

Muhammad and Barirah burst into the tent, but I didn't see them. I had laid Mother of the Poor on her pillow and covered my face with my hands.

"I recant my words!" I sobbed into my cupped fingers, into the dark place I had made there. "*Yaa* al-Lah, please ignore my prayer and send her back to us. I only wanted to show off, and now she's gone. I should have prayed for Umm al-Masakin, not for myself."

A hand squeezed my shoulder. I shrank away. I didn't deserve comfort. But Muhammad wrapped his arms around me and wouldn't let go.

"She's gone," I said. "She's dead, and it's my fault."

Muhammad stroked my hair as I had done for Umm al-Masakin the day we'd left Medina—could it have been just two days ago?

"Remember what you said then, A'isha," he murmured. "Al-Lah alone decides whether we live or die. The rest is vanity."

To covet glory on the battlefield while your sister-wife struggles to breathe—*that* is vanity. But I didn't correct Muhammad. He'd given up everything he'd ever had for al-Lah. He didn't know anything about vanity. Not yet.

Tharid and Moonlight

Medina, July 626
Thirteen years old

The loss of my friend Umm al-Masakin weighted my body like a great stone, pulling me down when I tried to get out of bed, stooping my back as I trudged from my hut to the cooking tent. In an attempt to cheer me up—and, probably, wanting to clean me up, since I'd lost interest in my appearance—Sawdah and Hafsa took me to the *hammam*, the public baths where Medina's women gathered to wash, groom, and share stories.

Outside, the day was strangely cool and overcast, mirroring my gloomy mood. To my relief, the baths were not crowded; only a few women soaked in the large rectangular pools lined with stone, which were filled from a nearby spring using copper pipes. Others reclined on stone slabs beside the waters and towel-dried their skin, or sat upright, clothed and scented, while their daughters braided their hair. Musk and sandalwood, lavender and rose tinged the moist air, overpowering the burnt smell of oil from the lamps on the stone walls.

Umm Ayman, Sawdah's sun-wrinkled friend and wife of Muhammad's son Zayd, greeted us with brittle kisses and fevered questions as we entered.

Why, she wanted to know, didn't the Prophet wear dark blue after the death of his dear wife?

"He says folks who mourn over dead Believers lack faith," Sawdah told Umm Ayman as we undressed and lowered our bodies into the bath. *Zainab sits at the side of al-Lah this very day,* he'd said the morning of her funeral, and forbade the city's wailing women to join our group as we walked to her grave site.

Why, Umm Ayman asked, did I look so bedraggled and red-eyed? Sawdah told her how fervently I grieved for my sister-wife."Not because she isn't faithful, by al-Lah, but because she misses Mother of the Poor. Those two did everything together."

Their words fell like blows on my head, pushing me down under the water. I remained there as long as I could, away from my sister-wives' dewy-eyed gazes. But, alas, I couldn't hide forever from Umm Ayman, whose eyes gleamed as if she knew a secret about me.

"Poor A'isha. You and your sister-wife shared so much, isn't that the truth? Including the Prophet," she said, nodding. "But now, with her gone, you share a little less, hmm? You lost a sister-wife but gained a husband, hmm? Maybe al-Lah will bless you with a child now. Then you can put to rest all the wagging tongues in the *umma.*"

I looked down at my hands, not wanting to insult Sawdah's friend with hateful looks.

"I would happily share Muhammad with Umm al-Masakin," I said, "to have her back with me."

Yet as my grief subsided, I began to see how shrewd Umm Ayman's insights were. With one less wife in the *harim,* I saw more of Muhammad than I had in a year: sword-fighting in the courtyard, riding horses togeth-er in the desert, and sparring with our tongues as we each strived to out-wit the other. Bolstered by his love, I began to feel more like a real *hatun.* But I made sure to keep my promise to Mother of the Poor and visit her beloved tent city from time to time.

At first, those visits were excruciating. Struggling to rise above my grief—and guilt—over Umm al-Masakin's death, I had little solace for the tent-dwellers who mourned and keened for her and begged me to recount her final hours. How could I talk about her death when I'd been partly to blame? I'd thought of my own desires above her needs, and al-Lah had taken her away. From now on, I'd strive to fill her place not only by caring for the tent-dwellers, but also by thinking more of others and less of myself.

That vow flew out of my head when, just three months after Mother of the Poor's death, Muhammad asked me to ready her apartment for a new wife. Sawdah's prediction was coming true: Ten months after the death of Muhammad's milk-brother, his widow Umm Salama would join our *harim*.

"They say she is a haughty one," Sawdah told me and Hafsa as we kneaded bread.

"Her story is the opposite of mine," Hafsa said. "While my father's friends declined to marry me because of my temper, they all wooed the lovely Umm Salama. My father and yours both proposed marriage to her, can you believe it, A'isha?"

My laugh was harsh, raising Hafsa's magnificent eyebrows. "She must be special indeed for *abi* to take that risk. Marrying a twenty-eight year old from the Makhzum clan would turn his *harim* into a hornet's nest." Umm Salama hailed from a long line of wealthy Meccan aristocrats.

Like Qutailah, she was a jealous woman. That was why she'd turned down my father's proposal, she'd said. To Umar she'd given no reason. She'd rejected Muhammad three times before he won her over.

"I am set in my ways, and my years are too advanced for me to change them," she'd told him. "Also, I am hesitant to move my children into a home that may not be as loving as the one they had with their father. And, third, I am averse to sharing my husband with other women. Abdallah loved me alone. I would writhe in jealousy to see the man I married even look upon another with desire."

But, unlike her other suitors, Muhammad persisted. He wooed her for months until she finally relented. "I am more advanced in years than you," he'd said in answer to her concerns. "And I have known, and loved, your children since their births. As for your jealousy, it is no obstacle. I will ask al-Lah to remove it from you."

Judging from her demeanor the day she arrived, his prayers had not been answered. Standing in the cooking tent with Muhammad, Umm Salama appraised me, Hafsa, and Sawdah with arrogant gray eyes that seemed to calculate our worth and find us all lacking. Jealousy shadowed her face even as she held herself erect. Were it not for the colors she wore—a robe of white over a dark blue gown—she might have resembled a date-palm tree, so rigidly did she tower over us.

"Brrr! I feel a sudden chill," Hafsa murmured, but I didn't answer. I was watching Muhammad's nostrils flare and his eyes gleam, as though he were a hungry lion and she his next meal. And I wondered: Could I, his Little Red, ever compare to this tall, elegant beauty?

With Umm Salama were four children: a baby sleeping in her arms, the sight of which made my heart pang with longing; two boys, one about fourteen, and one much younger, and a tall, quiet girl named Dorra, almost my age, who smiled at the pet goat I had tied to one of the tent stakes. I returned their smiles even as I felt my stomach writhe. How fertile was this new bride! Would it take long for her conceive an heir for Muhammad?

Of course, I'd had these same fears when Mother of the Poor had first married him. If she were alive, she'd be kissing the bride's hands and welcoming her to her new home. I couldn't go quite so far, but I reminded myself to treat our sister-wife with kindness until she proved unworthy.

"I will leave you all to acquaint yourselves while I attend to an urgent matter," Muhammad said. "*Yaa* Umm Salama, when I return I will show you your new apartment." His eyes flashed with a look I remembered from his first day with me.

"By al-Lah! He needs a handkerchief to catch all that drool," Hafsa whispered. Umm Salama lowered her gaze to the sleeping baby in her arms and her cheeks blushed a delicate pink. She, I noticed, was not smiling.

Sawdah cooed and clucked over the babe while I looked on wistfully, wondering what it would be like to have a little one of my own. The children went out to play in the courtyard as I led Umm Salama to a cushion in the "nest," as Hafsa had named the wives' corner. I poured the new sister-wife a glass of date water, inhaling the scent of rose oil as I drew near to her.

I and Hafsa looked at our hands and sneaked glances at the new bride. She resembled an alabaster idol with that pale skin and those high cheekbones. No wonder so many men had courted her after her husband had died! And it was no wonder that Muhammad, the most prominent man of all, had persevered for so many months.

"She is not accustomed to *harim* life," Muhammad had told me the night before. "You will need to explain everything to her." I'd brayed like a donkey: After one and one-half years in Muhammad's household, I only knew one thing for certain. I wouldn't play "parrot" to anyone.

"A bowl of dates isn't much of a wedding feast," Sawdah said, grinning in apology. "We didn't know you were coming today."

"*Yaa* Sawdah, we have some clarified butter, also. *Samn* and dates are perfectly appropriate for a last-minute celebration." I spoke with authority, to establish my status.

"We were hoping for a big feast, because then they'd kill a goat or a lamb," Sawdah said. "We haven't had meat for a long time."

Umm Salama frowned. Judging from her perfume and the sheen of her silk, I guessed she was used to mealtime spreads of lamb and pomegranates, cucumbers and saffron-scented rice. Did she realize how different her life would be here? More important, did she realize who was in charge of this *harim*?

"I am sorry to disappoint you," she said in a quiet voice. "The Prophet offered me a feast, but I declined. These days I have little appetite for celebrations."

A tear rolled down her cheek, dissolving the stiff mask she'd put on for us. I saw the face of heartbreak, and I forgot for a moment that she was my rival.

"Please forgive us," I said. "We didn't realize. You're still grieving for Abdallah. Yet you married Muhammad. Why?"

She lifted her head on that stalk of a neck and looked at me as though I were a spider crawling across the floor, which she might crush at any time—but chose not to, out of pity. "If ever you have children, perhaps then you will understand," she said.

Her baby began to cry, and Umm Salama turned to face the wall to nurse the child. I glared at her back. *If I ever had children?* Did she know that my marriage was unconsummated? My pulse beat frantic wings at the thought. In the eyes of the *umma*, an unconsummated bride was not a wife at all. And the only proper place for an unmarried virgin was in *purdah*— a place I'd avoid at almost any cost.

Yet even if Umm Salama hadn't known I was a virgin, her remark about *if* I ever had children was a cutting one, and deliberately so. After one and one-half years in Muhammad's *harim*, I should be expecting a child. Eyebrows were raising over my failure, as Umm Ayman's remarks in the *hammam* had made painfully clear. Some were speculating that I was barren, a shameful condition indicating the displeasure of the gods or, in our community, of al-Lah.

In a few moments, Muhammad came to the nest with a face as eager as though Umm Salama were a bowl of honey. He stretched out his hand to her and led her out of the tent. As she walked, with her baby in her arms, she held her head as still and erect as if she balanced a crown atop it.

"So why *did* she marry him?" I puzzled as soon as they were gone.

"Tut, A'isha, how is a woman going to take care of herself, and four young ones, too, if she does not marry?" Sawdah grinned. "Besides, you know how the Prophet can be when he wants something. As stubborn as a donkey."

"Al-Lah only knows why he would want *her*," Hafsa said. "A winter's night is warmer. I should have given them a blanket as a wedding gift!"

◆

Apparently, Muhammad tried very hard to warm his new bride. For seven days he closed himself up with her, not visiting the cooking tent, my apartment, or the mosque, except to lead the Friday prayer service. On the pulpit, he delivered his sermon with his mouth stretched tight and worry marching across his forehead like a funeral procession. When he arrived at my apartment the next day, I had strewn rose petals on the floor and in my hair, and I was ready to lift his spirits with a night of love—but he no longer needed cheering up. He swooped me into his arms and whirled me in a circle, then set me down, laughing, and sprinkled kisses on my nose and cheeks. He was acting very fatherly, but I didn't mind. After tonight he'd think of me not only as a woman, but as his true wife and, I hoped, the mother of his child.

"How happy you are!" I said. "You must feel as pleased as I do to be together again."

"I and Umm Salama have consummated the marriage at last," he said with a broad smile. "After six nights of frustration."

"Six nights?" He removed his turban and handed it to me. It was tied in a new way—with a long strip of fabric trailing down his neck and shoulders, like a tail. *Her* handiwork, I supposed. "Why did she delay?"

"Her infant is young and needs constant nursing." His color deepened. "Umm Salama had neither time nor energy for anything else."

"So, the baby finally got its fill?" I tried to sound nonchalant, but my voice was as stiff as Umm Salama's spine. "Or maybe Umm Salama's arms grew tired of holding it to her breast. Either way, congratulations." Hiding my flushing face, I turned away and pulled from my shelf the surprise I had made for him: a dish of *tharid*, Muhammad's favorite meal, fragrant chunks of goat meat and broth ladled over broken-up pieces of bread. It was time to change the topic of conversation—to *me*.

"See what my sister taught me to make while you were gone?" I said. "I hope you don't mind, but I confessed to Asma that you and I haven't consummated *our* marriage yet. She was very surprised."

"Was she?" Muhammad said absently, his eyes on the food, his nostrils flaring at the aromas of meat and spices.

"Very surprised. She said, 'But you're a woman now! How can he take new wives before consummating with you?' She helped me make this dish to tempt you."

He took a big bite, chewed with his eyes closed, and pronounced it *latheeth*—delicious. I let down my hair and arranged it over my shoulders as he slurped every morsel from the dish and then lamented that there wasn't more.

"I have something else just as tasty for you," I said, and whisked the dish away to settle myself on his lap. His breath smelled of coffee and cardamom. I cocked my head at him. "Have you and Umm Salama been enjoying a cup in the *majlis*?" I teased, to lighten the tone.

He laughed. "Her uncle asked me to share a drink with him. He discovered the difficulty I was having with Umm Salama. He took the child from her and hired a woman in the country to nurse it."

"And so, with the baby out of the way, you were finally able to finish your task?" My tone was harsher than intended, sharpened by humiliating memories of another night when I'd sat in his lap, blatantly offering myself to him while he'd blathered on about Mother of the Poor. But I was nearly fourteen years old now, and, some said, developing into a beauty. Muhammad should be melting into my eyes and groaning with desire, not reminiscing about his attempts to heat the blood of his chilly bride.

"I am telling you this for a reason, A'isha." The vein on his forehead began to darken. "Umm Salama is upset over the loss of her child. She was doing well—" his smile was fleeting "—until after the consummation. Then she cried all night."

"How romantic," I said, and pulled myself out of his lap to stand.

"*Yaa* A'isha, are you so cruel? This must be jealousy speaking."

"What do you expect from me? Advice?" I glared at him. "Leave the poor woman alone. Can't you see she's miserable?"

"Miserable?" He stood. "She has been very engaging with me. We have talked together all night long, then slept in each other's arms all day."

"That sounds quite cozy." I turned to the window. "It sounds like you two are great friends."

"We are. We were there together when Abdallah died. He was my milk-brother, you know," he said, meaning that, as babies, they'd been fed by the same wet-nurse. "I feel responsible for his death. I should never have allowed him to lead that caravan raid. The wound he received at Uhud had not healed completely, and it opened up and became infected."

"Responsible, you?" I said. "You told me yourself: Al-Lah alone decides when we live and die."

"That is what I know," he said. "What I feel, however, is another matter."

"So you married her to assuage your guilt?" My heart softened. I knew all too well these days how powerful a force guilt could be.

"That is only part of the reason. I will not lie to you. Umm Salama is special to me. She possesses all the finest qualities. Beauty. Modesty. Wisdom. Courage. Intelligence." I flinched at each word of praise. Did he think I lacked these qualities?

"We began to talk together, and it was as though time had taken wing. I did not notice the setting of the sun or the rising of the moon." Muhammad smiled like a man who has just enjoyed a meal. Which he had—the *tharid* I'd prepared. If there were any justice, I seethed, the meat would settle as heavily in his stomach as his words were doing in mine. "When you come to know her, you will find much to admire."

"Unrequited love is painful," I muttered, blinking back my tears.

"What do you know about it?" Muhammad snapped. I jerked my head around to look at him, but his glower made me look away again. Suddenly the room felt cold. I pulled my robe from its hook and wrapped it around me. "You know nothing," he said. "You have only met Umm Salama once."

"Twice," I corrected. "I saw her at Uhud, when she was tending to her husband's arrow wound. You should have seen the love in her eyes."

"Of course she loved him. We all loved him!"

"She still loves him." The vein between his eyes bulged at my words. "You don't believe me, do you?" I laughed, wondering how he could be so blind. The great military strategist knew nothing about women. "Maybe it wasn't the baby at all! Maybe she was putting off the consummation because she didn't want it. That's why she cried afterwards. She might be married to you now, but in her heart she's still the wife of Abdallah ibn Abd al-Asad."

Now Muhammad was the one who laughed—a rough laugh, like the scrape of gravel on the grinding stone. "What an imagination! You have been reading too many love poems."

"I don't need poetry to know about love. My love for you has taught me plenty about heartache."

"Your love for me? What love for me, A'isha?" He was shouting now, and his vein was throbbing and turning black. "The love that tries to sabotage each new alliance I make?"

"Alliance?" I snorted. "Is that what you're calling marriage these days?"

"It is both! Umm Salama's father wields much influence in Mecca. He can help us greatly."

"So *that's* why you married her—for her family connections! It's pure coincidence that she happens to be incredibly beautiful."

"Nothing is simple. Not any longer. The *umma* is growing in power. Power brings enemies. Every new alliance I form extends our influence in Hijaz and increases our chances of survival."

I scowled at him. Did he really expect me to believe he'd married Umm Salama for her ties to Meccan high society? "What about love, Muhammad? Is there room in your life for love anymore? Or are you too busy 'extending your influence'?"

His pupils were fierce pinpoints of rage. His nostrils flared, and his face bunched up like a fist. I staggered backward as he thundered toward me.

"Love?" he shouted. "Do you see any love? Because I do not! I see only a spoiled child who loves herself!" He snatched his turban off the windowsill and stormed out the door.

I stood in place for only a moment, gasping for breath enough to keep up with my racing heart. "Well, *someone* has to love me." I threw open my door and looked around.

"Muhammad!" I cried. "Come back!" I ran into the courtyard, searching for him, thinking perhaps he'd gone into the *majlis*, but it was dark. The mosque? I turned toward the entrance—and, in the window of Umm Salama's hut, I saw his profile flickering in the lamplight. I stood there with my mouth hanging open. He'd run to *her?*

I felt a scream rise in my throat. I closed my mouth against it, loath to give Umm Salama even this small victory over me. I turned to walk back to my hut, but I stopped after only a step or two. Dread filled me when I thought of another night in my room alone, while my husband dallied with his new plaything. *Al-Lah, free me from this wretched life!* I remembered Muhammad's words: *Do you see any love?* In truth, I did not. Was it love to cause such heartache as Muhammad was causing me?

Sorrow flooded my soul and spilled tears on my cheeks. If I were a man, I'd be riding through the desert now. No one would lock me away or call me "parrot" or judge my worth by the number of children I had. I'd be in charge of my life as only men could be, with their swords and their horses, their courage and their wits. And then I remembered: I had all those things, but still I wasn't free. Yet.

I ran to the stable, tears streaming down my face, where Scimitar stood as if waiting for me. "Let's go join the Bedouins," I said to her, and soon we were riding through Medina at full speed. The stars whooshed past in a blur. Scimitar's hooves pounded in time with my pulse. The wind rushed against my ears. Two men on horseback parted for me to pass. One of them called my name. His voice beckoned, familiar somehow, but I resisted the urge to halt. Instead, I drove Scimitar to gallop faster. No one would stop me. I leaned into the gusting wind. Sand stung my face, a rough caress. Then the world lurched, and I hurtled up into the air, my arms outstretched as though I were flying. I reached out to grab a nearby star but then I was falling, falling. The lap of the earth opened up for me, plump and soft, and I landed with my astonished face in a dune of sand still warm with the day's heat.

I heard my name again. A man's hands clasped my arms and pulled me up from my sand-bed. I imagined how I must look, with grains pouring like water from my hair and clothes, sand like white powder in my eyelashes and in my mouth. I spat, brushed myself off, and staggered, dazed by my fall. Strong arms caught me, and I gazed up into the worried face of Safwan.

"A'isha." My name sounded as round and full as the moon on his tongue—and I realized that it had been his voice I'd heard calling me as I'd ridden out of town. "Are you hurt?" He lifted a hand to brush the sand from my forehead and cheeks. The heat of his body pressed against mine like a lover's touch. I reeled, dizzy.

He stepped back and steadied me with his hands on my shoulders, then let go of me. I shivered and pulled my robe tight, all those parts of my body so warmed by his closeness now cold in the night air. The wind whipped around us, enclosing us in a private world of swirling sand.

"Forgive me, A'isha," he said, taking a step back. "I did not mean to impose upon you. I feared you were injured."

His voice and manner were so formal. Had I imagined those moments in his arms? I felt my face grow warm. How could I have let him touch me? I lowered my eyes, hoping he couldn't see my blush, and thanked al-Lah for hiding the moon's light behind a cloud.

I forced myself to laugh. "The only thing injured is my pride."

His hands hung by his sides, but his eyes continued to caress me. My heart began to race again.

"My horse." I looked to the east, to the north, everywhere except at those eyes. "Where is my horse? Scimitar!"

"I'm afraid she is gone. But I can return you to the mosque." His eyes caught mine at last and held me there as surely as if he'd wrapped his arms around me.

"That's a very kind offer—but I can't accept it." How people would talk if they saw me riding in from the desert on Safwan's horse!

Disappointment clouded his eyes. "Forgive me again. I was thinking only of myself."

I grinned, trying to lighten the tone. "Yes, how selfish of you! Making me ride your horse while you walk alongside it, all the way back into town."

But he didn't smile. "I was thinking of riding behind you, with my arms around your waist," he said. "Holding you close."

I loosened my wrapper, no longer cold. I turned away from him, knowing I should scold him for being so forward, yet flushing with excitement at his words. If only Muhammad would speak so sweetly to me!

"But I would gladly walk beside you for the pleasure of your company," he said.

"I'm honored." I scouted the vast, undulant terrain for Scimitar. "But we can't be seen together in the middle of the night. Where is that horse of mine? Scimitar! Scimitar!"

"Here, then." He walked over to his horse, a handsome, cinnamon-colored steed, and held the reins out to me. "Ride Bedouin into Medina, and tie him up outside the mosque. I'll walk alone, and I'll collect him when I arrive."

"But—you'll spend hours trudging through this sand! I have an idea." My pulse fluttered. Safwan watched me, waiting. His ardent gaze seemed to tie my tongue in place. I looked around for Scimitar again. "What if we ride together to the edge of town, and then I take your horse in alone?"

He smiled at last, and the clouds parted from the gibbous moon. As I was pulling myself up onto his horse, though, the rhythm of hoof beats sounded in my ear. With chagrin and relief I looked up to see Scimitar cresting a dune and running in our direction.

"There she is!" I cried as though elated. I leapt down to the sand and ran to her. She stopped in front of me and nickered, nuzzling my neck with her nose.

I mounted her and rode over to Safwan. His turban had tumbled from his head at some point this night, and his long, straight hair blew free and glossy in the moonlight. My heart throbbed in my throat.

"Scimitar," he said. "Isn't that a strange name for a mare?"

"Not when the mare belongs to A'isha bint Abi Bakr."

"Lucky mare," Safwan said. He reached out to caress her mane, then moved his hand over to mine and gently pulled it to his lips. His gaze pressed into me as his body had done just moments before, and his kiss seared my fingers. I gasped and yanked away, pulled up on Scimitar's reins, and galloped back to Medina—and to my marriage that, with all its problems, seemed a much less dangerous place than the desert tonight.

RIDICULOUS RUMORS

MEDINA, SEPTEMBER 626

THIRTEEN YEARS OLD

*A*mong Muhammad's wives, I was the only one who escaped the pinches and lewd remarks of Ibn Ubayy and his cohorts in the Medina market. Tired of the humiliation, my sister-wives began asking me to shop for them. I was happy to oblige, always eager to walk in the open air, reveling in my freedom. But when Umm Salama sent me for cow's milk, I rankled. What would be next? Ordering me to the well for her hair-washing water?

It wasn't the asking that bothered me, but the way she asked, with a lifted chin and her usual commanding tone. After her new bosom friend Fatima had started encouraging her to take my place as *hatun*, Umm Salama began asserting herself in the most irritating ways. For example, she now insisted that I nurse my runt lambs outdoors instead of in the cooking tent. She said she was afraid I'd infect her children with diseases from the tent city, but I knew she just wanted to be in charge.

As I crossed the courtyard to the cooking tent, I passed her and Muhammad reclining under the date-palm tree. He had his head in her lap, and she was dropping fat grapes into his mouth. Entranced by her fruit, he didn't see me pass. But she did, to my dismay.

"I need you to do something for me," she said. I hurried along as though I hadn't heard her, but then Muhammad called my name and I had to stop.

Umm Salama lifted herself off the grass like a swan taking flight and glided over to me. "My children do not care for the goat's milk that is drunk here," she said. "I have promised them cow's milk for their meal today."

She pressed a coin into my palm. "I dare not venture into the market myself, for fear of suffering at the hands of those ruffians." As if she were so pure that a single pinch would undo her virtue.

I turned pleading eyes to Muhammad, who had come over to join us.

"I was going to the tent city this morning," I lied.

"Surely you can delay your visit until the afternoon," he said. "For the benefit of Umm Salama's children."

He watched me closely, and I dropped my gaze. After our terrible fight the night I'd run off to the desert, I'd promised to trust his judgment in the future. He'd forgiven me, but not without some chiding. *I am not the same as other men, but I am a man,* he'd said sternly. I knew what he meant: He differed from other men in the way he treated his wives. He listened to our opinions and encouraged us to speak. But in the end, Muhammad was the ruler of the household and of the *umma*. He made the decisions for all our lives. And my duty, as his wife, was to submit.

The journey to the market lifted my sour mood. The morning sun kissed my face as I walked through Medina, and people I hadn't seen in weeks greeted me with smiles and embraces. The burdens of *harim* life grew lighter the farther I walked from the mosque, until even the smell of manure didn't bother me. Neither did the swarms of insects. *Kohl* on the eyelids might attract the glances of men, but, I'd discovered, it also repelled thirsty flies. I only hoped I didn't attract Safwan's glance today.

Remembering that exchange in the desert with him a few nights ago made me blush so hard I thought my hair would catch fire. What had he been hoping to accomplish by flirting with me so boldly? Did he really think I would betray Muhammad, God's holy Prophet, for anyone—even him? True, I'd fantasized about joining the Bedouins when he and I were young, but those had been children's dreams. I was an adult now, account-able to my family, my husband and, especially, my God.

Which made my behavior even more abhorrent.

Hadn't I vowed to forget about Safwan and focus on my marriage? Yet whenever I saw him, my intentions scattered like clouds blown by the hot winds of desire. My heart fluttered as I remembered his proposal to ride through the desert with our bodies pressed together on a single horse. I shook the memory away. Whatever Safwan was trying to do, he was des-tined to fail. I was the wife of God's Prophet. If Safwan didn't respect my position, at least I should respect it myself. And if I lost my intelligence whenever I was around him, I would have to avoid his company.

A cacophony of sounds jolted me out of my reverie. I'd arrived at the market. Goats bleated. Cart wheels clattered. Children ran and laughed and screamed, and their mothers shouted. Amid all the noise, I could barely hear the vendors beckoning, their voices lilting, as I passed their stalls. The savory aroma of roasting lamb brought water to my mouth—but I had to do without, since the coin Umm Salama had given me would pay for the milk and nothing more. I held my stomach to quell my pangs as I passed by the meat vendor's stall, wondering when I'd ever taste such a delicacy again. *Not soon*, a part of me hoped. Meat, in our household, almost always meant a wedding. I'd give it up for the rest of my days to avoid another one of those sad events.

Not that I needed to worry about more wives in our *harim*. We were full, according to Muhammad's own rules. He'd told his followers they could have only four wives each. I, Sawdah, Hafsa, and Umm Salama made four. There would be no more new brides in our household, thank al-Lah! It was too exhausting, establishing my position as first in the *harim* again and again. Plus, each marriage meant I had to wait a little longer between nights with Muhammad. He slept with each of us in turn: Sawdah one night, then me the next, then Hafsa, then Umm Salama, no matter whom he might prefer. He was determined to treat us all the same—an honorable goal, but impossible to attain, in my opinion. I was sure he looked forward to his nights with Hafsa and Umm Salama more than to his time with me. They gave him pleasures while I gave him only talk. Or—that was all he would accept from me. As for Sawdah, she'd become indifferent to their nights together.

"I cannot have more children, so what good does it do? I would rather work on my leather," she'd told me.

In truth, Sawdah earned a tidy income with her elegantly tooled desert boots, sandals, and saddlebags. Neither she nor her son hungered for meat or wore ragged clothes. We watched from the corners of our eyes, envious, when she counted her money from her sales.

"It's unfair," Hafsa complained to me privately. "We like nice things, too. Husbands are supposed to provide for their households, but ours provides for everyone else, instead."

"*Yaa* Hafsa, you need to spend a day in the tent city before you make that claim," I said. "People there die of hunger every week. Our stomachs may growl, but at least we're alive."

"I'm not talking about food. I want clothes. Look! I've had to mend this robe three times. And your gown is too small, A'isha. See how your wrists stick out from your sleeves!"

I wanted to tell Hafsa how the tent people wrapped themselves in goat skins or moved about under the blazing sun with nothing on their heads, but I knew how she felt. Our life wasn't as hard as she imagined, but it might have been easier if Muhammad paid more attention to matters at home.

I slipped my arm around her shoulders and gave her a squeeze. "That's our misfortune, being married to the Prophet of God," I teased. "His mind is in Paradise, so our bodies suffer."

Or, I reflected now, maybe the problem wasn't Muhammad at all. He didn't concern himself with us much, that was true, but he also demanded very little. Ours was an easy life, compared to those of the tent-dwellers or of women whose husbands beat them or who, like my mother, suffered abuse from a tyrannical first-wife.

Would I still think my life was easy if Umm Salama became the *hatun*? The child of wealth, she was used to being waited on. As Great Lady, she'd keep us all busy catering to her and her children. My spirits sank when I thought of spending my life in servitude to that stiff-necked princess. I tried to shrug off the notion, telling myself it would never happen, that Muhammad would never let me be treated that way. But I knew there was only one way to ensure my number-one status in the *harim*. I would ask Muhammad tonight to make an announcement recognizing me once and for all as his *hatun*. After that, no one would be able to challenge my place.

But there were other problems in the *harim*. We were hungry, we were threadbare, and, worst of all, we were bored—especially Hafsa, who had no other interests except henna decorating. In other *harims*, women's lives were filled with babies to raise. In Muhammad's *harim*, there were no babies, only children from previous marriages—and most of them older. We sister-wives spent our days in idleness, magnifying our few problems and grumbling at one another, when we could have been using our time to earn money for ourselves, as Sawdah did.

Entering the Medina market, I passed the stall of a woman hairstylist, and the idea flew into my head: Why couldn't Hafsa offer her skills with henna to the women at the public baths? Brides, especially, would clamor to have her filigreed peacocks and flowers adorn their hands and feet, and they would pay a nice sum for her artistry. The work would keep her happily busy, and with the money she earned she could buy a new gown for herself every now and then. I quickened my steps, eager to buy Umm Salama's milk and run home to Hafsa with my plan.

I found a vendor selling the milk and filled my skins, then turned to hurry back, my thoughts full of moneymaking schemes. But fragrances of flowers and spice beckoned from another stall, tempting me to sample some perfumes.

Dotting rose oil on my arm, I heard laughter behind me, followed by Muhammad's name and more laughter. I touched my hand to my sword. Was Ibn Ubayy nearby? No—these were women's voices. I pulled my wrapper about my face to hide, and listened.

"Imagine! She answered the door wearing nothing but a nightgown. The Prophet could see right through it," an elderly voice said.

"*Ai!* That modest man? He must have prayed for the ground to swallow him up," said her listener.

"She told me his eyes shone like two glowing lanterns, even as his face turned red."

"But why did she open the door to him?"

"She says she thought it was Zayd." The first woman snorted. "As if she would not know her own husband's voice at the door."

"She exposed herself to the Prophet on purpose? Is she not modest?"

"Zaynab bint Jahsh, modest?" The old woman cackled. "She ought to sprout the tail of a peacock! And now she is worse than ever. Since the Prophet saw her naked, all she does is preen before the mirror."

I gasped, then glanced over my shoulder: As I'd thought, the scratchy-voiced woman was Umm Ayman, Sawdah's friend and the first-wife of Muhammad's adopted son Zayd. With her was a short, squat woman with eyes that bulged like an insect's.

"The Prophet saw her naked?" the pop-eyed woman squawked. The perfume vendor lifted her eyebrows. Umm Ayman shushed her companion, and she lowered her voice—but not too low for me to hear. "But how?"

"When she opened the door in her nightclothes, he told her he would wait outside for her to get dressed. But then a gust of wind blew past and lifted her bedroom curtain. 'The breath of God,' she calls it. As if al-Lah willed it to happen. The Prophet saw everything, she said. *Everything!*"

"But how does she know what he saw?"

"She turned and saw him standing outside the window, flushed with desire. He covered his eyes with his hands, but it was too late. She threw on a gown and raced out the door to apologize, but he had already rushed away with a red neck. He was shouting, 'Praise be to al-Lah, who changes men's hearts.'"

"That is a strange thing to say. What does it mean?"

"I am not clever enough to figure it out, but Zaynab claims he is in love with her. Poor Zayd! She goads him about it day and night. 'Muhammad wants me,' she tells him. 'He has always wanted me, but now he is obsessed.' The Prophet is her cousin, and Zaynab says he would have married her long ago if his first wife, Khadija, hadn't insisted on being his only wife.

"'I waited years for that old woman of his to die, but you had to beg for my hand in the meantime,' she said to Zayd. 'Now I'm stuck with you, and all Muhammad can do is keep marrying other wives, trying to forget me.'"

"Poor Zayd!" Umm Ayman's listener clucked.

"By al-Lah, it breaks his heart to hear it. It breaks mine, too, to see my husband hurting. She wants a divorce so she can be free to marry the Prophet, that is what I think. Zayd would be happier without her, believe me."

Their voices faded. I turned to see them walking away with their heads close together, nodding and laughing—as the entire *umma* soon would be. Sawdah couldn't keep a secret for a day, but her friend Umm Ayman was worse: She couldn't keep her lips sealed for even an hour.

I hurried to the mosque to tell Muhammad about the rumors, far more damaging than anything Ibn Ubayy had invented. The blame Muhammad took for losing at Uhud was nothing in comparison. And, even though I knew her tale could only be half-true, others would be eager to believe every word, and to pass on the story with embellishments. Rumors only grow more spicy as they move from tongue to tongue. Soon everyone would be whispering "incest"—unless Muhammad stopped the lies before it was too late.

I found him in the courtyard with Umm Salama. He was stripped bare to the waist, and stood bent-over as she washed his hair for Friday services—my task.

"What delayed you, A'isha?" he said. "I had to ask Umm Salama to do your job today."

"I have urgent news," I said, panting from my long run.

"It will have to wait until after the services." He raised his dripping head and began toweling it dry. His arms were lean and muscular. The rippling of his chest muscles made my pulse flicker. I felt Umm Salama's eyes watching me, and I looked away.

"I must tell you now," I said. "Before the services." Umm Ayman would spread her gossip all over the *umma* by noon. The crowd filling the mosque would whisper about Muhammad even as he led the prayers. Perhaps if he knew about the rumors beforehand he could mention something in his sermon to deflate them.

"I am sorry, Little Red. There is no time. I will talk with you afterward." Umm Salama lifted a razor to trim Muhammad's beard. Their eyes met, and the intimate look they exchanged turned me on my heel and sent me out the door to my hut. After the services? Fine! Let the whole city talk. Why should I care?

Yet I trembled for him as worshippers filled the mosque. With my head down I listened for gossip about Muhammad and his son's wife. I saw Umm Ayman in the corner. I slipped against the current to move closer to her.

"I am the one who suggested she move out," she was murmuring. "The

Prophet told Zayd not to divorce her. You should have heard her scream when she heard that news! So I said, 'If you are so unhappy, sister-wife, then why not be the one to leave? No one has told *you* to remain in the marriage.' I even helped her pack her things—crying all the time, of course. If she knew how glad I was to see her gone, she might remain just for spite!"

Murmurs rustled through the room, and I looked up to see Zaynab bint Jahsh standing in the entryway. I tried not to stare at her, but my gaze kept returning like a bee to a succulent flower. She was every bit as beautiful as Umm Salama, but in a different way. Umm Salama was a gazelle, elegant and understated; Zaynab was a lioness, gleaming with power. Her eyes shone a startling gold, like ripe dates fresh from the tree, and her loose, dark hair curled wildly about her face, vining around her green silk wrapper.

As she entered the crowd, the murmurs ceased. People might gossip about her, but not to her face. Boldly she stepped to the front of the mosque, where the men prayed, and with a graceful flick of her wrists she unrolled her prayer mat. Clearly she didn't cringe in shame, and why should she? A transparent nightgown, a blowing curtain, a blushing Prophet—such ridiculous rumors!

Then Bilal's rich voice rang through the mosque. Muhammad burst into the room like a ray of sunlight in his white gown, red robe, and gleaming smile. His hair tumbled in glossy curls from beneath his white turban—tied again, I noted, with that tail of cloth that all the men were wearing now. His freshly scrubbed skin glowed, and his stride was as quick as a stag's. In a single leap he stood atop the date-palm stump in the front of the room.

From his perch, Muhammad scanned the mosque. His glance flickered when it met mine, as if he barely recognized me, before he graced Umm Salama with the warmest of smiles. My cheeks burned and I lowered my head. Muhammad, who had once called me "beloved," now treated me with a vague indifference since our fight over his new wife. After he heard my news of this terrible rumor, though, he'd be so grateful that he'd probably spend two nights with me. Then I'd finally have my chance to make him see that I'd grown up.

His gaze flitted like a moth from face to face—and then it lighted on

Zaynab, who stood directly beneath him. When I saw the burn in his eyes, the world seemed to shift under my feet. The rumors were true. If only a hand would reach down and pluck me from the room! I longed to rush forward and yank every curl from her brazen head. I wanted to scream at him for being so gullible. But I had tried pouting and shouting before, and all I had done was send him to another woman. The arms of Zaynab bint Jahsh were the last place I wanted him to go.

Zaynab was known throughout the *umma* for her extraordinary beauty as well as for her magical charm. Every man who looked upon her fell utterly under her spell, it was said. Zayd was foremost among them, or so we all thought. But she'd claimed that Muhammad was in love with her. If she joined the *harim*, how could I avoid being overshadowed, forgotten, turned into a servant? I was only a skinny, red-haired thirteen-year-old with narrow hips and a tart mouth. She was an oasis of a woman, lush, yellow-eyed and wild-haired. And cunning enough to seduce the holy Prophet of God.

I dropped to my knees and pressed my hands and forehead against my coarse woven mat, feeling the fronds cut into my skin. I blinked back my tears, stood, bowed, prostrated myself again. *How could You let this happen? Haven't You tested me enough?*

After the service, I paced in my room, wondering how to tell Muhammad about the rumors, worrying the sash of my robe into knots. Would he accuse me again of jealousy? By al-Lah, I wouldn't let it happen! I'd seen the flashing eyes of Zaynab bint Jahsh. She played a game for which I didn't know the rules—but I could guess them after hearing the story of how she'd seduced Muhammad. And in this contest, I held at least one advantage: I was married to Muhammad, while she was married to his son.

I met Muhammad at the door wearing only my night robe, with nothing but flesh underneath. When he entered I would let the robe slip to the floor and stand before him naked. He would forget about the woman he couldn't have, and embrace the new, young breasts of the woman he already loved.

My hand felt cold as I led him into the room. He was frowning. "Was there something urgent you needed to discuss?"

"Discuss? Not exactly. But it *is* urgent." I hoped he couldn't hear my

voice quavering. I fumbled with the ties that held my robe together, trying to loosen them.

"Please, A'isha, I have other concerns," he said. His voice sounded
rough and impatient. I hesitated, imagining the humiliation of standing
before him unclothed while he reddened and demanded I cover myself.
You have chosen the wrong time again, A'isha. Even if he hurried away, at
least he'd have the image of me seared into his mind. He would think
about me later, and maybe he'd feel that same fire I'd seen in his eyes two
years ago. My hands jerked the cord and I felt the knots tighten.

"Wait," I said, as he started to speak again. Frantically I worked at the
sash. A knock on my door made me jump, and my robe fell open—but he
had turned away from me. I scurried over to the screen in the corner of my
room while Muhammad answered the door.

"Father, help me! Zaynab has gone!" Zayd's anguished cry flew around
my apartment and out again. Then I heard muffled voices, followed by
silence. I stepped out from behind the screen. Muhammad had gone out
with Zayd and closed the door behind him, leaving the room as empty as
my open arms.

◆

Muhammad was gone for hours. When he returned, I met him in my silk
wedding gown. I'd brushed my hair until it sparked, and decorated my
hands with henna. I greeted him with a kiss and the sweetest of smiles.
Muhammad would never tell me anything if I pouted every time he tried
to confide in me. *A wise man knows his enemies,* my father had always said.
If I was going to prevent other women from stealing Muhammad's heart—
and my status in the household—I needed to know their tactics.

He circled the floor of my apartment, groaning and gripping his beard
with both hands as if pulling himself around the room. "By al-Lah, I do
not understand what is happening!"

As Umm Ayman had predicted, Zaynab had moved back into her parents' home, demanding a divorce from Zayd. Muhammad tried to visit her,
but her father wouldn't let him in. *Forgive me, Prophet, but her reputation
is at stake,* he'd said.

"I must speak to her," Muhammad said to me. "She is making a mistake. She thinks I will marry her, but I cannot."

"You already have your four wives," I said from my cushion.

He grunted and waved his hand as if to say, *Who cares about that?*

"She is my son's wife," Muhammad said. "It would be forbidden for me to marry her. Even al-Lah couldn't change that."

"Nor could Zaynab," I said. "Blowing curtains or not."

"Zaynab did nothing wrong. The wind simply moved her curtain aside."

"'The breath of God,'" I murmured, remembering Umm Ayman's words in the mosque.

"You speak the truth," Muhammad said. "If people must blame someone for it, they will have to blame al-Lah."

"Why would God cause such pain to poor Zayd, who has suffered so much? He spent years in slavery until you adopted him. He's not even your blood-son. Why would al-Lah take Zaynab away from him and hand her to you, who have so many blessings? And why would He give your enemies more ammunition against you?"

"Only al-Lah knows the answers to your questions, Little Red. In fact, I think I will pray tonight for His guidance." He kissed my forehead and turned away without looking into my eyes.

I sighed and crawled into bed—alone again—while Muhammad stepped through the door that led from my apartment into the mosque. He'd placed me close by when I was younger so I wouldn't be lonely or afraid. Now, lying in bed, I could peer through the open door and watch his prostrations and hear his prayers. I felt tempted to say a prayer of my own—*Send her back to Zayd*—but I told myself I had nothing to worry about.

Zaynab could plot and scheme, but she would never have Muhammad. "Changed heart" or not, marrying her would be too dangerous for him. God wouldn't like it, the *umma* wouldn't like it, and our few remaining allies in the desert wouldn't like it. They might stone the two of them to death, or exile them. At the very least, the *umma* would fall apart and Ibn Ubayy would be king of Medina at last. After all his work, would Muhammad throw everything away for a woman? Even now, as he prayed, he must know he would have to give her up.

For fifteen minutes I watched as Muhammad knelt in silence, squeezing sand in his fingers and letting it go, pushing his forehead deep into his mat as I'd done earlier. Then, to my horror, his body stiffened and he yelped. He fell backward to the floor. He writhed and trembled and moaned. His eyes rolled, and his limbs jerked.

After a few moments he lay still, panting quietly and glistening with perspiration, his eyes closed. I raced to him, my heart hammering, and pressed my hand to his chest, feeling for a heartbeat. "Muhammad?" I whispered.

He lifted his head and stared at me, his eyes wide and wild. Excitement ignited his smile.

"Al-Lah has spoken, A'isha. How wise He is! He has made everything clear to me."

My pulse calmed a bit. Muhammad had been having a revelation from God! I gazed at him in awe—that quickly turned to dread. From the trill in his voice, I knew he'd found a way to have Zaynab. I spread a smile thick as *hummus* across my lips. He sat up and gripped my hand.

"A'isha, al-Lah has given me permission to marry Zaynab. No—He has commanded it."

I didn't even try to hide my smirk. "Al-Lah certainly hastens to do your bidding," I said, widening my eyes. "You say He has given you permission to marry the wife of your son?"

"My *adopted* son. As you pointed out, Zayd is not a blood relation."

Panic rose in my breast, tearing at my throat. He *had* found a way! And al-Lah had helped him. Still, I kept my voice calm. "But it's the same thing in the eyes of the *umma*—in the eyes of Hijaz."

"That is the point." Muhammad was nodding, the way he did when I mastered a difficult sword-stroke. "We have been in error all these years. Blood children and adopted children are not the same. If I marry the woman with whom my blood-son has shared a bed, of course I am committing an incestuous sin. But if the son does not carry my blood in his veins, then why should I hesitate?"

Tears filled my eyes. How much longer could I pretend? Yet I kept smiling. "So you change the tradition. But, *habibi*, do you have to break Zayd's heart? Why can't you just recite your revelation and leave Zaynab for someone else to marry?"

His look said, *Haven't you learned anything?* "The entire *umma* is talking about her, Little Red. Some are saying she is pregnant with my child!

Who would marry a woman who has been so disgraced? I cannot let the slander continue against a member of my own family. If Zayd divorces her, the only way to stop the talk is to marry her."

The urge to flee swept over me, making me leap up and storm to my bed. Muhammad followed and lay down beside me with his hands under his head. He gazed at the ceiling as if it were a sky filled with stars. "My uncle and aunt will be very pleased. As will Zaynab, of course."

Of course. And me? I could only lie there beside my husband with my mouth full of woe. Hadn't he wanted *me* once? And hadn't he forbidden every other man in the *umma* to marry more than four wives? Apparently, though, the rules didn't apply to the Prophet of God—not anymore.

"Praise be to al-Lah, who changes men's hearts," I whispered.

I turned my back against him, refusing to let him hold me. *Why?* I prayed again. *Why won't You change his heart for* me?

And I fell into a fitful sleep with dreams of a man with long, shining hair and a face like a fine Arabian steed, with eyes for me alone.

13

Come Away with Me

*W*as there meaning in the rage of the wind that day, in the slap of the sand against our skittering legs? We scurried from the courtyard with our wrappers pulled close, hiding our faces from the sting, closing our eyes to the sight of our Prophet signing the marriage contract with his son's wife. The sky grew thick with dust, blotting out the sun, hiding the blasphemy, some hissed, from al-Lah's wrathful gaze.

Others remained loyal to the Prophet.

"To us, this union may appear unwise," my father said during the feast, as I poured water from a ewer into his yellow gourd. "But who among us can discern the intentions of al-Lah?"

"Al-Lah's intentions are perfectly clear." Ali stabbed the air with a bread crust. "By commanding this marriage, He has left no room for doubt: Adopted sons are not the same as sons by birth." He narrowed his eyes at my father. "And no man should place friends above family members."

Umar folded his arms and scowled at Ali.

"Unfortunately, interpreting the Prophet's revelations to fit our own needs has become a popular pastime in the *umma*," he said. "Some accuse Muhammad of doing the same in this instance."

"Treacherous words, Umar." Ali sagged into his cushion, his bark now a whimper against the powerful Umar's dissent.

"Is it treacherous to accuse the Prophet of being human?" Umar said. "Zaynab bint Jahsh is the jewel of Hijaz. Given the chance to have her, I could easily convince myself that it was God's will."

He glanced across the room at the laughing bride in her shimmering flame-colored gown and his own beady eyes seemed to ignite. Sweat dotted his face, and he licked his lips. As I watched him, his eyes shifted suddenly—accusingly—to me. Disconcerted, I brushed Talha's hand with mine as I poured water into his cup. The forbidden touch of his skin flustered me so that I splashed water into his lap, making Talha laugh.

Umar growled. "Mind your virtue, A'isha!"

I rushed away, flushing as furiously as if Umar had caught me flirting with Talha, whom I loved more dearly than I loved my brothers. Such was the mood in al-Lah's holy mosque that evening: lewd and leering, filled with bawdy jokes and winking speculations. *See how the Prophet lusts for his bride? It is a wonder he was able to wait four months to marry her.* With the sides of the cooking tent snapping like whips outside, men and women alike nudged one another, baring teeth and wagging tongues. *Of course he waited. He had to be certain that she did not carry his son's child, did he not?* I moved in the thick of the talk, pouring water into the guests' bowls and setting platters of meat before them, my hands trembling, my blood zinging. The insinuations made me yearn to attack some of them with my water jug, or to cut off their tongues. When a group of Khazraj men tried to draw me into their gossip, I *did* cut them off, with the only weapon I was allowed to use.

"Five women in his *harim*, while he limits us to four. Is that fair?"

"The Prophet of God must have special powers in the bedroom."

"Here is one of his wives. Let us ask her. *Yaa,* A'isha, how will your husband satisfy five women?"

I laughed, scorning them to hide my panic, for I'd wondered the same thing. With so many others to sate his desires, how would I ever become Muhammad's true wife?

"I was just serving your wives," I said, "and they asked a similar question:

'How can the Prophet satisfy five women when our husbands struggle with one?'" Their banter fell away like the glance of a modest girl.

In the close room, thick with the stench of unwashed bodies barely masked by cloying perfumes, the aroma of meat made my empty stomach twist. Needing to eat, I stepped gingerly among the men dressed in white and the women in their gaily colored gowns and made my way to the cooking tent.

I walked with my head down to escape the bawdy talk, yet the Khazraj men's question taunted me. How would Muhammad satisfy us all? I'd have to spend four nights alone now between visits. With each new wife, I'd have an even harder time catching his attention. Would he forget altogether about consummating with me?

Lately, when Muhammad lay beside me, a strange force tugged at my body, pulling me toward him. I would move close to him, and he would wrap his arm around me—but nothing more would happen. My skin tingled for his touch in spots he never approached. I'd lie there wondering what to do next, how to invite his caress. If I placed his hand there, or there, would he pull away in horror? If I asked him to make love to me, would he laugh and call me Little Red? While I lay there wishing and wondering, he'd begin to snore, indifferent to my charms.

Or did I even possess charms? I'd wanted to be a boy for so long when I was growing up that I'd ignored my mother and sister's advice about clothing, hair and makeup, and how to use my eyes to captivate a man. And with my awful reddish-brown hair and eyes like a murky pond, maybe I wasn't desirable to Muhammad. Safwan's fevered gaze that night in the desert flashed through my mind, sending heat to my cheeks. Would such an exciting man desire an unattractive woman?

"By al-Lah, is this a wedding or a funeral?" Safwan's voice jerked me out of my thoughts and into his gaze. His eyes pierced mine so boldly that I quickly glanced away, worried we might be noticed.

"I've never seen such sorrow on your face, not since the day your mother confined you to the house," he said. "Of course, it's understandable. You must be feeling very neglected right now."

I felt my skin heat like a flame fanned by a bellows. Remembering my vow, I glared at him, trying to ignore the way his sly smile set off his high cheekbones.

"Right now, I have plenty of attention," I said. "Unfortunately, it's unwanted." I tried to step around him, but he blocked my way.

"Unwanted attention is better than none, A'isha." His gaze intensified. "Besides, I'm not convinced that it *is* unwanted."

I ignored the whirling of my pulse. I denied my skin's familiar tingle. I quivered—in outrage, I told myself, at his rude behavior. Flirting with the wife of God's Prophet here in the middle of the mosque, for all to see! I glanced around the room and saw hundreds of eyes looking at Muhammad and Zaynab. I heard the clamor of arguments over al-Lah's will and the meaning of incest, saw Muhammad neglecting his meal while he gazed hungrily at his new bride, saw Ali staring at me and Safwan with the eyes of a predator about to pounce on its prey. I turned and, brushing Safwan aside, hurried out the door.

I ducked my head against the blowing sand as I headed to the cooking tent—but before I reached the entrance, hands tugged at my robe and a pair of arms encircled me. Safwan's body pressed against mine. I struggled, but he pulled me closer, as if we were tied in a knot. "Do you ever quit?" I said, but my words were lost in the wind.

He touched his lips to my ear. His warm breath made me shiver. "Never," he said.

He pulled me around to the back of the tent. He removed his turban as we walked, freeing his long hair to caress my face. His spicy sandalwood smell mingled with the choke of dust.

"What are you doing?" I gasped when we were out of the wind and out of sight of the mosque entrance. "Do you want us to die? They'll stone us if they catch us together."

"The Prophet would never let that happen, not to you. And you'd protect me."

I wrenched myself free from his hold. "If you deserved it."

He frowned. "Have you forgotten our years together as children, A'isha? Didn't we once think we would marry?"

"We were young."

"I've heard how you cried at your wedding. You *wanted* me."

"So what if I did?" I raised my voice, knowing the wind would sweep it away before it reached the mosque. "I wasn't allowed to make that choice, was I?"

"*Yaa* A'isha, I wish it had been me. If you were my wife, you wouldn't look so sad. I can see you're not happy with him. Five wives, and one of them like a daughter!"

"Zaynab's no daughter," I said. "She never was, even when she was married to his son."

"No. But you are."

His words sent an arrow through my heart. Safwan spoke truly. I *was* more of a daughter to Muhammad than a wife. Did Safwan know my marriage was a lie? I searched his face, but I saw no pity there—only desire, as I'd once seen in Muhammad's eyes.

"I don't know what you're talking about," I said.

"The Prophet is—how old? Fifty-eight? Old enough to be your grandfather, or even your great-grandfather. Too old for a spirited woman like you."

He moved closer to me. I would have stepped backward, but I was too near the tent.

"A'isha. I think about you all the time. I can't stop! It's as if I had a fever and walked around delirious, blinded by visions of your loveliness. I must have you, A'isha. Come away with me. We'll leave tonight."

He touched his hands to my shoulders, making me shiver, then slid his palms down my arms. I stood as if in a trance, looking up into his handsome face, listening to the words of love I had longed for so many months to hear from Muhammad.

"He has so many other wives," Safwan murmured. "How long will he miss you? Yet, with you as my bride, I'd never look at another woman. You would be my world. You *are* my world."

His face drew nearer to mine. His breathing was slow and deep. His hair fell forward like water against my hands, and I buried my fingers in its softness.

"A'isha."

His lips pressed against mine. His hands kneaded my arms. He kissed me again, coaxing my lips apart. I felt my body leap to life like an animal released from its cage. I collapsed against him and returned his kiss as the wind swirled around us. "*Habibati,*" he murmured—but then the image of Muhammad's face appeared before me.

Shame burned the backs of my eyes, flooded my skin like a fever. No one but Muhammad had ever called me "beloved." I pushed Safwan away, fled around the tent and into the stinging sand, and lurched into the mosque—where Ali stood in the doorway, watching me like the Evil Eye.

"What were you doing out in the storm?" he demanded.

"I went to the cooking tent where I could dine in peace," I said.

His lips twitched as if he suppressed a laugh. "Tell me, A'isha, on what did you feast tonight? Or should I ask *whom?*" Safwan slipped past us, his turban set neatly on his head. Ali stretched his neck to watch him duck into the crowd, and I fled to my apartment.

On the way I bumped into Umar, who scowled at me. "Your cousin Talha bragged tonight that he would marry you after Muhammad dies. Why would he say this unless you had encouraged him?"

I started. Talha, my future husband? It had never occurred to me. "I expect Muhammad to live for many years," I said coolly.

"I saw you touch Talha's hand when you poured his water," Umar said.

"That was an accident!" I cried, losing my temper.

"The way you women behave, it is no wonder the *umma* crawls with rumors about the Prophet."

I turned and walked away from him, holding my head high. Hafsa stood near my apartment door, her eyes wide. "*Yaa* A'isha, what did my father say to upset you?"

"He accused me of flirting with Talha."

"From what I saw, he suspects the wrong man."

I felt myself blush. "I don't know what you mean."

She poked me with her forefinger. "I saw you and Safwan leave the mosque together. Take care with him, A'isha. He's not a child anymore."

"Yes, I've noticed." I smirked, belying the crazed thumping in my breast. "But I think Umar is the one to worry about. Why is he suspicious of me?"

"He suspects every woman. Why do you think I was so eager to marry—both times? In his house, if a woman glances at the mirror she's plotting evil. He's upset about the scandal this wedding has caused. And he blames Zaynab, of course."

"Why shouldn't he? She seduced Muhammad."

"By al-Lah, are you agreeing with my father?" Hafsa pretended to swoon, then lowered her voice. "But you speak truly: My father is the one to beware. I heard him tell Ali today that the Prophet's wives should all be sequestered, to avoid more gossip."

"God forbid that from happening. We would kill one another if we had to stay indoors together all the time." Suddenly, the crowded mosque seemed too warm and close, as if the walls had shifted inward.

"Who's afraid of Umar? Not me," I said, wiping my damp palms on my robe.

"I am afraid of my father, and you should be, too," Hafsa said. "He knows how to command the Prophet's attention. And he can be very convincing."

◆

Although I shrugged and scoffed, the idea that we might be confined to the mosque sent fear racing through my limbs, reviving memories of how I had stood at my bedroom window and watched life march by like a caravan redolent of spices. Yet I couldn't believe Muhammad would agree to such drastic measures. Hadn't he given women more rights? Before *islam*, women were as chattel. Now we could inherit property, testify in hearings, and write provisions for divorce into our wedding contracts. Hadn't those rights come at al-Lah's behest? Muhammad's revelations proved that God valued women, also.

Yet it wasn't fear of imprisonment that made me pace the floor of my apartment that night. My mouth still burned, enflamed by Safwan's kiss. His seductions pricked my longings like blowing sands. *Come away with me. Tonight.* As if I'd leave the Holy Prophet of God for a mere warrior, no matter how persuasive! Yet Safwan offered something Muhammad could not: True freedom, to ride in the wind, to fight as a warrior, to choose for myself how to live.

Hadn't Safwan once held me rapt with his daring plots? He was only a warrior, true, but he was far from ordinary. Life with him would never be dull. We'd have adventures together every day. He wouldn't spend all his time with other wives. *You'd be my whole world.* If only Muhammad would make that promise!

I heard a knock on my door, the one leading into the mosque, and I felt my pulse flutter in my throat. Safwan wouldn't dare come to my room—would he? With a trembling hand I opened it, but it was only Muhammad, come to complain about his wedding guests.

"They finished their meals long ago, yet three men remain, arguing among themselves about the history of our incest laws," he said through clenched teeth.

"I'll bet Zaynab wishes she could disappear," I said with a smirk.

"She is enduring," Muhammad said. "She sits with her face to the wall, hoping the men will realize how badly they are behaving and depart. So far, they notice nothing."

As he spoke, he paced also, stomping up dust. I felt the urge to hold him in my arms—until I remembered why he was upset.

"Why not ask the men to leave?" I said. But I knew Muhammad would never do it for fear of offending his guests—or, worse, having them guess how eager he was to be alone with his new bride.

Another knock on my door. I cracked it open and peered out, holding my breath, praying it wasn't Safwan. To my relief I greeted a man about my height with round, anxious eyes and a mustache as stiff as if it had been dipped in candle wax.

"Good news for the Prophet," he said.

Inside my apartment, the messenger bowed and, in a high, quavering voice, told Muhammad that his guests had departed at last.

"*Yaa* Prophet, your beautiful new bride awaits you in her chamber." His eyes shone as if *he* were about to enter Zaynab's bed.

Muhammad's smile was so bright it brought tears to my eyes. He excused himself and hurried out into the courtyard with his visitor on his heels while I stood in the doorway, watching, my heart in my throat. The wind had ceased, and the night was chilly. The crescent moon gleamed like a dagger over Zaynab's hut. Muhammad looked over his shoulder, saw the man following him, and stopped suddenly. A titter flew from the little man when Muhammad whirled around to face him, his eyes snapping.

"*Yaa* Anas, I thought you said all the guests had departed."

"They have. Abu Ramzi, Abu Shams, and Abu Mahmud walked out together. They asked me to say good-bye to you."

"And you, Anas? Are you planning to spend the night with me and my new bride?"

The little man tittered again. "I am afraid I would be in the way. But if there is anything you desire . . ." He wiggled his eyebrows suggestively.

A gust of wind blew through the courtyard and knocked Anas's turban to the grass. He scurried after it, shouting. Muhammad slumped to the ground, shaking, and his eyes rolled like loose stones. I screamed and ran to him, having seen him like this before.

A door slammed and Hafsa raced toward us in her nightgown, her hair falling into her eyes. Together we helped Muhammad lay his head in my lap. He smelled of almonds and *miswak*. Sweat beaded his brow. His mouth moved as he tossed his head from side to side.

Umm Salama floated over in white like a pale cloud, one hand holding her wrapper tight around her face. She knelt down to hold Muhammad's limp hand. "Is he ill?"

"He's having a revelation," I whispered.

Anas dropped to his knees beside us. "I never meant to cause him harm, I swear it by al-Lah!"

Muhammad's trembling stopped, and the wind settled about our shoulders like a sigh. With a corner of my robe I dabbed the moisture from his brow. He opened his eyes, took in our hovering faces, and slowly pushed himself up.

"Are you still here?" he said to Anas. "Good. Then you can bear witness to al-Lah's pronouncement."

With our help he stood and then, with his eyes closed, spoke words I could have lived the rest of my life without hearing—words that changed everything for me, for all of us in the *harim*, forever.

He said: "Do not enter the Prophet's home unless you are invited, and leave as soon as you finish your meal."

He said: "When you ask his wives for something, ask them from behind a curtain. That is purer for your hearts and for their hearts."

And: "It is not for you to cause injury to the Messenger of al-Lah, or ever marry his widows after him. To do that would be something dreadful in the sight of God."

When he had finished, he turned and walked into Zaynab's apartment, closing the door behind him. Anas hopped from foot to foot, repeating Muhammad's words. I sat on the dry courtyard sand, clutching handfuls of it, and flinging it down. *Ask them from behind a curtain.* What did it mean? Would we in the *harim* need to carry curtains around with us everywhere?

Silence fell like a shroud on the courtyard as we sister-wives turned fearful eyes on one another.

"It looks as if we'll be spending a lot of time at home," Hafsa finally said, her voice cracking.

"All our time," Umm Salama agreed. She held herself as erect as ever, but I could see her hand tremble as she dabbed a tear from her eye. "How else are we to hide ourselves from view?"

"My father must have convinced Muhammad, after all," Hafsa said.

I puzzled over Muhammad's words as I walked back to my hut. Would I really be kept in the mosque, confined and hidden like a bird in a covered cage? I would rather die than face imprisonment for the rest of my life. Would my visits to the tent city be forbidden? I gasped for air, feeling as if a pillow covered my face.

In my hut I lay in bed and stared at the ceiling. Not allowed to marry after his death? Even God's Prophet couldn't live forever; he had told me so himself. Soon he would be sixty, and his remaining years would be as fingers on my hands. I would be a very young widow. Would I remain so for the rest of my life, never allowed to remarry, as lonely as the moon in a starless sky?

Come away with me, Safwan had said. *We'll ride away together, and never look back.* At the time, I'd thought he was possessed by a *djinni.* Now, though, Safwan appeared as an angel of mercy, sent to me from al-Lah Himself.

THE PRICE OF FREEDOM

*F*or three days after Muhammad's wedding-night revelation, my sister-wives talked endlessly about what his words might mean. Despair weighted me like a wet cloak as I listened to them agree that we'd all be confined to the mosque. In my room I prayed that, if I were to be imprisoned again, al-Lah would take me soon. I would rather roam free in Paradise than spend the rest of my life inside these walls.

Yet when Muhammad emerged from his time with Zaynab, he surprised us. The "curtain" he'd commanded for us was not a prison door, after all.

"Ibn Ubayy says he harasses you because he mistakes you for common slaves," he told us in the courtyard. "You must set yourselves apart by covering your faces. Then he will not be able to make such a claim."

Relief washed over me like a cool breeze, to hear that I wouldn't face another *purdah*. But then Muhammad described how we were to cover ourselves: From head to toe, every inch, except for a single eye.

"And so Ibn Ubayy and his Hypocrites are victorious," I said. Muhammad gave me a sharp look, but I was too indignant to care.

"Have you ever tried to move about with only one eye exposed?" I pulled my wrapper over my face and began to walk. A few steps later, I misjudged the location of the date-palm tree and kicked it with my bare foot. I released my wrapper to grab my throbbing toe, as my sister-wives watched in grim silence.

"Yaa Prophet of God, see what a time I'm having," I said with a wry grin. "Three steps, and I've already broken your rule."

Muhammad frowned. "This difficulty is not my intention," he said. "I will think more about this new requirement."

That evening, he and Umar discussed the hijab in my room—while I hid myself behind a screen, as now mandated.

"A woman's eyes are her most enticing feature," Umar said. "Even your wives know how to use them for seduction. Covering one eye is the only true way to avoid scandal."

His words rankled me, but I said nothing. How could I argue? I'd used my eyes with Safwan—not to seduce him, but to test my charms. And now, as Umar might have predicted, I fantasized about riding through the desert with Safwan, free from all the cares of the harim.

Yet I mourned privately about not being able to fight. I'd dreamt for so long of becoming a warrior and now, so close to my fifteenth birthday, al-Lah had taken the privilege away. When I complained in the harim, though, I found little sympathy.

"Yaa A'isha, these new rules benefit the umma," Fatima said, sitting with Zaynab and Umm Salama in their own corner of the tent. "How can my father build his empire and worry about you at the same time? It would be best if you remained at home."

"Not everyone benefits." Zaynab smirked. "Poor Safwan ibn al-Mu'attal will be bereft of her company."

"What you need is a child, A'isha." Fatima patted the baby boy she held to her breast. "Then you would be too busy to complain." My heart squeezed like a fist, but I rolled my eyes as if her words were ridiculous.

Sawdah clucked her tongue. "Yaa Fatima, mocking a woman for not having a child while you nurse your own baby? It would break the Prophet's heart to hear it."

"It breaks my heart, also." Hafsa looked askance at Fatima. "I have been in Muhammad's household nearly as long as A'isha, and I haven't given him a child, either."

Zaynab preened the dark curls wisping around her face and throat. "Two barren wives? That's more than a coincidence."

Hafsa's face reddened as if she'd been too long in the heat. "Are you implying that the Prophet isn't intimate with us? By al-Lah, I'll bring you my bed sheet after his next night with me, if you need evidence."

"As for me, I have nothing to prove," I shot back, my cheeks burning. "Especially to a woman who would seduce her husband's father."

"I desire no proof of anything." A smile hovered at the corners of Zaynab's mouth. "I know very well what a lusty man Muhammad is. But I do find it strange that, after several years with him, neither of you has conceived a child. Could it be the work of al-Lah? Perhaps He is waiting to sow Muhammad's seed in a more desirable garden." She patted her stomach.

I wanted to grab my sword and hack the laugh off her tongue. Umm Salama merely showed her tiny, secretive smile, as elusive as a shadow, but Zaynab tossed her hair and crowed like a raven. Around her neck she wore a beautiful topaz pendant, which set off her golden eyes. Muhammad now gave each new wife a necklace, courtesy of Abu Ramzi, the jeweler, who made them free of charge. I still wore the agate necklace my father had given me on my wedding day, yet I longed for a gift from my husband, something to mark me as his own. Even more, though, I yearned to be free of the *harim* and the taunts and sneers of Zaynab, Umm Salama, and their new friend Fatima.

My wish came true a few days later, when I was chosen to join Muhammad on an expedition. A man had tried to assassinate Muhammad but his hurled dagger had missed its mark, praise al-Lah! With Ali's twin-pointed sword aimed at both his eyes, the attacker confessed: *Abu Sufyan of the Qurayshi bribed my chief to kill your Prophet.* He came from the Mustaliq, a prominent Red Sea tribe. *If they find out I have failed, two thousand of my tribesmen are prepared to invade your city. They wait at the Well of Muraysi.*

"We must surprise them and attack first," Ali had urged, and for once Muhammad agreed with him.

As the troops readied for battle, Umar railed against Muhammad's tradition of bringing wives with him to battle. Thank al-Lah, he didn't prevail. Muhammad enjoyed women's company more than men's, and he didn't like to sleep alone. In appeasement, he agreed to bring only one wife. Ever concerned with fairness, he drew date-palm stems to determine which of us would join him—and, to my relief, I was the winner.

Yet, in another concession to Umar, I was forbidden to carry my sword. Umm 'Umara would be fighting in full battle regalia, I pointed out. Muhammad ruffled my hair as though I were a child. "Umm 'Umara is not my wife," he said. "And you would have difficulty fighting with your face covered."

On the evening of our departure, I faced another unpleasant consequence of the new rules: the *hawdaj* Umar had devised for me to travel in. It consisted of a seat resting on a pair of long wooden poles, surrounded by curtains. I pushed them aside and called out to Muhammad as he inspected the caravan.

"This *hawdaj* is uncomfortable," I said when he came over. "I'd rather ride my horse, or on a camel with you."

"You will be fine, Little Red. Princesses ride this way in India," Muhammad said. So I perched in my box on the ground and gripped the bars as servants tipped and teetered me onto the back of my camel. When the camel lurched to standing I held on, terrified, certain I'd topple over.

After a while I became accustomed to the swaying of the *hawdaj* and forgot about falling. Then my thoughts returned to Fatima's words, and Zaynab's laugh, and Umm Salama's sly half-smile. What a disaster it would be if they discovered my marriage had never been consummated! They would knock me down to the lowest position in the *harim*. I would be made their servant. Even Sawdah wouldn't be able to help me.

The only way I could ensure my freedom was to become Muhammad's true wife. Yet doing so now seemed impossible. Not only did two new women keep him busy, but plots against his life seemed to emerge every other day. Our loss at Uhud had weakened his support among the desert tribes, and his marriage to Zaynab had hurt his standing with the urban clans. With so much else to occupy his mind, it was no wonder he hadn't noticed the changes in my body or the desire in my eyes.

Perhaps on this journey Muhammad would notice me at last. For two nights and maybe three, he would belong to me alone. Consummating our marriage was urgent now, with Zaynab openly challenging my status in the *harim*. She, of all women, must not be the first to bear Muhammad's son.

On our first night we traveled like slow ships over the undulant waves of shifting sand. The following morning we set up camp at Muraysi, on the soft white beach of the Red Sea, and waited for the Mustaliq to arrive. I stood transfixed at the tent entrance, my eyes resting on the deep blue water, watching its waves rake the shore like fingers combing for treasure, listening to its soft sighs. A breeze skimmed the water and kissed my face wetly, tingeing my lips with salt. In the open, blue expanse of sea and sky I felt my body lighten as I gulped deep draughts of air. I grasped the fabric of my tent, giddy, fearing I might float away and, at the same time, wishing I could. I'd soar like the gulls wheeling overhead, free of constraints, free of everything except breath and sun and silver-finned fish, free to choose for myself what, how, when, and where.

Muhammad spent the day planning strategy with his commanders. He slept little, with his head in my lap, after fretting aloud for an hour over this battle. If we lost, Quraysh wouldn't need to use swords and arrows against us the next time we met. Their laughter would be enough to destroy us.

"We could defeat those fish-eating Mustaliq with our eyes closed," I said to Muhammad as I helped him strap on his helmet and shield. The Mustaliq lived easy lives on the Red Sea, where the climate was mild and the fruits grew abundant and wild. The mountains protected them from the Bedouin tribes we in the *umma* faced every time we ventured into the desert. "I hear the Mustaliq chief had to file the rust off his sword for this expedition."

Muhammad laughed and kissed me lustily—and I returned his kiss. That brief clutch with Safwan behind the cooking tent had taught me a few things. I pressed my body against my husband's, ignoring the roughness of his chain-mail suit, and I opened my mouth to invite his tongue to dance with mine. When we parted, Muhammad's eyes held the fire I'd been waiting to see again.

"You are full of surprises," he said.

I kissed him again. "After your victory, I'll show you more."

He turned away from me and strode toward the tent entrance.

"*Yaa* husband, where are you going?"

"To win a battle," he said. "As quickly as possible."

◆

I watched the fight from the camp, fingers twitching for my sword as if feeling for a lost leg. Muhammad had trained me so well I could defeat almost any man, but none of that mattered. I was not even supposed to show my face outside our tent. Once the battle began, though, I let my wrapper fall and, from afar, shouted encouragements to our men. We needed to win so all of Hijaz would know the price of treachery.

The fight started slowly. Arrows flew back and forth for an hour. From time to time I sneaked glances at Muhammad, who directed his troops from atop his camel. He glanced at me also, his eyes smoldering, making my pulse race more madly than any of our warriors'. Finally he rode over to Ali and spoke a few words. In the next moment the guttural cries of men thirsty for blood curdled the air and our fighters were running across the beach, waving our green flag and their swords. I held my breath, fearing for our men's lives—then laughed to see the Mustaliq archers drop their bows and flee. A few of their swordsmen attempted to fight, but our men trampled them like a stampede of horses. The black-and-yellow standard of the Mustaliq fell, and our men swarmed their camp, shouting and looting tents and chasing down the women who tried to escape.

For once I didn't mind not being in the thick of the action. I had excitement of my own to prepare for. Judging from the looks he'd been sending me, Muhammad would return very soon. With a light heart I slipped into our tent and cleansed myself with water from my goatskin bag. I brushed my hair and crushed lavender against my bosom. Holding up a cooking knife to serve as a mirror, I lined my eyes with kohl. I fastened my agate necklace around my throat, then fingered the milky white stones and admired their glow against my sun-kissed skin. Abu Ramzi couldn't have fashioned a more gorgeous piece of jewelry.

Then I waited. I rolled out our sheepskin bed and strewed cushions upon it, then arranged myself seductively. When he walked in, Muhammad would find me ready. Aroused by our army's easy victory and the sight of me spread like a banquet on his bed, he would shed his chain-mail suits, lie down beside me, and cover me with his body. At last I would know what Sawdah meant when she winked, and why Hafsa wiggled her eyebrows at the mere mention of a night with Muhammad. And then, al-Lah willing, I would have the son I wanted—at last.

After a while, I lay down, trying to calm my impatient heart's gamboling like a lamb in my breast. Outside the sun hurtled upward like a shot arrow and the Red Sea lapped at the sands in rhythms as ancient as the Earth. What could be delaying him so long? After a victory, he'd oversee the dividing of the spoils—but how much booty would the Mustaliq carry on a battle expedition? I stood and paced the floor, walking in circles as I'd done so many mornings while in *purdah*. In some ways, little had changed for me since then. I'd thought I'd gain so many freedoms by going to live with Muhammad, but here I was again, trapped by the *hijab* and wearing a path in the floor with frustration at not being able to control even the smallest aspect of my life.

I moved to the tent entrance, poked my head through the flap. The camp slept, as though deserted. I grabbed my wrapper and pulled it around me, then ventured outside to search for him.

Empty tents rested under the midday sun. Their open flaps shivered occasionally in the breezes that wafted from the Red Sea. Like a shadow I moved among them, afraid to be seen and chastised by the likes of Umar.

From the edge of the camp nearest the sea's shore, I heard a shout. Tentatively, trying to see through just one eye, I followed it and heard rough laughter. As I drew closer to the clamor I peered around the edge of a tent. Our men crowded together under a large canopy, many of them gripping the arms or waists of women and laughing as their captives struggled. "I have tamed this one already," Ali bragged as he ran his hand up and down the torso of a girl about my age. She stood motionless with her eyes closed and tears streaming down her cheeks.

"Look, *habibati*, how meekly Ali's slave submits to him," another man said as he wrestled his captive in place.

"His sword is not the only thing about Ali that is double bladed," another man said, and laughter filled the air.

"Are two blades necessary to subdue these Mustaliq daughters? Then tell me this: Why does the Prophet's slave kneel at his feet when he has yet to touch her?"

Then I saw Muhammad standing deep inside the tent, bending over a heart-stopping woman who knelt at his feet.

Her hair was the color of a brass bell. Her mouth was a red bow. She wore a blue gown that glittered as if she had been rolling in diamonds. Muhammad gazed at her, rapt, as if she were a snake-charmer playing a tune with her beseeching eyes.

"I agree, it is not proper for a princess to become a slave," he said. "But these are strange times. Nothing is as it was even a few months ago."

"I beg you, Prophet of al-Lah, do not send me into slavery," she said in a voice as light and refreshing as rain. "See how soft my hands are? Look at my skin. It has never been touched by the sun. I have lived a life of ease. Slavery would kill me."

He was, in truth, looking at her skin. Alarm jabbed me with a sharp finger.

"My warriors fought bravely for me today," he said. "Am I to tell the man who claimed you that he must now forfeit his prize?"

She lowered her eyes, pulling his gaze downward to rest on her ample bosom.

"I am at your mercy," she said. "I will do whatever you desire."

Desire? Muhammad was having so many of them at that moment, they clashed like lightning bolts on his face. I could have spoken his next words before he even thought them.

"There is a way," he said. "I can save you from slavery and avoid offending my men if you will do this one thing."

Hope lit her face like sunlight. She lifted her dimpled chin to beseech him. I felt my plans for the evening—for my life—slip away like sand though my fingertips. A falling sensation swept over me, and I grabbed a tent pole for support.

"Anything," she said. "I am your humble servant."

He sank to his knees before her and took her hands in his. His eyes caressed her face as if he had loved her all his life.

"Marry me," he said.

I let my wrapper drop away from my face and fled from the ugly scene, of men pawing women, of Ali kissing the neck of his new slave while she stood passively sobbing, of Muhammad proposing marriage to yet another beauty. She would consent. She had no choice. Marriage would be the price of her freedom, although I could have told her that our lives were anything but free. Did she know she'd be imprisoned as Muhammad's wife, bereft of her fineries, subsisting on a diet of barley mush and dates? I careened against tents as I ran, toppling their supports. My wrapper flew like a sail about me, revealing my hair and my contorted face, but I didn't care. What use was it to try to please a husband who thought so little about pleasing me?

"A'isha!" I heard my name, but I kept running. Let Umar go into convulsions over his precious rules! "A'isha! Wait!"

I ducked into my tent and let the flap fall shut behind me. A man's hand drew it aside.

"You don't have to say a thing, Umar," I said in a broken voice, but it was Safwan who stepped inside.

"I saw you spying on Muhammad," he said in a low voice. "And I know why you cry. Poor A'isha." His words of sympathy made my tears pour like water from a spout, although I tried to blink them back. With a soft sigh he pulled me into the circle of his arms and held me as I cried. He caressed my hair with his fingers, murmuring. Then, when I'd ceased sobbing, he lowered his lips to my eyes and my cheeks and kissed away my tears.

"Sweet A'isha," he said. "Come away with me. Tonight. I have the perfect plan."

Like a slap, his words jolted me back to reality. I yanked free and pulled my wrapper over my hair.

"Yaa Safwan, do you wish to die? Leave now, before someone catches you here."

"My only wish is for you, habibati." That endearment again. This time, though, my heart warmed to hear it.

"Listen," he said. "Our victory was so swift that our army isn't tired. And the Prophet is eager to take his new princess back to Medina to marry her. Forgive me," he added when he saw me wince.

"The Prophet has commanded us all to pack our tents and prepare to leave tonight. But I'll remain behind, as a scout, to watch for the return of the Mustaliq men. Here's my idea: When the caravan stops at the Wadi al-Hamd oasis, you find a way to stay behind. The curtains on your hawdaj will keep anyone from noticing you're gone—and when they do, we'll be far away!"

A satisfied smile spread across his face, reminding me of when we were children and he would invent some devious plot sure to land us all in trouble. But in those days, all we faced was a scolding or maybe a slap if we were caught. Now, the stakes were much higher. If we ran away, we'd face permanent exile from the *umma* or, if we were hunted down and captured, we might be stoned to death.

From outside the tent, Umar shouted my name. Safwan's hands grew cold. "Al-Lah save me!"

"Shhh! He'll hear you. Come with me," I whispered. I yanked him behind my screen with me. "Bend down, or he'll see you." I could feel his hand trembling in mine.

"You may enter," I called out.

"What if he comes back here?" Safwan rasped.

"Calm yourself! He's not going to come back here. Not seeing me is the whole point of this screen."

"Did you say something, *yaa* A'isha?" Umar's voice rumbled.

"I said, 'I hate this screen.'"

"It is for your own protection," Umar said. "You will learn to appreciate it, in time."

"I doubt it," I said. Safwan had stopped trembling, praise al-Lah, but then he did something far more dangerous: He lifted my hand to his lips and began kissing my palm, sending shivers up my spine and into my voice.

"Did you come here to discuss the new rules?" I called out.

"You sound unwell," Umar said. I pulled my hand from Safwan's lips.

"I'm . . . tired, that's all. What do you want?"

"The Prophet has sent me to tell you we will leave immediately," he said. "Pack up your belongings, and prepare for the tent to be dismantled."

"Where is Muhammad? Why couldn't he tell me this himself?"

"You will learn why soon enough." I heard the tent flap swish, and when I peered around the edge of my screen Umar was gone.

"Get out of here now, Safwan! Muhammad may be on his way."

"Will you wait for me tonight?"

I looked up into his eyes, listening for my heart's answer. Then I knew our time had run out.

"Leave," I said.

"I will look for you, A'isha. At the Wadi al-Hamd. Under the highest date-palm."

"We shall see," I said. "Now, go."

Safwan leaned down and brushed my lips with a treacherous kiss, then ducked out into the frenzy. I knew he wouldn't be noticed. After all, he was the one who'd taught me how to spy.

"I'll see you tonight," I said softly, when I knew he couldn't hear. "Maybe." Then I turned to the bed and began packing up my dreams for another night, with another man.

AN UNPICKED FLOWER

*A*s our caravan departed for Medina, my mind wavered with each sway of my camel's back. Safwan's offer of escape made my pulse leap in anticipation. With him I'd be able to live out my dream of freedom, for hadn't we conjured that notion together long ago? Yet my heart trembled at the thought of leaving Muhammad. Would al-Lah strike me dead for abandoning His Prophet?

I leaned back in my seat, dizzy with indecision. Muhammad had been my morning of light for as long as I could remember. We had always had more of a father-child relationship, it was true, but I depended on his friendship. Yet unless he changed his view of me from child to woman, I'd never have the control over my life that I needed. The longer his caravan of wives grew, the slimmer my chances of catching his eye, of conceiving his heir, and of holding my place as number one in his *harim*. How could I endure the dread gathering like a dark cloud in me with each new marriage? Yet—how could I bear losing Muhammad, never to see or touch or talk with him again?

When he came to visit me in my *hawdaj*, I would decide. When I saw his face, I would know what to do. Maybe he would apologize for leaving me waiting in our tent. *I was disappointed, also, A'isha,* he would say. *I did not want another wife, but I had no choice.*

My intentions shifted with my body, back and forth, leave or stay, Safwan or Muhammad, as our caravan rode into the night, torches flaming against the deep, their lights glimmering in the wild eyes of desert rats, the light defining rocks as rocks and not jackals about to pounce or, worse, dagger-wielding Bedouins. We illumined the sands as brightly as if the sun shone in the sky, but peer and yearn though I might, I couldn't glimpse Muhammad. At last I asked the driver of my camel where he might be.

"He accompanies his new bride-to-be, the princess of the Mustaliq," the driver said. "Shall I have him summoned for you?" I dropped the curtain and slumped in my seat.

At the Wadi al-Hamd oasis, the caravan stopped for a few hours' rest— and Muhammad finally came to me. Or, I should say, he walked past my camel and thrust his face through the curtains for barely an instant.

"Greetings, A'isha. I am glad to see you are well," he said—and then disappeared again.

"Wait!" I pushed the annoying curtains aside and called out to him. "*Yaa* Muhammad, come back!" I saw the flicker of a frown before he summoned a smile and strode over to me. I forced myself to smile, also. Everything depended on these next few moments. I reached for his hand and stroked it gently with my fingertips.

"I've been expecting you, *habibi*," I said as sweetly as possible. "Are we stopping to camp? You and I had plans for the evening, remember?"

His eyes darted to the front of the caravan, where he had been riding with his new princess. "That will not be possible."

"Muhammad, you hardly slept yesterday. Surely you'll come and lie down with me for a little while, at least." I burned with shame at the whine edging my plea.

"I have others to take care of for now," he said. "Two hundred women and their children have joined us from the Mustaliq camp."

I flung his hand away. "When did you begin worrying about the welfare of war prisoners? No—don't bother. I know the answer. When you became betrothed to one of them, isn't that right? Aren't you planning to marry a Mustaliq she-dog?"

"She is a princess, A'isha. Juwairriyah, the chief's daughter. Having her in the *harim* will be valuable for us. Think about it! Today her people wanted to kill us. When she becomes my wife, the Mustaliq will be our allies."

I hesitated. For the *umma*, an alliance with the Mustaliq would be very good indeed. For me, though, another sister-wife would be as useful as a hump on my back.

"I saw the Mustaliq fight," I said. "Wouldn't you rather have them helping our enemies?"

"They belong to the biggest tribe in Hijaz," Muhammad said. "They hold much influence. This is the work of al-Lah! First He handed us an easy victory, then He awarded me the chief's daughter. This marriage will be good for the *umma*, and for *islam*."

"Praise al-Lah, then!" I said, smirking, although my heart seemed to crumble. "But why do you have to be with her tonight?"

"She is unbelievably beautiful." His eyes lost their focus for a moment, as though he were gazing into the distance. "As long as she remains with me, she is safe. But if she were to escape, there would be no one to look out for her. And if she were harmed, her father would become a terrible foe."

"The poor thing," I said. Rage unraveled my voice, but I knew I'd lose him if I showed my anger. "Send her to me, and I will watch her."

Muhammad shook his head. "You would watch her run all the way back to Muraysi."

"Why don't you come and watch me, instead?" My smile was meant to seduce, but it felt as though hands were pulling it too tight. "Maybe *I'm* planning to run away."

"I do not have time for this nonsense, A'isha. If there is anything you need to discuss, it will have to wait until we are home. Now I must go and make a place for Juwairriyah to sleep."

Al-Lah forbid that her soft princess hands should be roughened by unrolling a bed! While Muhammad hurried off to care for his bride-to-be, I lugged my sheepskin to a grassy spot and spread it out, muttering. The sweet fragrance of jasmine wound around me like a vine, choking me. The nighttime breeze heaved a mournful sigh, rattling the heads of the date-palms. The rustle of their fronds made a sound like feet running across the desert sand. The moon blazed a trail of light that obscured the stars.

I shivered under my camel's-hide blanket and snuggled deep, wishing for Muhammad's arms to keep me warm. But no, he was busy tonight— again. Just when I'd been on the cusp of his desire, just when he'd begun to glimpse the woman in me! But it was useless. Muhammad would never love me except as a daughter. I'd been a fool to think I could change his love, that I could forge it with my own fire into something deeper and more mature—into something that would produce a child for me and an heir for him.

In his eyes, *I* was a child. How long before my new sister-wives noticed? Then I'd be forced to spend the rest of my days serving, pleasing, smiling, cringing. Caring for their babies instead of my own. Pain twisted my stomach, clenching me like a fist. Then I remembered Safwan, and the pain seeped away. He'd offered to free me from all this, to take me away to a place where we would make our own rules. I sighed and curled around that thought, cupping it like a warm flame in my belly. Safwan would arrive soon, and I would be waiting for him. The rest was in the hands of al-Lah.

◆

Losing the caravan was surprisingly simple. I handed my bedroll to the men packing my camel, then I stepped into the *hawdaj* and, with a clamoring heart, waited for them to turn their backs. As they tied on our beds and amused one another with exaggerated verses about the battle with the Mustaliq, I slipped away across the still-warm sand to hide behind a dune. I weighed so little, I knew the men wouldn't feel the difference as they lifted the *hawdaj* onto the camel's back. And since no one but Muhammad was allowed to look behind the curtain, I faced no danger of discovery. He wouldn't return to me tonight, not if it meant tearing himself away from *her*.

From my hiding place I heard the cry to move forward, and the camels' belches and the clanking of cooking pots as the caravan resumed its journey home. This afternoon they would arrive in Medina, set down my *hawdaj*, and wait for me to emerge. My pulse surged as I imagined the shock on my attendants' faces when they realized I was gone. What would Muhammad think then? Would he remember my frown and my words about running away? Would his heart cry out for me? Or would he turn red with rage and leap on his horse, then tear across the desert in search of me? I looked frantically about for a hiding place. But could I hide from the Prophet of God?

The sister-wives would come rushing out at the news that I was gone. Sawdah would wave her arms and rustle the curtains as if I might be hiding in their folds. Hafsa would weep, fearing that I was lost to her forever. Umm Salama and Zaynab would have to force their tears. Without me in the *harim*, they'd compete only with each other for Muhammad's heart— unless they found a new rival in the princess Juwairriyah.

As for the men, what an uproar my disappearance would cause them! Umar would burst with fury, especially when Safwan turned up missing, also. *Women are good for only one thing: trouble*, he would say. *That is why I keep mine locked up at home.*

Ali would be thrilled to see me gone. He'd goad my father: *It is unfortunate that your daughter has brought such shame upon you, Abu Bakr.* He'd try to push him out of the circle of Companions. And my *abi*, who loved me best, would be so torn with grief he wouldn't resist. My disappearance would destroy his friendship with Muhammad, for how could he face him after this?

The honor of the entire family depended on its women. My father, mother, sister, and brothers, even Asma's husband Zubayr and their son, Abdallah—all would suffer because of my actions. They'd endure finger-pointing, whispering, rude laughter, public poems about Safwan and me. They'd become known as the family of the adulteress who'd deceived al-Lah's Prophet. My mother would wear dark blue and scratch her face with her fingernails, then try to forget I'd ever lived. In the eyes of the *umma*, I would be dead. No—worse than dead. Speaking my name would be forbidden. No woman would ever name her daughter "A'isha" again.

"What have I done?" I leaped up and ran to the place where the caravan had so recently stood, but it was gone, sailing across the vast, rippled sea of moonlit sand to another wedding—and wedding night—for Muhammad.

"Stop!" I jumped and waved my arms, calling Muhammad's name. I shouted and screamed until my throat grew raw, and I strained with watering eyes to see the line of camels, horses, and men dwindling into the distance. As they shrank I felt myself grow larger until, overwhelmed by my deed, I lay on the ground. There I shivered in the cold and pondered the stars fading against the bleeding dawn. No one—except al-Lah—knew what I had done.

Forgive me, I prayed. *Help me.* Yet not even God could change my actions. Nor was I sure I wanted Him to.

The truth was, my life in Medina had become unbearable. The *umma* might whisper, my parents might mourn, my sister-wives puzzle or sneer, but none of them could judge me. None of them had spent six years in *purdah,* clawing at the walls and vowing never to become imprisoned again. None of them had lived in constant fear of losing the few freedoms they possessed. I felt like the girl on the seesaw again, fighting off attackers with a wooden sword—but the game had gone on too long, and I was tired. When Safwan arrived, I'd find respite at last.

Tall, handsome Safwan, with the chiseled face of a purebred steed and hair as thick and glossy as a horse's mane. Soon he would come galloping across the desert, kicking up sand, and whisk me away to another life. Where would we go? To Ta'if, with its beautiful gardens of roses and its famous vineyards? Or Damascus, perhaps, the glorious city I'd heard so much about. In a great, bustling place like that you could lose yourself and start anew, and no one would even ask questions.

A poignant light spilled across the sky. The rising sun colored the air with warmth. Grass and leaves brushed my cheek like Muhammad's beard. The deed was done, and at last I could rest. In my dreams, Muhammad rode up on al-Qaswa, his white camel, laughing with relief at finding me there. *I have decided to give up all my other wives for you, my A'isha,* he said.

His soft kiss thrilled me. I opened my eyes to see him—and found Safwan lying next to me instead.

"My A'isha," he was saying. "At last, you belong to me."

His lips were so sweet and his breath so warm. I let my eyes flutter shut again as I returned his kiss, as chaste as a child's. I felt a stirring under my skin, and I raised my tongue to touch his. With our bodies we brushed each other lightly—my breasts to his chest, his thigh to my most intimate place, my toes to his shins. An aroma like musk rose from his body. My moan of pleasure surprised me, luxuriant as the purr of a cat stretching in the sunlight.

"My Safwan," I said—but the words sounded strange, as if someone else were speaking.

Yet they must have awakened something inside him. His eyes widened, and he growled before attacking my throat with lush, wet kisses. Shudders wracked my body, squeezing back the cry that pushed against my throat. By al-Lah, I wasn't ready for this! He was moving too fast. I thought of Muhammad, his gentle kiss that first day, how he'd let me go at the first sign of fear. Safwan grabbed my breasts and squeezed them hard. I jerked away, but he tugged at my chemise and pulled it open, exposing me. The hunger on his face made me cry out. I pushed his hands away and sat up, pulling the fabric back together to cover myself.

He frowned. "What are you doing?"

"What are you doing?" I said, panting, stalling for time, struggling against the anger I knew I shouldn't feel. Of course Safwan would expect to make love with me. The desire had been there for me, also—but like a glimpse of brightness from the corner of my eye.

His expression shifted first one way, then another, mirroring his confusion. "I'm doing what we came here to do."

My mouth went dry. I hadn't come to this oasis to consummate our friendship. I'd come here to escape. Seeing the passion on Safwan's face, though, I realized that to achieve my desire, I was going to have to accommodate his.

Suddenly shy, I averted my gaze to the grass between us. "C-could you go more slowly?"

"We don't have much time," he said, crawling toward me. "Someone could come back looking for you."

I tied my shirt decisively. "That would be a disaster. We'd better wait."

"I've waited long enough for you, A'isha." When he kissed me this time, his mouth was hard. His pointed tongue darted into my mouth like a lizard's. He pushed me back onto the ground and pinned me with his body.

"I've dreamed of this for so many years," he said. "Ever since that day at Hamal and Jamila's window. Remember?" I glanced up at him to see if he was joking, but his gaze was so intense I had to look away.

"Safwan, I was just a little girl," I said.

"You wanted it, too," he said. "You wanted to marry me, remember? You were supposed to be my wife." He pushed his hand between my legs, making my blood scream. I tried to squirm away but his hand increased its pressure, hurting me.

"The Prophet picked your flower, but the fragrance is mine to enjoy now," he said, and thrust his tongue into my mouth again.

I struggled to push him away, but he was too heavy. He grunted as he ground his mouth against mine and tugged at my gown, pulling it upward across my calves, my knees, my thighs. I kicked and writhed, trying to escape and wishing for my sword. I felt his fingers on my bare skin, burning me. I flailed my hands, grabbed long strands of hair, and yanked as hard as I could. He yelped—and, my mouth freed, I could finally speak.

"My f-flower has not been picked," I said, gasping.

His body stiffened. He pushed himself up and stared down at me. "What did you say?"

"My marriage has not been consummated."

Safwan sat up abruptly, cursing. Trembling, I slid away from him. He was laughing—a rare sight, I suddenly realized—and shaking his head.

"You always were the worst liar imaginable," he said. "By al-Lah, tell me the truth!"

So I told him: about the day I'd moved into my new apartment, about how my girlish fear had put out Muhammad's fire. I didn't tell him about the times I'd tried to seduce Muhammad and he'd patted my head and called me "Little Red," or how I'd held back tears in recent nights as he'd slept with his back to me. "In his mind, I'm still a child."

"By al-Lah, I wish you'd told me this sooner!" His tone was bitter. I stared at him. When had I been able to say anything to Safwan? He'd filled our every moment together with his declarations of love.

"Yes, I'm sure if you'd known, you would have attacked me more gently," I snapped. Clearly my feelings were far from his thoughts.

He stood and brushed the sand from his gown. "The Prophet is going to kill me," he said. "If al-Lah doesn't strike me down first."

"If I'd had my sword a few moments ago, I might have done it myself," I said.

Above me, Safwan paced and glowered. "A virgin," he muttered. "If I take you now, it will unman the Prophet completely."

"Safwan, he doesn't care! That's why I'm here with you now."

He stopped. His eyes searched mine. "I thought you were here because you loved me."

I felt my stomach clench. Did I love him? I'd never considered the

question. Years ago I'd practically worshipped him. He'd been my rescuer, coaxing me out of the cage that was my girl's destiny. Because of
him, I'd dared to dream of a life different from my mother's: a life of
adventure, in which women and men rode, and fought, together. But did
I love him?

"Please don't be offended." He held out his hand to help me stand. He
wrapped his arms around me and pulled me close. Musk and cinnamon,
coarse cloth, a racing heartbeat. "You took a great risk by waiting here for
me. If that doesn't prove your love, nothing will." He kissed me again but
I hung limp in his embrace, pondering his question. Did I love him?

"A'isha, feel how crazy you make me!" He pressed my palm to his chest
so I could feel his heart's frenzied knock. "By al-Lah, you won't have the
same problem with me that you've had with the Prophet. I want to possess you right now, under this tree."

"Didn't you say we should go? If someone catches us here, we'll be
killed."

"That's true. And Ubaynah ibn Hisn is expecting us tonight. They're
not far away." He puffed out his chest. "They were planning to raid the
Prophet's caravan, but I talked them out of it."

"Ubaynah ibn Hisn? He's with the Ghatafan!"

He grinned. "We join them tonight. Ubaynah said he would be thrilled
to have us on their side."

I took a step back from him. "But they're friends with Quraysh!"

"Which makes them even more powerful. The Prophet will never be
able to take you back—not without a war."

I took another step back. "You'd fight against the *umma*?" I remembered my promise to al-Lah—to protect the *umma*—and panic scrambled
my thoughts.

"I'd fight anyone for you." He stepped toward me, but I moved away.
He frowned. "They're Bedouins, A'isha. We'll live the life we've always
dreamed."

"Sleeping in tents, always moving around, never bathing. Turning
brown and wrinkled from the sun. Drinking camel's milk. What kind of
life is that?"

"You liked the idea once. It was all you ever talked about!"

"When we were children, yes. But I've grown up."

"Yes, and your mouth has grown, too." He glowered at me. "Since when do wives talk back to their husbands? We'll do as I say."

He turned and walked to his horse. I stood in place. He swung himself up into his saddle and rode over to me, his expression hard.

"I'm not going to fight for the Ghatafan," I said.

"Don't worry. They don't allow their women to fight."

"You're not going to fight for them, either."

He narrowed his eyes. "No silly girl is going to tell me what to do."

Rage rushed through my veins like hot steam from a boiling cauldron. "Silly girl? Don't you ever call me that again. I'm a warrior, Safwan. A warrior!"

He leaped down and stood before me with his arms crossed over his chest. "*Yaa* A'isha, have you forgotten which one of us is the man?"

"Do you see a man here? I see only a traitor." Still seething with anger I reared back and, with a mighty force, spat on his chest.

Safwan's hand aimed for my face, but I saw his open palm coming. I ducked out of the way and stood triumphant while he stumbled forward.

"Fighting against the Prophet would be betraying God," I jeered. "I have no desire to burn in Hell. But if you're so eager to, then go a-"

This time he moved quickly. He had hold of my shoulders before I could finish my sentence. His grip was fierce. His eyes blazed. He spat when he spoke, hitting my eyes with a fine spray. His breath smelled like lemons and rue.

"I'm running away with the virgin bride of God's holy Prophet!" he shouted. "I think Hell-fire is already a certainty for us both."

16

QUEEN OF THE HARIM

MEDINA, FEBRUARY 627

*S*afwan's words hit me like blows, stealing my breath so that I couldn't speak, filling my eyes with tears and my mouth with bile. Doubling me over to spit up regret and fear. Afterwards, he handed me a water skin for rinsing my mouth, then helped me up onto his horse—but before I could swing my leg over its back I began to retch again.

Sickness hurled me to the ground, and the sun kept me there, stomping me down with its heat. Safwan carried me to the grass and pitched his tent in the shade. Inside it, I lay on his sheepskin and curled up like a child in the womb, groaning with pain but not daring to speak the thought that tortured us both: Al-Lah's punishment had already begun.

I had forgotten my pact with Him, my promise to defend the *umma* against our enemies. Instead, I'd thought only of my own desires.

Forgive me, I prayed. *And please let Muhammad forgive me.*

I returned to Medina the next day on Safwan's horse with the *umma's* accusations pelting my aching head. To protect me from the storm of scandal, Muhammad sent me to my parents' home, where I contemplated with horror the sin I had almost committed. Death was the penalty for adultery—not a swift, merciful death by beheading, but stone by stone, painful and slow, agonizing. Given the rumors already flying through the *umma*, I couldn't be sure I'd escape that terrible death. But at least I would die knowing I'd been true to Muhammad. When he joined me in Paradise he would know the truth also.

In my parents' home I prayed daily for al-Lah's mercy, begged Him to spare my life and to restore me to Muhammad. Each day flowered with hope—would Muhammad visit me today?—then dropped its petals like tears. The weeks dragged on like a funeral procession. My father barely spoke, and shifted his glance aside when he saw me. My mother, on the other hand, speculated about my fate, speaking freely with Asma or the few friends who would risk being seen entering the dwelling of an accused adulteress.

"What A'isha did was foolish," *ummi* would say. "But does she deserve to die for it?"

What loyalty! It's no wonder I spent most of my time in the bedroom. As in my father's other homes my parents kept a dark house, one that banished the sun's heat by blocking its light, creating an atmosphere as uplifting as a tomb. I missed the large, light cooking tent in the mosque courtyard with its banter, however barbed, among sister-wives while children shrieked and ran among us. My mother and Qutailah, by contrast, barely spoke to each other throughout the day.

I longed for a visit from Hafsa or even Sawdah. Muhammad had forbidden them to come to me, at Ali's urging. My sullied reputation might affect theirs, he'd told Muhammad.

"They are to stay away until your name is cleansed," my father told me.

"But I have done nothing wrong," I protested. My father averted his eyes.

"What hope is there for me if my own father doesn't believe I'm innocent?" I fretted to my mother as I helped her knead dough in the kitchen.

"What we cannot believe is that a daughter of ours would do something so stupid," she snapped. "That story about losing your necklace was clever, but it didn't fool me. What were you thinking of, running away with that boy?"

Exposed, I felt my face grow hot. "Controlling my destiny," I said.

"Controlling what? Are you possessed?" Her eyes flashed.

" 'Control your destiny, or it will control you.' Don't you remember telling me that, *ummi?*"

Her laugh was as sharp as acacia thorns. "By al-Lah, are you fourteen or four? Only a child—or a silly young woman—would entertain such fantasies. Women control nothing in this world, A'isha."

"But you said—"

"I was a fool!" She slammed the dough onto the counter, her face red. "I thought life could be different for you. The Prophet is a kind and gentle man who, I thought, would allow you to live as free as the wind."

"He would." I spat out my bitter words. "But he isn't the only one giving orders at the mosque. Umar distrusts all women, Ali and Fatima hate me, and two of my sister-wives want to make themselves the *hatun.*"

"Do not let that happen." My mother gripped my arm with a floury hand. "That Zaynab bint Jahsh could be a real tyrant. I would rather die than have you live as I do, A'isha." Her gaze fell to my belly, and her features hardened. "Bear your husband a son, and all your problems will be over."

Her accusatory tone made my blood rise. "Do you think I'm not trying?" I snatched my arm away from her.

"Not hard enough, from what I see. You've been with him more than two years, and what do you have to show?"

I cringed, feeling as humiliated as if she'd slapped me in the face. "I have nothing—I admit it, all right, Mother?" I cried in a choked voice. "By al-Lah, some things I can't do by myself!"

She stepped closer and stared at me as if I were a stranger. "What are you saying?"

I turned away, embarrassed by her searching gaze, disgusted with myself for blurting out my secret. I'd never confided anything to my mother, who'd been too involved with her own problems. Now, when I didn't want to talk, she was eager to listen.

"I'm going to lie down." I took a step toward the kitchen door, but she grabbed my arm again.

"*Yaa* A'isha! I must know. Is the Prophet unable to—to—" She blushed as she searched for a delicate term.

My laugh was harsh. "I only wish that were the problem." As much as I dreaded her judgment I knew I'd have to tell her the truth. Otherwise, the rumor would run rampant through the *umma* that Muhammad was impotent. He would be a laughingstock, more thoroughly unmanned than if all his wives had run away.

"Muhammad doesn't want me, not in that way," I said in a tiny voice. "He never has."

"Your marriage is unconsummated?"

I nodded, wincing, dreading her angry words. She'd blame me for this failure. And why shouldn't she? If I hadn't trembled in fear that first day, Muhammad would have made love to me, and I'd be holding his child in my arms this very moment, the proud *hatun* of his *harim* and honored mother of his heir.

After a long silence, her hand pressed my shoulder. Her tenderness surprised me so much, I forgot my embarrassment. When I lifted my face, I saw that she was crying. Not the great, heaving sobs I'd held back for fear they'd make me look guilty, but two lone tears rolling down her cheeks.

"You poor child," she said, her voice clogged with emotion. "No wonder you left him."

She opened her arms and enfolded me in barley flour and linen cloth and lavender. In the circle of her arms, safe and secure at last, I was finally able to release the tears that had been building up inside me, to let them burst forth in a sweeping torrent, flooding from my eyes and heaving my chest in wave after wave of remorse over wrong choices and broken dreams, and fear of a future that might hold a terrible death for me.

For many minutes she held me, patting my back and stroking my hair with a stiff hand accustomed to working, not consoling. At last when my tears had run dry and my hiccupping breath fell in a long, ragged skein, she loosened her hold.

She smiled gently and wiped my face, then led me into the courtyard. It was empty save for a lone nightingale perched high in the pomegranate tree, filling the air with its sweet *chirr, chirr, chirr.*

We sat on the grass together, and she reached for my hand as though it were a cherished gift. She gazed into my eyes. The love I saw there filled my heart near to bursting.

"Do not worry too much about the Prophet," she said, stroking the back of my hand with her fingertips, sending warmth to my heart. "I have seen the affection on his face when he looks upon you. It will not be long before desire fills his heart, also."

"I wish I felt as confident as you," I said. "But his new wives are so beautiful. I don't know how I can compete."

"A'isha!" My mother opened her mouth in astonishment. "Have you no mirror, child? Do you not realize how you have blossomed? By al-Lah, you grow lovelier every day. Who among those women has hair like fire, or eyes that change color with her moods? You will surpass them all, A'isha, and the Prophet's mouth will water for you."

"If I ever see him again," I said, blinking back more tears as I yanked blades of grass from the earth.

"He will come. And when he does—" she gave the back of my hand a light slap "—you must convince him of your innocence." She paused. "Are you innocent?"

I straightened my back, indignant. "How could you even ask?"

She waved her hand. "What is done is done, and it is not my business. Whether you are innocent or not, you must make the Prophet believe you are as pure as Mecca's well of Zamzam. Only then will he take you back. You can do it, A'isha! You must. The future of the *umma* depends on it. Already they fight in the streets over you, and it will be worse for us all if Muhammad divorces you."

The unspoken alternative—stoning—hung between us like a sword we were both afraid to touch.

"I would like to do as you say, *ummi*. But I'm not sure I can convince Muhammad of anything. Why would he believe me?"

"You are the only one he will believe, child. And then, when he takes you back—A'isha, do everything in your power to conceive." She gripped my hand so tightly I winced.

"The bond between mother and child is the strongest bond of all," she said. "And if you are truly loving, then you will find the love you want. Unlike the love of a man, which changes over time, the love of your child will never diminish. Even you and I—" she relaxed her hand, although it trembled still, "—are linked by our love for each other. No one and nothing can ever take that away."

And so my mother renewed my dreams for the future. I began again to imagine myself the queen of Muhammad's *harim*, the mother of his curly-haired boy, an infant all warm and smelling of milk and with cheeks too plump not to kiss all day and night. But, by al-Lah, I was not the Virgin Maryam! To bear a child I would need to consummate my marriage with Muhammad.

Yet—confined in my parents' home, forbidden to go to him, how would I attract him to me? Barirah was my answer. As a servant, she could go anywhere she pleased. She brought me fresh reports every day: Ali had found a willing witness in Zaynab's sister, Hamnah, who fabricated tales about me and Safwan. Zaynab cleverly kept her distance, insisting that I was virtuous, as far as she knew. Meanwhile, war nearly broke out between the Aws and the Khazraj over whether Safwan and I should be killed, and who would hurl the first stone. And in the market, Safwan lost his temper during one of Hassan ibn Thabit's slanderous poems and attacked him with his sword.

At night, tears pooled on my windowsill. I'd gaze out at the moon Muhammad loved so much and wonder if he was looking at it also. Did he think of me? Or was he finding comfort in Zaynab's arms? Jealousy stung me, but I shrugged it off. Self-pity had caused me nothing but trouble. It was time to face the facts: Men would be telling me what to do for as long as I lived. I might not like their rules, but I couldn't escape them. Safwan couldn't rescue me from servitude; nor, I'd discovered, did he really want to. The Prophet of God himself couldn't loosen this yoke, not without losing the support of men like Umar, who clung to the old ways.

Running away had been futile. Wherever I went, life would be the same. Resisting my chains only seemed to tighten them. Yet all around me women found ways to slip those bonds, to discreetly flout the rules and then return to their so-called captivity before anyone noticed. I was smarter than Umar and Ali together, a better warrior than most men, as beautiful as any woman, and the daughter of Abu Bakr al-Siddiq. I held the power to live life as I pleased—not by fighting or running, but by using my wits.

I would have to find a way to live within the confines of my womanhood. To be a warrior, like Umm 'Umara, but in a battle that was uniquely mine. If I wanted my freedom, I'd have to fight for it. My first step would be to clear myself of these charges. But how? For once, my mind failed me—and so I turned to al-Lah.

I fell to my knees and prayed for hours, begging His forgiveness for my impulsive act, asking Him to show me the way to win my husband's trust again. Finally, exhausted, I fell asleep on the floor of my room, and God sent His answer to me in the form of a vivid dream.

When I awoke, I plucked a sprig of lavender from our courtyard and asked Barirah to present it to Muhammad.

"Tell him I rub my skin with this fragrance every day in anticipation of his visit," I said. Then I adorned my hands and feet with henna, painting red and purple leaves and flowers on my skin.

She returned that evening. "He says nothing, but he lifts the flowers to his nose and smells them."

The next day, I sent a cup of water. "Tell him I fill this cup with my tears every day from missing him." Then I had my mother's servants wash my clothes and scent them with lavender.

That evening, Barirah still brought no reply.

"He drinks the water and says there is no salt. I tell him you cry so much, the salt is all used up."

The third day, I sent a poem. Barirah frowned at the date-palm leaf on which it was written. "I cannot read this."

"Neither can Muhammad. Tell him it is a private poem, meant for his ears alone. Tell him I long to recite it to him in person."

An hour later, Barirah came running into my room, her eyes shining.

"He comes today!" she cried. "Quick, mistress, we must dress you."

In former times I would have rushed around in a panic, anxious to be ready when he arrived. But those weeks in my bedroom had given me much time to think. In particular, I'd pondered Zaynab. She acted like the world's most desirable woman—like a woman worth the wait—and Muhammad seemed to agree with her. Yet she was no lovelier than me or Hafsa. The difference came in the way she presented herself. She carried herself as if she were a valuable work of art to be gazed upon but not touched. And she mesmerized Muhammad. His gaze followed her, and his hands were always reaching out for her—gestures she coyly eluded, admonishing him to "wait until tonight, habib."

So I took my time dressing for Muhammad's visit. Barirah heated a tub of water in my parents' bath, where I sponged my body and cleaned my hair. Then I dressed in the cream-colored gown my mother had sewn for me, and I swept my hair away from my face with a set of shell combs. I fastened my agate necklace about my throat, the one I'd claimed to lose in the sand the night the caravan left me behind—but then I removed it. It would only remind Muhammad of our troubles.

As I was about to apply my makeup, *ummi* flurried in.

"*Yaa* A'isha, give thanks to al-Lah! The Prophet has arrived."

I smiled coolly. "Please tell him I'll be out in a little while."

My mother gasped. "But A'isha! The Prophet expects you now. You must come at once!"

"I've been waiting three weeks to see him," I said. "I'm sure he can wait a few minutes for me."

Half an hour later I stepped into the living room, where lamps like so many moons illuminated exquisite tapestries hanging on its walls. My arms dripping with fragrance. My hair shimmering like fire. My face made up like an exquisite flower. Muhammad's eyes kindled a flame the instant he looked at me. *You're the most gorgeous woman he knows.* I straightened my back and lifted my chin. "*Ahlan,* husband."

He stepped forward, more fully into the light. I suppressed my gasp. He had become so frail and gaunt—not the mighty Prophet of al-Lah, but a mere man. His shoulders sagged as if the frame that held him had broken. Before, I might have teased him, might have said, *I'm the one who's supposed to be sick, habibi.* The new me said nothing. I did not throw my arms around his neck, although I yearned to embrace him. I was his favorite wife. He was supposed to approach me, not the other way around.

He cleared his throat. He glanced at my parents, who stood against the wall. My mother twisted the rings on her fingers and grimaced. My father looked away.

"Tell me you were faithful to me, *habibati,*" he said. His voice sounded thin, like water leaking from a cracked vessel. "One word from you is all I need."

I hid my doubt behind a haughty gaze. I remembered how he'd looked at me when I'd told the story of losing my necklace in the dunes. If I lied now, Muhammad would know. Yet if I told the truth, it would be worse for me than lying.

"I have recovered from my illness. Have you come to bring me home?" My calm, clear voice surprised me.

"You look well, A'isha," was his vague reply.

"Should I flatter you," I teased, "and say you look well, too?"

I gave him a coy glance, but his eyes only drooped.

"You look as if you hadn't slept these past three weeks," I said.

"My dreams are too tortured for sleep."

"I have been waiting for you, husband. I have been praying to al-Lah, hoping He would send you to me."

"Al-Lah has abandoned me."

My mother sucked in her breath, reminding us that she watched. My father shook his head at her and pressed a finger to his lips.

"I have prayed, but He turns His back to me," Muhammad said in a choked voice. "I do not know what He would have me do now. I do not know what is true and what is false anymore."

Guilt flooded me, but I clung to what I knew. In waiting for Safwan at the Wadi al-Hamd oasis, I'd made a terrible mistake. But I hadn't cheated on my husband. And I'd realized, there in the desert with Safwan, how much I truly loved Muhammad.

"Do you believe I'm guilty?" I hated the tremor in my voice. Muhammad admired women who were strong and confident, not whining and cringing.

"I do not know what to believe," he said. "Others have come forward, telling tales of seeing you and Safwan together. He is a handsome young man, and you have a history with him."

"Has no one spoken on my behalf?" I turned to my parents. "*Ummi, abi?* Won't you vouch for my innocence?"

My father's face was a stone carving, except for his tear-brimming eyes. My mother twisted her rings and shifted her glance between Muhammad and me. "We know how unhappy you have been, A'isha, with your marriage unconsummated."

I laughed. "My own parents think I'm an adulteress. But they don't know me nearly as well as you do."

Muhammad frowned. "Does your mother speak the truth? Have you been unhappy?"

"Of course I've been unhappy!" I raised my voice, forgetting my parents, forgetting my newfound poise. "Haven't you noticed? Haven't you heard my complaints?"

The vein on his forehead bulged. "I have been busy, as you may have noticed."

I laughed again. "Busy finding new wives to marry. You're right—that's hard work! Meanwhile, the one who loves you the most sleeps alone, neglected."

"No more neglected than my other wives, A'isha. I divide my time equally among you."

"Wife? How can you call me 'wife' when you've never been intimate with me?"

"I am waiting, out of consideration for you."

"Waiting? For what? For me to beg you, or take you by force?"

"For you to grow up," he said darkly. "From the tone of this discussion, it appears that you have some distance to go."

I turned my back to my parents, then untied the bodice of my chemise and pulled it open, revealing my breasts. Muhammad's eyes widened in surprise—and then, to my delight, the flicker of desire began to dance on his face.

"I'm not a child anymore." Having made my point, I laced up my chemise.

He looked into my eyes again. His expression tightened.

"Did Safwan make you a woman in the desert?"

Heat flooded my skin. "How eager you are to believe these rumors!" I said. "You said yourself that I'm not ready for consummation, yet you suspect me of giving my virginity to another man. Of course, Safwan doesn't think of me as a little girl."

"Did he make you a woman?"

"I was a woman before any of this happened. I've been waiting for you to make me your wife."

"By al-Lah, A'isha!" Muhammad cried. "Were you unfaithful to me with Safwan or not? Tell me you were not, and I will proclaim your innocence to the entire town."

"Tell him, A'isha," my mother urged from her corner. "Tell your husband you are pure."

"Why should my husband believe me, when my own parents don't?" I said. She lowered her eyes, and I turned my gaze back to Muhammad. How could I say what he needed to hear? I'd waited for Safwan under the date-palms. I'd almost run away with him. Wasn't that a kind of infidelity?

The dream al-Lah had sent me came back as clearly as if I'd just awakened, telling me what to say next, and what to do.

"If I tell you, 'Yes, I did what they accuse me of,' you'll divorce me and al-Lah will punish me for lying," I said. "If I say no, you may stand up for me, but you'll always doubt me in your heart. So I will say nothing. There is only One who can clear my name."

"But Safwan has disappeared!" my mother cried.

"Do you think I need Safwan to plead my case?" I straightened my spine, reminding myself: I was the queen of Muhammad's *harim* and of his heart. "I have the most persuasive One of all on my side. Al-Lah will speak for me."

"I told you, I have tried praying," Muhammad said.

"Perhaps you should try listening," I said. Then, with my head high, I walked toward the entryway.

"*Yaa* A'isha, I command you to come back," my father boomed. "Your business with your husband is not finished."

I turned to face them all. "I have said what I have to say, *abi*. The matter is in al-Lah's hands now." I looked at Muhammad. "When He has vindicated me, I will happily return to the *harim*—as your true wife."

My task completed, I glided from the room, hoping they couldn't see how my legs trembled. I pulled aside my curtain, took a shaky breath, and went inside, where I fell onto my bed and covered my head with my pillow. *It's in Your hands, al-Lah. I trust You to help me.*

It had been the greatest performance of my life—and the most dangerous. Muhammad would return, but in what capacity? As a loving husband with his arms open wide, or—al-Lah forbid—as a stern judge, condemning me to death?

17

BEWITCHED

he inexorable sun trudged upward, dragging the day in its wake. Outside, a vulture's cry impaled my waning hopes. On my divan of blue and gold I lay in wait for Muhammad, fending off despair, refusing Barirah's solace, eschewing the evening meal. How could I face my parents after defying them so confidently this morning?

Muhammad should have returned for me before now. Where had I erred? Perhaps I should have insisted I was innocent, as he'd asked. I could have told him that Safwan didn't take my virginity. But Muhammad would want the full truth. He might ask how I'd *really* ended up in the oasis with Safwan. No, I'd been right not to say anything. He would come back for me. But when?

A clamor at the front door made my heart jump. Muhammad! Through my window I saw eight men, including Ali and Hamal, waving swords and demanding that my father hand me over.

"The wells are drying up, and the dates shrivel on the trees," an Aws man snarled. "Al-Lah withholds the rain to punish us for the sins of your daughter."

A rock flew past me, barely missing my head. I dropped my curtain of blue beads and hid against the wall, trying to hear my thoughts above my heart's hammering. Blood-lust raged in the voices of those men. Could my father fend them off, one against ten? They'd cut off my head and parade it through the streets before Muhammad finished his prayers.

"*Yaa* Ali, has the Prophet sent you?" my father asked, as calmly as if they had come for coffee.

"The Prophet has done nothing. That is the problem, Abu Bakr. That daughter of yours has bewitched him. He has been in anguish since she returned from the desert."

"The *fahisha* has brought a curse on the city," the Aws man cried. "Al-Lah demands justice!"

"Bewitched?" I heard my father chuckle. "By al-Lah, Muhammad was in my house this day, and I saw no signs of bewitching."

"The Prophet was here?" Hamal spoke. "We have heard nothing of this."

"He is making a decision about A'isha's guilt or innocence," my father said. "We expect him back soon. What if he declares her blameless?"

"Safwan ibn al-Mu'attal has disappeared," the Aws man said. "Only a guilty man would run away."

"You may speak truly," my father said. "Or you may be mistaken. Either way, the Prophet will not be pleased if he returns today and finds you have killed his favorite wife. If he declares her guilty, he will punish her soon enough. But if he finds her innocent, then you have committed murder, my friends. You would all be dead before the sun sets."

"Muhammad would be grateful," Ali said. "That girl has been trouble since the day she arrived in his home."

Hamal cleared his throat. "*Yaa* Ali, if the Prophet is going to decide today, then we should wait for his verdict."

"If we kill his wife, the Prophet might kill us," the Aws man said. "And we would go to Hell for eternity."

To my relief, their murmurs and grumbles faded as they walked away. Then Ali's voice hissed through my curtains and slithered over my bones.

"*Yaa* A'isha, you might have tricked the Prophet, but you have not fooled me," he said. "I have seen you and Safwan together, remember? If the Prophet finds you innocent—al-Lah forbid it!—I will watch your every move for the rest of your days."

◆

The sun was a bird with an injured wing, lurching painfully downward, staining the horizon with blood. Digging my knees into my prayer mat, I begged al-Lah to send my husband the revelation he needed to set me free and take me home, away from all the doubts and shame.

As I prayed, my voice cracked with the weight of my deeds. Why would al-Lah help me after what I had done? I'd dreamed of a life without Muhammad even while I lay next to him at night. I'd schemed to run away with Safwan, never even thinking about how my husband—and my family—would suffer.

When I'd told Safwan I was a virgin, he'd stopped his advances. But what if he hadn't? What if he'd continued pulling up my skirt and pushed himself inside me? I would have deserved it. Then, having consummated with Safwan, I'd be living with him among the Ghatafani Bedouins right now, doing his bidding—and Muhammad, stripped of all dignity in his followers' eyes, would be the same as dead. Ibn Ubayy would have taken Medina at last, and that would have been the end of Muhammad, and the *umma*, and *islam*.

I began to cry, imagining Abu Sufyan's army riding into Medina, seizing Muhammad, torturing him to death, slaughtering all the Believers who remained with him. Would my parents have been among them, or would my disappearance have sent them slinking away in shame?

"*Yaa* al-Lah, forgive my selfishness," I prayed. "I know I deserve to die. I deserve to lose Muhammad. But for his sake, and that of the *umma*, please show my husband I'm innocent."

I began to cry. "And please help me to accept the life You have chosen for me, and to live it in ways that bring honor to You and to Your Prophet. Yet—" an ache rose in my chest, as if chains weighted my heart "—I beg you, God, please help me to seize my destiny, to become the woman I yearn to be."

I cried so much, I could have filled that cup I'd sent with Barirah. When I finished I lay on my mat, exhausted. And then I had a revelation of my own. Not the direct kind such as Muhammad experienced, with al-Lah speaking through his mouth. For me, it was like the drawing aside of a curtain, sending sunlight pouring into the darkened rooms of my soul.

I hadn't left the *umma* for Safwan. I'd never dreamt of his kisses or his

loving arms, but of desert rides wild and free and, later, of a life of equali-
ty with my husband. It was an impossible dream, my mother had said.
Even now, though, I didn't believe her. Hadn't Muhammad declared,
when I was a baby, that girls were as valuable as boys? Al-Lah had wanted me to live, and He'd called me to fight. He'd given me the sword and
the skills of a warrior while Ali and Umar and other men like them and,
yes, women also, including my mother, forbade me to use them. They were
the ones I'd run from, they and their ridiculous inventions such as *purdah*
and *hatun* and *durra* and their traditions of male superiority that made
chattel of women.

Power was what drove them all, including Muhammad. In truth, it was
what I desired, also: the power to live freely, to fight for my *umma*, to control my destiny. Being a woman meant I couldn't seize this power by force,
and I certainly wouldn't gain it by running away. Muhammad had married
every one of his wives, starting with me, for political gains. My best
chance for empowerment, I saw now, was to become politically useful to
him. If I could earn his respect and his trust, I could become his advisor. I
might also be able to help the *umma*, fulfilling my promise to al-Lah with
my intelligence instead of my sword.

My pulse drummed an exuberant beat. Me, advisor to the Prophet of
God! I knew I could do it, and do it well. How many times had I spied on
the men in the *majlis* with ideas spinning through my head? Muhammad
would listen to me if I proved myself worthy. Even that jackal Abu Sufyan,
it was said, consulted his shrill wife, Hind, for political advice.

I must have fallen asleep, for when I awoke the rich, red light of the
fallen sun bled into my room, and the wing of the angel Gabriel slid over
my cheek and out the window.

"The Prophet!" Barirah crashed into my room, arms flapping. "He calls
for you. Look outside."

I heard a shout as I arose, followed by clamoring voices. Muhammad
stood in my mother's garden with his arms outstretched, his smile leaping
like a flame, his hair flung about his head as if he'd just awakened from a
long sleep. Around him, men and women of the *umma* ululated and threw
themselves to the ground, shouting their thanks to God.

"*Yaa* A'isha, al-Lah has sent me a revelation at last," Muhammad
called. "You are innocent of any wrongdoing!"

Relief washed over me like a cooling rain. "Praise al-Lah," I breathed, and let the curtain drop.

I sent Barirah for my robe and pulled my hair back, reminding myself of my vow to become Muhammad's helpmate. To gain his respect, I would have to command it. And if I wanted him to treat me like a woman, I would have to act like one. I dried my tears and washed my face, giving myself a chance to calm down before going to greet him.

Barirah came in with my robe. I slipped it on, then covered my hair with my wrapper. My mother rushed in with a face as eager as a child's.

"Muhammad is waiting for you. Come and thank him," she said, and practically pushed me toward the front door, where my father stood smiling at Muhammad, who in turn beamed at me like a man presenting a precious gift.

"*Yaa* A'isha, I've come to take you home and make you my true wife," he said.

I lowered my eyes quickly, hiding my joy, fearing he'd see triumph, which would have raised me above him, or gratitude, which would have placed me at his feet. Neither of us was responsible for this change, anyway. Al-Lah had made it all possible. The triumph belonged to Him, and so did my thanks.

"I will gladly accompany you, husband," I said. "But first, I'm going to the mosque."

"What are you talking about?" my mother cried.

I kissed my father's beard. "Thank you for your protection during this difficult time. Will you please call for a camel so I may ride home, as befits the wife of the Prophet?"

It was a ridiculous request; the mosque stood next door to us. But I was determined to reclaim my dignity. My father grinned, but my mother seized my shoulders and stared at me with wild eyes.

"*Ai!* The Prophet has saved your life today. Are you too proud to thank him?"

"Muhammad didn't clear my name. Al-Lah did," I said. "Al-Lah is the one I'm going to thank." Then I gave Muhammad my most winning smile. "And when I return to my room, husband, I hope to find you waiting there."

"Hearing is obeying, *habibati.*"

A Glance in the Mirror

*H*ow quickly the heart changes! Desire burned like a fire
in Muhammad's loins, unquenchable in one night, or two, or three. As for
me, the pain of consummation soon melted away—Muhammad was so
gentle, I hardly felt the scorpion's sting. To be in his arms, skin to skin,
was the bliss I had longed for all my life. Now my husband's very glance
filled me with pleasure, and I understood at last the grins and sighs and
innuendoes that swirled like cinnamon in the cooking tent whenever
Muhammad sequestered himself with a new wife.

Afterward, lying in the circle of his arms, I listened with a full and
quivering heart to his declarations of love and his tender promises for the
future.

"When I heard that you were missing from your *hawdaj*, I felt as if my
life were ending," he murmured, stroking my hair. "All color seemed to
drain from the sky, and all the heat from the sweltering day. For the first
time in my life, A'isha, I felt truly afraid. My first thought was to ride out
in search of you immediately."

My stomach shifted as I imagined him galloping up to find me lying in
Safwan's arms. Of course, by the time Muhammad had discovered me

missing I was vomiting in the dirt and holding my belly, alone, in the shelter of Safwan's tent.

"What made you change your mind?" I asked.

"Ali. He convinced me that it would be foolish to set out in the midday heat. In truth, I was weary and in need of replenishment. When the day had cooled, Ali sent Abu Hurayra in search of you." He frowned. "In retrospect, it was not a good decision. Being unfamiliar with the path, Abu Hurayra lost his way."

I couldn't suppress my smirk. If Ali had truly been interested in finding me, he wouldn't have sent a newcomer from Yemen to search for me. But I kept my suspicions to myself. Ali couldn't hurt me now.

"It's fortunate that Safwan's horse has a more refined sense of direction than Abu Hurayra's nose," I said.

"Fortunate, yes. But it does not surprise me that you returned in safety, for al-Lah chose you for me long ago." Muhammad caressed my face with his coppery eyes, making me glow. "The angel Gabriel once showed me your face in the palm of his hand. I knew we would be together until death."

"And afterward." Heat surged under my skin and spread through my chest.

"A'isha, every woman I have ever loved has left me. My dear Khadija, who believed in me from the first and who gave me Fatima, died only a few months before you and I became betrothed. Before that, I lost my mother when I was six."

My heart beat only for him as I imagined the sorrow of the boy Muhammad, orphaned at such a young age, for his father had died before he was born. "That must have been terrible for you. Do you remember her?"

"As if she lived yesterday." His eyes grew misty. "She was beautiful and filled with joy. No one ever made me laugh so much—until you came along." He squeezed my hand and gave me a tremulous smile.

"At least you had your uncle Abu Talib to take care of you." Ali's father had raised Muhammad as his own son, inspiring Muhammad, years later, to return the favor and care for Ali.

"But not right away. In those first years after *ummi*'s death, my life was a procession of ever-changing sorrows. My grandfather took me to live

with him in a house with little light, for he was nearly blind. No longer
was I allowed to play with my friends or to go outdoors except to draw
water from the well. Instead I became my grandfather's servant."

I exclaimed over this news and pulled him close Like me, Muhammad
had been imprisoned at a young age—had lost his childhood before he'd
had a chance to enjoy it. "Then you must know how I felt, being locked
in *purdah*."

"I tried to change your father's mind, to convince him such drastic
measures were unnecessary, but he feared for you," Muhammad said.

I sighed and lay my head on his chest. "We were not children for long,
were we, *habibi*?"

"Our lives have been difficult, yes. But you and I are survivors. That is
one reason I admire you, why I love you more than my own life. Like me,
you are a fighter."

"Control your destiny, or it will control you," I said.

Muhammad nodded. "You speak the truth. That is why I have risked so
much for *islam*, why I have given up everything to come to Medina. I must
worship according to al-Lah's wishes, not those of Quraysh."

I sat up, sensing the opening I'd been waiting for. "And I want to fight
in battle—" Muhammad winced—"as I know I cannot do, and to be the
official *hatun* of your *harim*, which I know I can. With your support."

He wrinkled his brow. "But you are already the *hatun*, are you not?"

"Yes and no. I have taken the position, but not all your wives respect
it. Some say I'm too young to lead the household. But if you tell them
yourself, they'll have to respect my status.

Muhammad tapped his forefinger against his chin and studied me as if
I were a puzzle that needed solving. "My leadership of the *umma* was given
to me by my followers."

My jaw dropped. "You're not going to help me?"

"The *harim* is not the man's domain, but that of the women," he said
with a rueful smile. "If you want to be *hatun*, you must earn the privilege
from your sister-wives."

◆

As disappointed as I felt to learn Muhammad wouldn't declare me his *hatun*,
I was delighted at all his attention after I became his true wife. He lingered

in my apartment seven days and nights, as befitted a virgin bride—although, as far as anyone else knew, we were merely celebrating my safe return home. We might have spent every moment giving love to each other if not for the constant interruptions. Messengers brought gifts from the *umma*, congratulating me for my return: figs and honey, pomegranates and *tharid*. Muhammad adorned my hair with an opalescent comb made of shells from the Red Sea, and I admired my reflection in a brass hand-mirror Hassan ibn Thabit presented along with a new poem praising my many virtues.

But not everyone was pleased to have me back. On my third day with Muhammad, as I lay in his arms and sucked grapes from his fingers, and dreamed about the child that could not be long in coming, Umm Salama came to my door.

I stood as regally as my short frame would allow.

"Welcome home, sister-wife," she said. "I am pleased to see you looking so well after all you have endured."

"I'm sure you are."

"Forgive me for intruding, husband." She turned to Muhammad. "But I have not seen you in several days. Had you forgotten that last night was your night with me?"

"I have been keeping A'isha company since she arrived," Muhammad said. "As you said, she has been through a terrible ordeal."

She looked at me without expression. "I understand."

When she had gone, Muhammad pulled me close for a kiss. "Being my true wife has its disadvantages, also. Now you will have to contend with the jealousy of your sister-wives."

"Disadvantage? After years of being the jealous one, it's a nice change." I slipped my arms around his waist and kissed him again. "One of many nice changes."

Another knock on the door made us both laugh. "Lack of privacy is another disadvantage," I said. "All of Hijaz seems to be at our door today."

Fatima stormed in with a face as pinched as a rat's.

"*Yaa* Father, Umm Salama is very upset," she said. "Zaynab also. You are paying too much attention to your child bride. The rest of us are feeling neglected."

"What's the matter, Fatima? Doesn't Ali keep you entertained?" I said. Muhammad shook his head at me. I pressed my lips together.

"It's not fair to the rest of us, *abi*, the way you favor her," Fatima said.

Muhammad gave his daughter a tender look. "*Yaa* Fatima, do you love me?"

"You know I do, Father. More than anyone in the world."

"Then do you not love whom I love?"

"Yes, but—"

"Good." Muhammad's smile broadened. He lifted my hand to kiss it. "Since I love A'isha above all others, that means you love her, too. So naturally you do not want to hurt her feelings with these accusations, or by keeping me away from her."

"But Zaynab—"

"Zaynab can take care of herself. I know you two have become close friends, but she does not need to send you on her behalf. You can tell her I said so when you see her again." He held open the door, and Fatima huffed out.

"You've done it now," I said. "Zaynab is next."

Moments later there she stood, chilling the room with her cold stare, filling it with the fragrance of thorny roses.

"I have come to make a protest," she said. Her eyes moved over the baskets of food, the silks and linens, the jewels and hair combs that spilled over the floor of my room. She picked up the mirror from my table and eyed her reflection lovingly. Yet when she put it down the tenderness had vanished from her eyes.

"If you are going to complain about my time with A'isha, I have already heard it from the others," Muhammad said.

"Look at all the treasure piled at her feet—for what? For acting like a fool!"

"If foolish behavior earns treasures, then Zaynab's apartment must be filled with gold," I said.

"Muhammad, this brings shame to the rest of your wives. Please tell the people of the *umma* to stop sending gifts to A'isha," Zaynab said. "We like honey and pomegranates also."

"Refuse these gifts and insult those who would congratulate A'isha? I cannot do that."

"You spoil her!" Zaynab cried. "She has only to lift a finger, and you run to her side as if she were a baby."

I laughed. "With that pout, you're the one who looks like a baby." Then I remembered that Muhammad had asked me to be quiet.

Looking at me, he swept an arm toward Zaynab. "I have been defending you all afternoon, with little benefit," he said. "Would you like to speak on your own behalf, A'isha?"

"Only to point out the destructive nature of jealousy," I said, smiling sweetly at Zaynab. "And to remind you that your sister Hamnah's lies are just that: lies."

Zaynab's skin turned as pale as the moon, and her eyes flashed in outrage.

"I had nothing to do with Hamnah's accusations," she said, lethally calm. "If she thought she acted on my behalf, she was mistaken."

She lowered her eyes and glided out the door, closing it behind her. I looked at Muhammad and saw, by his lifted eyebrows and shaking head, that I had gone too far. I lowered my gaze, chagrined by how easily I'd fallen back into my old, impulsive ways, despite swearing to Muhammad that I had changed. I'd never win the trust of my sister-wives if I continued to speak without first measuring my words. By blaming Zaynab—unjustly, it seemed—for her sister's actions, I'd certainly made an enemy of her at a time when I should be making friends.

Frantically I glanced around the room. My gaze fell on the bronze mirror, and an idea flew into my head.

I snatched up the mirror and dashed into the courtyard. "Wait!" I cried. Zaynab halted in the dappled shade of the ghaza'a tree and turned to me with eyes so cold they made me shiver.

"Yaa Zaynab, forgive my harsh words," I said, venturing a smile. "I've heard how you refused to slander me. Please accept this as a token of my gratitude."

I held the mirror out to her. She looked down her nose at me as she took it, as if she were doing me a favor.

"I have done nothing for you," she said.

"You defended me."

"My sister and I saw you walking into my wedding feast with Safwan ibn al-Mu'attal snapping at your heels," she said. "Lust was smeared all over your face, and his, too. But when Muhammad asked me, I said I did not believe you would be unfaithful to him. However, I did not do that for you."

I frowned. "For whom, then?"

"For Muhammad!" Two messengers paraded past us with gifts in their hands, headed to my apartment. Zaynab leaned closer and lowered her voice so they couldn't hear.

"I would love to see you disappear, like your lover Safwan," she murmured, her tone deceptively silky. "But you should have seen Muhammad these past weeks, when he thought he might lose you. It would kill him to know the truth. I kept my knowledge to myself, so he wouldn't be hurt."

"You could have been the first-wife in this *harim*," I said, blinking at her in confusion. "You would have had everything you wanted."

She sneered at me as if I were a dung beetle destined for the bottom of her sandal. Her gold eyes flashed. "Everything," she said, "except Muhammad's happiness."

I shook my head, trying to understand.

Her laughter stung my face like sand. "It's called 'love,' A'isha. Perhaps someday you'll try it."

A GATHERING STORM

MEDINA, MARCH 627

*O*n the desert, the *samoom* is the most dreaded of storms. It's the poison wind that whips the sand into pillars we call *zauba'ah*. These "devils" lash the sky, blocking the sun, and whip the sand into a fury like a surging, windswept sea. The *samoom* rushes across the desert like the most ravenous beast, devouring all in its path, chewing up houses and spitting them out, then cleaning its teeth with trees ripped out by their roots. The sight of those enormous towers of whirling dust sends even the most godless desert traveler to his knees in prayer, for those fortunate enough to miss the crushing force of the *zauba'ah* are certain to die an even more agonizing death by suffocation as the frenzied sands rise and fling themselves down in great waves, smothering everything in dunes nearly as high as the yellow, grit-laced clouds.

Few have survived the *samoom*. Those who do, miraculously, begin their tale with their first sighting of the *zauba'ah* where the whirling towers join at their pinnacles, sucking the stars from beyond the pale and ripping the heart from the Earth. Although we sat in my apartment and the sun sparkled outdoors in a flawless sky, I saw in Muhammad's dilated eyes

the vision of the *zauba'ah* that day when Safwan told him of the gathering storm he'd witnessed to the south.

There he stood in my apartment, Safwan, my childhood playmate and,
more recently, my betrayer. From behind my screen I seethed as I watched
him greet Muhammad, his face not so handsome, I realized now. Were the
ashes in his complexion meant for me, whom he'd wooed to the edge of a
precipice, then left dangling? I glared at him, quivering like a drawn bow
with an arrow of rage notched on its string. Yet I also knew he wasn't
entirely to blame for what had happened.

It's called "love." Perhaps someday you'll try it. As much as it grated on
me to admit it, Zaynab had spoken the truth about me. I did have a lot to
learn about love. I loved Muhammad, but I realized now that love was
more than a feeling. Love was something you did for another person, like
Zaynab's speaking up for me so Muhammad wouldn't be hurt. Love was
something I was going to do for Muhammad from now on.

Had Safwan learned this lesson? Judging from the plaintive looks he
sent my way, the answer was "no." Given the chance he'd ride away with
me again, leading me to a destiny that was no more mine to control than
if I were a camel. And if we were caught again, he'd disappear, leaving me
to my fate, just as I'd nearly left Muhammad to his. I burned with shame
at the realization.

When he'd finished his ablutions, Muhammad settled his turban on his
head and beckoned Safwan to sit with him.

"*Yaa* Prophet," Safwan said, "now is not the time for sitting down." His
lips had turned white, and the urgency in his eyes sent fear rippling
through my blood. "I bring distressing news. Abu Sufyan is marching to
Medina with an army of ten thousand men."

"Ten thousand?" Muhammad gripped the windowsill. "Are there so
many men in Mecca now?"

"The Nadr march with them. Also, the Kaynuqah." The Jewish clans
Muhammad had banished for conspiring against him. Ali had insisted
they should be killed, but Muhammad had refused. *Our mercy will make
allies of them.* Unfortunately they'd become allies of Abu Sufyan, instead.

"Also—they have the Ghatafani."

My lips curled, although I found nothing amusing in this news. If I'd followed Safwan, he and I would be with them now, coming to attack our *umma*. The realization filled my mouth with bitterness.

Muhammad stared out the window as if straining to see the advancing army. "What do they desire, Safwan?"

"To kill us all—even our children," Safwan said. "I heard their poets foretell Muslim blood filling the streets."

The vein on Muhammad's forehead throbbed as he paced the room. "Kill us all?" he growled. "Will Abu Sufyan never learn? He faces his own death for this act."

He sent Safwan to fetch my father and Umar. I flung myself from my hiding place to bury my face in his scented beard.

"Ten thousand men?" I said. "Can even al-Lah defeat such an army?"

"It will require a miracle. If only I had more notice! We could have sent for help. We could have built a wall to protect our eastern boundary." High cliffs and black rocks surrounded Medina on three sides, but on the east the broad, flat desert lapped like the sea at the edge of our oasis town.

An idea flew into my head—and I decided to reveal it. Here was my chance to help Muhammad and my *umma*! My heart raced with excitement—but before I could speak, Umar and my father entered, sending me back behind the screen as Muhammad told them the news.

"Ten thousand!" My father's voice quavered like an old *shaykh*'s. "How soon will they arrive?"

"In six days, at their current pace," Muhammad said.

My father blanched. "How many warriors can we gather in such a short time?"

"Three thousand, at most," Umar said. His eyes were wide and vacant, as if he watched a scene unfold that no one else could see.

"Three thousand. That means we cannot go to meet them as we did at Uhud," Muhammad said. "Our only hope is to remain here, and allow them to besiege us."

"By al-Lah, that will not be a siege but an invasion! An army that size will slaughter us all." Umar wiped his face with his handkerchief and pressed his cheek against the cool wall.

"*Yaa* Umar, would al-Lah let the *umma* be destroyed?" Muhammad said quietly. "Would He have brought us to Medina only to be annihilated by Quraysh? No. We can prevail."

"We have friends in Abyssinia, but they could not join us here so quickly," Umar said.

"Can we fight until the Abyssinians arrive?" my father asked.

Umar's laugh was harsh. "Outnumbered more than three to one, and with no barrier between us? We might fend off our attackers for ten minutes, al-Lah willing."

"If we trained our women to fight, we would add to our numbers," Muhammad said.

"And then, when the battle ended, would they put down their weapons and submit to us again? I do not wish to take that risk," Umar said.

"The Quraysh threaten to kill even our babies," my father pointed out. "What mother would leave her children in order to fight?"

"I see only two choices," Umar said. "Desert the city or prepare ourselves for death."

"Desert the city? And go where?" my father said.

"We might be able to hide in the mountains, but for how long?" Muhammad said.

"You speak the truth. Abu Sufyan is determined to put an end to *islam*. By al-Lah, his hatred consumes him! He is Satan in the flesh." Umar thrust a fist into the air.

"Perhaps God will send a storm to blow them back," my father said glumly. "Or a flash flood to drown them all."

"I wonder if we have time to build a wall?" Muhammad said.

"We would need six days just to gather up the stones." My father shook his head. "We might as well dig a moat like the Abyssinian king, except we have no water to fill it."

Now was the time for me to speak. I took a deep breath to quell my clamoring pulse, and asked Muhammad's permission.

"*Yaa* Prophet, we are engaged in a serious discussion," Umar grumbled. "Can you not keep your wife silent for even a few moments?"

"I have a suggestion," I said. "A good one."

"A woman's role—" Umar began, but Muhammad waved his hand to silence him.

"Please, A'isha. We have exhausted all ideas of our own."

"Build a moat without water," I said. "A huge trench around the edge of Medina. If it is deep and wide enough, it will stop anyone who tries to cross it."

Umar's face reddened. "*Yaa* Prophet, do you understand now why I require silence from my wives?"

A long pause followed. My father pulled at his beard. Muhammad moved back to the window and stared at the sky as if waiting for al-Lah to write an answer there. I peered around the edge of the screen, holding my breath, willing him to see the beauty of my idea. At last he turned and smiled at me, making me want to leap with joy.

"A'isha's plan has merit," he said. "An enormous trench could save us. If we build it correctly, no one will be able to penetrate Medina. Praise al-Lah for you, A'isha!" Muhammad strode over to me behind the screen, kissed me on the mouth, then bounded out into the sitting area, shouting and exclaiming. I smiled with pride, knowing I'd moved up a notch in Muhammad's esteem. If this trench worked, could he fail to ask for my advice in the future?

"Tell Bilal to summon every man and boy in the *umma*," Muhammad said. "We have much digging to do. Praise al-Lah! We are saved."

◆

For the next six days I girded myself for battle. This invasion, I knew, was the event for which al-Lah had called me. For the first time I felt a clear sense of my mission. I had already helped defend the *umma* with my trench idea, and now I would confront our enemies with my sword and dagger, filling that trench with Qurayshi blood. It was time for Abu Sufyan to pay the ultimate price for what he'd done to Raha, and to the rest of us.

When Bilal sounded the call to battle I stood ready. I donned the helmet and shield I'd begged from Talha and strapped on my sword. With my hair tucked into the helmet I looked like a boy. No one would send me back to the mosque to cower with the other women of the *umma*— waiting, helpless, for slaughter.

I ran through the streets, my feet racing with my thrumming pulse. Ululations, shouts, whinnies, and the clang of metal couldn't drown out the drum of my heart in my ears. Terror snatched at my throat like the teeth of a crazed dog and hammered the city like a hailstorm. It made the men roar in defiance and hoist their weapons. It beat the heads of women until they sobbed and ran from their homes, clutching their babies. Jamila rushed past me, carrying two young children, her eyes frantically searching for a place to hide them. All around her, mothers stuffed their young ones into doorways, through windows, and high into trees, hoping that an invader with evil in his heart and a dagger in his hand wouldn't look there. A smell like sex, faint yet pungent, rose from the moil.

My feet carried me like true arrows toward Muhammad, who darted to the city's eastern edge as if his double chain mail were weightless. In the roiling dust and churning crowds I nearly lost him, but shouts from the men ahead pulled my eyes to the red feather Umar wore in his helmet and my father's own gray head, bare, as always, until the last possible moment.

The last thing I wanted was to be noticed. If anyone recognized me, I'd be sent home and placed under guard at the mosque, to be certain I remained there. Not for me the task of sitting passively and wringing my hands in worry. Al-Lah had chosen me to fight, not to cower like a girl. And, after the debacle with Safwan, I needed to prove myself to the *umma*.

I hid behind a boulder as immense as an elephant and peered around it, trying to see whether the Qurayshi army had arrived, but a high bank of dirt blocked my view of the desert. I strapped my shield to my arm and climbed into a thorn tree. A shout rang out and then, like the flood bursting through the great Marib dam, a sea of men came pouring over the ridge far ahead of us. Our warriors scrambled into position behind the embankment, forming a line all the way to the high stone wall around the neighborhood of the Qurayzah, one of the few Jewish clans remaining in Medina. They'd sworn allegiance to the *umma*, but they wouldn't fight on our side, for they refused to kill their Nadr and Kaynuqah kinsmen.

Our troops stood silent, bows and arrows ready, as the dark swarm blanketed the land before us, men rushing and clamoring red-faced for our blood, their horses whinnying and rolling their eyes. I clutched the hilt of my sword and braced myself, preparing to fight. When the invaders approached so near we could almost feel their breath on our faces, they stopped, staring at the enormous trench our men had dug, a chasm as wide and deep as a *wadi*, impossible to cross.

"Why do you stop, you idiots?" Abu Sufyan thundered up on his horse, bulging over his saddle like a sack of grain. Almost too late he saw the trench yawning like a grave. He yanked back on his reins, skidding his horse to the edge.

He heaved himself down to the ground and stood at the trench's lip, surveying our work with his mouth twisted in disgust.

"Muhammad ibn Abdallah ibn al-Muttalib!" he shouted. "What cowardly device is this to keep my army at bay?"

"*Yaa* Abu Sufyan, you thought you would surprise us. But we are the ones with the surprise," Muhammad called back.

"This is not doing battle honorably. Why do you not come out and fight like men, instead of cowering behind this hole you have wasted your time digging? Or do you fear your precious al-Lah will not protect you?"

"Al-Lah protects us already," Muhammad said. "Who do you think is responsible for this glorious trench?" Our men began to yell, shouting praises to God. Someone shot an arrow up and over the berm; it rose in an arc and fell among the attackers. More arrows followed, hissing like serpents and spooking the horses. I heard a scream and saw a man pitch sideways with an arrow stuck in his throat. A horse whinnied and reared, pierced in the flank. The iron sea of men tumbled and crested as skittish animals flailed and sidled, tossing their riders to the ground or over the rim of the trench into an instant grave.

Ali ran over to the tree where I'd perched. "What are you doing up there?" he snarled. I tried to answer him, but my leaping pulse blocked my throat. Of all the men to discover me here, why did it have to be him? I clambered down the tree to face his outrage, but he was so preoccupied he just ordered me home.

Cursing, I stormed back to the mosque. How could I have let myself be spotted? I'd thought Ali would be at the trench with his troops. He'd tell Muhammad I'd broken the *hijab*, and I'd lose Muhammad's trust again. Now my husband would certainly post a guard to prevent me from leaving the mosque, condemning me to sit at home and wring my hands while a battle raged outside our walls.

When I saw Muhammad in the courtyard later that day, his expression was sober, but, thank al-Lah, not furious. "I admire your courage, A'isha," he said. "But you have already contributed much to our defense with your trench idea."

"How could I ever do enough for you?" I dabbed the moisture that had popped onto my lip.

"Bringing harm onto yourself would harm me, also," he said. "Please, A'isha, stay here to guard the mosque. Our women and children would be soothed by your protection."

Umar stormed into the courtyard, his chain mail clanking, and seized Muhammad's beard. His eyes looked stricken, as if someone had just died. I held my breath.

"Huyayy, the leader of the Nadr clan, has entered the gates of the Qurayzah," he said. "There can only be one reason for this visit: access to Medina."

Muhammad shook his head. "The Qurayzah have given me their pledge to remain neutral in this conflict. Their leader Ka'ab is a trustworthy man."

"He also hates to fight," Umar said. "Would seeing ten thousand men at his gate cause him to break his pact with us?"

For the second time that day, I saw fear's dark wing fall across Muhammad's face.

"If the army gains access through the Qurayzah gate, the *umma* is doomed," he said. "By al-Lah, Umar, I hope you are wrong." Gray strands appeared as if by magic in his hair and beard. The skin under his eyes sagged. He shuffled away with his shoulders stooped, shaking his head and muttering.

"*Yaa* husband!" I cried. "Where are you going?"

"To pray," he said. "I suggest you both do the same."

Poison Wind

Twenty-five days later

*T*wenty-five days felt like twenty-five years. Fear became a familiar flavor, mixed daily into our bread. Sawdah wept at every sunrise, certain it would be her last. Hafsa hid in her hut, refusing to emerge, taking her meals alone in her apartment. Zaynab scowled at anyone who dared to look at her. Umm Salama held her children in her lap and rocked them all day, humming a dismal tune and frightening the color from their poor faces.

As for me, I sharpened my sword every morning. "You're going to wear out the blade," Zaynab snapped.

"Then I can use your tongue to fight with," I said. "It's sharper than any sword."

She didn't laugh. No one did during those twenty-five days. Even the children lost their glee: They walked instead of running, and their little mouths quivered. I carried meals to Hafsa for relief from the gloom, but the darkness under her eyes and the pallor in her voice made the cooking tent feel festive in comparison.

Ten thousand murderers lingered outside our city. They toyed with us the way a cat teases its prey before it pounces. Laughing at us, they urinated and defecated into the trench. They threatened to roast and eat our children, elaborating on the tenderness of the meat and lamenting the foulness of Muslim flavor. They sang lewd songs about Muhammad's wives and what they planned to do to us before killing us. They staged mock battles between the Qurayshi and the Believers, with the "Believers" oinking and grunting like swine.

"Such humiliation should not be endured," Ali would grumble to Muhammad after a long day of watching the enemy's displays. "If you would only allow us to strike them with our arrows, they would remain in their camp."

"Conserve your arrows," Muhammad would say. "We may need our weapons yet. Abu Sufyan seems determined to find a way in."

And in truth, he did find a way, as we learned on the twenty-fifth day. That's when Safwan came to the mosque with news: Ka'ab, the leader of the Qurayzah tribe, had agreed to open his gates to the invaders. "My Ghatafani source says Abu Sufyan is preparing his troops," he told Muhammad.

Watching and listening from my apartment, I leaned against the doorway, dizzy with fear. Abu Sufyan was preparing his troops—to slaughter us all!

"I cannot believe this of Ka'ab." Muhammad shook his head. "Less than one year ago he shared a bowl of milk with me and promised his allegiance."

"But his people were allies with the Nadr for many generations before we arrived," Ali said. "Then we exiled the Nadr."

"Now Ka'ab is afraid you'll do the same to the Qurayzah," Safwan put in.

"We will do worse than that to those treacherous dogs!" Ali shouted. For once, I agreed with him. If we lived through this terror somehow, I'd happily sever Ka'ab's head myself.

Muhammad excused himself to pray, asking Ali to gather his Companions in the *majlis* and to find food for Safwan.

"It will not be extravagant," Ali said. "Our stores are nearly depleted."

"The invaders are also hungry," Safwan said. "Abu Sufyan promised them an easy victory, so they only brought a two weeks' supply of food." He grinned. "Of course, the Bedouin warriors are accustomed to hunger pangs, but you should hear the Qurayshi complain." I glowered at him as he snickered. If not for me, he'd be getting ready now to invade Medina.

Muhammad thanked Safwan and departed. Ali went to summon the Companions, promising to return shortly. Left in the mosque alone, Safwan glanced toward my door—which I shut hurriedly and, when he knocked, refused to open.

"My heart still longs for you, A'isha," Safwan said through the door.

"Is that why you left me to face the *umma* alone?" I choked.

"The Prophet sent me away. He didn't want me here to remind people of our night in the desert together."

"And so you went to your old friends the Ghatafani."

"By al-Lah! The Prophet asked me to spy on their talks with Abu Sufyan. I wouldn't have left you otherwise, A'isha."

I kept silent. Yet my heart did soften toward him—a little.

"I hope you will forgive me," he said. "I would like for us to be friends."

A tear seeped from my eye. "That can never be," I murmured. After that, all was silent. Safwan was gone.

I sat on my cushions for a long while, mourning our lost childhoods. How innocent we'd been in those days, imagining a life free of restraints! In truth, our destinies had been set for us since birth. We might be able to shape the future, but we couldn't escape it, no matter how far into the desert we rode.

Now, when my own future seemed about to end, I once again faced the impossibility of escape. If death awaited me today, then so be it. I couldn't flee from my fate; nor did I want to. But I could act bravely, wielding my sword, fighting to the end. I swallowed my tears, summoning my courage. If the Qurayshi invaded, they wouldn't find me sobbing and begging for mercy! I'd fight like no woman those soft-bellied merchants had ever seen.

I fastened my sword to my belt and headed to the *majlis* to listen to the men's talk.

"The enemy troops are massing at the trench," Ali barked. Bluster as he might, he couldn't hide the fear in his voice. Outside the *majlis*, my knees trembled so hard they knocked against each other.

Muhammad seized Ali's beard, embracing him. "Prepare to fight," he said. "And have faith in God."

The men hurried out the door, not even seeing me. When Muhammad emerged, I flew into his arms. "Let me come with you, *habibi*," I said through my tears. "I want to die fighting by your side."

He wrapped his arms around me and kissed the top of my head. I could feel his heart racing as though it would leap from his chest. His body quivered in my embrace like a shot arrow.

"My A'isha," he said. "You are the bravest of all my warriors. That is why you must remain in the mosque with the women and children. You can give them courage."

"Some comfort, waiting for slaughter!" I said, beginning to cry. "Do you expect us to huddle in the mosque and pray for a miracle? Arm us with weapons, at least, so we can send our enemies to Hell before we die."

"Hearing is obeying, *habibati*." His voice cracked. "I will send Talha with all the extra daggers, swords, and shields we possess."

Muhammad pulled me closer and kissed me with such passion, I had to gasp for air when his mouth left mine. Then he loosed his hold and pushed me gently away.

"Al-Lah be with you, husband," I said.

"And with you, my warrior-bride." He gazed intently at me with liquid eyes. "Now, go and prepare our women to join God's army. I will see you in the next world, if not in this one."

How I wanted to sob! Were we all to die like sheep at slaughter? If Muhammad were killed, would I even want to live? *Please, al-Lah, keep him safe.*

Shaking all over, I went into my room to strap on my dagger and don my helmet. When Talha arrived at the mosque with a sack full of weapons, he gave me the first smile I'd seen since the siege began.

"By al-Lah, cousin, I have never seen a lovelier warrior," he said. "Our enemies will be fortunate to have their throats slit by such a pretty hand."

"Who's slitting throats? I'll be whacking off heads," I boasted. His smile softened like melting butter, and his eyes moistened. Shrugging off proper behavior, I stood on tiptoe to kiss his cheek, in thanks for the friendship he had shown to me over the years.

As the women began to arrive, I handed them weapons at the door. "It's not going to bite you," I said to Umm Ayman, who stared at her sword with wary eyes.

"You can grasp it firmly; you won't break it," I told Jamila, who dangled her dagger like a ribbon from a limp hand. "That's the way, *ummi*," I said as my mother grasped the hilt of her weapon and thrust it, wild-eyed, into an imaginary foe.

Sawdah ran up, puffing and perspiring. "Hafsa still won't come out of her hut," she said. "It doesn't seem right to leave her in there alone."

Zaynab strode up to me with her eyes flashing. "What do you think you're doing?" she demanded. "Are you the wife of the Prophet of God, or a common street fighter like Umm 'Umara?"

My cheeks blazed. "Umm 'Umara saved Muhammad's life at Uhud."

"While you ran around making a spectacle of yourself. And now, look at you. Armored head to toe like a . . . a . . . boy!" She shook her head in disgust.

I lifted my chin, already knowing the real reason for her protest. While I'd been exiled in my parents' home, Zaynab had set her sights on the *hatun* position. That had become apparent to me when she'd challenged me in my apartment, in front of Muhammad. Now she couldn't bear to see me wielding a power she didn't possess. Of course, our struggle over a title wouldn't matter once our bodies lay in heaps in the dirt.

Umm Salama stepped forward with her arms around her children Dorra and Omar. Her oldest son, Salama, had turned fifteen and had joined the ranks of the warriors, and her baby girl was safely nestled in the arms of a Bedouin wet-nurse somewhere in the desert.

"Zaynab speaks the truth," she said, remarkably calm for a woman about to die. "We women were meant to give life, not to destroy it. What kind of example will it set for my children to see me spilling the blood of men?"

I couldn't believe what I was hearing. My heart slammed against my breast like a bird caught in a room. "Example? For whom? Unless we fight, no one here will live to tell how you died," I said.

"I agree with Zaynab and Umm Salama." Fatima glared at me, jealous of her father's love to the last breath. "If I must die, I would rather do so with dignity."

I shook my head in disgust and dropped my bag of weapons to the floor. "Do as you wish. Cower in the corner when our murderers arrive, with my blessing. As for me, let it be said that A'isha bint Abi Bakr died the way she lived: fighting!" I left the mosque, trembling with rage, and went to find Hafsa.

She sat in the darkest corner of her apartment, hugging herself with crossed arms. "Why is al-Lah doing this to us?" she cried.

Compassion spread like warm milk through my breast. I knelt beside her and enfolded her in an embrace. She didn't respond at first, but when I began to sing to her I felt her body relax, and when I told her it was all right to be afraid, that we were all afraid, she sighed and placed her head on my shoulder.

"Fear is normal," I said. "The question is, what are you going to do with your fear?" I pulled out the weapon I had brought for her—an elegant, curved dagger with a bronze handle and a blade that flashed even in the dim light of her room.

"Let your feelings flow out through your hands and into this dagger. Then, when it's full, stick it into your attacker's belly—and watch your fear empty itself into his eyes as he dies by your hand!"

Timidly she accepted the dagger from me and hefted its weight. She turned it over, examining it. She pushed it forward in a hesitant stab. Then she dropped the blade and burst into tears.

"I don't know what to believe anymore. I'm so confused."

I picked up the dagger and curled her fingers around its handle. "Yaa Hafsa, many of us are confused. But there is one thing we all know: Everyone dies, sooner or later. We don't have a choice about that. But I and you do have power over how we die. I would rather go fighting than cringing. What about you?"

Something stirred in her eyes. She wiped them with her sleeve and sat up a bit straighter.

"How do I use this thing?" she said, lifting the blade. "Will you show me?"

I stood. "In a few minutes, I begin giving lessons. You are invited to join us in the mosque." As I left her room, she was reaching for her robe.

Back in the mosque, I was astonished to see all the women, including Zaynab, Umm Salama, and Juwairriyah, clumsily hefting swords and shields at the feet of my mother, who stood on Muhammad's tree-stump pulpit and shouted improvised verses about killing and maiming our enemies.

"*Yaa* A'isha, come and give us a lesson!" *ummi* cried when she saw me walk in with Hafsa at my heels. She held out her hand and pulled me onto the stump. I raised my sword and began to teach. In moments every woman in the room was practicing sword fighting and envisioning herself a warrior. On the edges of the room the children sat in clusters, clapping and cheering as if we were playing a game.

To my delight many of the women learned quickly—even those who'd resisted at first. Umm Salama proved a canny opponent, detached enough to think, rather than feel, her way through a fight. Zaynab, on the other hand, was as impulsive as Ali, but without his skills. She fought with the ferocity of a tiger, but I feared she wouldn't last long in a real battle. My mother was indomitable, and she laughed as she fought against the hapless Qutailah as though she were having the best time of her life. Sawdah danced with her sword, light-footed and graceful, easily overpowering Umm Ayman. The clank of swords and the grunts and shouts of women filled the room until, at last, we decided to stop and rest. It would do us no good to exhaust ourselves before the real fighting began.

I and Hafsa, newly energized, rounded up the children to help us in the cooking tent.

"We might as well cook everything," Hafsa said, eyeing our last sack of barley. "We'll need the energy for the fight, and there's no use leaving anything for Quraysh when it's over."

When we returned to the mosque bearing huge bowls of grain, we found the women prostrating themselves on the floor. My mother gestured toward the date-palm stump.

"*Yaa* daughter, we need a prayer, and you are the one to lead it," she said. Zaynab rose and made a noise of protest, but when my mother thrust her chin out in defiance, she lowered herself to the floor again. Her eyes hurled daggers at me as I nervously climbed atop the pulpit.

I felt as tiny as an ant in that silent room. I opened my mouth to pray, but my lips trembled too much for words. How could I stand here in place of Muhammad, the Prophet of the One God? Yet hadn't he asked me to comfort the women of his *umma*? Here was my chance to prove myself worthy.

Al-Lah, please provide me with the right words. I opened my mouth again, and this time they rang out as true as the cries of Bilal from the rooftop.

"Give us the heart we need to protect our children and our *umma*," I prayed. Serenity filled me as though I were an empty vessel. "With You on our side, we will be victorious."

After our meal the women lay down to rest, their hearts too fearful for sleep. Asma's little boy Abdallah begged me for a story. I sat on the tree stump and held my arms out to him, and he crawled into my lap. Then, warmed by his breath, I began to recite. One poem after another, whatever came to mind: love poems of old, verses of revelation from al-Lah to Muhammad, poems of heroic deeds at Badr and Uhud, and poems of longing for Mecca, our motherland, which filled the mosque with sniffles and tears.

And then from outside we heard a rumble like the hooves of one thousand and one horses. A screech like the wind tore through the streets. Panic seized me—they were coming! The end was near. Tears filled my eyes as I said my good-byes, but I gave myself a shake. If anyone lived to tell this tale, they'd say A'isha died a warrior, strong and proud, not sobbing in fear and self-pity.

Sawdah cried out. Fatima's baby began to wail. I lifted the sleeping Abdallah and carried him to Asma. My sister's eyes brimmed, luminous with fright. I stepped back atop the stump and pulled my sword from its sheath. It sang and quivered in my hand, joined by the songs of swords all around me as they were lifted into the air.

We stood in place for what seemed like hours, sniffing the air like dogs on point, listening for those first feet pounding, watching for those blood-lusting eyes. My pulse sped through my body, slowing time. I heard the breaths of the women, smelled the tang of the barley we'd eaten and the dust we'd kicked up with our feet. The air was uncommonly cold, although sweat covered my body. Chilled, I clamped my jaw shut to keep my teeth from chattering.

Then, from outside the mosque entrance, we heard a clatter and a yelp. I tensed, waiting for the onslaught—but nothing. I strained my ears, listening, but heard only a long, loud roar that ebbed and flowed like the Red Sea.

With trembling legs I stepped down from the stump and walked slowly through the room, weaving among the taut, tense women, aswirl in the fragrances they'd perfumed themselves with this morning, not knowing whether this day would be their last. Long, panting breaths filled the mosque. Not a single hand shook, although many faces glistened with tears.

Inside the mosque, the area around the entrance remained empty; no one wanted to be the first to greet our enemies. I stepped into the vacant space as though taking the stage. Every woman's eyes watched me sidle to the doorway. As I neared the entrance I could see the cause of all the noise outside: A *samoom* flung dust against the houses and ripped up date-palm roofs. Sand filled the air in swirls, and in the distance *zauba'ah*, dust devils, spiraled and twisted and blotted the sun with a cloud the color of sesame paste. I saw no sign of soldiers or anyone else. I craned my neck to peer up and down the street, but the scene was the same: deserted.

I let out a whoop. "We're not under attack! It's a *samoom!*"

Relieved sighs whooshed through the room like air from a punctured ball. I heard the rustle of clothing and the scrapes of swords being sheathed. And then, before I pulled my head inside, I saw them coming.

Dark shapes in the distance grew larger as they neared. Like ten thousand whirlwinds they raced through the storm, heedless of the blowing sand and palm branches slamming to the ground.

"Prepare your weapons again!" I shouted. "The enemy approaches."

Hafsa hurried up and stretched her neck to see, also. "They're coming for us," she said.

So they were: ten thousand killers running straight to the mosque, elbowing each other aside, shouting and laughing, racing ahead then being pulled back by others. How similar their armor appeared to ours! They must have torn it from the dead bodies of our *umma's* warriors. I growled low in my throat and gripped my sword, hungering for Qurayshi blood. Looking for Abu Sufyan.

Then, in the front of the mob, a familiar figure emerged—a compact man, curly bearded, and with the most beautiful smile in all of Hijaz.

"*Yaa* A'isha, give praise to al-Lah!" Muhammad waved his arms, flashing his blade. "He has destroyed the enemy camp with His *samoom.* Abu Sufyan, as we predicted, has taken his army and fled. The siege is lifted, and we are rescued!"

The Harim Divided

*T*he entire desert buzzed with the news: The Prophet Muhammad had defeated an army of ten thousand without a casualty on his side. Converts to *islam* poured as thick as honey into Medina. Bedouin chiefs, including the leader of the Ghatafan, now clamored to be his friends. The Negus, king of Abyssinia, sent one hundred camels in congratulation. The Egyptian holy chief promised his most beautiful courtesans to Muhammad. Only one month ago all of Hijaz had called him *djinni*-possessed, but now the Prophet of al-Lah stood with the world at his feet. I stood by his side, and tried to hold my place against the conniving Zaynab.

I'd grown in Muhammad's esteem because of my trench idea, praise al-Lah, and also for the way I'd helped the women to defend themselves and their children. "If it weren't for A'isha, you would have found us huddled on the floor and blubbering like little babies," Sawdah had told Muhammad, who'd nodded at me as if he'd expected nothing less. None of us mentioned how Zaynab, Umm Salama, and Fatima had challenged me.

My mother had changed their minds. After I'd left the mosque for Hafsa's apartment, *ummi* had asked who agreed that fighting was more desirable than begging. As women clamored around her, taking swords and daggers, Zaynab spied a blade with a silver scorpion clutching its handle. She grabbed the sword from my mother's hand and lifted it up with gleaming eyes, admiring its beauty.

"*Yaa* Zaynab, if you are not going to use that sword, hand it to someone who will," my mother snapped. But Zaynab was entranced and wouldn't let it go. Moments later, Umm Salama's children urged her to take a sword and protect them, their eyes wide with fear. Once Umm Salama had capitulated, Fatima decided to fight, also.

Sawdah's tale of how I'd empowered the women brought tears to my father's eyes, and my mother's demonstration of her swordsmanship made him smile. Yet not all Muhammad's Companions were impressed. Umar barked at his wives to drop their weapons before they harmed themselves, and Ali scolded Fatima for endangering their child with such a sharp object. "You should have known the men would protect you," he said as he led her out the door of the mosque.

My father chuckled at his Companions' reactions. "I suppose you will want to take command of the household now that you have had a taste of power," he said to my mother. Her face lit up at the idea. She turned to the pale, haggard Qutailah, who held her sword as if it were a stinking fish, and took the weapon from her.

"Come, sister-wife. It is time we went home," my mother said imperiously.

Umar's wives followed him from the mosque with their heads high and smiles on their lips. Even Zaynab, seeing how Muhammad's eyes shone when he looked at me, hoisted her sword and bragged to him about how she'd planned to skin the Qurayshi attackers alive. As she cut her eyes at me, I wondered if I'd created an even more formidable foe for myself.

I thought I had enough worries, but al-Lah must not have agreed, for He sent me another very soon. A few days after the Battle of the Trench had ended, I and Muhammad were in my room when Ali arrived. His hands gripped the arms of a *houri*-eyed woman with a beauty spot like a quince seed on her right cheek and rage in her dark eyes. Ali shoved her toward Muhammad.

"A gift from your warriors," he said. "Raihana, the Qurayzah princess."

She hurled a stream of spittle that landed on Muhammad's beard. Ali cried out, but Muhammad raised his hand to silence him.

"You murdered my father, my husband, and my brothers," the woman snarled. "I'd rather die, too, than become your whore—like this one." She flung her hand toward me without a glance.

I winced at the hatred in her voice. Yet who couldn't understand her anger? After Abu Sufyan's army had fled, devastated by hunger and the *samoom*, our warriors had attacked the Qurayzah neighborhood and killed all its men in the most brutal act Muhammad had ever ordered. "We cannot risk their betraying us as the Nadr have done," he'd said. Yet I could see sadness in his eyes as we watched our men hack off their heads and push their bodies into the trench.

I shared his sorrow, yet I supported Muhammad's decision. The Qurayzah leader, Ka'ab, wouldn't have shed a tear over our massacre. In truth, he'd tried to help our enemies. And if Muhammad had shown them the same mercy he'd given to the Nadr and Kaynuqah clans, our men would have rebelled. They needed to take revenge on the treacherous Qurayzah.

His gaze steady on Raihana's face, Muhammad dabbed his beard with his sleeve. When he had finished, he told her he regretted causing her grief. "I do not require you to choose between marrying me and death."

"If you plan to send me into slavery, kill me now," she said. "Death by beheading would be more merciful than rapes and beatings. I'm an unskilled princess with soft hands and a sharp tongue, neither of which is valued in a slave."

"I will not make a slave of you, daughter of Ka'ab," Muhammad said. "In spite of his recent treachery, I admired your father. Out of respect for him I will allow you to live here, in my *harim*—but not as my wife until you have converted to *islam*."

Foreboding filled me, but I bit back my protests. Muhammad's warriors had given her to him, and so he couldn't reject her. But to bring this venomous creature into the *harim*? I would have sooner kept company with a serpent.

"Marry you, and forsake my Jewish God?" Raihana's laugh scraped like sand over a fresh wound. "I will never do that, even to get my sons back."

"You have not lost your children," Muhammad said. "They may live with you here."

Raihana lowered her eyes, but not before I saw the tears cupped on her lashes like dewdrops on blades of grass. Ali prodded her with his sword. "See how kind our Prophet is?" he said. "Why don't you thank him for his generosity?"

She glared at Ali. "Why should I thank him for giving to me what is already mine?"

◆

"What kind of man is Muhammad?" Raihana asked that evening in the cooking tent, where we sister-wives hid from the men building her hut. "A killer or a lover?"

"He only kills those who deserve to die," I retorted, still stung by her "whore" remark. "Luckily for you, he's not so choosy about whom he loves."

She pursed her full lips at me. "Jealous?" she said. "You needn't worry about me. I'm not interested in your false Prophet."

"False!" From the corner where she played with the children, Sawdah cried out. Her face reddened like a pomegranate as she pushed herself to standing and lumbered over to us. "The Prophet is the truest man in all of Hijaz."

Raihana smirked. "A true pretender. Claiming to be the prophet our Jewish Book foretold. Would God anoint an Arab over one of His own chosen people?"

Sawdah tutted and lowered herself to sit in the "nest" with me, Hafsa, Juwairriyah, and Raihana. I leaped into the discussion, relishing the role of Muhammad's defender.

"Would a pretender risk everything he owned?" I glanced around at my sister-wives for support. "Muhammad had a wealthy wife, one of the most beautiful homes in Mecca, four daughters, and a life of ease. Why would he want to change his life unless he had to?"

"Oh, I see. God forced him to do it," Raihana said, rolling her eyes.

"As a matter of fact, He did," Hafsa said.

"It was the angel Gabriel that forced him," Sawdah said. Her voice dropped to a mystical hush, and she told the tale the rest of us knew so well—how Muhammad had become the Prophet of al-Lah.

In a cave atop Mount Hira, Muhammad was sitting in meditation and praying to his family's gods when a sound like thunder shook the walls. A booming voice echoed through the cave. "Recite!" it commanded.

Muhammad fell prostrate with fear, wondering if fasting had made him delirious. Then, in the dark, a pair of hands squeezed his throat, choking him. "Recite!" the voice shouted again, and the hands released him.

Shaking so violently he could barely stand, Muhammad stumbled to the cave's entrance, wanting a glimpse of his attacker, wondering if it might be a *djinni*. What he saw stunned him: A great, glowing figure of a man—the angel Gabriel—straddled the horizon, blocking the moon and stars. Muhammad fell down in a trembling heap.

Raihana scoffed. "A *djinni?* Surely no one believes this ludicrous tale."

Zaynab strolled in with Umm Salama at her side and Fatima in the rear like an attendant. She stood over me with a contemptuous smile.

"I have just heard a most interesting rumor," she said.

I tensed. "Did it involve a man's daughter-in-law and a curtain?" I asked, glaring up at her.

"That old bit of gossip has long been disproved," Fatima broke in.

"This is a new tale. Judging from its source, I'd say it's true," Zaynab said. "Your mother's sister-wife told me. Has anyone else heard it? About Muhammad's child bride being too afraid to consummate their marriage until recently?"

Hafsa's eyes bulged at me, warning me to restrain myself. Sawdah shook her head and told Zaynab she shouldn't listen to gossip. Fear crept up my neck. According to tradition, which linked marriage with consummation, Zaynab had been Muhammad's wife for longer than I, which gave her more rights to the *hatun* position.

"Maybe it wasn't fear that stopped Muhammad, but that skinny child's body," Zaynab taunted. "You still look like a child to me. And, as we saw during the siege, you still act like one." Her eyes glimmered. "Like a boy who can't wait to become a man."

Hafsa clamped her hand over her mouth, signaling to me, but I was too enraged to hold my tongue any longer.

"*Yaa* Hafsa, did you hear something?" I said, keeping my tone casual. "A strange squawking sound, like a parrot?"

Zaynab sucked in her breath. "We'll see who's the parrot in this *harim*," she snapped. She turned to my sister-wives. "Let's take a vote right now."

She marched over to her group's corner and took a seat. "All of you who want A'isha to be your *hatun*, remain there in her court. Those of you who support me, come and sit here."

Umm Salama followed her without a pause, and Fatima, of course. The three of them sat facing us.

I grinned. Fatima didn't count. With Sawdah, Hafsa, and Juwairriyah on my side, I had the majority. I flashed Zaynab a look of triumph—but she was smiling eagerly at Juwairriyah, who had moved over to her corner

"I and Juwairriyah became good friends while you were throwing your-self at Safwan," Zaynab said to me. She swiveled her head to address the women by her side. "As *hatun*, sister-wives, what task should I make A'isha perform first?"

"Why not have me count your votes?" I said archly. "I see two others, besides your own." I looked around at my group. "By al-Lah, we have the same number!"

"*Yaa* Zaynab, don't designate yourself the *hatun* yet," Hafsa said. "You need one more vote."

Zaynab raised her eyebrows at Raihana. "There's still another member of this *harim* to be heard from," she said. "Lovely Raihana." She flashed her most dazzling smile. "Welcome to our home, sister-wife. Whom would you rather have leading this *harim*: me, a woman of maturity and intelli-gence, or this impulsive little brat?"

Raihana laughed. "Don't expect me to choose sides in this fight," she said. "I've already witnessed too many battles. Besides, I'm not married to Muhammad, so I'm not a member of this *harim*. And, God willing, I never will be."

MUTINY AT MECCA

he confrontation with Zaynab had been a close call. One more vote in her favor, and I would have been shoveling out the toilet that afternoon. It was time, I decided, to conceive a child. Knowing my plight, Sawdah had begun whispering remedies: A suppository made from the desert plant *khuzama* was supposed to help a woman's fertility. I'd try it when Muhammad came to me next. Soon, al-Lah willing, I'd bear his son.

But before we could have our night Muhammad announced plans for a pilgrimage to the Ka'ba, to thank al-Lah for saving us in the Battle of the Trench. Because the Qurayshi might try to stop us from entering Mecca, he would take just two wives along: me and Umm Salama. Before long, though, Zaynab had convinced him to bring her, also: *You know how I always loved Mecca, habib.*

The idea of sharing a tent with those two was so unpleasant, I almost declined to make the journey. But I longed to see Mecca again. And I wasn't about to let Zaynab become a *hajja*, one who had made the pilgrimage, without my doing the same.

We left at dusk, one thousand men, seventy camels to be sacrificed to al-Lah, plus more camels, donkeys, and horses carrying sacks of barley, bags of dates, cooking pots, tents, rugs, clothing, bowls, *kohl*, flowers, daggers, water skins, hopes, memories, and prayers for a peaceful reception in our motherland. Although, as usual, braggarts swaggered about and recited verses about how we'd bring Quraysh to its knees if its leaders tried to stop us from entering the city.

But Muhammad wasn't looking for a fight. He'd decided to go to Mecca because of a dream: Our men in white robes streaming into the city, drinking from the sacred well of Zamzam and circling the Ka'ba like a river.

"Al-Lah is calling us to Him," Muhammad told me.

The timing was perfect for such a bold move. The *samoom* that had shredded Abu Sufyan's camp on the eve of his army's invasion had convinced all of Hijaz that *islam* was a mighty power. Many of the converts who had come to Muhammad since the Battle of the Trench hailed from Mecca, and all told Muhammad the same tale: Abu Sufyan was losing the respect of Quraysh. Some advocated replacing him with al-Abbas, uncle to Muhammad and Ali.

"Our people are weary of losing battles and caravans to Muhammad," one convert said. "Many would like to make peace with you."

We left Medina buoyed by the cheers and ululations of the women, children, and *shaykhs* who lined the street. Our men's eyes outshone the scattered stars; the desert air exhilarated us all as the caravaners sang and cheerfully urged their camels onward, eager to see their beloved Mecca again. But by the tenth night, tensions cracked like stiff whips around us. The donkeys lowered their heads and refused to budge. The horses reared and spooked. The camels belched their weird, garbled noises, like the rantings of demons. The men muttered about a Qurayshi attack, and they grumbled about Muhammad's prohibition against carrying weapons on the journey. Only daggers were allowed, for slitting the throats of the sacrificial camels.

"We could not fight a flock of birds with these puny toys," I heard the driver of my camel complain. "If Quraysh attacks, we might as well lie down and let them kill us."

Probably because of the grumbling, Muhammad consecrated the camels that final night instead of waiting until we arrived in Mecca. We wives watched from our tent as he walked the first camel amid the camp, calling out, "God is great!" Cheers and shouts dispelled the gloom that had shrouded us. Then, with a stick of *kohl*, Muhammad marked the girl-ish face and strong haunches of his animal with lines, squiggles, and circles.

"*Labaykh al-Lahumah labaykh!*" he cried, announcing our arrival to God, as he placed a garland of bright flowers on the camel's neck.

Soon the entire camp bustled as sixty-nine other men paraded the remaining camels. With their long eyelashes and flowered necklaces, the beasts reminded me of women made up for a party. Tomorrow, our one thousand pilgrims would lead them into Mecca, the sacred city we faced in prayer five times a day. At the Ka'ba they would offer the animals to al-Lah.

We slept, and then, even as the sun struck our eyes and hearts with heat so intense we could barely breathe, we prepared to ride the few remaining hours to Mecca. We'd enter the city while the Qurayshi war-riors dozed away the hottest part of the day. Or so we thought.

I heard the hoof beats first, then the shouts. Sitting in my *hawdaj*, I parted the curtains to see our scout riding at full speed through the shim-mering heat, waving his whip and kicking his feet against his horse's flanks. When he arrived, Umar handed him a water skin. He gulped messily, sloshing liquid onto his clothes. Then, gasping, he told us that Khalid ibn al-Walid was on his way with two hundred fully armed fighters.

Rumbling erupted like thunder among our men. "By al-Lah, we will tear them apart with our bare hands!" Umar shouted.

Only Muhammad appeared unfazed.

"Alas for Quraysh!" he said, shaking his head. "War has completely devoured them. It would have done them no harm to simply let us come and worship. But they can think only of fighting and killing. In that way, we are already victorious."

He turned to my father. Did anyone among us know a different route to Mecca? My father went to find out. I and my sister-wives followed Muhammad to our tent. In moments Ali and Umar burst in, ranting.

"We should have brought our swords!" Ali cried, sweating and striding in circles inside the tent. "I told you, cousin, that Quraysh would attack us. They have not yet learned the power of *islam* and they will not—not until we shame them the way we did at Badr."

"I do not want to kill our relations anymore," Muhammad said. "Al-Lah will grant us peace. Today He has shown me a vision of myself standing in Mecca with a shaved head and the keys to the Ka'ba in my hand. In my dream, my clothes were spotless. Mecca will be ours, and without a drop of blood spilled."

"Has the heat made you dizzy?" Umar said. "Khalid ibn al-Walid killed many of our men at Uhud. He is a ferocious fighter, very bloodthirsty. If he catches us, we will die!"

"Al-Lah willing, Khalid will not overtake us." My father stood in the doorway. "We have found a Bedouin who knows an alternate route. He promises we will not encounter a single Qurayshi on our way to Mecca."

Ali glared at my father as if he were an intruder. "But Khalid ibn al-Walid has spies, also," he said. "When he discovers our path, will he not follow us? *Yaa* Prophet, without arms to protect ourselves we are doomed."

"The alternate route is rugged and broken, covered in thorns," my father said. "Serpents hide among the rocks. Our guide says the Qurayshi will not follow us there."

"Weak merchants." Umar's laugh stabbed the air.

"We are accustomed to hardship, thanks to Quraysh," Muhammad said. "Such a path would be difficult, but not impossible."

"For the men, yes. But women are another matter," Umar said. "They are too frail to withstand a journey through that country."

"A'isha? Zaynab? Umm Salama? Will you speak to these doubts?" Muhammad said.

"I can do anything a man can do," I said. Muhammad grinned.

"And I can do anything A'isha can do," Zaynab added.

All waited for Umm Salama, who sat with her hands folded in her lap, her back as straight as if she were made of stone. As the daughter of a rich man, she probably worried about getting calluses on her hands. Then I chastised myself for such unkind thoughts. After all my visits to the tent city hadn't I learned compassion?

As if she could hear me thinking, Umm Salama lifted her gaze to meet mine.

"I have given birth to four children," she said. "Is there any man in

Hijaz who can make that claim? A few bumps in the road are nothing in comparison."

I wanted to laugh at the blush that spread across Umar's face. "By al-Lah, Prophet, if these were my wives they would not speak so audaciously."

Umm Salama nodded. "*Yaa* Umar, I am aware of your attitudes toward women," she said. "It is why I refused your offer of marriage."

◆

Our route carried us over sharp-toothed lava beds choked with thorny weeds. Our progress was slow and lurching, and several of our horses bruised their hooves or forelegs on the rocks. A serpent spooked Umm Salama's camel, and it fell to its knees, but she never made a sound. No one complained, male or female: A stubbed toe was a knife in the heart.

At last we reached al-Hudaybiyyah, the Sanctuary outside Mecca where we could camp in safety. As the men set up our tent, Muhammad led Umm Salama, Zaynab, and me to the overlook. There we feasted our eyes on Mecca, spread below like a cloth filled with jewels encircled by a necklace of black mountains. Although the terrain was dustier here than in Medina, the city was much bigger and brighter-looking. Colorful canopies dotted the bustling market and homes of stone gleamed white under the sun. Whitest of all sparkled the Ka'ba, flanked by the twin hills the men would run between as part of the worship ritual.

Ali rushed up, excitement sharpening his features. "With Khalid and his men out of the way, we can ride into Mecca unchallenged," he told Muhammad.

"I want to enter in peace, and I want to depart in peace," Muhammad said. "We have one thousand men. If we march in unannounced, the people of Mecca may think we are invading them. The Qurayshi may be merchants, but they are also Arabs. They will fight. No, we will need to send an emissary to Abu Sufyan to announce our arrival."

Ali followed us to our tent, gesturing and arguing, until my father interrupted with the news that Suhayl ibn Amr, a friend of Muhammad's from Mecca, approached on horseback with three men wearing chain mail.

"He says he wishes to speak with you alone."

Muhammad's smile illuminated his face "Suhayl, my *sahab*," he said. "This is a good development."

"But he still clings to the old ways." Umar scowled. "Are we now nego-
tiating with idol-worshippers?"

That evening, while Muhammad talked with his visitors, Zaynab and
Umm Salama sat in the tent and reminisced about Mecca, ignoring me. I
contented myself with my spindle, listening. In a low, sad voice Umm
Salama spoke about the last time she'd seen her father.

"When I and my husband Abdallah tried to leave for Medina, my
father forced me to stay behind. Abdallah's father took Salama from us,
claiming our son belonged to him. How I begged them to let us go! But
they would not listen to the pleas of a woman. So I went to the people of
Mecca."

Wearing the dark indigo robe of a mourner, she walked to the market,
sat on the ground, and wailed. She wept and tore her clothes and prayed
to al-Lah before the entire marketplace. When the sun began to set and
the market closed, Umm Salama walked back to her parents' house. The
next day she did the same, and the next—every day for a year.

"My father forbade me to go to the market, but I refused to listen, just
as he had refused to listen to me," she said. How the townspeople gos-
siped! They said her mind had flown away.

"Finally, when *abi* could no longer endure the shame, he brought my
camel and my son to me and ordered me to leave the city immediately. I
could not even say good-bye to my mother. I wonder if she will want to
see me again."

I stared at Umm Salama as she spoke, awed by her courage. On the sur-
face she seemed so compliant, so obedient. Yet hadn't she stood up for the
women who came to Muhammad, complaining about their husbands'
harsh treatment? Maybe she'd learned the same lessons I had—that for a
woman to have any power over her life, she had to seize it with both
hands.

After a while Umm Salama fell asleep, leaving me under the watchful
eye of Zaynab, who refused to slumber. I longed to slip out and spy on
Muhammad's talk with Suhayl—information that could make me useful
as his advisor. The minutes dragged on while Zaynab watched me squirm,
sending sly smiles to tell me she knew what I had in mind.

At last I mumbled that I needed to relieve myself and, donning my
wrapper, made my escape to Muhammad's tent.

Of course his Companions hadn't allowed him to meet Suhayl alone, without any protection. I wasn't surprised to see a crowd of men in his tent, but I was amazed to hear them shouting at Muhammad.

"*Yaa* Prophet, you cannot sign this!" Umar was yelling. He waved a sheepskin with writing on it. "This agreement is an insult to *islam*."

Ali nodded; Uthman and my father sat on the ground with their faces locked and their arms folded, saying nothing.

"To sign this agreement with Quraysh is *islam*, submission to al-Lah," Muhammad said quietly. "We must put our pride aside and do as He instructs."

"Does al-Lah allow Quraysh to strip away your position?" Ali said. "Why does the contract fail to name you as God's Messenger?"

"I do not know Muhammad as anyone's Messenger," Suhayl said. "To me, he is simply Muhammad, son of Abdallah ibn al-Muttalib. He is a man, not a god."

Ali rushed forward and pressed his dagger to Suhayl's throat. "Say that again, and you'll soon discover for yourself who is a god and who is not."

"Release him!" Muhammad sprang to his feet, his face darkening. The vein between his eyes throbbed; the tendons in his neck bulged. Ali yanked the dagger away from Suhayl's throat and pushed him to the ground.

"My apologies, Suhayl." Muhammad helped Suhayl to stand. "Ali's love for me overwhelms him."

"I have never seen a man so worshipped by his people," Suhayl said. "When a hair falls from your head, they vie to catch it. When you utter a sound, their talk ceases. Whom do they really worship, al-Lah or Muhammad?"

"As you said, Muhammad is a man. He is not God," my father said. "A man makes mistakes. Al-Lah does not."

"*Yaa* Prophet, you are making a very big error here, it seems," Uthman said. "Agreeing to halt our raids on Qurayshi caravans? The *umma* will starve."

"Al-Lah will provide for us," Muhammad said. "Losing the proceeds from our raids is a small price to pay in exchange for peace with our brothers."

"Abu Sufyan is no brother of mine," my father said. "Do you forget how he wanted to slaughter us all?"

How I wanted to cry out in my father's favor! Remembering the scene from my bedroom window that night, how Abu Sufyan had treated Raha so roughly. All these years later, his cruelty had only increased, along with his girth.

Curses and oaths careened through the crowd. Muhammad smiled at Suhayl, who was signing the sheepskin. Muhammad took the date-palm stem, dipped it in ink, and drew a crescent moon next to Suhayl's name. "That will suffice as my signature," he said. He turned to his Companions. "The pact is official. At dawn we will thank al-Lah with our sacrifices."

"Here or at the Ka'ba?" Ali said. He held his arms rigidly at his sides.

"At our camp, of course." Muhammad's voice was as calm as if he discussed the weather. "We have just agreed not to enter Mecca until next year."

My spirits sank. Not enter Mecca? After traveling all this way, eleven days of heat and dust and lurching camels? We'd all tended visions of the sacred Ka'ba as we'd journeyed, and yearned for repose in the bosom of our motherland. Now Muhammad was saying we had to leave. A cry of outrage rose in me, but I held it back. My task was to support him—but what if he was making a terrible mistake?

"I have agreed to nothing!" Ali shouted, and stalked away. I jumped back into the shadows moments before he passed. My heart pounded as I ran back to our tent. Inside, Zaynab combed her hair by candlelight.

"What a long time you spent relieving yourself," she said. "Just like the night you lost the caravan, hmm, A'isha?"

I was too upset to respond. I slumped in my bed and tried to sleep, but I could only toss about as I puzzled over what I'd seen and heard. Did Muhammad understand what he'd done? Suhayl had spoken truly: Ever since the Battle of the Trench, the people of the *umma* practically worshipped Muhammad. He possessed as much power as a king.

Any other man would be satisfied—but not Muhammad. "How can I rest knowing my own people are destined for Hell?" he would say. But I knew their salvation was only one of his concerns. He wouldn't be happy until he had the respect of Quraysh again.

Was their acceptance worth losing the *umma*? By signing this pact against the wishes of his Companions, Muhammad had taken a great risk. If his closest Companions protested it, how would the rest of the men respond? As for Abu Sufyan, I could imagine the smile on his face when he read the treaty. I'd heard how he'd been boasting since the trench disaster: *Not even the Prophet of al-Lah could amass an army of ten thousand.* The obvious retort was that one hundred thousand men were nothing when God was on your side, but alas, Muhammad wasn't the bragging sort.

Now, it seemed, he wasn't the fighting sort, either. But why? And this treaty included a promise to stop raiding Qurayshi caravans. Without the loot from those raids, how would we in the *umma* buy food and clothing? Those riches would fill Abu Sufyan's purse, instead—and buy Bedouin friends for his next attack on Medina.

In spite of my dislike for Umm Salama, I dreaded giving her the bad news the next morning. She awoke early full of excitement, which drained away like milk from a broken bowl when I told her we wouldn't be entering Mecca this year.

Zaynab smirked at me. "How do you know, A'isha? Did Gabriel visit you while you were relieving yourself?"

"What does it matter?" I snapped at her. "Muhammad has submitted to Quraysh, and for no good reason. Abu Sufyan wouldn't dare attack us now, not after the Battle of the Trench. He thinks we used magic to cause that terrible storm."

Umm Salama toppled her cup, spilling water onto the sand. "We cannot always understand the ways of al-Lah. We must believe in Muhammad."

She spoke the truth, I knew. Yet I also understood the anger of the men. From our tent door that morning we watched Muhammad call for the sacrificial ritual to begin—and watched every man in the camp turn his back on him. Muhammad cried out again, but they stood mute as if they heard only the wind.

His face darkened. His worried gaze flew around the camp and landed on me. His troubled eyes seemed to grope like the hands of a blind man as they locked with mine. The scuff of sand under his heavy steps sounded like ripping cloth. I pulled the tent flap aside, and we sister-wives made room for him to enter.

"I do not know what to do," Muhammad said when he was inside, his voice hoarse from shouting. "*Yaa* A'isha, my helpmate. I need your advice more than ever."

"The solution is obvious." I'd devised a strategy for him in the night, while I'd tossed and turned in my bed. "You have to renounce that pact and lead us into Mecca as you promised."

Muhammad's jaw dropped. "So you take their side against me?" He tore at his beard. "By al-Lah, has everyone abandoned me?"

I looked to Umm Salama for support. She'd been so disappointed by this agreement. But she moved to Muhammad's side and clasped his hands in hers.

"A leader does not renounce his pacts, A'isha," Zaynab said. I scowled at her, my face flooded with heat.

"Please, husband, allow me to speak," Umm Salama said. "I have advice that may serve you."

Muhammad nodded, and she continued. "The solution is simple. As Zaynab has said, a leader is one who leads. If you want your men to shave their heads, you must shave yours first. If you want them to make their sacrifices, you must sacrifice your own camel first."

"And if they do not follow?" Muhammad said.

"Pray," Umm Salama said. "Perform the ritual. Then, if you have pleased no one else, you will have pleased al-Lah. Is He not the reason we have come here?"

The wrinkles of worry in Muhammad's face smoothed as if caressed by a hand. "Your wisdom is my comfort," he said with a weary smile. "I will do as you say. As for the rest, I will trust al-Lah."

He stepped outside and pulled out his dagger. "*Labaykh al-Lahumah labaykh!*" he cried. He stretched his long curls out from his head with one hand, and sliced the hair from his scalp with his dagger. "God is great!" he called.

"This is ridiculous," I snapped. "Muhammad is going to look more foolish than ever. He has made a mistake, and he needs to admit it. The men want to go into Mecca. I thought you wanted it, too."

"I did want it," Umm Salama said. "But mostly I desire the best for Muhammad, always. That is the pact I signed when I married him."

I lowered my gaze, contrite. Umm Salama spoke truly: Unflinching support was a wife's duty to her husband. Again, I'd let my emotions control me.

My father looked over his shoulder and saw Muhammad's shorn head, his bright excited face, his arms thrust toward the sky gripping the dagger and his tufts of hair. "*Al-Lahu akbar!*" Muhammad cried. "God is great!" My father gave a shout and ran over to him, pulled out his dagger—I gasped—and sliced off his silver hair.

"God is great!" my father called.

In another instant Talha had joined them, and Uthman, and Umar. And, yes, Ali. Soon the entire camp roiled in a haircutting frenzy as everyone shouted and praised al-Lah. Tears slid in rivulets down Umm Salama's face, making her beauty shimmer. Zaynab watched proudly, her hands lifted as Muhammad stepped upon a large rock and led a prayer of thanks to al-Lah for His goodness and mercy. One thousand men fell to their knees around him and pressed their foreheads into the ground, facing Muhammad and Mecca. Meanwhile, I hid my face and cried, but mine were not tears of joy.

I had failed Muhammad, and I had failed al-Lah. *Think only, and cast aside your feelings.* When would I learn to apply this lesson not only to sword fighting, but to life? Until I learned to control myself I'd never be able to control my destiny.

LIARS AND SPIES

MEDINA, AUGUST 627 AND 628
FOURTEEN, THEN FIFTEEN YEARS OLD

*P*eace. It slipped through the *umma* like a cooling breeze. Filling our mouths, our chests, our bellies. Soothing our fears.

We Believers had faced attack for as long as I could remember: from Quraysh, from Ibn Ubayy and his Hypocrites, from the Mustaliq, from our Jewish neighbors, from an ever-changing mix of Bedouin tribes. We'd stood up to them all, vanquishing some enemies and making friends with others, except for Quraysh. Now, with this peace treaty, we'd struck an uneasy coexistence with them.

Once the furor had died over the pact, I had to admit it was a good idea. The *umma* needed time to heal its battle scars, to settle down and to strengthen. Our army took advantage of the lull to train and recruit new warriors. My life, on the other hand, was anything but peaceful.

Since our aborted pilgrimage to Mecca, Muhammad's demeanor toward me had cooled. He'd accepted my tearful apologies without a smile, making me realize I'd have to work hard to gain his trust yet again. At night I wept into my empty hands and prayed for al-Lah's guidance—and also for a son. Bearing Muhammad's heir would soften his heart toward me. It might also help me reclaim the status I'd lost in the *harim*.

Zaynab had assumed the role of *hatun* before we'd started back to Medina, giving orders to the camel-drivers and overseeing the packing of our tent. When I protested, she shot me a cold stare.

"You've betrayed Muhammad—twice," she said. "That disqualifies you from leading his *harim*." Umm Salama stood beside her, regal and long-necked, lifting her eyebrows at me. Rage crashed through me, and I would have hurled myself atop them both, fists flailing, but a quiet voice that could only have been al-Lah's whispered in my mind's ear. *Think only, and cast aside your feelings.*

"Instead of standing there with your mouth open, why don't you make yourself useful?" Zaynab said. "Roll up our bedding, and carry it to the car-avan for loading."

My very bones tensed, but I could see that I had no choice. Zaynab spoke the truth: I had betrayed Muhammad, and didn't deserve to be his Great Lady. Shame filled the pit of my stomach as I rolled up our beds—a job for servants—and then, holding my wrapper over my burning face, walked to my *hawdaj*. There I hid for what seemed like hours, crying over my wrong-headed advice to Muhammad and the loss of my status that would result. When I'd exhausted my tears, the swaying of my camel jolt-ed me to my senses. Was I going to let one mistake make a servant of me? Zaynab might have the upper hand now, but that wouldn't last. Somehow I would prove myself worthy of my sister-wives' trust as well as Muhammad's. Unlike Zaynab, I wouldn't have to seize the *hatun* position. My sister-wives would give it to me. Then no one, not even Zaynab, would be able to take it away again.

One year later I was hauling water from the well for Zaynab's hair, curs-ing. By telling everyone about my disloyalty to Muhammad, Zaynab had coaxed Raihana and even Sawdah to support her as *hatun*. And I? I wasn't even the parrot. I was at the bottom of the heap, running to the market when she ran out of *kohl* and having to apologize if I didn't return quickly enough; serving her the bread I'd baked and hearing her criticize it; wash-ing her clothing; emptying her chamber pot. My only relief came during her afternoon naps when, shaking off my own need for sleep, I'd sling a bag of barley or dates over Scimitar's back and ride off to the tent city.

By nightfall, I was exhausted—too tired to give much pleasure to Muhammad, but not daring to complain to him about my plight. The one time I'd mentioned Zaynab's tyranny, he'd told me he was too occupied with his own affairs to concern himself with *harim* squabbles.

"If you want to be a leader, A'isha, you must learn to master those who would master you," he said.

In truth, Muhammad did have more pressing worries. Our peace treaty with Quraysh included their allies, but not everyone respected it. Incensed by our killing of his Qurayzah cousins, Huyayy, the leader of the Nadr, had boasted of plans to "cleanse the excrement of *islam* from Medina." Something had to be done, or Muhammad would lose the respect of the other desert tribes.

Muhammad's face looked haggard, and his eyes held no spark as he led his army out of Medina to confront the Nadr. He was tired of fighting. We were all tired. Worry dragged the corners of my mouth down as I watched the caravan march away. How could he defeat anyone when he looked so defeated?

Tension spread through the *umma*, straining the already-tight *harim* almost to breaking. Raihana's snide comments, once so amusing, became as irritating as sand in a bed. Zaynab had missed a monthly bleeding, and made a point of measuring her waist with a rope every day, making me want to strangle her with it. In a few weeks, to my relief, her blood flow returned. Fatima's crooning over her baby, and her pride in her own thickening stomach, carrying another child, grated on everyone's nerves until, one day, Hafsa hurled a dish at the wall behind her head.

"Get out!" she shouted. "Can't you see you're crowding us with your baby and your expanding belly and your smug fertility? Go home and gloat to your doting husband!"

Something had to change. While Sawdah rushed over to beg Fatima not to leave and Zaynab berated Hafsa for being rude to the Prophet's daughter, I thought again about the dangers of idle time. Boredom, not babies, was the reason for our bickering. Yes, I had my trips to the tent city and Zaynab to serve, and Umm Salama had four children to care for, but Hafsa, Juwairriyah, Zaynab, and Raihana had little to do. The only one among them who kept busy—and who never complained—was Sawdah, who filled her hours tooling leather and making items to sell at the market.

I had an idea that would solve the problem—and, perhaps, enhance me as a leader in my sister-wives' eyes. But I would need to present it at the right time, in the right way. Otherwise, Zaynab and her clan would reject it.

When I walked into the cooking tent and saw Umm Salama displaying a threadbare garment—"Behold, my only gown!"—I saw my chance. But for my plan to succeed, I'd have to make my sister-wives think it was their idea.

"How can Muhammad walk with pride through Medina when his wives wear rags?" Zaynab said.

"Being impoverished doesn't mean having no pride," I said. "Many of the tent people are very proud."

"Yes, but they did not choose their poverty," Umm Salama said. "Our husband forces ours upon us."

"Sawdah doesn't wear rags," I said.

"And why not, I wonder?" Zaynab gave a snort at my stupidity. "She has a trade, while we have none."

"How sad," I said with a sigh. "A *harim* full of women, and only Sawdah has a skill."

Hafsa gave me a puzzled frown. "*Yaa* A'isha, you know I'm a henna artist."

"The best in Medina," I said. "But would someone pay for that?"

"I don't see why not," she said. "Many brides hire artists to adorn their hands and feet for their wedding night."

"They have hair stylists, too, but I could do a better job," Juwairriyah said.

"And the makeup! By al-Lah, it's a wonder their husbands don't faint with fright when they remove their veils," Zaynab scoffed "I, on the other hand, could transform a camel into a vision of beauty. Isn't that a skill worth paying for?"

It was like leading sheep to the shearing pen. In moments my sister-wives had hatched my plan: They would hire themselves out as tire women to prepare brides for their wedding ceremonies. Umm Salama would make lace for their veils, and Raihana would embroider their gowns. I even agreed to make cloth with my spindle and loom, thinking to earn a few *dirhams* for the tent-dwellers. Aside from hunger, I had few problems that money could solve. And with drought still sucking the life from Medina's date-palms and grasslands and drying up our springs, there was little food to buy.

"I already know who our first customer will be," Hafsa said to me later, as we cleaned the dishes from the evening meal. "I heard Umm Ayman say today that Muhammad is going to marry again. You'll never guess who. The daughter of that traitor Huyayy!"

"Don't believe everything that old gossip says," I told Hafsa with a laugh. "Muhammad went to Khaybar to teach Huyayy a lesson, not make him an ally by marrying his daughter."

But I was wrong. When Muhammad arrived in Medina, he not only brought Saffiya bint Huyayy with him, he was already married to her.

Breaking every tradition, he'd unwrapped his pert-chinned, slant-eyed gift the night he'd acquired her—and, according to rumor, every night since. Watching them together, I could easily see why Muhammad lusted for her: As they rode into Medina on one camel, she stroked his arms winding around her wisp of a waist. Her eyes laughed even when her lips didn't, and when Muhammad helped her down from the saddle she winked at him.

"She's only a child," Hafsa said as we sister-wives watched the caravan's return.

"She's not much older than you, A'isha," Zaynab said. "Now you'll have someone your own age to play with."

"I'm not impressed," I said to Hafsa, ignoring Zaynab and Raihana's snickers. "This new wife is not the kind of woman to hold a man's interest for long."

"She certainly holds the Prophet's interest now," Juwairriyah said. "He did not look at me like that on our wedding day."

"He has never looked at anyone like that," Zaynab said. "Except me."

"As I said," I retorted, "she won't hold his interest for long."

Secretly, though, I seethed to see this new wife's dainty hand in Muhammad's large one and her flirtatious gazes commanding his attention. But I shook off my jealousy, knowing this marriage would force the Nadr and their relatives, the Kaynuqah, to fight on our side in the future. Besides, being nearly my age, as Zaynab had said, she might be an ally for me. Then, when Muhammad brought her into the courtyard to meet us, I noticed a fading yellow bruise under her right eye, and my heart softened toward her.

Or it did until Raihana, her cousin, asked her how she'd acquired it. "Was that the work of Muhammad's holy henchmen?" she quipped, arching an eyebrow.

Saffiya giggled and blushed ever so delicately. "Oh, no," she said in a voice that warbled like a songbird's. "My husband gave it to me." She glanced up at Muhammad and giggled again. "Not you, honey hive, my other husband."

Muhammad traced the bruise lightly with a finger. She gazed into his eyes so knowingly, I felt my face burn.

"Before you came to me, Prophet, I dreamt that I would be yours. In my dream, the moon lowered itself down from Medina to make love to me. When I awoke, I told my husband Kinana about it, and he struck me with his fist." Her voice wobbled as if she were drunk. "He said, 'Whore! You want to marry that Muslim prophet?' I didn't know what he meant. I didn't understand the dream." She smiled at Muhammad through limpid eyes. "Now I do."

"By al-Lah, what a show," Zaynab said in the courtyard, when they had gone to "rest," in Muhammad's words.

"What a performance, you mean," Raihana said. "Saffiya bint Huyayy is a born manipulator."

"Did she call him 'honey hive'?" Hafsa said.

I thought again of how this new wife might help me. "I thought she seemed nice," I said feebly—drawing a gasp from Hafsa, who stared at me as if I'd grown another head.

Sawdah approached then, wiping her forehead with her sleeve. A tall, masculine woman with large hips and prominent cheekbones—where had I seen that face before?—walked regally behind her.

"Where is the Prophet? Is he here yet?" Sawdah said.

"He went to bed with his new child-bride." Zaynab smirked at me. She and the rest of the sister-wives strolled to the cooking tent, leaving me and Hafsa in the courtyard with Sawdah and the stranger.

"A new bride? By al-Lah, what a mess!" Sawdah came over to us, wringing her hands. She glanced nervously at her charge, who'd seated herself under the date-palm tree. "This is awful," she said in a low voice.

"If I disturb the Prophet, he will get mad, but if I do not disturb him, then *she* will get mad."

"Who? That man in woman's clothing over there?" Hafsa whispered.

"Who is she, Sawdah? Not another wife, I hope." I was joking, but the worry on Sawdah's face told me this was no occasion for humor.

She gestured for me and Hafsa to step closer. "She says her name is Umm Habiba bint Abu Sufyan."

Drawing in my breath, I scrutinized the woman, who stared stonily back at me. The daughter of Abu Sufyan and that shrewish Hind? What was she doing here?

Sawdah lowered her voice further: "She says she is the Prophet's wife."

Alarms clanged in my head like a thousand jarring bells. What trickery was this? I couldn't imagine what Abu Sufyan was scheming, but I knew it was nothing good.

"By al-Lah, does Abu Sufyan think Muhammad is a fool?" I said loudly, drawing Umm Habiba's disdainful gaze. "*Yaa* Umm Habiba, tell your father his latest plot against the Prophet of God is his most pathetic one yet."

Muhammad's voice rang from above. "It is no plot, A'isha." He smiled down at our visitor from his apartment over the mosque, then climbed down the date-palm tree growing beside it. On the ground, he extended his hands toward Umm Habiba, who returned his gaze boldly.

"*Ahlan wa sahlan*, Ramlah," he said, using her given name. "I did not expect your arrival until a month from now."

"I was so eager to leave Abyssinia, I rode ahead of the caravan." Her voice sounded as shrill as her mother's, but Muhammad didn't seem to notice. He bestowed her with the heavy-lidded love looks I now realized wouldn't last. Each new wife enthralled Muhammad at first, but when the newness wore off, he'd turn his attention back to me. Or so I hoped.

I counted the number of nights until he would lie with me again. With nine of us in the *harim*, would I now have to wait eight nights between visits to my room?

"Excuse me, Muhammad, but how can this marriage be?" Hafsa asked. "Have you traveled on a magic carpet while the rest of us slept?"

"The king of Abyssinia has married us by proxy," Muhammad said. "With my permission." He turned to Sawdah to discuss sleeping arrangements for his new wife, and Hafsa and I began walking to our huts.

"Why would Muhammad marry the daughter of his most dangerous enemy?" I said. Hafsa shook her head, as mystified as I.

My old suspicions began to nag me again. After the trench disaster, Abu Sufyan's Bedouin allies had deserted him for Muhammad. Meccans were flocking to Medina to convert to *islam*. Muhammad could have crushed Abu Sufyan if he'd so desired. But he'd signed a peace treaty, instead, giving our enemy time to build new alliances. Now that our raids on his caravans had stopped, Abu Sufyan would be able to collect more wealth. Soon he'd be able to buy the allies he needed to mount another attack on the *umma*.

Positioning his daughter inside Muhammad's *harim* was a brilliant ploy.

"By al-Lah, this marriage is no coincidence," I said as Hafsa opened the door of her hut.

"I hope you're wrong," she said, "but I fear you speak the truth. If Umm Habiba is a spy, al-Lah help us."

"Don't worry," I said. "I'm going to watch her more closely than Ali watches me. If she's a spy, we'll find out before even al-Lah knows it."

THE BLACKAMOOR'S BLADE

MEDINA, APRIL 629
SIXTEEN YEARS OLD

For many months I kept my eye on Umm Habiba, convinced her marriage to Muhammad was no coincidence. She was a spy for her father, I was certain. Abu Sufyan would stop at nothing to destroy Muhammad, peace treaty or not, because he needed false gods to bring worshippers and their loot to Mecca. He'd sent his daughter here to help him, and I'd be the one to expose her.

Yet I didn't have much time for spying, not with Zaynab's demands filling most of my days. I waited on her like a slave, scrubbing her clothes with soap and resentment, keeping my head down when she scolded me for invisible stains on a flawlessly cleaned garment. Even as hatred throbbed in my skull I said as little as possible to her, reminding myself to *think, not feel*, and waiting for my chance to send her toppling from her throne.

Then one day, an even more worrisome threat arrived from a most unexpected place: Egypt.

Bilal's shout pulled the entire city outdoors to gawk at the caravan marching through our gate. We sister-wives stood at the mosque, our faces covered and our senses resonating at the sights, sounds, and smells: tin-kling bells like shy giggles from the camels' ankles; the sultry rattle of tam-bourines; women whose blue-black hair swung like the fringe on a Persian carpet; men in pleated skirts with braided hair and pointed beards, hoist-ing on their shoulders an enormous ebony box.

I and Hafsa laughed at the men's made-up faces, but my humor soured when two women rode past on camels, their bodies barely covered by their tightly fitted bodices and transparent skirts. How immodestly they dressed, like slaves for sale at the *suq*! These must be the courtesans the Egyptian ruler had promised to Muhammad months ago.

"I thought Saffiya had no shame, but she's a virgin compared to these two," Hafsa said. "They seem to enjoy the eyes of our men on their bodies."

"They're used to being ogled," I said. "They're concubines in the palace at Alexandria."

"Very loose morals." Saffiya pushed her way into our conversation. "See the women shake those tambourines? They shake other things, too, to entertain the men at court."

The caravan halted. A man stepped forward and bowed to Muhammad. He wore no shirt or robe over his fair skin, only a wide ham-mered gold necklace and a fur sash. A gold belt encircled his waist over a white skirt that fell almost to his ankles. A gold band gripped his upper arm, and gold rings pierced his ears. Strangest of all, *kohl* lined the rims of his eyes and painted the corners nearly to his temples. Hafsa and Saffiya giggled, but I *shushed* them when he began to open his parchment scroll and read.

"In honor of your military victories and religious influence, the Muqawqis of Egypt, our governor, sends his homage and his praise, as well as gifts. Please accept this box filled with myrrh, frankincense, cardamom, cinnamon, and perfumes of crocus and lily." The men lifted the lid and fragrances swirled like dreams about our heads, drawing murmurs from the crowd.

The messenger continued reciting his list of gifts: a mule and a saddle, ceremonial clothing of gold cloth, precious jewels, and two entertainers from the Muqawqis' court.

The camels bearing the women knelt, and the men helped them dis-mount. The messenger stepped up to one of them, a dark-haired beauty with blood-red lips and copper-green shading on her eyelids, and escorted her to Muhammad.

"Prophet, I present Sirin, favored courtesan to the Muqawqis, and his most excellent dancer." She lowered herself to the ground, not quite touching the dirt with one knee. I half-expected her to lose her balance and sprawl in the street. Instead, Muhammad was the one who nearly fell over, as her ample bosom threatened to spill over her low-cut bodice. The back of Muhammad's neck flushed a deep purple.

"He won't keep her," I said to Hafsa. "She's too brazen."

When the messenger presented the second courtesan, though, I felt my throat constrict. This woman's hair was as golden as the sun, and tumbled in curls about her face and shoulders. Her eyes were a deep, fathomless blue, like no eyes I had ever seen.

"Maryam, Sirin's younger sister and the court's most gifted singer," the messenger said. Shyly she lifted her gaze to Muhammad's face. Her cheeks dimpled when she smiled, and when she greeted him, her voice sounded like falling water.

Hafsa *hmphed*. "Foreign and exotic, eyes the color of sky, hips and belly as round as pillows, and a voice like a nightingale's. How are we to compare with her?"

"Muhammad would not marry a courtesan," Umm Salama said—but even her normally calm voice had unraveled. "I heard him promise one of these women to Hassan ibn Thabit."

"Are you suffering from sunstroke?" Raihana laughed. "Muhammad is not going to give her away."

In truth, we were the ones Muhammad abandoned. His evening visits to my room grew more hurried and distracted than ever, and, judging from the sullenness tingeing my sister-wives' eyes, I knew their nights with him weren't going well, either. Umm Salama hardly spoke even to her children after her night with him. Zaynab did nothing but complain and criticize: My bread was too crusty, she hadn't had a new gown in a year, the cushions in the oven tent were as hard as stones. After Hafsa's night, Raihana made her usual snide remarks, and Hafsa threw a bowl at her head.

Meanwhile, the Christian concubine Maryam moved as blithely as a golden cloud through our stormy *harim*, singing as she prepared her *tharid* for Muhammad, which he praised as though it had come directly from Paradise.

Muhammad would have married her, but she refused. She said she didn't want to give up her Christian religion, but I knew she enjoyed the freedom of moving through Medina unveiled. None of ibn Ubayy's men pinched her or made lewd comments the way they'd done to us. Muhammad's new power had everyone intimidated, even the Hypocrites.

"I don't understand it," Hafsa fumed as she drank galangal water with me and Saffiya in my apartment. "That woman has Muhammad transfixed. Is she a sorceress?"

Whatever she possessed, it was far more potent than magic. Spells and charms fade, but her hold on Muhammad grew stronger. Then one night he failed to visit my room, leaving me hugging myself with cold arms and begging al-Lah to plant a seed in me Himself, as he'd done for Jesus' mother.

Jealousy clawed at me with sharp talons. I resisted, reminding myself that to gain Egypt's friendship was an impressive coup. Quraysh would never invade us now, knowing that such a powerful country had pledged its aid. Yet did Muhammad have to spend all his time enjoying his gift?

A knock on my door interrupted my thoughts. Barirah brought word that Muhammad was meeting in the *majlis*. "He does not know when he will come to bed. He tells you not to wait up."

Relief calmed my indignant heart. It wasn't Maryam who kept Muhammad from me tonight, after all. I slipped on my robe and slid into the night, curiosity tugging me like an insistent hand. Hiding outside the *majlis* entrance, I heard my father's agitated voice.

"Twenty Ghatafani men were herding their sheep near Mecca when they were attacked by a group of Qurayshi allies. Bedouins," my father said. "Some Qurayshi were involved, so we assume Abu Sufyan gave his approval for the raid."

The peace treaty, broken! My heart sank. This would certainly mean another war with Quraysh.

As if to confirm my fears, Ali spoke. "Let us amass the biggest army we can muster and march on Mecca," he growled. "Treaties are nothing but words. Force is the only language Abu Sufyan understands."

I slinked out of the mosque when their talk had dwindled, and almost bumped into a grinning Saffiya. "I have news about Maryam," she said. "News you'll find very fascinating."

"Maryam?" She had my attention now. "What news?"

"Take me to your room, and I'll tell you everything," she said. "But first, you have to tell me what you heard in the *majlis*."

In my apartment, she shrugged to hear the talk of a Meccan invasion. And why should she care? A Jew, she had no ties to that city. Her secret, on the other hand, interested me greatly.

"Poor Maryam couldn't bear our teasing for another day," she said with a wink. "Muhammad has given her a house to live in outside the city."

"Praise al-Lah," I said. "Maybe now Muhammad will forget her."

"She wouldn't suffer much if he did," Saffiya said. She lowered her voice as though the walls had ears. "I watched the men move her belongings into her new home today. When they left, a black-skinned man knocked on her door—and she let him in."

"You are jesting," I said.

Saffiya shook her head, smiling. "I waited to see how long he would stay. He never came out. As far as I know he's in there now, doing who-knows-what with her."

I gasped. This news, if true, was a terrible threat to Muhammad. His following was growing, but his status as a powerful leader was still new. A scandal could harm him beyond repair. If Maryam was entertaining another man, Muhammad needed to know.

The next evening I slipped through Medina with my wrapper pulled close and walked to the sheep pastures on the edge of town. With my pulse clipping my throat, I climbed into a tree on a rise overlooking Maryam's house, a mud-brick house shaded with ghaza'a and acacia and pomegranate trees, and a yard of blooming lavender. After a short while, the door opened, and she and Muhammad stood in the doorway. I watched with burning eyes as Muhammad pulled her close for a passionate kiss. The tangle of her hair and the smudge of her lips made it clear how they'd spent the afternoon. He gave her a last, lingering gaze, then mounted his camel and rode toward town, his face as dreamy as a sleep-walker's.

My face burned with resentment. No wonder Muhammad had no energy for his wives! A man of fifty-nine had only so much to give, and he was bestowing it all on his concubine. As I dwelled on these thoughts, a large figure as dark as a shadow emerged from behind the house and approached Maryam's door. She was already smiling when she opened it to him. Another moment, and he was inside.

In my apartment that night, I felt as though I might burst with the thrill of my discovery. But Muhammad's scowl held my tongue for the time being.

"I am not pleased with the way you all have treated Maryam," he said. "You have driven her out of the mosque with your jealousy."

I snorted. "By al-Lah, when you hear my tale, you'll wish we'd driven her all the way back to Egypt." I told him what I'd seen, but he shook his head, glowering, and called for Ali.

"A'isha says a man is keeping company with Maryam," Muhammad said as I hid behind my screen. "Hurry to her house and find out if this rumor is true. Be discreet. We do not want to frighten her visitor away before we learn the facts, nor do we want to insult Maryam if the tale proves false."

"A big black man?" Ali's tone was mocking. "Your imagination knows no bounds, A'isha." I felt my face flame as he strutted out.

Muhammad was still frowning as he closed the door. "Yaa A'isha, why would you spy on Maryam? Why do you mistreat her?"

I stiffened. "I'd heard a nasty rumor about her and a blackamoor. I knew you wouldn't want another scandal. What would all these kings and princes say about a leader who can't control his own harim?"

"Is Maryam the one I cannot control?" He peered at me as though my face were a cryptic scroll. "I have asked you many times to set aside your jealousy, but you continue to challenge each new woman I bring into the harim."

"I've been very gracious to share you with so many women." I glared at him through my tears. "Especially since my chances of conceiving a child grow smaller with each new addition."

He slapped his fist against his open palm. His eyes snapped. "Maryam has been tormented by all of you since the day she arrived. Your tauntings have driven her out of the harim, so that now she has to live in isolation. Why do you do this, A'isha? Do you not believe me when I say I love you best?"

"You have all my affection," I said. "Why do I have to share yours with nine other women?"

"We have been through this many times. Maryam is a gift from the most powerful man in Egypt. He honors me—me!" His eyes shone. "The king of Yemen is sending me the most beautiful woman in his country to marry, the daughter of one of his important ministers. What should I reply to him? 'No, thank you. A'isha does not like to share.' What impression would that make on the Byzantine emperor?"

"So, you have your eye on Byzantium now," I said. "They're Christians, aren't they? Do you think they're going to cast aside their churches and statues and their prophet who rose from the dead?" His expression told me that was exactly what he hoped.

I wiped the water from my eyes. "Where is the Muhammad I used to know? Turning hearts to al-Lah was his only desire. Now your nights are filled with flesh and perfume, and you dream of ruling the world."

"Turning hearts to God is still my desire!" he cried. "Every marriage I make, every concubine I accept, is for the good of the *umma*, for protection against our enemies. And my strategy is working. We have new converts every day, more souls saved from Hell fire. Egypt, Byzantium, Persia, Yemen: Someday soon all these nations will bow to al-Lah. It is for Him that I strive, and for the *umma*. If I thought only of myself, I could have lived on Khadijah's fortune until the end of my days."

"But that wouldn't have been nearly as thrilling as sitting with the world at your feet," I shot back. "And marrying only four wives, as you've allowed everyone else, wouldn't be nearly as pleasurable as having ten in your *harim*."

"Pleasurable? Trying to please ten jealous women? Do I look like I am enjoying myself?"

A rap on the door interrupted us. I moved behind my screen, and Ali stepped into the room with a grin splitting his face.

"Your smile tells me all I need to know," Muhammad said, shooting me a dark look. "Obviously, the rumors are untrue."

"No, they're true enough," Ali said. "Someone has been visiting Maryam, just as A'isha reported." Satisfaction filled my throat with a chuckle—that died when Muhammad slumped onto a cushion, his eyes staring bleakly at the floor.

"*Yaa* Ali, why do you laugh?" he said, his voice as stiff as a corpse. "Do you mock me?"

"No, cousin. When you hear my tale, though, you will laugh, also." He sat across from Muhammad and clapped a hand to his shoulder. "Your concubine has a visitor, and it isn't a woman. But neither is it a man."

His eyes brightened as he told of peering carefully into Maryam's window, as Muhammad had directed. Inside—behold! A large black man combed her hair and sang with her.

"You should have heard them, Prophet. His voice was as sweet as any woman's, and it mingled with hers as if they were two lovebirds singing a duet. She leaned into his arm and closed her eyes in ecstasy while they trilled away."

Muhammad's face grew darker with every word. I grew teary-eyed, sorry for causing him this pain, but also relieved to think that she would soon be gone and Muhammad would be free from scandal.

"Did you arrest him?" Muhammad said through gritted teeth. "By al-Lah, I will have his head this night."

"I did. I burst into the house with my sword lifted." Ali leapt to his feet and whipped out his sword with a *zing*. "I seized him by the throat, since he had no beard. You should have seen him cry!

"'Save your tears for Judgment Day,' I told him. 'Al-Lah will not be generous with one who has stolen what belongs to the Prophet.'"

"You spoke truly, Ali," Muhammad growled.

"Maryam was weeping, also. She told me he was her servant, but I said I did not want to hear her lies. Then the man spoke in his own tongue and pointed to his crotch."

I sighed deeply and slumped to the floor, guessing how Ali's tale would end. Muhammad wouldn't send Maryam away, but he would be annoyed with me for spying on her. Once again, by trying to help him I had hurt myself. When would I learn to watch and wait instead of leaping to conclusions?

"Then," Ali continued, "the black man fumbled with his waist string and dropped his skirt. I was infuriated! 'I'll cut off your testicles for that insult,' I said. But he bent over and pointed to his backside—and, by al-Lah! I saw that someone had already done the deed."

Ali began to laugh so hard he almost dropped his sword. "*Yaa* cousin, you have nothing to worry about. Your concubine's sheath is safe from the eunuch's blade."

25

AN HEIR FOR THE PROPHET

*M*uhammad had accused me of jealousy toward Maryam, and, yes, I envied her blue-and-gold allure. More distressing, though, was his lack of desire for me after she'd arrived. To conceive his child I needed more than fond kisses and weary smiles.

With so many women, Muhammad should have sired enough heirs to form his own personal army. Sawdah was long past the childbearing age, but the rest of us made a tree full of ripe fruit waiting to be picked. In the *harim* we eyed one another's bodies jealously, knowing that she who bore the Prophet an heir would enjoy a special place in Hijaz. And when Muhammad left for Paradise, his son would hold the *umma* in his hands, to guide and rule as his father had done, and his mother would live as a queen in this life and the next.

Stoked by competition, cruelties flared hotter than the cooking fire.

"I awoke this morning feeling lightheaded," Saffiya announced, slanting her eyes. Laughter squawked, vulture-like, from Zaynab's corner.

"That is no sign of pregnancy," Raihana retorted. "You truly *are* light in the head."

I, on the other hand, kept my symptoms to myself until I could be sure. Missing my monthly bleeding was hardly proof of pregnancy. My blood flow had ceased before, caused by hunger, Sawdah said. Yet after weeks of nausea and my second missed period, I began to nurture secret hopes.

Competitiveness aside, the *harim* was a busier, and happier, place these days as my sister-wives sewed, spun, tatted, embroidered, crushed flowers for dye, tried new lip colors and blended fragrances in anticipation of their first paying work as tire women. Sawdah had told Umm Ayman about the enterprise, and in only a few days the wife of the wealthy landowner Harun ibn Malik had hired them for her daughter's wedding at a good price.

While my sister-wives worked and chattered about how they'd spend their earnings, I slipped off to Sawdah's hut. When she opened her door to me, she gasped in delight.

"You waited long enough to come, by al-Lah!" she said. "Have our prayers been answered?"

She laid me on her bed and pressed her hands against my belly as if feeling a melon for ripeness.

"Mmm-hmm," she said. "Just what I thought."

She pulled my legs apart and peered between them as if she could see into my womb. "Yes," she said. "Yes."

She hefted my breasts.

"Filling up. A good sign."

Then she examined my tongue, gazed into my eyes, and made the pronouncement I had not even dared speak in the mirror: I was pregnant with Muhammad's child.

My heart seemed to take wing, lifting me in great, excited leaps. At last, a baby of my own to love, to play with, to sing to, to hold and cherish and to give me grandchildren in my old age! I skipped around the room like a joyous child. At last I'd escape my servitude to Zaynab! Bearing Muhammad's heir would place me in charge of the *harim*, out of her control forever. I threw my arms around Sawdah's neck and embraced her.

"Praise al-Lah, He has saved the best for the youngest," she gushed, grinning hugely, when I finally let her go. Then, fingering her Evil-Eye amulet, she added, "May His will be done."

I kissed her again, then ran across the courtyard to Hafsa's hut.

"You're not going to believe this!" I cried when she opened her door—
but the wild gleam in her eyes and the flush in her cheeks stopped my bur-
ble of excitement like a hand clamped over my mouth.

"Have you come with a strange tale, A'isha? Ha, ha! I have tales of my
own. Alas, they're too sordid to repeat."

She turned and disappeared into her hut. I followed and shut the door
behind me. Her apartment was like mine, except darker—Hafsa hated the
heat—and the walls and windowsills were bare. I smelled dust and a trace
of musk—Maryam's scent. As my eyes adjusted to the dim light, I noticed
bits of broken clay clinging to her walls and, on the floor, shards of pots
and bowls.

"What happened?" I pointed to the piles of broken clay. Hafsa glared.
"Yaa Hafsa, is there a body hidden somewhere?"

"By al-Lah, I wish there were two!" A tear trickled down her cheek, but
she wiped it away. "Yaa A'isha, Muhammad has ordered me not to tell a
soul, but I must talk to someone. Why should I keep his tawdry secrets?
Let him divorce me. I don't care! Then at least I wouldn't have to share
my bedroom with that Egyptian harlot."

Then she told me: She'd spent the afternoon with a throbbing
headache at her mother's house, sipping sherbet and being fanned by
servants.

"You know I can't bear these stifling summer days," she said. "But I had
no idea how hot it was in this apartment."

When she returned to the mosque, her face and hair damp with sweat,
she headed to her hut for a nap.

"When I opened the door, I found Muhammad and Maryam lying on
my bed, kissing and embracing."

I gasped. "You walked in on them together?" Heat rushed through me
as I tried to imagine the scene. "What did they do?"

"They didn't even know I was here until I smashed a bowl into the wall
over their heads. That got their attention, ha, ha!" Her laughing mouth
was a gash of pain. "I threw another, and Maryam clutched her clothes to
her breast and ran out the door. Muhammad begged me to calm down
before I brought the entire umma running. That's all he cared about,
A'isha: his reputation! His desire to be king of Hijaz has made him forget
his compassion and his good sense."

A knock sounded at her door. "This hut has seen more visitors in one day than I've received all year," Hafsa grumbled as she yanked it open. Muhammad stood in her doorway, his smile tentative.

"I have come to ask how you are feeling, Hafsa."

"Why? Are you afraid I'll tell my sister-wives how I found you making love to your concubine in my bedroom?"

"We were not making love. We were only embracing. May I come inside?"

So—Hafsa *had* caught Muhammad in her room with Maryam! This was the worst kind of insult. My temper spiked with hers.

"That was quite an embrace," Hafsa snapped. "So intense, you had to lie down. Or is that how the Egyptians do it?"

"Maryam was feeling faint. That is why I brought her into your hut. I did not think you would mind."

"What was she doing here? Doesn't she have an entire house to herself?"

"Hafsa, I do not wish to have this conversation in the courtyard. May I please come inside?"

"Fulfill your desires," Hafsa said. "As you always do."

I greeted him with a glare, not bothering to hide my anger.

"I have come to speak with Hafsa in private," Muhammad said to me. "Leave us, please."

"Leave? Why? I already know everything. Except your excuse, of course."

The vein between his eyes throbbed. "Did I not ask you to keep our conflict between us, Hafsa?"

"You had company in the committing of your deed," she said. "Why should I suffer for it alone?"

Muhammad's countenance darkened. "We did nothing! But you have betrayed my confidence. How can I live with a wife I cannot trust?"

"Did you ask this question before you married Abu Sufyan's daughter?" I said.

"Keep out of this, A'isha. Did I not ask you to leave us?"

"Please remain." Hafsa arched an eyebrow and looked down her long nose at Muhammad. "I would like a witness."

"I was only kissing Maryam." Muhammad's tone was flat. "We were celebrating her good news."

"Maryam's going back to Egypt?" I said.

"She is not going anywhere," Muhammad said. "She is bearing my child."

I willed my fluttering pulse to calm down. Maryam, pregnant also? Just as Muhammad's desire for me had been diluted by her, so, now, would his excitement at my news. Yet—my own joy would not be affected. A child was the one thing Maryam could not take away from me.

Hafsa cawed like a crow. Muhammad smiled at me as though his mouth were filled with sweet cream. He wanted a son more than anything.

"Congratulations, husband," I said. "This is a special day for you. In truth, I'd say it's doubly special. Because I discovered today that I'm pregnant, also."

His smile disappeared. The vein on his forehead bulged. "By al-Lah, I never imagined such audacity, even from you," he said. "Are you so desperate for my attention that you must fabricate tales?"

I reeled at the insult, but only for an instant. Within me beat the heart of my child, quickening my courage and my tongue.

"I follow your example, Prophet," I said. "You have become quite adept at the art of fabrication."

"When have I lied to you?"

"Not five minutes ago, you said you were only giving Maryam a kiss when Hafsa walked in. Yet, according to Hafsa, Maryam grabbed her clothes as she ran from the hut."

"She was feeling faint," Muhammad said. "She had removed her robe."

"Also, you say you treat all your wives equally. Yet when have you done so? Your true wives wait for affection that rarely comes, while you sow your seed in a woman who refuses to marry you."

"Enough!" Muhammad yelled. "You have said too much, as usual, A'isha."

"Then I will speak," Hafsa said. "We are tired of broken promises and empty beds."

Muhammad glared at her. "Accustom yourself to an empty bed, Hafsa," he said. "Since you have broken my confidence by telling A'isha what I asked you not to, I will respond by breaking my marriage contract with you. When I have spoken with Umar, you may take your belongings and rejoin your father in his home."

Hafsa's face turned so pale, I rushed over to catch her in case she should faint. "How could you speak of divorce when you've forbidden your wives to remarry?" I said, glaring at him.

"Al-Lah made that prohibition, not I." His eyes held only darkness. "And the revelation spoke of my widows, not wives divorced from me. Any wife I release would be free to marry again."

Bilal's call from the roof of the mosque sent confusion across all our faces. Muhammad flung open Hafsa's door and strode into the courtyard. I started to follow, but I remembered Hafsa and stopped to reassure her.

"Don't worry," I said. "He's only angry. And that was just his first repudiation. He won't make the other two." For a man to divorce his wife, he had to declare the intention to her three times.

"No, you spoke the truth," Hafsa said. "We women of Hijaz are like tail-wagging dogs compared to Muhammad's exotic Egyptian feline of a mistress." Tears streamed down her cheeks. "It's impossible to compete."

The contest was about to become more intense. Bilal's cry had announced the arrival of that much-awaited caravan from Yemen, the one bringing a new wife for Muhammad. We trudged like stones rolling across the grass to see her. Neither the colorful silks adorning the camels nor the incense scenting the air could arouse even a comment from any of us.

Murmurs rustled through the crowd, heralding the bride-to-be. We watched her in silence at first, as though listening to a poem that told of high cheeks like figs, of eyelashes as long as a lover's kiss, lips as full and dark as forbidden wine, skin like coffee, and a bosom like the twin hills of Mecca.

"Say good-bye to your husband, sister-wives," Raihana finally said. "This new toy won't lose its appeal anytime soon."

"She is an exotic flower drawing every eye," Saffiya complained.

"By al-Lah, another foreigner to make us all seem common," Hafsa said. "Raihana speaks the truth. We'll never see Muhammad again."

"*Yaa* Hafsa, where is your spirit?" I stared at her. "You've never been so quick to submit."

Hafsa's face slumped. "Look at her, A'isha!"

I looked—and saw Muhammad help his new bride-to-be down from her camel. Her smile outdazzled the jewels dripping from her throat, ears, arms, and ankles—a smile that didn't reach her eyes—but it was those gently swelling breasts, rising like soft cushions from the scoop of her gown, that tugged at Muhammad's gaze.

"Don't be fooled by her suggestive clothing. She's a complete innocent, with a father more strict than Umar," I murmured to Hafsa and Saffiya. "She's harmless."

Then as Muhammad instructed her servants, I saw her eyes move to the face of her escort, a tall man in clothing of gold thread with a fine long nose and eyes that seemed to shoot daggers into the back of Muhammad's neck. Fear contorted the woman's face as if she were screaming and her lips moved beseechingly, but the man's face hardened and his jaw ticced.

In the next moment Muhammad stood and smiled at her. Both she and the escort beamed so benignly I wondered if I'd imagined their exchange.

I would have to find out. "I think we should befriend this one," I said to Saffiya and Hafsa. "Let's offer to help her prepare for the wedding."

"You want to be her tire woman?" Saffiya shook her head. "Pregnancy must addle the brain."

Hafsa eyed me suspiciously. "What's running through your mind?"

"I'd like to get to know her. Wouldn't you?" I gave Hafsa a pointed look. She shrugged. Later, when we were alone, I'd tell her what I'd seen. My instincts pointed to danger—but before I could go to Muhammad I'd have to know more. He wouldn't believe me otherwise, and I couldn't afford another mistake.

I linked arms with Hafsa as she and I walked toward our huts. "*Yaa* Hafsa," I said, leaning close to her ear. "There are all kinds of ways to prepare a woman for marriage."

Conspiring with the Enemy

lone in my room that night, I waited for Muhammad and fretted over his words to Hafsa. Would he utter the remaining repudiations and send her back to Umar? My breath tore in my throat, frayed by the notion. If Muhammad would divorce Hafsa, the daughter of his close Companion, were any of us safe? Was I?

In spite of my turmoil, my stomach demanded food. Since I'd become pregnant, my appetite was a deep, unfillable well. I stepped out to the cooking tent, but in the courtyard I stopped at the sight of shadows sweeping like crows' wings across the night. I heard the snap of a twig and flattened my body against the wall, watching for the pounce, listening for the snarl or growl of something wild. Their watering holes sucked dry by the drought, jackals had begun haunting our streets at night in search of water. Sawdah said when they became this desperate, they'd hunt humans to drink our blood.

I heard a muffled cry. Across the courtyard, a dark figure slumped to the ground. When it arose I saw that it was no jackal, but something far more sinister. My heart drummed its warning as I discerned the outline of a man stumbling from hut to hut, pulling curtains aside and peering into windows. I watched him stare into my apartment and, finding no one there, move quickly away. When the light crossed his form, rage snarled in my breast.

It was Abu Sufyan who peered in the windows, grinning at what he saw in Hafsa's apartment, lingering at Zaynab's, then waving excitedly at the window of his daughter Umm Habiba. He waddled around to the front door and waited there until she opened it, then slipped inside. And I was the only one who'd seen him enter.

So Umm Habiba *was* a spy! How many times had her father visited her these past months? Had she helped Abu Sufyan plan the Bedouin raid on those Ghatafani shepherds, the attack that had broken the peace treaty? Had she passed information to him that our army was preparing to invade Mecca?

Like many in the *umma*, I worried that Quraysh would attack us first. When I'd told Muhammad this, he'd said he wasn't afraid.

"We have become too mighty for Abu Sufyan to fight, let alone conquer," he said.

What would he say when I told him of Umm Habiba's treachery? Would he believe me? He'd scoffed today when I'd told him I was carrying his child. "Desperate," he'd called me. Why would he listen to me now?

I ran to the *majlis*, where Muhammad and his Companions dined and talked politics with his new fiancée's escort, the Yemeni emissary. I caught my father's eye and summoned him away from the meal, then told him in a hushed voice what I had seen.

"Abu Sufyan, here?" His body tensed. "We must alert Muhammad." He turned to head back into the *majlis*, but stopped. "Are you certain it was him, A'isha?"

"Of course I'm certain!"

"Did you see his face?"

I faltered, trying to remember. "I saw his fat body," I said. "And I saw him walk into Umm Habiba's hut."

He stroked his beard. "I will go and investigate. But our dinner is nearly finished. If Muhammad comes out, will you tell him where I have gone?"

Alarm jabbed me with its bony finger, and I grabbed his arm. "No, *abi*! You can't go alone. It is too dangerous—"

He patted my shoulder. "I and Abu Sufyan used to do business togeth-er," he said. He leaned close to whisper, "His fighting skills are atrocious."

As I waited for Muhammad to emerge, worry and excitement tugged my thoughts in different directions. Would he believe me when I told him what I'd seen? My accusations against Maryam had made him sus-picious of me. He now saw me as a jealous schemer determined to destroy his other marriages. In fact, he couldn't be further from the truth. I hated sharing him with so many, but I knew the value of each alliance. Yet where Umm Habiba was concerned, I had good cause for suspicion. Would my discovery of her father's visit redeem me in Muhammad's eyes?

About ten minutes later, the men stepped out of the *majlis* in twos and threes, talking among themselves, unaware of the presence of their enemy in our household or of the danger lurking in the eyes of the Yemeni emis-sary. I stood in the shadows with my wrapper over my face, waiting for Muhammad. When he appeared, I asked him to follow me to my apartment.

Inside my apartment, I let my wrapper drop. "Umm Habiba is a spy," I said. Before I could continue, his anger swept like a storm over us both.

"Damn your accusations!" he said, gritting his teeth. "If I hear another slander from your lips about your sister-wives—"

"This is no slander." I forced myself to speak calmly although his anger shook me. "I saw Abu Sufyan in the courtyard. My father has gone to con-front him."

"Abu Sufyan?" Questions gathered on Muhammad's brow.

"He sneaked into the hut of his daughter. The one he sent to spy on us."

Muhammad glowered. "Umm Habiba is no spy."

"And I'm not a redhead."

"She has been a devout Muslim for many years. Abu Sufyan tried to kill her husband after he converted. The two of them fled to Abyssinia years ago."

"And without her husband, what is she now?" My voice rose in protest. "Her father's enemy or his ally?"

"Her hatred for Abu Sufyan has caused her much pain. If he visited her, it was without her permission."

"So that's why she wanted to marry you," I hurled, wanting to hurt him as his disbelief had hurt me. "Not to spy on Abu Sufyan, but to punish him." His low growl told me he was about to shout again, but my father's knock interrupted us.

His smile was grim as he entered and bowed to Muhammad. "Congratulations. Your enemy is vanquished. Abu Sufyan trembles at rumors of a Muslim invasion. Although he will not admit it, he has come to plead for mercy."

Muhammad took a deep breath and looked at me. Contrition flashed in his gaze before he returned my father's smile.

"This is in truth good news," he said. "But why did he not approach me with an official delegation?"

"After his men broke our treaty, he did not know whether he would be in danger," my father said. "He left his bodyguards at our gates to avoid attracting attention and asked Umm Habiba to relay him safely to you. She refused."

Muhammad shot me another look—this time, of triumph. "She is a loyal and devoted Believer," he said. Then he frowned. "Abu Sufyan should have known that. Yaa Abu Bakr, is there a trick? Why has he taken the risk of coming here alone?"

"He has insurance." My father's voice hoarsened. "His son Mu'awiyah occupies my father's home in Mecca, uninvited and refusing to leave. Abu Sufyan is holding my abi hostage."

Muhammad's vein darkened, but he clapped a hand on my abi's shoulder. "Do not worry, Abu Bakr. Your father is safe. Not a single hair on Abu Sufyan's head will be touched." My father's face relaxed, though worry still filled his eyes.

"As for Abu Sufyan's pleas for mercy, I would like to hear them myself," Muhammad said. "Let us go to him now. I think we can claim Mecca for al-Lah in a way that is merciful."

"After all the times he's tried to kill you?" I blurted.

"He is my cousin, and now my father-in-law," Muhammad said, all business, as he turned toward my door. "Yaa A'isha—" he kept his back to me, and his voice pulled itself tight at the edges, "—you and I have not finished. Please wait for me here."

◆

It was late by the time Muhammad entered my apartment. I'd paced my floor for hours, trying to think of a way to listen in on his talk with Abu Sufyan. But I didn't want to break Muhammad's command to wait in my room for him. His trust in me was too damaged for me to risk his wrath again. I fumed, wondering what I had to do to repair our relationship. Discovering Abu Sufyan should have pleased him, but accusing Umm Habiba had harmed me more. *Please, al-Lah, give me the chance to prove myself.*

He rolled into my room like a brush fire. "Your jealousy has become untenable. If I cannot depend on your support, at least, in this *harim*—"

"Do your other wives oppose you also?" I said, my voice surprising me with its even tone. "Perhaps you're at fault."

He raised his eyebrows at my impertinence. "At fault? For which offense? Each of my wives has a different complaint."

"Some of us have much to complain about," I said bitterly, hoping he would ask me what I meant so I could tell him of my servitude to Zaynab and how I dreaded rising from my bed every day. But Muhammad was too immersed in his own problems to consider mine.

"Juwairriyah has not had new clothes in a year," he grumbled. "Saffiya dislikes the food that Sawdah prepares. Hafsa dislikes Maryam. Umm Habiba dislikes you."

"What a coincidence! I feel the same about her."

His smile was humorless. "Umm Salama will barely speak to me, and Zaynab will not leave me alone. Raihana dislikes everyone except Zaynab, and everyone dislikes Saffiya."

"By al-Lah, what a tangle!" I said. "I can understand why you're eager to marry again."

"That is not so, A'isha. I am resigned to it."

"Resigned? Was that the look I saw in your eyes when you beheld your Yemeni bride's heart-stopping face?"

He frowned. "I will not lie and say I feel resigned about spending time with her. But I would not have sought another wife."

"Why trouble yourself when they flock so readily to you?"

"You speak truly." He sighed. "Al-Lah has already given me more than my share of women."

I took his hand in mine and pressed it to my breast, letting him feel the urgent flutter of my heart's caged wings. "Why marry this new one, then? Send her back to the Yemeni king."

"And risk his displeasure? Never." He pounded his fist on the windowsill. "We need Yemen's allegiance. With it we can ride into Mecca without worry or bloodshed."

"But Yemen is allied with Quraysh," I pointed out. "They've traded together for generations. How many of their caravans have we raided?"

"All that ended with the peace treaty. The trade route is open now."

"Peace treaty?" My laugh was harsh, for I could see Muhammad was determined to proceed with this marriage. "Your friend Abu Sufyan has broken it, remember?"

He pulled his hand from my grasp. "I sealed another agreement with him today."

"Truly?" I stared at him, incredulous. "That's like placing your hand in a lion's mouth and trusting it not to bite you."

"He will honor this pact, or he will pay with his life." Muhammad grasped my shoulders and shone his eyes at me. "Mecca is ours, A'isha! We are taking her back for al-Lah. In return, Abu Sufyan will remain as leader—as long as he obeys me."

"Invade Mecca?" Panic gnawed at my insides. "But you said you were tired of killing brothers and cousins."

Muhammad lifted his hand to stroke my hair. "You have nothing to fear, A'isha. No one who converts to *islam* will come to any harm. And when they see the size of our army, they will all convert—even Abu Sufyan."

BROTHERS OF JOSEPH

THE NEXT DAY

With Abu Sufyan hidden away, I was unable to listen in on his talks with Muhammad. As much as I distrusted him, I consoled myself that at least Muhammad was aware of the dangers he posed. The Yemeni emissary, on the other hand, seemed to have everyone fooled—except me.

I was suspicious of his story. Muhammad's territory, such as it was, included a few thousand devoted subjects, a few vanquished tribes, and a handful of inconstant Bedouins. Why would the Yemeni king suddenly shun his longtime ally Abu Sufyan in favor of Muhammad, whose religion he hadn't embraced? Since the trade route from Yemen to Damascus had been reopened, what did he gain from an alliance with us?

Each time I remembered the look of terror Muhammad's bride-to-be, Alia, had given the Yemeni emissary, my hair stood up on my neck. And why had the emissary sneered as he'd watched Muhammad kiss the beautiful Alia's hand?

I arose and dressed myself early the next morning, intending to learn more about our guests. A rap on my door made me race to open it with a pounding heart, fearing that evil had already occurred—but it was only Zaynab.

"We have a wedding feast to prepare," she said. "We need you in the cooking tent. Now!"

I followed her across the courtyard clasping my hands, wishing they circled her neck, and turning my eyes to Alia's hut. In the flash of the rising sun I spied the glimmer of gold in her doorway before the door clicked shut. My breath stopped. That robe belonged to Nu'man, the Yemeni emissary. He was in her room at this very moment. I had to find out what they were plotting. But how, with Zaynab hovering over me?

"Are you sleepwalking?" she said. She clamped my arm with her fingers and yanked me along to the cooking tent. "We have work to do, you lazy child."

Inside the tent, Sawdah's face flushed when she saw Zaynab handling me so roughly. "By al-Lah, be careful with her!" she cried, running up to us and pulling Zaynab's hand away. "Our A'isha is carrying the Prophet's heir," she said, beaming, to the entire room.

A stunned silence followed. Zaynab's eyes grew three sizes larger, and her open mouth trembled. Umm Salama looked down at her hands. Raihana rolled her eyes and said, "Praise al-Lah, the race to impregnate is ended."

Sawdah came rushing up with a tray of dates, barley mush, and coffee. "*Yaa* A'isha, will you take these to Alia?" she asked. I took the tray, glad for an excuse to check on the Yemeni bride-to-be and her escort.

Outside her hut I set down the tray and looked around. The courtyard tents where Alia's maids and guards slept were quiet. I crept around to a window in the back of the hut and peeked through the curtains. Inside, Nu'man held Alia's hair in one hand, pulling it back to expose her neck, and was running his dagger lightly across her throat. Her eyes were wild, her skin colorless.

"You have no choice, *habib*," he said. "Not if you want to keep your pretty head."

"Go ahead, slit my throat," she choked. "Muhammad's men will kill you next, and we can burn in Hell together."

He let go of her hair, but his eyes continued to strangle her. "You took my money. Now I want the services you promised."

She rummaged in the pouch at her waist and flung a handful of coins at him. "Here is your repayment. Now release me from this dreadful deed! God will punish me forever if I kill His Prophet."

My heart flip-flopped. Kill Muhammad! I wanted to run to him with the news—but I'd have to learn more for him to believe me this time.

The emissary's eyes glittered as brightly as the coins, which he let drop to the floor. "You should have worried about your immortal soul before you took my money."

"I had to pay my father's debt." She looked at the floor. "Those men you sent would have killed him."

"And they will yet, if I command them to," he said. "Which I will do, unless you keep your promise."

Alia mumbled something that must have been assent, for Nu'man laughed and thrust his dagger into the sheath under his arm. "Let us go over the plan one more time," he said. "Tell me everything you intend to do."

"I must drug his wine and give it to him before the consummation."

"That is correct."

"But—" her mouth quivered. "I have discovered that the Prophet does not drink wine."

"Put it in whatever he drinks, then."

"I do not think he will bring his bowl of milk to my apartment. And the drug will be too easily detected in water."

"Hmm." Nu'man tugged at his beard. "Then I suppose you will have to complete the consummation."

"Make love with him and then kill him? Nu'man, I cannot! It is too heartless."

"I would not worry about Muhammad. At least he will enjoy his final night in this world." He licked his lips. "If anything goes wrong, scream, and I will rush to your aid."

I shuddered to think of that awful scene, Alia consummating with the man she was supposed to kill while the man she hated waited outside. Her mouth twisted, but she said nothing.

"When he is asleep, you slip out the door and come to my tent," Nu'man said. "I will creep to the hut with my dagger, and *unh!* The Prophet will be no more. My camel will be waiting outside the mosque, and before the rest of the household awakens, you and I will be gone. Then I will sleep peacefully at last, knowing my caravans are safe from Muslim raiders."

I let the curtain drop, fearing they'd hear my pounding heart. Assassins! The Yemeni emissary was a murderer, plotting against Muhammad's life the same as Abu Sufyan had done, and for the same reason: money. They'd kill him this night unless I could find a way to stop them. But how? *Al-Lah help me*, I whispered. *Show me the way*.

I tiptoed around to the door of her hut, knocked, and entered with the tray. Without her makeup or jewels, I noted, Alia wasn't nearly so beautiful. She was going to need a lot of work before the wedding tonight. And then, as if a veil had been lifted from my eyes, I suddenly saw the perfect way to thwart their plot.

"*Marhaba*," I said as I set the tray of food before her. "I am A'isha bint Abi Bakr, favored wife of the Prophet Muhammad, and your future sister-wife."

"*Marhabtein*," she said. "I am Alia."

"I hope you will allow me to help adorn you," I said. "We could use the time to get to know each other better. Also, my sister-wife Hafsa is unparalleled at the art of henna. She has offered to adorn your hands and feet."

Alia blinked in confusion. "I have servants for that."

"But it is our gift. When we finish, you will surpass even your natural beauty. Think of the impression you'll make for Yemen!"

"But—" She glanced nervously at the emissary, and he nodded. Then she turned to me with a slight smile. "I would be delighted," she said. "Sister-wife."

As soon as I left her hut I ran to Saffiya's, searching for Muhammad. "He arose early and went to the *hammam*," she said. "What's the matter, A'isha? You look so pale."

I turned and ran, ignoring her questions, thinking only that I had to reach Muhammad—not about how I might accomplish that while he bathed in the men's *hammam*. Women, of course, were forbidden, as the attendant with the laughing eyes told me when I reached the door.

"Please summon him. It's urgent," I said, but he shook his head.

"I am under orders not to disturb the Prophet," he said, clearly amused. "Unless it is a life-and-death matter."

"But it is!" I cried. "Please, tell him A'isha is here, and it's an emergency."

As I waited I paced the hard-packed dirt outside the baths, replaying the scene I'd witnessed in Alia's hut, going over every word, looking for some other, saner interpretation. It seemed far-fetched even to me, who'd heard every detail of their plan. But there had been no mistaking that poor woman's words or the lust in Nu'man's eyes as he'd talked about spilling Muhammad's blood.

The door opened and I whirled around, ready to throw myself at Muhammad's neck and tell him all I'd seen and heard. Instead of my husband, though, I found myself facing Ali's mocking eyes.

"The Prophet is preparing for his wedding, A'isha," he said. "He doesn't have time for jealous wives today."

He stood with his feet apart, caressing his sheathed sword as though he contemplated using it on me. I glared at him, wishing for my own sword. How satisfying it would be to bring Ali to his knees! As for now, though, I had neither the time nor the patience for fighting, or even for arguing.

"*Yaa* Ali, I asked to see Muhammad," I said. "I have urgent news."

"I told you, he's busy," Ali said. His grin widened. "What's the matter now, A'isha? Is Alia a spy, like Umm Habiba? Or have you conjured something new?"

My expression must have startled him, for he stepped closer to me and stared into my eyes. "Behold your face, A'isha, with its look of a naughty child whose lie has been discovered. I am well acquainted with your tactics in the *harim*, even if Muhammad is not."

My heart began to pound very fast. "Ali, I must see Muhammad! His life may depend on it."

"I swear by al-Lah, if you try to disrupt this alliance with Yemen, I will make your life miserable," he said. "I have tried to persuade Muhammad to ban you from the wedding, but he is unwilling. I warn you, though, A'isha: I have eyes, and ears, everywhere. One false word or deed from you, and I will make sure you are confined to your room until the marriage is consummated."

I whirled around and rushed through the streets, fury blinding me to the curious eyes of passersby. That self-important ass, blocking my access to my husband! Muhammad couldn't have known I'd wanted to see him, or he would have come to me. I thought of going back and waiting until he emerged, but decided against it. What if Umar was with him? Al-Lah help me if he spotted me loitering outside the men's baths!

Soon my steps slowed, and I pulled my wrapper about my face, con-templating Ali's jeers. As much as I hated him, his words had served a use-ful purpose. He'd made me realize how foolish I might appear to Muhammad if I went to him with claims of an assassination plot. I'd just accused Umm Habiba of being a spy for her father, and I'd been terribly mistaken. Before that I'd falsely called Maryam an adulteress. Because of my blunders Muhammad hadn't believed me when I'd told him I was car-rying his child. Why would he believe me now?

If I said anything about Alia except in praise, Muhammad would only grow angrier. Then Ali could easily convince him to shut me away. If that happened, I'd never be able to carry out my plan—and Muhammad would die tonight.

◆

To help prepare Alia for the wedding I recruited Hafsa, the only sister-wife I trusted. When she heard about the assassination plot, her eyes flashed with a familiar, temperamental fire.

"I'd like to thrust a dagger between those precious breasts of hers," she said.

"Patience, Hafsa, is the key to success," I said. "If we kill her, her emis-sary will simply find another way to assassinate Muhammad."

She gripped my sleeve. "But what if your plan fails, A'isha? Shouldn't we tell someone?"

I told her about my attempt at the men's *hammam*, and about Ali's scorn.

"Don't let that bag of wind stop you from alerting Muhammad," Hafsa said. "If something happened to our husband, it would be your fault."

"Nothing is going to happen to him if I can help it," I said. "But I won't be able to do anything if Ali has me locked away."

"Tell your father, then, A'isha. You can't do this alone."

I nodded. "My father, of all people, might believe me. If not, though, don't worry: My plan is a good one. And if it doesn't work, I have anoth-er. That murderer will never get close to Muhammad."

I left her and went to *abi*'s house. I found him, to my surprise, in his *majlis* with Abu Sufyan. "You're letting him stay *here?*" I said when he came out to greet me.

He ran trembling hands through his hair. His eyes were vacant, staring at me but not seeing. "By al-Lah, he will not leave my sight as long as my father is his hostage."

I seized his beard, trying to grab his attention. "I need your help, *abi*. This new bride of Muhammad's—"

"A'isha, did you hear what I said? I am busy. I have no time for your intrigues."

"But this is serious!"

His eyes focused on me at last—in a glare of outrage. "Serious!" he shouted. "You know nothing of serious. Your domestic squabbles are of no interest to me now, A'isha, do you understand? I have my father's life to worry about. Now, leave me!"

He turned and rushed into his *majlis*, leaving me feeling as if I'd just been caught in a *samoom*. My father couldn't help me, after all. Despair swirled around me, but I took a deep breath and summoned my wits. I would save Muhammad myself.

That afternoon I tried to keep my hands steady and my voice light as I and Hafsa primped and painted and coifed the bride-to-be until she dazzled even us with her beauty. I flattered Alia and gave her sisterly advice while Hafsa, gritting her teeth, adorned the bride's hands and arms with sharp-toothed serpents and thorny roses—very fashionable, I assured her.

The next part of my plan was crucial to its success. Knowing how Alia had been blackmailed into her role, I almost hated to do it. I consoled myself by thinking of Muhammad, and my love for him formed a hard shell over my heart.

"Now remember," I said as she stood to leave. "When the time comes for your consummation tonight, don't submit to Muhammad right away."

"Be coy," Hafsa said. "That's how he likes it."

"Resist his advances—while giggling, so he'll know you aren't serious," I said.

"Men relish the role of pursuer," Alia said. Then she gave us a sly smile. "That is what I have heard."

"Muhammad will lose interest in you if he finds you an easy conquest."

"But what if I frighten him away?"

"Frighten the Prophet? The mightiest warrior in Hijaz?" Hafsa's laugh was scornful.

"Just as he is about to achieve the consummation, cry out, 'I take refuge in al-Lah from you!'" I said, wiggling my eyebrows at her. "His reaction will surprise you."

In truth, I had already seen the phrase's effect on Muhammad. During one of our evening coffee hours with him, Saffiya had told a disturbing tale from the *umma*'s raid on her tribe. A cousin had begged for mercy as one of our warriors stripped off her clothes. "I take refuge with al-Lah from you!" the woman cried, but the soldier hadn't paused in his attack. In truth, Saffiya said, he'd called her an impostor and treated her more roughly than before.

Muhammad's face turned as pale as milk when he heard the tale. "Who is that warrior? He will certainly burn in Hell for that transgression."

"But the woman wasn't a Muslim," Zaynab said.

"Do you think only Muslims can call on al-Lah?" Muhammad said. "Anyone who does so should be protected."

Looking in her mirror, Alia practiced her line.

"I take refuge with al-Lah from you," she said, and frowned. "Are you certain that will excite Muhammad?"

"You will be amazed at the effect," Hafsa said. She smirked as the unwitting Alia walked out of her apartment and into the mosque, toward the trap that awaited her.

◆

"Praise al-Lah," Zaynab muttered at the wedding, "the bride's marriage gown, at least, does not plunge down to her navel."

"*Yaa* Zaynab, did you think you invented that form of seduction?" Hafsa teased.

"Mine was an off-shoulder nightgown," Zaynab said. "And no, I did not invent it, but I perfected it."

"I thought she was going to burst open like springtime when she came down off that camel yesterday," Raihana said.

"They have much to learn about modesty in Yemen," Umm Salama said.

Maryam didn't participate in our talk, but stood off to the side, splendidly dressed in white linen and long jeweled earrings, and sending us cool sideways glances. But I felt sure her loneliness was well compensated when Muhammad smiled sweetly at her across the room. I caught his eye, also, but he quickly glanced away, making my own eyes burn. Perhaps after I'd saved his life he'd love and trust me again.

Please al-Lah, please let my plan work. As the rest of the *umma* feasted, disastrous scenarios pushed aside my hunger. What if Alia failed to say the phrase I'd taught her? Then she and Muhammad would consummate the marriage, and, as always after lovemaking, Muhammad would fall into a deep, satisfied sleep from which even the angel Gabriel couldn't awaken him. Cutting his throat would be an easy task.

I tried to comfort myself: Wouldn't I be waiting nearby, ready to defend Muhammad with my sword? Yet my mind was so preoccupied with worries that I hardly tasted the exotic Yemeni food everyone else said was so delicious: Juicy hunks of goat in a peppery broth; a yogurt-and-cucumber salad pungent with garlic; a spicy-hot relish; sweet bright slices of ripe mango. I picked at my food, knowing I should fill my belly, but my thoughts honed in on the night ahead as if I were preparing for battle. Muhammad had looked so happy as he'd gazed down into his bride's face, blissfully unaware of her treachery.

We wives approached him for kisses and congratulations after the meal was finished. When I beheld Muhammad's smile, my throat felt as if a blade were pressing against it. And poor Alia's arms trembled as she embraced me.

"I have not forgotten the phrase you taught me," she whispered.

"Don't forget to say it, or he may not be able to consummate." I blushed to utter such a slander on Muhammad's manhood.

The night stretched out like a terrifying dream. I'd planned to crouch behind Alia's hut, listening to the conversation within. That way, I would know whether my plan had succeeded. If she failed to say the words, I'd spring out with my sword before the emissary could even touch the door handle.

But as I neared the apartment, my sword hidden under my robe, I saw the figures of men, one at each corner of the building. That wily Nu'man had posted guards—not against evildoers from outside, but to protect the ones within.

Broken clouds muffled the moonlight like an assailant's hand. I crouched in the shadows beside Umm Habiba's hut next door, straining to hear the murmurs and whispers filtering from their bedroom.

"Nothing to fear," I thought I heard Muhammad say.

"Thrilling kisses," she purred.

His hungry eyes. His devouring mouth on her flesh. His fingers unty-ing her, unwrapping her. I shook my head, scattering the images, but they drew themselves again, delineated by his animal moans, her sultry laugh-ter. She sounded anything but innocent. Had she forgotten her ploy, or cast it aside? I prayed she wouldn't forget her line.

"Say it!" I whispered, crouched in the dark, dabbing the moisture from my face, willing my thudding heart to be quiet so I could hear.

I heard her gasp, sharp as a dagger, and his deep laugh. By al-Lah, had he shown himself to her?

"Say it," I rasped. *Help, al-Lah! Please, don't let her forget.* If she failed to say her line, I would be powerless to stop him. The guards would over-whelm me, and Muhammad's life would be lost, unless I found a way to get near that door.

I glanced around the courtyard, looking for answers. Why hadn't I tried harder to get help? I'd been afraid no one would believe me. How foolish those fears seemed now! Even the suspicion of a plot might have made Muhammad more careful, or might have put my father on the alert. I'd been so confident I could rescue Muhammad. Now it was too late to seek help, and Muhammad might pay the ultimate price for my vanity.

The clouds shifted again, unsheathing the moon. Its light bathed everyone in the courtyard—including me. I stepped back into the shad-ows, but my movement had caught the attention of the front-door guard. Without a sound he sprang across the grass and seized me by the hair.

"Come with me," he rasped, and, with his hand over my mouth, yanked me toward the emissary's tent.

My eyes filled with tears from the pain in my scalp but somehow I man-aged to reach for the dagger under my arm. As the guard jerked me along I formed a plan: Once we were out of sight of Alia's hut I would shove the blade into his belly, then don his clothing and post myself at the door. That way I'd have no trouble stopping Muhammad's murderer.

But before we got very far a screeching wail pierced the night, a terri-ble sound like cats before a fight. The guard stopped and turned, still hold-ing me, and I turned with him to see Muhammad stepping into the court-yard, his clothing in disarray, his head bare—and the tearful Alia, in a diaphanous gown, clinging to his arm. In the distance the clatter of galloping hoof beats rose, then faded.

My heart smashed against itself, clamoring to be heard. I struggled with the guard, wanting to scream out a warning to Muhammad. He stood without a weapon and surrounded by assassins, unaware of danger.

"*Yaa* Muhammad, beware!" Hafsa ran into the courtyard with Umar and Talha, who brandished swords. Seeing them, the guard released me and rushed toward Alia, waving his own sword. Nu'man was nowhere to be seen.

"Muhammad, watch out!" I cried. "They're assassins!" But no one heard me.

"I didn't mean it!" Alia cried. "Your other wives told me to say it. They said you would like it, those she-dogs! Please do not send me back home. I will do anything!"

She flung her arms around his waist, then his legs. Muhammad reached down and pulled her gently to her feet. She entwined her arms around his neck, but he pried her loose and handed her to the guard.

"My bride has sought refuge from me with al-Lah," Muhammad said. "I must obey her wish and send her home untouched."

The guard frowned. "But you heard her say she did not mean her words," he said. "She was deceived."

"It does not matter," Muhammad said. "The words hold the same power regardless of her intention."

"The king will be insulted." The guard thrust the sobbing Alia forward, jostling her against Muhammad who stepped back and fended her off.

"Will al-Lah allow me to marry one who has sought His protection from me? The decision is not mine to make," Muhammad said. "I am deeply sorry."

At that moment the tear-streaked bride spotted me standing in the courtyard. She tried to yank herself free of the guard but had no better luck than I'd had.

"A'isha!" she screamed. "You did this to me. *Yaa* Prophet, there she is, the one who tricked me. And that one, also!" She pointed to Hafsa, who returned a glare.

"It was an assassination attempt," I said.

The stricken look on Muhammad's face as he turned his eyes to me almost made me wish I were the one being sent away instead of his new bride. Yet if he knew the truth, he'd laud me as his savior.

"Muhammad," I said, my voice beseeching. "You have to believe me. Nu'man was going to kill you tonight!"

"Enough!" he shouted through lips that trembled.

"No, you must believe me." I looked around for Nu'man, intending to accuse him, but he hadn't appeared. I recalled the sound of hoof beats after Alia's scream, and I knew he'd gone.

"Where's Nu'man?" I turned to the guard, whose hard eyes told me he'd known of Nu'man's plans. "He ran away, didn't he?" I turned to Muhammad, triumphant. "Only a guilty man would flee."

The guard released Alia, who now stood sobbing quietly, and bowed to Muhammad. "The emissary sends his farewell," he said. "The king called him back to Yemen this afternoon on urgent business."

Muhammad's face darkened. The vein between his eyes throbbed. He glared at me, then at my sister-wives, who'd floated into the courtyard like so many ghosts.

"It does not matter which of my wives did this deed, for any of them would have wished to," he said, sweeping his hand to include all nine of us. "These women are like the brothers of Joseph, who sold him into slavery. Loving themselves above all others, they would betray the one who would never do them harm."

He turned and marched back into the hut that had been Alia's, slamming the door behind him. Hafsa and I turned to each other with eyes full of panic. "He will divorce me now, for certain," she murmured.

I said nothing, but trudged to my hut feeling as if a foot were pressing on my chest. Hafsa wasn't the only one who had to worry about divorce. When Muhammad had looked at me tonight, I'd seen his love shatter into one thousand and one fragments. Only a miracle could save us now.

HONOR AND GLORY

On the confusion following the incident with Alia, the Yemeni caravan departed before I could explain to Muhammad what had happened. Umar had rebuked Hafsa for believing my "outlandish" tales about Alia and Nu'man, while Muhammad asked the emissary to send his apologies to the Yemeni king.

As for me, I waited anxiously to convince Muhammad that I'd saved his life by deceiving his bride. But how could I tell him anything? He avoided me as though I were a leper. For three evenings I waited for his visit, yet he spent his nights with Juwairriyah, Raihana, and Saffiya, instead.

I barely left my apartment. I didn't want to answer my sister-wives' questions. I couldn't even answer my own. Why, I agonized, had I risked Muhammad's life? I'd never felt so afraid as I had when the Yemeni guard was dragging me away from Alia's hut. I'd thought I could protect Muhammad by myself, but my plan had nearly failed. What if it *had* failed? If Alia hadn't followed my ridiculous advice, Muhammad might be dead, and I would be at fault.

If Muhammad died now, the *umma* would die also. We'd buzz about like a beehive without its queen, and Abu Sufyan would have little trouble soaking the streets of Medina with the blood of Believers. And I and my sister-wives and their children—plus my baby—would be sold as slaves, the children separated from their mothers, the women enduring the humiliations of men with hard eyes and cold fingers prodding our secret places.

I'd taken risks for Muhammad, but not only for his sake. I'd done it for myself—I'd rather die than live as a slave—and for the *umma*. Now, it seemed, the price for my foolhardiness was Muhammad's love, for he looked away whenever I glimpsed him in the courtyard, and he failed to come to my apartment even for his nightly visit. I felt as empty as if my soul had flown away.

Three days after Alia's departure, Muhammad sent word that he was leaving. He, my father, Ali, and Zayd were on their way to meet with the Ghatafani. He sent my father to say good-bye to me.

"Our departure is hastily arranged," *abi* explained, averting his gaze. "Muhammad has no time to visit with you now."

"But he must!" I cried. "I have something important to tell him."

"The Ghatafani chief demands Muhammad's presence immediately," *abi* said. "He wants revenge against Quraysh for the killing of his tribes-men and the breaking of the peace treaty. He is angry about Muhammad's latest agreement with Abu Sufyan."

Who could blame the chief? Muhammad had negotiated only for him-self, apparently forgetting the pride of his Bedouin allies. Yet the Ghatafani would be easily assuaged. The real danger to Muhammad, I feared, lay with the Yemeni.

In just a few hours Muhammad and my father would be traveling in the desert, vulnerable to attack. Would Nu'man give up so easily when he had traveled so far to kill Muhammad? I was certain that he and his group lurked nearby, waiting to fulfill their evil mission.

"*Abi*," I said. "You must warn Muhammad. That woman he nearly mar-ried was an assassin." I told him the entire story, from spying on her with Nu'man in her hut to thwarting their plot with my advice. As I spoke, his face reddened.

"Why have you waited so long to tell me this? Muhammad could have been killed!"

"I tried to tell you," I said. "I tried to tell Muhammad. But no one would listen."

He frowned. "Forgive me, A'isha. I should not have dismissed you. I am as much to blame for all this as you are."

"Yet my plan worked, didn't it, *abi?*" I lifted my head proudly. "Muhammad is alive."

My father closed his eyes and pressed his lips together. I waited for his rebuke, reminding myself that it didn't matter what anyone, even my own *abi*, thought about me or what I'd done—as long as they kept Muhammad's neck safe from the Yemeni's blade.

When he opened his eyes, I thanked al-Lah to see that his expression had softened.

"*Yaa* A'isha, I have often wished your brother Abd al-Rahman had some of your spark," he said. "I used to wonder why al-Lah had wasted all that intelligence and courage on a female."

"Unfortunately, courage seems to be admired only in men," I said, lowering my eyes so he couldn't see how his remarks stung me. So my father thought my efforts to protect Muhammad had been wasted. If I'd been a man, he'd be beaming with pride at me right now. As a woman, I was an embarrassment.

"You are wrong," he said, calling my gaze to his broad smile, his shining eyes. "I have more respect for you than for both my sons combined. You have not let being a woman prevent you from fighting for your *umma*."

"Yet still I am criticized," I said. "If I were a man, I'd walk around in a glow from the praise."

"Glory," my father scoffed. "Is that what you want? It is not difficult to obtain. Ask Abu Sufyan. Glory is as easy to grasp as a dagger. It draws attention to its bearer like a blade flashing in the sun. Honor, on the other hand, requires discipline and compassion and self-respect. It often works silently, without recognition or the desire for it. Honor comes only after years of effort and, once grasped, is even more difficult to hold."

"Which makes it more precious," I guessed.

He lifted his eyebrows as if he could only now see me clearly. "As precious as a courageous daughter."

He stepped forward and clasped my elbow, greeting me in the way of men. I clasped his elbow in return, choking back my emotion, accepting the tribute he'd bestowed on me. We could never be equals—he was, after all, my father—but in that moment we were Companions, each with the same purpose: the protection of our Prophet and of the *umma*, and of our freedom to worship our God in peace.

"You saved Muhammad, and you did it brilliantly," he said. "In doing so, you saved the *umma* also." My eyes brimmed with tears of gratitude as he pulled me close for a coffee-and-cardamom embrace.

My heart seemed to swell in my chest until it filled my throat, keeping me from speaking. My father was proud of me for what I'd done! He'd grasped my elbow and praised my cleverness. I buried myself in his arms, in his long, henna-dyed beard, in the love and trust I felt beating in his heart. Then he released his hold and turned to leave.

"I must go and confer with Muhammad now," he said. "In the meantime, we should keep your news a secret. It would only worry the *umma*."

"All I care about is Muhammad's approval, and no one else's—except yours," I said. "What if he doesn't believe you?"

"Do not worry, A'isha. He will not only believe your tale, but his heart will soften toward you when he realizes what you have done for him—for all of us."

"What about Nu'man, *abi*? Do you have a plan?"

He frowned. "Not yet, but I wonder—do you have a strategy for me to present?"

I stared at him, not sure I'd heard correctly. My father, asking me for advice? Was he teasing me? But his face held only respect. The plan I had already formed in my head sprang readily to my lips.

"I would send our scouts in all directions to find the Yemeni encampment. It has to be nearby," I said. "Don't you think so?

He nodded. "By al-Lah, I do."

"Have Ali and Zayd and some of their best men sneak up on them tonight, before you leave on your journey. Then send Nu'man's head on his sword to the Yemeni king."

◆

With Muhammad and my father off to appease the Ghatafani, Umar took command of the *umma*. Normally we in the *harim* cringed at this arrangement. As much as Umar enjoyed devising new restrictions on Muhammad's wives, he seemed to like enforcing them even more. But this time, with so many new converts in Medina, he was too busy arbitrating disputes, finding housing, and recruiting warriors to worry about the *harim*. At least for a while.

As for us, we were busy with our new enterprise. The wedding of our first client, Ghazala, was less than two weeks away, and my sister-wives had a gown to sew and adorn, face paints to mix, fragrances to extract, henna to prepare. They tested their concoctions on one another, then refined them. This would be their first paying work, and they intended to make the bride's mother faint at the sight of her daughter's beauty. The praise she would spread afterward would send every bride in Medina to the Prophet's wives.

I didn't help them much. I still felt queasy and tired from my pregnancy, and I spent much of my time in the tent city. Our three-year drought had only worsened the lives of the tent-dwellers. People died of hunger and disease, women and babies cried, men hung their heads in despair. How could I help any of them? Yet I kept trying. Every few days I'd lead Scimitar, loaded with barley and dates, across Medina to their sad enclave, where the people welcomed me as warmly as if I were one of their own.

Each time I returned from my visits with Umm al-Masakin's poor, my sister-wives would sit me in the cooking tent's "nest" and display their accomplishments. Umm Salama would lift the veil from her face with a flourish, showing off her made-up eyes, or Zaynab would bare her arms to show Hafsa's latest design. I'd never heard my sister-wives laugh so much, or talk so eagerly together. For the first time ever, I looked forward to going home.

A few days before the client Ghazala's wedding, I came home to a surprise: Raihana rattling her tambourine and Sawdah playing her *tanbur* while the gentle Juwairriyah danced in the bride's gown, a confection of green and gold, her hands and arms adorned with peacocks whose tails seemed to shimmer with color. As she moved she wafted a perfume of cardamom and rose, Raihana's invention; and then, to my delight, removed her wrapper to reveal her brass-colored hair wound in a shining series of coils, eyes so dramatically lined with *kohl* that they seemed to leap off her face, and lips not only stained a fetching red, but as moist and glimmering as if she'd been kissing dewdrops.

"By al-Lah! I'm glad Muhammad isn't here to see this vision of loveliness," I said, laughing but only partly joking. My sister-wives laughed, also, and Hafsa leapt up to join Juwairriyah's dance, twirling and flipping her hair and writhing her body like a serpent, surprising us all. In the next moment Zaynab was dancing and making up a song about *dirhams* and the new gowns they would buy, while Saffiya snapped her fingers and jerked her head from side to side, holding out her hands and beckoning me to join them.

Exhausted by the demands of my pregnancy, I demurred, but Hafsa danced over and pulled me to my feet. Then Umm Salama stepped into the circle, and even Umm Habiba. Soon we were all dancing and laughing and clapping to Sawdah's plinks and Raihana's clinks, which grew faster and faster until I forgot my weariness and my sister-wives became a blur. We bumped into one another and shrieked and sang until the cooking tent must have looked as if a *samoom* whirled within.

Immersed in clamor and joy, none of us heard Umar's thunder. Sawdah must have spied him in the entryway, because her music was the first to cease. Raihana's rattle stopped next, and then we all ceased dancing and turned to our musicians, perplexed. We followed their dread-filled gazes to Umar, his hands planted on his hips and his face curled into a sneer that told us we were doing something very bad.

The room was silent for a moment and then, remembering the rule against seeing our faces, he commanded us all to cover ourselves. When we had done so, he entered the tent, picked up Sawdah's *tanbur*, and broke it over his knee. Sawdah cried out, and some of us gasped, but no one spoke. The blustery Umar intimidated even me, especially now, when I carried a vulnerable child in my womb.

"The Prophet would not like this music," he said, his voice rough.

He spoke the truth: The modest Muhammad enjoyed a private show, but he disapproved of public performance. Yet not all the sister-wives trembled in fear at Umar's thunder.

"It is fortunate for the Prophet, then, that he is not here," Umm Salama retorted in a cold, clear voice. I stared at her: Was she possessed by a *djinni*? No one spoke back to Umar.

"He will be here soon, and there will be trouble when he learns of this party you have put on!" Umar cried. Then his eyes took in the mortars and pestles and colored powders and inks, the bottles of fragrant oil, the scraps of cloth and cutting knives and thread, all scattered at his feet like lost hopes.

"Where did you find the money for all these trinkets and frills?" He spied a purse of silver coins on the floor: Ghazala's mother's down-payment for supplies. Hafsa reached for it, but he grabbed it away from her.

"Daughter, you did not get these *dirhams* from me! Did your mother give you this? If so, she stole it from me, and I am taking it back."

"I didn't get it from *ummi*," Hafsa said in an almost-whisper. "Nor does it belong to you."

"Who, then? Certainly not from the Prophet."

"The Prophet has no money to give, *abi*."

"Just tell me where you obtained it, by al-Lah!" He raised his fist. "Answer me, or—"

"No!" I flung myself in front of her, shielding her with my body. "She's not yours to strike, Umar, not anymore. And Muhammad doesn't beat his wives."

"Move out of my way, A'isha." Shadows gathered on his pocked face as he lifted his fist.

I thrust my chin out at him, pretending not to be afraid even though my very breath trembled. "Would you strike me, and risk injuring the Prophet's heir?" I challenged.

Umar's mouth opened. His eyes widened like full moons. I patted my stomach and smiled, and watched with satisfaction as he moved his hand slowly down to his side.

"*Yaa* Umar, that money belongs to Umm Jibrail, the merchant's wife," Umm Salama said, stepping up to stand before him. "She has given it to us to buy these materials. We are going to be her daughter's tire women."

The money pouch fell to the floor. Umm Salama's hand dived to snatch it up.

"The Prophet's wives working for pay?" Umar frowned.

"We are helping Muhammad by helping ourselves," Zaynab said.

"That cannot be." He shook his head. "I forbid it."

I sucked in my breath. Hafsa stepped forward. "*Abi*, no! We've promised Umm Jibrail. We've already spent her money, see?"

"You have wasted her money. I will talk with her husband today and tell him there has been a mistake."

"Then you will speak falsely," Umm Salama said. "We have made no mistakes."

Umar's laughter seemed to quake the sides of the tent. "You made a mistake when you planned this affair without consulting your husband," he said. "By al-Lah! He has let his wives command the household, instead of taking charge himself. But women will not rule as long as I am in control."

In my ears a door slammed, and I felt the hot whirr of caged wings in my chest. Helplessness filled my mouth like a fist.

"An impressive display of power, Umar," Raihana drawled. "As is that belly of yours. Tell me, gold-ringed one, what was your feast today? Lamb? Rice with saffron?"

"We had barley mush," Juwairriyah said. "And two dates each."

"*Yaa* Umar," I said, finding my voice again, "if you're going to stop us from buying food, you should at least share yours with us."

"And those nice gowns your wives possess," Zaynab said. "That green one I saw Hafsa's mother wearing last week would look stunning on me."

"Silence!" Umar waved his arms as if he would knock us all down. "You are the Prophet's wives, not mine."

"You speak truly," Umm Salama said. "And only Muhammad can forbid us to work for Umm Jibrail."

"By al-Lah, I say you will not leave this mosque! Whoever tries it will be whipped—in the middle of the market."

"*Yaa* Umar, they don't mean to cause any scandals," Sawdah said, fingering her Evil-Eye amulet and darting her glance from his face to the floor. "The girls are hungry, that is all. You know what a bad drought we are in. And the children here are all growing up. Without any babies to care for, there is not much for them to do."

"These are not my concerns," Umar growled. "I said you will not leave the mosque, and I mean it. I will post guards outside the doors to ensure you obey me."

I laughed out loud, unable to believe his audacity. Standing before us in his rich tapestry of a robe, his breath smelling of lamb and cumin and honey, depriving us of a few measly pieces of silver! I looked about the cooking tent and saw the old, familiar lines pulling like harness ropes at my sister-wives' mouths, felt the gaiety that had quickened our limbs and our hearts flee from the tent like frightened birds. A fierce protective urge rose within me.

I pulled my dagger from my belt, wishing I could erase my sister-wives' sorrows with my blade. "Don't worry, sisters. I'll deliver your gown and prepare the bride myself."

"I will have you bound and imprisoned first," Umar said. As he advanced toward me, my sister-wives beat him back with their slaps, and soon the very heavens must have quaked from the cries of nine outraged women and one—Sawdah—shouting for peace, and one stomping, snorting, yelling man brandishing threats as empty as his heart.

What a sight must have met Muhammad's eyes when he walked into the cooking tent at that moment! I don't know how long he stood there watching the melee before Saffiya cried out his name and broke from the crowd to flee into his arms. The sound of his murmuring to her, so quiet it was a miracle that it could be heard at all, silenced the tent as if he had uttered a magic spell.

He stood in the slanted evening light with his hair splayed all about him, curling madly from his turban and fringed with gold to match his eyes. His smile looked eerie, out of place under the darkening vein on his brow. And yet—I wanted to shout, to cry—he was alive! *Thank you, al-Lah, for guarding him from harm.*

"*Afwan*, Prophet," Umar said, his face reddening. "Excuse me. I was trying to instill some discipline into this loose *harim*."

"Loose! He means 'enterprising,' husband." Smiling proudly, I told him of my sister-wives' business—but the vein between his eyes began to bulge and throb.

"You cannot allow your wives to solicit money from the *umma*," Umar said. "It will make you appear weak."

"By al-Lah! I suffer even now in my own esteem," Muhammad said. "Have my wives planned this without consulting me?" His eyes were stern. "I thought you respected me more."

"*Yaa* Prophet, I feel disrespected when I put on my threadbare clothes," Umm Salama said.

"What's so respectful about forcing me to wear the same gown for almost two years?" Raihana said. "I was a princess when I came to you, and now you make me live like a pauper."

"Do any of you wear holes in your clothing?" Muhammad said. "Are you cold or indecently covered?"

"How do you define 'indecent'?" Zaynab cried. "I have two gowns, both of them so faded that they drain the color from my face. I can't bear to see myself in the mirror. By al-Lah! I would rather walk around without any clothes at all."

"*Yaa* Prophet, do you hear how your wives talk?" Umar's face was as red as raw meat. "This impertinence begs for a whipping."

My blood surged at Umar's cruelty. Here was the man who'd robbed me of my freedom by convincing Muhammad to make me cover my face, and who'd cheated me of my chance to fight for my *umma*. Now, because we weren't as meek as he preferred, he wanted to scar our bodies with whips.

"*Yaa* Umar, do you think the Prophet's wives are animals?" I shot back. "First you cage us, and now you want to beat us."

Muhammad turned puzzled eyes to me. "You know al-Lah ordered your *hijab*, A'isha," he said. "You witnessed His revelation to me in the court-yard."

I smirked, remembering that revelation all too well: How it had fol-lowed Muhammad's scandalous wedding to Zaynab, how frustrated he'd been by the delay of his consummation. How his revelation, in essence confining us all to the *harim*, had closed in upon me like the dark, cold walls of a tomb, nearly driving me into another man's arms.

"Yes, I witnessed it," I said. "I saw everything—including your trans-formation from a liberator of women into an oppressor of them. *Yaa* Prophet, was that also the work of al-Lah?"

FACES OF HOPE

MEDINA, JUNE 629

*A*s soon as I'd made my retort to Muhammad, I regretted it. Anger swarmed like hornets about his face, and his eyes told me there was nothing I could say or do to appease him.

Despair made me want to bite off my tongue. I'd been waiting two weeks for him to return, hoping to see love and forgiveness in his eyes—and then I'd made things worse by opening my mouth. *Why do I always have to have the final word?* Muhammad, on the other hand, appeared to have no trouble keeping his thoughts to himself. Before I'd finished speaking, he'd turned and walked out of the tent, his only reply the stomping of his feet in the entryway as he kicked the dust off his sandals.

I cried out to him, my voice a hollow thud. I ran to the tent entrance but he raised his hand as he retreated, signaling me to keep my distance. How I longed to fling myself around him the way the Yemeni beauty Alia had done! But I knew him too well to even try.

My heart weighted my chest like a stone as I watched him stride to the date-palm tree and climb the rungs fastened to its trunk, up to his apartment in the attic over the mosque. He climbed nimbly and effortlessly as if he might keep going up and up, all the way to Paradise. But he stopped when, in a choked voice, I called out and asked him what he was doing.

"I am going to contemplate the future," he said. "You all would be wise to do the same."

Contemplate the future? Gathering behind me, my sister-wives urged me to ask him what he meant. But I didn't dare. I feared I already knew the answer.

"*Yaa* Muhammad, when can I talk to you?" I called.

He continued climbing as if an invisible hand lifted him from rung to rung. "After I have finished my consultations with al-Lah."

"About our future?" Saffiya cried in a trembling voice. He stopped again and studied us with the eyes of a father about to discipline the child he loves.

"About your future, yes," he said. "And about my future also."

"*Yaa* Muhammad, for how long will you remain in your room?" Zaynab called out.

"Today is the first day of the month," he said. "On the last I will return and tell you my decision."

He placed his hands on the windowsill of his room, climbed inside, and was gone.

"Decision?" Hafsa said. "What decision? Does he mean that he might not divorce me, after all?" In all the activity of the past weeks Muhammad had not yet spoken to Umar about her.

"You think he's going up there to think about you? He'd be back in thirty minutes instead of thirty days," Raihana said. "The Prophet isn't shutting himself away to ponder his future with just one of us. In his eyes we're all riding the same, lame camel."

"Raihana speaks truly," Umm Salama said as we moved back into the tent. "If Muhammad divorces one of us, he will divorce us all."

A loud gasp, then a stifled sob interrupted our commentary—and Sawdah, red-faced and clutching her Evil-Eye amulet, fled from the tent.

Umar, forgotten when Muhammad had walked in, raged past like a stampeding bull, knocking me aside.

"By al-Lah, he will not divorce any of you, not if I can stop him." He stamped to the tree and climbed its rungs much more slowly than Muhammad had done, and with a great deal more puffing and sweating.

I lifted my eyebrows at Hafsa, who looked as startled as I felt. "Umar, defending us?" I said. "Will the moon and the sun change places next?"

"*Yaa* A'isha, he is not defending us," Umm Salama said. "He is defending the *umma*. If Muhammad divorces us, think of the consequences. Who would follow a man who could not command his own household?"

◆

Chills scuttled across my skin in the next few weeks whenever I imagined Muhammad's coming down from his apartment and casting me out of his life. I thought of how his face would look, broken and full of shadows, like the stony ridge of Mount Subh at dusk, and a hole seemed to spread through my chest. He was the only husband I'd ever known, the only man I'd ever loved. My sister-wives moved like spirits about the *harim*, their eyes haunted, but their pain was nothing compared to mine. They were widows, some with children, all with memories of life before Muhammad, of some other love, perhaps. For me, life before him was a blot on the page, as inscrutable as the existence of my soul before birth. He had always been there, as my mother and father had been. And, for as long as I could remember, he had been my friend.

If only I were a nightingale! I'd fly to the top of that date-palm and perch on those fronds and sing my song of repentance to him for the cruel way I'd treated Maryam, who carried his child also. I'd trill my long notes of thanks to al-Lah for the heir that would be ours, and I'd hold those notes until he believed me and until he joined me with his own throaty song. I'd sing and sing of my love for him, a love so deep and pure I could not fathom life without him, a love that so longed to protect him from harm that it kept me ever vigilant for spies and assassins, a love that had caused me to err, yes, but that had also saved his life.

But alas, I was no bird, and the only way to Muhammad was up that tree—a route Umar had made clear was forbidden to everyone. And with Believers and *ansari* crowding the base of the tree night and day to bend their necks and gape their mouths like baby birds in hopes of a glimpse of Muhammad's turban, there was no chance for me to speak to him.

My feet carved a rut into my floor as I paced, agonizing, wondering what Muhammad was thinking, what decisions he might reach in his attic apartment with no one's influence except that of Umar, who brought him his daily meal. Would he truly divorce me? Panic rippled through me, making me jittery, depriving me of sleep. If Muhammad cast me aside, I'd lose my baby, for children belonged to their fathers. I clutched my pillow to my breast, remembering Umm Salama's tale of mourning for her lost son, wrested from her arms by her husband's family. I'd be alone for the rest of my life, for who in the *umma* would marry a woman scorned by the Prophet of God? Would I have to live with my parents again?

I had to prevent this divorce, but how? Every day I grew more desperate to tell Muhammad my story, so that he would know I'd always acted out of love for him and not only jealousy. Staring out my window at the guard Umar had posted under the tree, I felt as helpless as I had those years in *purdah*.

"Do not worry, A'isha," *abi* said to me one day. "I told Muhammad of the Yemeni plot and how you saved his life. He was distraught, at first, that you did not alert him to your discovery. But I think he had forgiven you by the time we returned to Medina." Some consolation his words offered! And from the waver in his voice I could tell he, also, was worried about what Muhammad might do.

After a while Muhammad's visitors began to tire of gawking. They still crowded the base of the tree to gossip and speculate about him, but by day's end only a few stragglers remained. When night cloaked the court-yard the last of them would trail home, leaving the guard to stand sentry alone. *Please, al-Lah, send him away*, I prayed, but as the weeks dragged on and the guard remained, I decided to grasp the camel by the nose—with Hafsa's help.

One night, when the moon gave only a sliver of light, Hafsa ran up to the guard and tugged at his sleeve. "A shadow!" she said, gasping. "I saw it moving behind my hut. And when I went to my window to see, I heard a crashing in the bushes. Come quickly!" Her performance was quite impressive. From my hut I watched the guard leave his post to investigate—and then, dressed in my dark red robe, I scurried across the grass and up the date-palm tree.

Stealthily I climbed, keeping my gaze on Muhammad's window, not daring to glance down for fear I'd be overcome by dizziness. Heights had frightened me ever since my first, frantic ride in that swaying *hawdaj* years ago. But too much was at stake to let that stop me from seeing Muhammad.

I found him sitting with his legs crossed on the clay floor, staring out a side window. His head was bare, and his hair was as tangled as my emotions. I yearned to throw myself in his lap and bury my face in his beard, as I'd done so often—yet, at the same time, I wanted to respect his need for solitude.

I leaned into his window and whispered his name, hoping he would invite me in. He didn't move, only sat and stared like one of the stone statues outside the Ka'ba.

"*Yaa* Muhammad!" I rasped, but he still didn't respond. By al-Lah, had his spirit left his body? I was about to call his name more loudly but the crackle of dry grass pulled my gaze to the base of the tree far below, where the guard had moved back to his post. I could just make out his turban, like a pale stone in the faint moonlight, before my stomach turned, queasy from the height. My heart raced, and a cold sweat beaded my face. I grabbed the windowsill and gulped the night air until the world righted itself again.

Through it all Muhammad sat motionless. Was he in a trance?

"I had to come and see you, *habibi*," I said, keeping my voice low so the guard couldn't hear. "Before you decide my fate, you need to know why I've acted as I have."

His back straightened, making me believe he was listening. Now was the time to tell Muhammad how much I loved him, how I'd only wanted to protect him from harm, how al-Lah had called me long ago to fight for him and for the *umma*.

Instead, though, I found myself relating a different tale, the story of a little girl betrothed without her knowledge to a much older man, a man so prominent that her parents locked her in *purdah* much earlier than usual to give her special protection. I told him how I'd cried and paced the floor, restless for the sky and the spicy warmth of the sun on my skin. I told how I'd watched Qutailah abuse my mother and vowed not to let the same thing happen to me, and how desperately I'd craved attention from my busy father. I didn't tell him how I'd dreamt of Safwan's rescue or how I made up verses about riding the desert with him, free from *purdah* and parents and anyone else who had the power to lock me indoors.

Like that nightingale, I sang to Muhammad of the shock and fear of walking into my wedding and finding him there, the man I'd loved more as a father than a husband. I told him how lonely I'd felt in that room filled with relatives and friends, all of them beaming with pleasure and pride for me, all praising the tears they thought I cried over leaving my parents while in truth I was grieving over the loss of my dream. Married to Muhammad I would never ride as free as the wind over the desert dunes, making my own laws, living my own life free of my neighbors' rules.

"They were childish dreams," I said, "but they were mine. And they were my only true possessions, for what else can a girl own? Even her body belongs first to her father and then to her husband."

A voice inside warned me to stop, that I was saying too much, but, by al-Lah! I could not. It was as if a dam had burst inside my heart, and all the sadnesses and disappointments in my life came gushing out through my mouth. I told Muhammad how frightened I'd been to see him sitting there in the groom's place at my wedding, and how I'd tried to run away but my mother had stopped me with her strong arms.

"Once I was in your lap, I felt happy," I hastened to add. "I knew you would always take good care of me. And I thought you would take me to your home and my confinement would end."

But it had not ended. I was doomed to nearly three more years of *purdah*. I told Muhammad how I couldn't wait for my menarche, for then I would be able to leave the dark, stifling prison that was my parents' home and ride away with him into the city, where as his wife I'd be able to walk freely in the market and feel the sun on my face and hands whenever I wished.

"My dreams of becoming a Bedouin had faded, but my yearning for freedom did not," I said. "And then you veiled us, hindering our movements. By al-Lah! You might as well have put blinders on us."

All these restrictions, we were told, were meant to protect us. It was the same excuse I'd been hearing all my life. It made no difference that I, an accomplished sword-fighter, could protect myself.

"That's why I said such angry words to you in the cooking tent the day you returned," I said, my voice catching. "Forgive me, but I've never believed that God meant for me to live in a cage. If it's a sin for me to say these things, al-Lah forgive me. He knows my heart. As you do now, my love."

Still he sat motionless, barely blinking. "Muhammad!" I cried, starting to sob. "Say something to me. Anything!" He did nothing, made no sound, just sat and stared into the night.

"*Yaa* Prophet, what is going on up there?" The guard's voice rose, but I didn't dare look down. "You! What are you doing? Come down!"

"Muhammad," I said, beginning to tremble. "Muhammad, please."

"Come down here now, or I will shoot!" the guard shouted. I heard Hafsa cry out, and then Sawdah, and soon the entire *harim* had gathered at the bottom of the tree to watch me descend.

My tears fell like hot raindrops onto my sister-wives' upturned faces as I slowly made my way down the tree. Muhammad had reached his decision where I was concerned, that was clear. How heartlessly he'd listened to me bare my soul, reveal my fears and my sorrows, and beg him for forgiveness, without even a glance or a nod of acknowledgment! I might as well have been a gnat buzzing about his head.

My tears dripped down my chin and rolled down my neck, tickling me. I stopped to wipe them away, but all I did was dampen my fingers so that they could barely grasp the copper posts that had been hammered into the sides of the tree. I stopped again to wipe one hand on my robe, and the other hand lost its hold—and then I was falling so fast my cry of alarm couldn't even escape my mouth before I hit the hard, parched ground.

30

Free at Last

I heard several gasps and Sawdah's "By al-Lah!" before the dear old mother was crouching beside me, cradling my head in her hands and feeling my temples for a pulse. I knew I'd have to withstand hours of nursing and Evil-Eye rituals if I didn't get up right away, so I forced myself to stand, ignoring the pounding in my head and the dull ache in my abdomen.

"I'm unharmed." I forced a laugh. "Only clumsy."

"What were you doing up there?" Zaynab said, flashing her eyes at me. "Trying to convince Muhammad to divorce everyone except you, I suppose."

"Not everyone. I'd be happy if Hafsa and Sawdah stayed." I glared at her. Then I made my way to my apartment with Hafsa and a clucking Sawdah close behind.

"I'm afraid your wish won't come true where I'm concerned," Hafsa said once we'd entered my apartment.

"Muhammad's not going to divorce you." I held onto the wall so I wouldn't fall over.

"He threatened to, remember?" Hafsa said.

"By al-Lah, he wants to divorce me, also!" Sawdah unrolled my bed with a face as grim as death.

"Not you, Sawdah." I reached over to pat her back, and nearly toppled. "You've raised Muhammad's daughters, and me, also. Besides, you're the only one of his wives who doesn't complain."

"Maybe I should have spoken up more, then," she said. "Last month he asked would I be happier in my own house, free to marry someone who would have physical affection with me."

"Physical affection?" Hafsa blurted. "You and Muhammad don't—" Sawdah's *hmph* cut her off.

"What does an old woman like me want with that stuff? I had my fun with my first husband, as-Sakran. When he died, I did not want anybody else. I wanted to be with him in Paradise."

Slowly they helped me walk to my bed while Sawdah talked.

"When the Prophet asked me to be his wife, I knew he just wanted someone to take care of his house and his girls, but I was honored. It meant losing my chance to be with as-Sakran again, but I knew he would understand."

"He's a true martyr," Hafsa said. "Giving up his life for Muhammad, and then his wife."

"Now as-Sakran has a beautiful young *houri* in Paradise, and I am supposed to live with the Prophet in his castle, next door to al-Lah. But if he divorces me, I will not get anything!"

She wiped her tears, smearing dust across her cheeks and upper lip. Hafsa lifted the corner of her gown and cleaned Sawdah's face. "Muhammad, divorce you? We won't allow it," she said.

A sharp pain pierced my womb, like menstrual cramps more severe than any I'd ever imagined, making me cry out. Wetness ran down my leg. I looked down to see blood on the floor. I moaned, then heard the cries of my sister-wives as I fell. When I opened my eyes again, I was lying on my bed, drenched with perspiration. The smell of blood filled my nose and mouth. Sawdah was kneeling between my legs and wiping my thighs and private parts with a warm rag. She handed it to Umm Salama, who dunked it in a basin and wrung out pink water. I dug my nails into my palms to distract from the anguish spreading like heat through my body.

"I'll dab the moisture from her skin." Zaynab took a dry cloth from the stack. I remembered my words under the date-palm, awful words because I knew divorce would be as tragic for Zaynab and the other sister-wives as

for me. I closed my eyes, not wanting to see her satisfied smirk at the sight
of me in pain or, worse, her sympathy which I didn't deserve.

"Is she in danger, Sawdah?" Hafsa said, sniffling.

"Her body will be fine. It is not that unusual to lose the first one. But
her spirit is what I worry about, poor thing. She wanted this baby so much."

Wanted? My baby, gone? A taste like bitter herbs covered my tongue.
I splayed my fingers across my womb, felt a fluttering like wings.

"Now not even she is safe from divorce," Raihana said.

"By al-Lah, Raihana, are you so heartless?" Zaynab snapped. She
pressed the cloth against my forehead, my cheeks, my neck, making soft,
cooing sounds although she couldn't have known I was listening. My
baby, dead! *Al-Lah, how could you let this happen?*

"For you to lose Muhammad is nothing, Raihana," Hafsa chimed in.
"You aren't even his wife. A'isha married him when she was a young girl."

"Losing Muhammad would be difficult for all of us," Juwairriyah said.
"When I think of returning to my family as a divorced woman, I want to
hurl myself off a cliff."

My baby. Hot tears rolled down the sides of my face. No little toes to
tickle, no big eyes to gaze into, no soft baby cheeks to kiss. Had he fingers
or toes yet? I had been carrying him not quite three months. Had he a
heartbeat, or ears to hear the songs I'd sung to him?

"I want to see him," I whispered, but no one heard me. And then I
thought of the miscarried babies I'd seen at the tent city: partially formed,
grotesque little creatures, more like nightmares than humans. Suddenly I
was glad my request had gone unheeded. I wanted to remember my son as
I'd imagined him: curly-haired like his father, and laughing, like me, running through the grass with his stick-sword and his friends, riding his
horse in a flurry of sand and shouts. And revering his mother above all
women. He was gone, my little man. Who would love me now? Whom
would I love above all others after Muhammad had gone to Paradise and
left me behind? Who would save me from a humiliating life as Zaynab's
servant? A dark wind blew through the hole in my body where he'd nest-
ed, bringing fresh tears to my eyes.

"At least you have a home to return to," Raihana said. "All my clan is
either dead or enslaved. What will happen to me? I'll poison myself before
I become some man's chattel."

I wanted so badly to sob, but my sister-wives had troubles, also. Should they have to bear my burdens? Divorce, I was learning, would devastate them in ways I, at least, didn't have to fear. If Muhammad cast me aside, I could return to my parents' home, where I would be fed and clothed. Umm Salama's family lived in Mecca, as did Umm Habiba's. Neither could return without giving up *islam*, yet they might starve if they remained in Medina. To survive they would have to marry again, but who would want them after the Prophet of God had shunned them? Even worse for Umm Salama, she had small children depending on her. How would she feed them?

Zaynab and Hafsa would return to their fathers' homes—but Zaynab's father was growing old, and would not live much longer. His brother—Zaynab's uncle—would marry her mother then, according to tradition.

"I have never liked the way he looks at me, as though I wore no clothes," I heard her say. "Living in the same house with him would only bring trouble. Al-Lah protect me from that fate!"

Hafsa dreaded a life with Umar, and who could blame her? He'd abuse her for bringing such shame on his head.

"His beatings will be terrible," she said. "Eventually, he'll kill me—or I'll wish I were dead."

As I listened to their fears, my tears dampened my pillow. Zaynab, blotting my perspiring face, didn't notice, to my relief. How could I bear their consolations now, when I had nothing but despair to offer them? What I really wished was for them to leave, so I could grieve for my lost baby in peace. My womb felt numb, violated by death's cold hand. My little man.

Their talk wearied me. *Please, al-Lah, send them away.* But why was I praying to God? He could have protected me from that plucking hand. Like Muhammad, He had turned His face from me. I was alone in the world. Tears gathered in my nose and eyes, but how could I mourn in a room full of others' heartache?

Sawdah pulled my gown back over my legs and dropped the rag with a plop into the bowl of water.

"I wonder if we ought to call the Prophet," she said. "He would want to know about poor A'isha."

I opened my mouth to speak, but my "no!" snagged in my throat. I squeezed Zaynab's hand. "She awakens!" she cried. I open my eyes and lingered on the faces of my sisters, all gathered around me like a beautiful bouquet. My heart flooded with love for them, even for Umm Habiba, who stood apart and frowned in concern, for Maryam, who was smiling, and for Zaynab, who clutched my hand as if I might be swept away by a *zauba'ah*.

"Let Muhammad finish his prayers," I said in a choked voice. "He can't do anything for me now." In truth, I didn't think I could bear the pity in his eyes, not when the last time I'd seen him he'd refused to look at me.

"But he will be a comfort to you," Sawdah said. "Let us call him, child."

"No!" I snapped. Seeing Muhammad would only break the pieces of my heart again. My sister-wives stared at me.

"What happened up there in the date-palm tree?" Raihana said.

"Nothing." In truth, that was the problem, but I didn't feel like talking about Muhammad. Would he blame me for the loss of our child? In a way, it had been my fault. If I'd heeded his command to leave him in peace, I wouldn't have fallen from the tree. How could I bear his blame? I would shatter like a rock under the hammer's blow.

"Watching Muhammad mourn will only make me feel worse," I said. I smiled at the women crowded around me. "And I have all of you here, my sisters. Who could be more comforting?"

They tended to me every moment for days, feeding me, bathing me, telling me stories, helping me heal. At night they left me alone to rest— but in truth, I slept very little. My lost child filled my dreams: the bubbling laughter I would never hear, the milky fat face I would never kiss. Early one morning I awoke in tears and remembered Muhammad. The month was nearly over. Tomorrow he would come down from the attic and reveal his decision. What would he say? Would he be sorry to learn that I really had been carrying his child? Or would he be relieved that I had lost it, freeing him to divorce me?

How one moment, one slip, had changed my world so completely! Against the bleak landscape of my baby's death, the possibility of divorce now seemed less terrible to me than it had before.

I considered my options. If Muhammad divorced me, I could marry someone else—Talha, perhaps, who'd bragged at Zaynab's wedding feast that he would make me his wife someday. With another husband, I'd contend with three other wives, at most, since the limit was four for ordinary men. And I'd be free to roam with my face unveiled.

Maybe, with a different husband, I could conceive again. My little man, gone! My stomach knotted at the thought of my baby's death. I sank to my knees, intending to pray, but I doubled over and wept, instead. Conceiving a child with Muhammad had taken so long, with his energies divided among ten women and his stamina diminished by age. If he kept me, would I ever bear him a son?

I heard a man's shout and stood to yank my curtain shut. Not yet time for the morning prayer, and already neck-craners were gathering in the courtyard! But no. In the slow blooming dawn I saw Muhammad trudging toward my hut, practically glowing in his white gown. The light in his copper eyes was subdued, like stars behind clouds, and the lines in his face pulled at his skin. He looked for all the world like a messenger bearing bad news, and my first impulse was to hide from him, or to run into the mosque and out the door. I'd had all the sorrow I could withstand.

But a true warrior doesn't flee, and in spite of the restrictions against my fighting I still considered myself a warrior. So I walked to my door and flung it open, facing my destiny with my chin thrust forward. Here came the man who'd ignored my pleas for his love and sent me, sobbing, down the date-palm tree. Hadn't he caused the tears that had sent me hurtling to the ground? Nothing he could do now would hurt me more than that.

"Ahlan, yaa Prophet," I said. "What a surprise to see you here today! You said you'd return in a month, but it has only been twenty-nine days."

The clouds parted from his eyes for a moment, revealing a glimmer. "This month, A'isha, has twenty-nine days only."

I refused him the smile he sought, as he'd refused to acknowledge me in his attic apartment. Holding my back as stiff as an arrow, I turned and walked inside as though I didn't care whether he followed me or not. I heard the door *whoosh* shut and turned around to face him. To face my destiny, which he held in his hands, because nothing of mine belonged to me.

His eyes searched mine, as if he were the one with the questions. His hair in damp ringlets, his sweet, fresh-bathed fragrance. His hands reaching out as if to hold me.

"You look pale, A'isha. Have you been ill?"

I closed my eyes. Summoning my strength.

"I thought you would have heard," I said. "Didn't Umar tell you?"

"I have spoken to no one except al-Lah this month. I vowed on my first day to listen to Him only."

"Is that why you ignored me when I came to see you?"

"You ignored my request to be left alone."

My sob surprised me, sharp and sudden as breaking glass. "You ignored my request to talk with you before you left. I had so many things to tell you! But now it's too late."

He stepped close to me and laid his hands on my shoulders. "Too late for what, *habibati?*"

I jerked away from his touch as if his hands were flames. How I'd longed for his solace these past days, as I'd grieved for our lost child! Now, though, as he stood before me with divorce on his mind, I had no desire for his comfort. His kindness would only make me cry, and I didn't want my eyes to be wet when he told me his decision. I was A'isha bint Abi Bakr, and I groveled before no one. No matter how much I loved him.

"Your son is dead, Muhammad."

He clutched at his beard. "Maryam—"

"No, not Maryam!" I took a deep breath, and when I spoke again it was in a calm, quiet voice. "Not Maryam. Me. I had an—accident, and I lost our child." In spite of myself, I began to cry. "He was almost three months old, and I loved him so much, and now he's gone and I have no one. He would have been so wonderful, Muhammad. He would have been ours."

I pressed my hands to my face, capturing my tears and hiding my shame, hoping he wouldn't ask me how it had happened. If I told him I'd fallen from the date-palm tree, he'd know it was my fault that our baby had died.

I felt his arms slide around my shoulders, and I buried my face in his beard, breathing in sandalwood and *miswak*, relishing the comfort I'd missed and would never, after this morning, feel again.

"A'isha, I am sorry," Muhammad said. His voice tore like cloth on a thorn tree, and I looked up to see his eyes spilling tears. "I should have been there. I should not have left you."

"Except you didn't believe I was pregnant. Why would you? I'd been acting like a child until then, accusing Maryam of having a lover, calling Umm Habiba a spy, fighting assassins to show what a warrior I am."

"You saved my life." His eyes were luminous. "Your courage continues to astound me. And now I know how brave you have always been. Being married to me was more difficult for you than I imagined."

His resigned tone sent a shudder through my blood, but I managed to give him a faint smile. "Why do you speak in the past tense, *habib?*" I said, keeping my voice light. "Aren't we still married?"

He gave me a long, quiet look. I held my smile up like a shield.

"That depends on you," he said.

"On me?" I forced a laugh. "You're mistaken about that, husband. Our marriage contract doesn't give me the power to divorce, only you."

"I am giving you that power now."

Pressed against him, I could feel his heartbeat like pounding fists against his chest. I looked up into his pooling eyes and saw my own open-mouthed reflection.

"The decision is yours to make, A'isha." My heart thrummed like powerful wings. I saw that his tears were gone, and that his face had stiffened as if he wore a mask.

"What decision?" I said.

"You can choose me and this life, or you can divorce me and marry someone else."

My stomach writhed. What strange game was this? His face was such a blank, I couldn't read his emotions. I pulled away from him and walked to my window. Outside, the sun lifted its face to the new day.

"I don't understand your game. If you want to divorce me, husband, please say so."

"It is no game, A'isha. I had vowed to listen only to al-Lah, but He opened my ears to your words the other night. When you left I wept tears of anger for my own ignorance. How little I have known of you! I did not know how miserable those years in *purdah* were for you."

"And you restricted my freedom later," I said. "It hardly seems fair, when I'm as good with a sword as anyone."

"The *umma* watches my every move, and so do my enemies. They watch you also."

"Let them watch! I've never cared what anyone else thinks."

"As the favored wife of al-Lah's Messenger, you must learn to care. I love your spirit, *habibati,* but others do not." In a few strides he'd closed the distance between us and stood before me at the window. "A'isha, as long as you are my wife you will have to hide yourself away, out of the glare of gossip and away from the threats of my enemies. I cannot afford the distractions or the added dangers."

"And I can't live like a bird in a cage," I said.

"No one is caging you. You are free to fly away now, if you wish. It was never my desire that you, or any woman, should be forced to marry me."

"Did you think I chose you at age six?" I huffed, impatient with his naivety. "Did you think I could even make a choice at that age?"

"I did not think about it at all, I am sorry to say. Your words from the date-palm tree showed me many things I had not known. Without the freedom to choose your own destiny, you are nothing more than a slave, A'isha. And you know I do not keep slaves."

"What are you saying?" My voice snagged in my throat.

"You are free, A'isha. To choose." He stepped to the cushions in the corner and settled himself, waiting.

As thoughts and emotions collided in me I turned again to the window, trying to make sense of Muhammad's offer. I, choose my destiny? That was like giving a camel the choice of which pasture to graze in. The morning breeze carried the fragrance of lavender, and I breathed it in, remembering my girlhood days wandering the hills and picking flowers. Divorced from Muhammad, I could do so again, without hiding behind a screen in my own home and without having to hold my wrapper over my face. As a free woman I could marry again if I chose or I could remain single.

Safwan still watched me with haunted eyes whenever I ventured out. He'd eagerly marry me—but he'd be even stricter than Muhammad. Talha would be a kind and respectful husband, and I could be happy with him. But how happy? Would I bubble with laughter and song at the thought of seeing him, as I did with Muhammad? Would my skin zing with lightning at his touch, or my body quiver from a single kiss?

I turned to Muhammad, who sat with crossed legs and eyes closed, his brow lined with worry, his mouth a thin line. Here was the man I had loved all my life, the man who'd taught me to fight, who'd shown me the ways of passion, who'd fathered the child I'd lost because of my love for him. With Muhammad, I was truly free—to speak, to dream, to make mistakes, to be myself. I might not be the queen of his *harim*, but I was the Great Lady of his heart. And now he'd given me the freedom and the power to choose my own destiny, the greatest gift anyone had ever given to me. In doing so, he had made me completely, utterly his own.

I knelt before him and removed the turban from his head. His eyes opened, and I saw fear race through them like a cold fire. I lifted his hand and pressed it to my cheek, and the fire went out, quenched by his tears.

"I choose you," I said.

He lowered his mouth to mine, and we drank each other deeply as if our love were the rain we'd been praying for these past years. I pressed my head to his heart, hearing it beat for me, feeling my pulse keep time with the murmurs and sighs that were his own love's song.

"A'isha," he murmured. "My beloved."

He kissed me one last, lingering time. It was a kiss that promised many more in the days and years to come. Then, too soon, he untangled himself from my arms and reached for his turban.

"Don't go yet, *habibi*," I begged. "Tarry with me awhile."

His eyes brimmed with love. "I will return," he said. "Very soon."

I felt a stab of jealousy until I realized that his smile was a grim one. I knew he didn't want to leave me but that he had a duty to perform. I remembered my sister-wives' tears as they'd nursed me and fretted over their futures, and fear for them sprang me to my feet to stop him.

"Muhammad, wait!" I said. He turned to me, and I clasped his hands. "Are you going to divorce your other wives?"

The vein on his forehead darkened. "That is what you desire, is it not?"

I lowered my gaze, ashamed of the person he thought I was. "At one time, it might have been. But not now. My sister-wives—they're all so frightened." I told him what I'd heard as they'd nursed me, how their lives would be as dust if he cast them aside. "They need you, Muhammad." I swallowed my own fear and met his gaze. "Even more than I do."

The vein on his brow disappeared in the tracks of his broad smile. "My A'isha," he said. "A woman at last." His words spread a warm glow from my heart to my fingertips, and I pulled myself a little taller.

He turned to leave again, but I halted him with a touch.

"Please don't tell my sister-wives what I've said about them. They spoke privately, among women, and they may not want you to know their fears."

His nod was curt. "On the other hand," he said, "they may be pleased to hear how you spoke on their behalf. And this is one pleasure I would not want to withhold from them."

◆

I waited for an hour, pacing more trenches in my floor. When Muhammad returned to me, would he bring good news or bad? Some said it would save the *umma* if he divorced us all, that it would stop the speculation that he was weak where women were concerned. Others said it would destroy *islam* by breaking the ties Muhammad had built with his marriages. As for me, I knew only that losing Muhammad would destroy my sister-wives.

The knock on my door made me jump. I raced to answer it—my heart throwing itself against my chest. In the doorway stood Muhammad, his face grave—and, clustered behind him, all the women of the *harim*, their eyes spilling tears. Sorrow covered me like dirt over a grave, and I cried out, knowing they were lost.

Zaynab stepped forward, her plump arms outstretched, her gold eyes flashing. "We have heard how you pled for us to our husband," she said. "Now—" a sob caught in her throat, snagging her words, "—we have come to thank you, and to make you our *hatun*."

I opened my mouth, but, in my astonishment, no words would come. Then, in one motion, my sister-wives joined Zaynab in stretching out their arms to me, then folding themselves in a deep bow. Muhammad stood in their center, his wild hair flying, his smile leaping like light from his face before he whisked off his turban and bowed nearly all the way to the ground.

TEN THOUSAND FIRES

*E*ach day was an unfinished thought. Night was a secret bursting to be told. People spoke in hushed tones. Questions marked all our faces.

Our invasion of Mecca was close at hand, and as eagerly anticipated as the next rains. *Why does the Prophet delay?* my sister-wives would ask me. I'd shrug, pretending I knew nothing. In truth, Muhammad had kept our departure date a secret even from me. He planned to surprise the Meccans with our army. Yet I could guess why we tarried, for I saw the answer in Muhammad's eyes when he laid his hand on Maryam's swollen belly. He was waiting—we all waited—for a child.

I wasn't jealous. I had nothing to fear now from this child or from my sister-wives. Since they'd made me the *hatun*, no one could take my status away, not even the mother of Muhammad's heir. Nor should anyone want to, for I governed the *harim* fairly, forgoing the revenge I'd vowed against Zaynab, whom I hated no more. My sister-wives had honored me. Would I treat them dishonorably in return?

In truth, I admired Zaynab for giving up the position. She'd resisted at first, Hafsa said, but then, after meditating and praying, agreed—and convinced Umm Salama to support the change. *It is a small gesture, compared to the effort A'isha has made on our behalf,* Zaynab had said.

We were no longer enemies, but my troubles were far from over. Now that I was the *hatun,* Ali criticized me more than ever, commenting on the chaos in the cooking tent as if it were new, spitting out the food I cooked and claiming it tasted like poison, and following me to the market like a persistent shadow in hopes of catching me in some sin that would degrade me and my father in Muhammad's eyes.

Muhammad took little notice of Ali. His only thoughts were for the baby. "He's patient, like his father," I teased Muhammad, who fretted constantly about the lateness of the birth.

"Babies have been being born since Eve had her first young one," Sawdah told him. "It will come in al-Lah's time, not ours."

Time stretched thin and quivering, ready with a birth of its own. A group of horses escaped from their pens and galloped into the mosque, where they injured a praying man with their flailing hooves. Meanwhile, Maryam, unconcerned with our impending invasion, sang and laughed as though each day were the first of spring. I and Sawdah walked every morning to her home, fretting over another battle with Quraysh and worrying over our loved ones in Mecca until the whitewashed bricks of Maryam's house came into sight. Like everyone else in the *harim,* I'd been glad to see her exiled to the country, but now I envied her. Here she tended her own flower garden; through her window she could view the craggy orange-black cliffs ringing Medina. Here she could rest her mind, away from the demands of the burgeoning *umma.*

Every day in Medina brought more mouths to feed. Muhammad's influence was spreading like sunlight across a land darkened by ignorance. Converts to *islam* poured into Medina, few of them with knowledge of farming. These new *umma* members suffered as we had at first, from the Medina fever and, most of all, from empty purses.

As Muhammad's *hatun,* I was supposed to provide their first meal. Under my direction, barley simmered constantly, and servants presented bowls of it to as many as fifty people a day. We wives ground the meal, hauled water, made bread and milked goats as we wore the new veils Umm Salama had fashioned to free our hands.

The tributes to Muhammad from foreign leaders had dwindled, for there were only so many kings in our world. Muhammad sent Zayd and a few others to invite the Byzantine emperor to accept *islam*, but they were mocked and jeered out of Constantinople. Then, in the desert, tragedy struck. The emperor's warriors pursued our men and killed them all. Zayd's death haunted the *umma*, causing even Zaynab to cry copious tears. Umm Ayman carried her grief like a flag, stumbling glassy-eyed through the streets and shrieking Zayd's name as though a *djinni* tormented her.

Muhammad held his own sorrow close, as he always had, retreating to his apartment for several days and emerging to utter a hoarse prayer over his body. Then he disappeared into the *majlis* with his Companions for long meetings.

On his visits to me Muhammad spoke not only of Zayd, but also of the Byzantine emperor's rejection. We couldn't count on help from that wealthy empire. The drought that had plagued us since before the Battle of the Trench persisted still. Our allies would have to pay a tax to Medina, or we'd starve to death.

"Yet there are many, like the emperor, who think us insignificant," Muhammad said. "Few will agree to pay a single *dirham* until we prove our strength by ruling Quraysh." Seizing Mecca was crucial to our survival.

For our visits to Maryam's home, I and Sawdah carried my replenished medicine bag and Sawdah's incenses and charms. I went reluctantly, at first, out of duty to Muhammad. But soon Maryam's home became our oasis within the oasis. She and her eunuch, Akiiki, welcomed us into her house filled with green plants and plush red and gold carpets, with blue and purple and yellow and green cushions strewn about like flower petals. A tapestry on the wall depicted a haloed Virgin Mary on an ass, her belly plump with her child under a star bursting forth from the heavens. A window looked out over pastures where ewes and lambs grazed and frolicked, luring me out to play. But I had more important tasks to attend: The massaging of Maryam's hands and feet, which suffered from poor circulation, and of her belly, where Muhammad's child seemed intent on kicking its way out.

Not once did I hear Maryam complain: Not when the child bulged against her skin, making it shiny and taut. Not when it weighted her steps to make moving about a chore. She'd hold Akiiki's arm when she walked, laughing.

"My baby's house is growing nearly as large as his mother's," she would say. "He will have to come out soon, though, for my body has no windows."

Going home was the most difficult part of each day. We'd say our farewells with light hearts, then stroll arm-in-arm through the fertile gardens and rolling meadows until the city enveloped us again in stink and gloom. Our covered faces marked us as Muhammad's wives even to strangers, and we inevitably found ourselves dodging those questions—*Why does he delay? When do we go?*—and averting our gazes from anxious eyes.

One evening, as we took our last breath of sweet air and pulled our wrappers tight for the descent into Medina, we heard shouts from behind. Akiiki, looking like an animated stick, ran toward us with waving arms. He spoke no Arabic, but his expressive gestures were easy to understand. As he spread his hands over an imaginary bloated belly and thrust them downward, we knew the child was coming. Sawdah waddled back to Maryam's house with the eunuch while I fled into town to fetch Umm Hanifi, the midwife.

I found the old woman attending a labor in the tent city, her hands coaxing a slippery babe from between a woman's legs as if she were pulling a plant, roots and all, from the soil. At the sight of me children and old men patted my robe, searching for the barley and dates I usually brought. I promised them food tomorrow, but they would not leave me, and in their hunger I thought they might devour me, instead.

"*Yaa* Umm Hanifi, the Prophet's child is coming soon," I shouted to her over the fray. "Sawdah sent me to fetch you to Maryam's house. Her labor pains are coming hard and fast."

She nodded as if I'd announced the time of day and pulled a long knife out of the sheath on her belt.

"Sawdah knows what to do," she said as she sliced the cord holding the child to its mother. "Look for me on my donkey when I have bathed and rested."

Back at the house I found Maryam sweating and gasping on her bed with Muhammad holding one hand and Akiiki holding the other. Sawdah handed Muhammad a palm-frond fan, and he waved it over Maryam's hot face.

"You had better start the fumigation, *yaa* A'isha," Sawdah said. "Umm Hanifi will move at her own pace, but we can get things started."

Maryam moaned. I lay my hand on her stomach and uttered a silent prayer to al-Lah for her comfort. *Forgive me, also, for my envy over this child,* I asked. *Please do not let it harm the baby or its mother.* As though in response, I felt a ripple like water flowing over a sharp rock.

"What a kick!" I said, making Muhammad and Maryam smile. "Your child is a fighter, *yaa* Maryam."

"It has to be a boy, by al-Lah," Sawdah said. "No girl was ever so boisterous—except maybe you, A'isha." She sucked in her breath and reached for her amulet. "Male or female, whatever al-Lah desires," she added quickly.

I rummaged in my bag for my mortar and pestle, then a pouch filled with goldenroot. This I would grind with frankincense to mask its pungent odor, then smolder in my brazier to fumigate Maryam's private parts. The vapors would protect the baby from infection—if the midwife ever arrived.

"What, by al-Lah, is taking her so long?" Muhammad cried, after sending Akiiki out for the fifth time to look for Umm Hanifi. The eunuch shouted something unintelligible. I ran to the door to see the portly midwife riding across the meadow on a slow donkey, dressed for a celebration in a colorful gown that billowed about her in the afternoon breeze, earrings dangling to her shoulders, her eyes heavily kohled and her lips rouged a bright red. Hundreds of Believers crowded around her, tossing flowers in her path and ululating their good wishes.

Inside, I told Muhammad what I'd seen. "While the midwife basks in the *umma*'s love, Maryam teeters in the maw of death!" he cried. I had to stop myself from laughing. Was this the mighty Prophet of God? He could learn a lesson or two from the eunuch Akiiki, who, though excited, was managing to remain calm.

Maryam's eyes twinkled, while Sawdah shook her head in disgust. "Warriors are the worst," she murmured. "They kill and maim without a care, but the sight of a woman giving birth makes their blood tremble and their stomachs quake."

Umm Hanifi walked into the room as imperiously as any queen. Sawdah waved a handful of coriander and began her incantations against the Evil Eye. The midwife's face sharpened to a stern point at the sight of Muhammad and Akiiki in the room.

"Be gone, and let the women do their work!" she cried, waving her muscular arms. "If we need the aid of a man, we will summon al-Lah."

In truth, we summoned Him many times during the long hours that followed. The labor was hard and long, but the only screams came from Sawdah, who railed against the evil forces holding the child from this world.

"You're allowed to express your pain, *yaa* Maryam," I said as she crushed my fingers in her grip. "You don't have to be brave."

Tears rolled down the sides of her face. "It does hurt. But if I cry out, Muhammad might hear me and worry about his child."

At last the time came for us to help her into the birthing chair, where she pushed and strained and grunted as Umm Hanifi rubbed her stomach and legs.

"This baby does not want to enter this world," the midwife said, frowning. "A short life is the usual interpretation."

Sawdah shrieked, then grabbed her coriander bundle and waved it in front of the midwife's mouth, "sending those evil words away before they could reach the child," she told me later.

Any malign spirits remaining in the room surely would have flown away when we began our earsplitting ululations announcing the baby's arrival, setting off trills and cheers among the Believers surrounding the house. Maryam cradled the wizened child and gazed at him as if he were the most beautiful sight she'd ever seen. I swallowed my tears, refusing to think of the child I'd lost, denying the taunting voice inside me that whispered that my status as *hatun* meant nothing now, that the infant was a boy and Muhammad would love him—and his mother—most of all, no matter how many children I might bear. Love, I reminded myself, was not a contest. Nor was it a dish of *tharid*, to be divided up and devoured until it was gone. Giving love away only made it increase. I smoothed the damp hair from Maryam's face and she squeezed my hand.

"May you be next, A'isha," she said.

◆

Ten thousand campfires: That was Muhammad's strategy for subduing Quraysh. Our army spread itself around the city of Mecca and built one fire for every man to emblazon the hills with light and make us appear as numerous as the stars. I and Muhammad stood at the edge of the al-Hudaybiyyah overlook and gazed in wonder at the bright lights at our feet, listened to the shouts of the warriors warning the Meccans that tomorrow would be ours.

"Imagine what the Quraysh are thinking now." Muhammad's quiet laughter tickled my ear as he squeezed my waist. "They cannot but know that al-Lah has arrived."

His eyes shone with another kind of fire. His kiss tasted of metal and spice. I breathed him in, smoke from the cooking fires and *miswak* and dust from our long journey. "At last, *habibi*, you're going home," I said. "And when you arrive, you'll rule. Abu Sufyan won't challenge you now."

In truth, Abu Sufyan's eyes bulged with fear when Ali escorted him to our tent that night. Inside, he fell to his knees and flung his arms around Muhammad's legs, making Saffiya shriek. Ali grabbed his robe and yanked him backward, then pressed his dagger against the fat man's throat.

Abu Sufyan shook like a candle-flame. "I beg you, son of Abdallah, do not destroy Quraysh!" he cried in a choked voice. "Be merciful to your people."

"My supporters will be spared, Abu Sufyan." Muhammad's tone was casual, as though his enemies were always barging into his tent. "As for you, I have not heard any professions of faith from your lips."

"How can I profess faith in your God and betray my people?" Abu Sufyan croaked. "I am the leader of Quraysh. Their gods are my gods."

"And their Hell is your Hell, you sniveling coward!" Ali scraped his blade across Abu Sufyan's neck, shaving off wisps of red-gray beard. "Profess al-Lah's Prophet here and now, or die."

"Wait!" Abu Sufyan's beard quivered. "I have seen the light of al-Lah in Ali's blade. The truth is revealed to me! There is no god but al-Lah, and Muhammad is His Messenger."

"Liar!" Ali pushed Abu Sufyan to the ground and spat on him. "Can such a speedy conversion be sincere, Prophet?"

"Only al-Lah knows the hearts of men." Muhammad extended his hand to Abu Sufyan. "I accept every man who calls me Prophet. Arise, Abu Sufyan, and welcome to the *umma*."

Disappointment clouded Ali's eyes. He'd wanted to kill Abu Sufyan—and, in my heart, I'd wanted it, too. At last, when he faced punishment for his wicked deeds, he'd needed only to say a few words to become blameless in Muhammad's sight. Yet, I had to remind myself, as Muhammad's *hatun*, my job was to support his decisions, not to doubt them.

Behind our screen, I and Saffiya listened to the men discuss the plans for the next day. Our entire army would march into the city, followed by our women. Anyone who opposed us would be crushed.

"Yet we would prefer to enter in peace," Muhammad said. "We have come to claim Mecca for al-Lah, not to make war."

Abu Sufyan's eyes darted from Ali to Muhammad. He licked his thick lips.

"Most of us have agreed to your terms," he said. "But a few young hot-heads vow to fight you. They are no threat, of course. You will be able to overcome them easily without losing a man."

Muhammad smiled at him and nodded: This was the kind of information he wanted. "Already you prove a worthy ally, Abu Sufyan," he said. "Your friendship will be well rewarded."

The night wore on. Throughout the camp, fires sputtered and gasped, succumbing to the dark and the cold. Inside my tent I felt the warmth of our own fire's waning light against my cheek. Through my closed eyelids I watched their flickering images, like shadow puppets dancing their way into Mecca. The motherland. The city I hardly remembered. Home. Anywhere Muhammad was, there was my home. *He* was my home.

His kiss awakened me even before Bilal's summon to the morning prayer. The sun had barely brushed the sky, but I leapt up and pulled on my pure white gown. When Muhammad had led the pilgrimage to Mecca on the anniversary of his peace treaty, he'd taken Umm Salama and Zaynab but left me behind, punishing me for failing to support his pact. Now, having regained his trust, I would at last visit the famous Ka'ba, built by Ibrahim and his son Ishmael so many years ago, with its mysterious black cornerstone dropped to the Earth by al-Lah Himself.

"The Ka'ba was built for al-Lah, not for the idols that profane it now," Muhammad said. "Today we return it to Him."

Waiting for our turn to enter the city's gates, we women sat on our camels and watched the procession. Nearby Abu Sufyan stood with his adviser, al-Abbas, uncle to both Muhammad and Ali. From my vantage I could see, and hear, the two men laughing as the Banu Muzayna jostled past, spitting and shuffling in their bare feet.

"We surrendered to this?" Abu Sufyan jeered. Al-Abbas smiled and said nothing.

"The laughter of Quraysh frightens me more than this ragged crew," he said of the Sulaym, with their dusty robes and rotting teeth.

But when the men of Medina marched past in perfect formation, fully armored, with their splendid, green-hooded horses, Abu Sufyan was silent. Muhammad's army was nothing to laugh at, as he well knew.

At last Talha came to lead the women through the gate in Mecca's high stone wall. Nearly all the *umma*'s women rode in *hawdajs* now, commanded by their husbands to endure the teetering ride in imitation of the Prophets' wives. Through my curtain I could see that Mecca was nothing like Medina. The air smelled pure and fresh, if a bit dusty from our camels' hooves. The houses of stone and pale clay shone in the sun. The market, in the shadow of the dark, bulky Mount Hira, looked forlorn with its long rows of stalls emptied of vendors, but festive banners crisscrossed the sky over its street. I recalled, faintly, the bustle of the place on an ordinary day: its jingling bells and smells of meat and incense, its lowing cattle and twittering caged birds, its beckoning merchants and men and women bargaining in strange tongues.

We stopped before the Ka'ba, a large cube-shaped building so starkly white it might have been freshly washed for us. Although I'd seen it many times as a child, I'd been too dazzled by the market to pay it much attention. Now, though, my spine shivered as I stood on the black flagstones circling its base. As spotless as it appeared, the roil of horses and men seemed intent on dirtying it, sending swirls of dust into the air as the *umma*'s warriors smashed their blades on the hundreds of idols perched on pedestals around it.

Muhammad stood in the Ka'ba's doorway, his smile disheveled, his hair curling in the sweaty air, his right hand hoisting his sword. "The Ka'ba is cleansed!" he cried. "*Al-Lahu akbar!* God is great!"

From the Ka'ba's rooftop Bilal echoed his cry. The women's camels knelt, and we emerged from our curtains, barefaced before God, and joined the wave of Believers dropping to the sand and stretching out their arms. Our shouts of praise soared as if on the wings of a hawk, wheeling higher and higher to the God who had brought His Prophet home at last.

We stood to watch Ali wrap a black turban about Muhammad's head. He handed him a white flag, which Muhammad waved as he ran—not daring to walk, lest Quraysh think him weak—three times around the Ka'ba, then twice between the city's sacred hills. Then, his moist face gleaming, he raised the flag to the roar of men and women who lifted their swords and handkerchiefs and hands in return.

The crowd parted at the base of the Ka'ba's steps, making way for my father. He ascended carefully, holding the hand of a very old *shaykh* who hobbled with a cane, and whose clothes and skin hung loose from jutting bones.

"My father stands ready to profess his faith in al-Lah and His Messenger," *abi* announced. I hurried to his side to greet my grandfather for the first time in my memory. Seeing me there, Muhammad held out his hand, and I ascended the steps to sit beside him at his right hand.

Soon the greetings of Believers and long-lost family members filled the air with joy.

"*Ummi!*" Umm Salama cried, and ran to embrace a tall woman in pale silk with her own prominent cheekbones. Ali presented al-Abbas, who held out to Muhammad a young woman with a thick cloud of black hair.

"Will you do me the privilege of marrying my daughter Maymunah, and joining our families again?" he said. I narrowed my eyes, watching her closely. Al-Abbas was Muhammad's uncle, but he was also Abu Sufyan's closest Companion. Might he use his daughter to try to harm Muhammad?

Uthman herded an entire family to kneel at Muhammad's feet. Talha brought his father—my mother's brother—making my mother gasp with delight. But when Abu Sufyan accompanied his pinch-faced wife Hind up the stairs, the *umma* hissed.

The bulge between Muhammad's eyes throbbed as he glared down at her. I cringed, recalling how she'd shrieked with laughter at Uhud as she'd lifted our general Hamza's bloody liver to her mouth. Ali charged up the stairs with his double-bladed Zulfikar quivering in his hand.

"You whore of Hubal," he growled. "I'll spill your blood all over these steps."

To Ali's astonishment and mine, Muhammad raised a hand to stop him.

"*Yaa* Hind, your husband has pleaded for your life today," he said. "Before I decide your fate, I want to know: Do you recognize me as God's Prophet?"

Aghast, I looked at the ground, hiding my disapproval. Would Muhammad capitulate to the evil Hind as he'd accommodated her treacherous husband?

She lifted glittering eyes to his—and spat on his robe. I trembled with the urge to lunge at her.

"I, forsake the mighty Hubal and the glorious al-Lat for a son of Hashim?" she cried. "Unlike my weak-livered husband, I am no traitor to my gods. Nor will I pretend to believe for the sake of saving my pitiful life. Do with me as you will, Ibn al-Muttalib."

Jeers pelted her, but Muhammad lifted his hand again, quelling the noise.

"Your husband has prayed for al-Lah's mercy, and God has decided to grant it, whether or not you convert," Muhammad said. "Go home with your husband, and do not cause any more trouble. Al-Lah's patience is infinite, but mine is not."

Hind's eyes grew as round as her astonished mouth, and her body began to quake. Her legs collapsed and she fell to her knees, then pressed her face shamelessly into Muhammad's lap. His cheeks reddened as if someone had lit a fire in his mouth, and my own face flamed, also.

But when she lifted her head and I saw her tears, my anger quelled. Pride poured into me like water filling an empty vessel. Muhammad had known what he was doing. By granting Hind her life, he'd won her allegiance.

"After all I have done against you, you would let me live?" she said. "What kind of man are you, son of Hashim? By God, I have never known such kindness." She stood and lifted her arms toward the sky, as if to embrace the entire *umma*. "I hereby proclaim your God as my God, Muhammad ibn Abdallah ibn al-Muttalib, and you are most certainly His Prophet."

And then, his enemies vanquished by force and forgiveness, Muhammad at long last, after decades of anguish and rejection, heard his kinspeople and his enemies shout his praises. One by one, every *shaykh*, every grandmother, every warrior and wife, every girl and boy in the city dropped to the stone steps at his feet and declared Muhammad the Prophet of the One God, then walked away with a red spot on the forehead from pressing it into the stone. Some grinned like jackals; others nursed sullen frowns. Many looked exhausted—but not Muhammad, who stood all night under the full moon to accept the homage of his people, his face brighter than the light from ten thousand fires.

And I? I led the wives, with Talha before us, back to our camp and slept the long, peaceful sleep of the first wife of the most powerful man in Hijaz.

The Keys to Paradise

uhammad was so proud of his son, anyone might think he'd fashioned him with his own hands. "Isn't he a handsome boy?" he'd say as the rosy-cheeked Ibrahim yanked at his beard. And then, with a wink, "Note how he resembles me, A'isha."

I'd tilt my head, eyeing the baby's golden curls and indigo eyes, and frown. "I see no likeness," I'd tease. "Are you sure he's yours?"

In truth, Ibrahim was like his father in just about every way. He never seemed to be still, even when he slept, and he never let anything stand in the way of a goal. Sawdah loved to tell how he took his first step as she and Maryam watched: Frustrated with trying to chase Abu Hurayra's cat on his hands and knees, he'd pulled himself upright and hurled his body across the floor to catch it. And, like his father, Ibrahim loved women. He made the rounds through the *harim* more often than Muhammad.

As for me, I loved him as much as anyone in the *harim*, despite my failure to conceive another child with Muhammad. I'd been jealous, yes, when he was born, and my arms ached with longing for a baby when I watched Maryam cuddle him. But as much as Muhammad doted on his child, his love and respect for me seemed only to grow as the years passed, easing my fears that he'd discard me for his concubine and freeing me to adore Ibrahim the way I did my nephew Abdallah. Besides, I'd learned from Muhammad how powerful love and forgiveness could be—far more so than jealousy and hate.

Then one day, Ibrahim fell ill. Fever burned his skin as though he'd swallowed not just one sun, but one thousand and one, and his eyes grew as dazed and shiny as if they'd turned to glass. Muhammad spent every moment at his side, growing thinner and more haggard every day. When the time came for Friday service my father offered to take Muhammad's place, but Muhammad declined. "Perhaps my prayers will help him," he said.

Moments after the service had ended, Sawdah and I had begun preparing the daily meal when Akiiki ran into the oven tent, gesturing crazily and gibbering in his broken mixture of Arabic and Egyptian. I and Sawdah grabbed our medicines and ran—or rather, I and Akiiki ran under the clouds racing like dark horses overhead while Sawdah hefted along far behind us, shouting through the winds for us to go on, not to wait, she'd be there in a minute or two.

But there was no need for Sawdah to hurry. I knew it as soon as we entered the house and saw Maryam holding the stiff little bundle in her arms and pressing it to her chest.

"He is cold, that is all," she said. "I need to warm him up."

I reached for him but Maryam drew away.

"I've run all the way from the mosque," I said. "See? I'm so warm I'm perspiring. Give him to me, and I'll try." His fist grasped the *ankh* pendant Maryam wore under the sapphire necklace Muhammad had given her. A faint blue sheen edged his lips. His body was a chunk of wood or stone in my arms. I placed my hand over his nostrils, feeling for breath, knowing there'd be none. I cried out just as Muhammad threw open the door and rushed into the room.

"I heard there was trouble," he said. He glanced at Maryam's stricken face, then turned panicked eyes to me. I couldn't speak for my tears so I held the child out to him with trembling arms.

He took the baby and fell to his knees. He covered Ibrahim's cheeks with kisses and shook him until I feared he'd harm the child—until I remembered that it was too late, and my sobs wracked me so that I also sank to the floor.

"Al-Lah!" Muhammad cried. "Al-Lah! Why have you taken my son from me? Did I love him too much? Al-Lah! Give him back, and I will love him less. Take me, instead."

Outside, a crash. A smell like the sea blew in through the open door. Wet splats hit the roof as Muhammad's tears fell on Ibrahim's still face. In Medina the men would dance, lifting their faces to drink in our first rainfall in years. Sawdah appeared in the doorway, clothes clinging to her drenched body, her broad smile as ephemeral as a child's life.

◆

At the funeral Muhammad prayed over Ibrahim's body with vacant eyes. His voice droned as if his soul, too, had flown from this world. Maryam huddled against the weeping Akiiki, her blue eyes swimming in their own stormy sea. We sister-wives stood around her in the still-pouring rain, shielding her with our robes from the storm.

Her grief made me almost glad I had never given birth to my child. Hadn't Khadija birthed two of Muhammad's sons, both of whom had died as infants? I'd heard the whispers circling through the *umma*: *It is not al-Lah's will for the Prophet to leave an heir.* If that were so, and I'd borne a son, how much greater would my pain have been to lose him now! As it was, my heart still ached for my little man. But no one's grief was more wrenching than Muhammad's.

For days, weeks, months, no one could console him. Darkness veiled his eyes, and he eluded us all like a shadow under the new moon. We begged him to eat, but he prayed instead, kneeling on his attic floor and awaiting God's comfort. We offered to hold him in our beds at night, but he slept in the cemetery, next to Ibrahim's grave.

One night in June, four months after Ibrahim's death, he arrived in my room at dawn. I moved in a fog through the morning prayer, having waited up for him. When I'd finished my prostrations, I slumped onto my bed, moaning. Muhammad sat beside me and held my hand, touching me for the first time in weeks.

"Oh, my head," I complained. He stroked my forehead with his fingertips, and the pain disappeared.

"No, A'isha," he said. "It is, 'Oh, *my* head.'" He tried to smile, but it looked more like a grimace.

"You've been grieving too long for a child you'll see again in Paradise," I said. I sat up and patted my lap. "Come and rest."

"You speak the truth, *habibati*." He stood to set his turban on the windowsill, then nestled down against me. His eyes flickered like waning fires. "I will see Ibrahim again, and soon."

"You, my love? A strong and healthy warrior? Al-Lah willing, I'll die before you."

"A'isha." His voice lowered. I leaned forward to hear him. "If you died before me, would you allow me to put the shroud on you and pray over you?"

"And leave you to feast with your other wives? I've changed my mind." I forced a smile, teasing. "I will not die first."

"You speak the truth."

I smoothed the hair away from his forehead. "Muhammad, your skin is burning! Did you build a fire at the cemetery to warm yourself?"

"My energy has been diminished since Ibrahim's death. My head aches so acutely, I can barely see." He closed his eyes and pressed his fingers against his temples. "A'isha. Al-Lah gave me a choice last night: Either the keys to my kingdom and the treasures of this world, or meeting Him in Paradise soon."

"By al-Lah, I hope you chose your new kingdom and its treasures!" My voice quivered like the string of a plucked *tanbur*.

He opened his eyes, but his gaze was far away. "This world's wealth stands as a barrier to al-Lah," Muhammad murmured. "I would rather go now, before too many possessions block my path to Him."

"There is little danger of that, my ascetic one." Tears clotted like blood on my tongue. My hand moved mechanically over his forehead, detached from my whirling thoughts. What could I say to bring him back to me? *Help me, al-Lah, before he is truly lost.*

"Don't be so impatient for Paradise, my husband. Eternity lasts forever, but I'm only nineteen years old. I have many days and nights remaining in this life. Would you be so cruel and leave me alone now? Tarry with me a while longer, *habibi*."

"It cannot be, A'isha." He closed his eyes. His breathing slowed. His

right arm twitched. His lips blurred. The vein between his eyes pulsed
gently, giving off a faint blue glow. "I have made my choice." Soon his
snores filled the room like music, accompanied by my sobs and prayers.
Please don't take him from me, not yet.

My legs grew numb, but I never moved. Two calls to prayer passed.
Hafsa called at my door, but I didn't answer. I sat with my eyes affixed to
Muhammad's face as if he were a star in the night sky, leading me home.
If his days were numbered, I wanted to fill my memory with him now,
before death snatched him away.

When he awoke that evening, his fever had broken. His smile fluttered; his eyes danced.

"I thought your frown had conquered your face," I teased. *Thank you,
al-Lah, for hearing my prayers.* "And your sickness, *habib?* Has it gone
away?"

"I am feeling well enough to visit my wives." He made his way to the
wash basin, where he brushed his teeth and cleansed his face. I rewound
his turban for him, then placed it on his head.

"I have neglected you for too long, A'isha," he said. "Forgive me." He
pulled me into his arms and kissed me so deeply his turban tumbled to the
floor. I clung to him, drinking him in the way we'd lifted our thirsty
mouths to the rain the day Ibrahim died. Then, when Muhammad had
left, I rolled out my prayer mat and gave thanks to al-Lah until my knees
ached.

At last the rumblings of my stomach sent me to the cooking tent.
Crossing the courtyard, I heard a cry. The door to the hut of Maymunah,
Muhammad's new wife from Mecca, flew open, and she appeared, shouting for help. I ran to her aid and found Muhammad slumped on her floor,
moaning and white-faced. The aroma of meat hit me, and I noted, in the
corner of the room, a dish half-filled with *tharid.* Had she put something
in that dish to sicken him? I ran to Muhammad and touched his face. His
skin burned with fever. His eyes winced with pain.

"Oh, my head," he moaned.

The other sister-wives rushed in, flapping and cooing, crowding
Maymunah's elegant apartment. Her father al-Abbas had provided well
for her: carpets, frankincense, silk curtains, velvet cushions, jewels dripping from her ears to rival the onyx necklace Muhammad had given her.

Ali and al-Abbas pushed their way in and helped us stretch Muhammad out on Maymunah's soft feather bed.

"This is a good place for you to rest," I said, but Muhammad shook his head.

"This is not Maymunah's night," he said. "Whose night is this? Is it yours, A'isha?"

"That was last night, remember?" I squeezed his feeble hand.

"When will it be your night again?" he said.

"Don't you be worrying about that, Prophet," Sawdah said. "Get your rest. We will stay here with you all night, if that is what it takes."

He moaned and clutched his head. Umm Salama placed her hand on my arm. "*Yaa* A'isha, do you have anything for headaches in your pouch?" she asked.

"Yes, by al-Lah, relieve his pain!" Zaynab cried. She sank to the floor and pressed her wet cheeks against his ankles, cascading hair over his bare feet.

I raced to my hut for the pouch, then back again. There I fumbled through my medicine bag, spilling half the contents onto the floor. Rose oil. I snatched up the vial and unstoppered it, then trickled it over Muhammad's forehead.

"This will help," I said as I massaged the oil into his skin. "You'll be better soon, my love."

"No," he said with a faint smile at me. "That is not true, A'isha. I made my choice. Soon I will be with Ibrahim." Over my head, the whir of wings. I glanced up; al-Abbas was staring with lifted eyebrows into Ali's startled face.

In a while Muhammad's headache subsided. He stood shakily and, with his arm around Ali's shoulder, made his way slowly to Hafsa's hut.

"This is not necessary," Hafsa said as she followed close behind. "I wish you would simply rest, husband."

He continued this way for a week. Struggling through his pain to lead the Friday prayer service. Defying his fever to stumble from one wife's apartment to the next. Ignoring our pleas for him to forget about us, to take care of himself. As he'd said, I knew his fate was sealed. But when my sister-wives consoled one another with news of this joke he'd made or that meal he'd eaten, I kept my knowledge to myself.

Then one morning Saffiya entered the oven tent with a face full of woe.

"Muhammad asked for you all night, A'isha," she said.

Hafsa looked down at her clasped hands. "He did the same on his night with me. But I was too selfish to tell you."

"'Who am I with tomorrow?' he kept asking on his night with me," Zaynab said.

"'When will I be at A'isha's hut again?'"

"He wants you, A'isha," Hafsa said. She sounded small and far away.

"Of course he wants her!" Sawdah said in a thick voice. "Have you heard how he talks? The end is near for him. He wants to be with the one he loves most."

A sob burst like a bubble from Saffiya's lips. "Dying?" She covered her face with her hands. "Our Muhammad, slipping away! What will happen to us?"

"Who will take care of us?" Juwairriyah said. "We cannot remarry. Where will we go? What about our children?"

"It's useless to worry about that now," Raihana said.

"If only there were something we could do for him," Hafsa said.

"There is." Umm Habiba leveled her gaze at me. "Yaa A'isha, take my night with Muhammad tonight."

"I will do the same," Maymunah said quietly.

Soon all the sister-wives had given up their turns with him so that Muhammad could spend his last days and nights in my bed. If any of them did so begrudgingly, I'm sure they were gratified by his enormous smile at the news.

"Al-Lah will bless you all for this, after I am gone," he said. "I will see to it personally, when I sit by His side in Paradise."

I wept bitter tears as he spoke. How freely I would have given up all my nights with him to keep him among us! He couldn't even walk to my room. Al-Abbas and Ali had to carry him, and when he fell from their grasp, I felt myself falling, also, as though I tumbled from a cliff toward a jumble of sharp rocks.

The threat of Muhammad's death drew us in the *harim* more closely together than before. Umm Salama's powers of organization kept us from falling apart; she instructed Hafsa and Raihana on the amount and types of foods to prepare for the visitors who streamed in to my apartment. She suggested Sawdah call the best caregiver in Medina to prescribe treatment for Muhammad. I listened to the nurse's advice, but my trembling hands could not administer the palliatives. Umm Habiba, for all her foreboding airs, turned out to be a capable assistant, clear-headed enough to do the job for me. To ease Muhammad's convalescence, Umm Salama arranged entertainment: I recited poetry; Hafsa danced; Sawdah strummed her *tanbur* while Maryam sang to him, relaxing his tightened brow.

Meanwhile, the *umma* began to tear apart as if invisible hands pulled it in different directions at once. His eyes red-rimmed, my father sat with me one night while Muhammad slept and told me of the struggles that had begun. Men of the Aws and Khazraj tribes, rivals for the leadership of Medina before we arrived, were fighting in the public market over who would rule when the Prophet died. Immigrants to the *umma* whispered rumors of impending Bedouin attacks and another Qurayshi invasion against a weakened Medina.

"The people need to know who will lead them if Muhammad dies," my father said. "But he has told me that he wants al-Lah to decide."

To me, the choice of a leader was obvious: My father had stood by Muhammad's side from the very beginning. He'd been the first man, with Ali, to convert to *islam*—and he was far more diplomatic than the brash, impetuous Ali. He'd sent food and supplies to Muhammad after the Meccans banished the Believers to the desert. He'd stood up for Muhammad at meetings of Mecca's leaders, and helped him escape assassination. He'd given him his favorite daughter—me—to seal their friendship. He'd helped him plan every caravan raid and battle, and had fought by his side despite Muhammad's protests that the risk was too great, that my father was too valuable to the *umma* and to Muhammad to lose.

I begged my father to let me speak to Muhammad on his behalf, but he refused. Others weren't so principled. One evening as I returned to my hut after the daily meal, I heard al-Abbas and Ali within, arguing so loudly I could hear them through the closed door.

"*Yaa* nephew, there is no need to wring your hands," al-Abbas said. "I am only suggesting that you ask him."

"By al-Lah, how can you speak about his death while he still lives?" Ali cried. Al-Abbas shushed him, and he lowered his voice. "It does not seem proper."

"I have seen members of the al-Muttalib family die before," al-Abbas said. "I do not like the looks of Muhammad now. He reminds me of his father, who died of pleurisy."

"Pleurisy? No, that is no way for a Prophet to die," Ali said. "I would rather he were killed in battle."

"Unfortunately, you cannot control how he dies," al-Abbas said. "However, you may have some power over what happens afterward. Do you want to succeed him, Ali? Do you want to rule Hijaz and restore our clan to its former status?" His voice sounded low and cunning. I remembered the tray of tharid in Maymunah's apartment and wished I'd taken some to test for poison.

"You know I want to succeed him," Ali said. My heart fluttered at the thought. With Ali in charge, what would become of my family, or of me? "But how can I ask him to name me? Then he would resign himself to dying. By al-Lah! I would rather that he lived." Ali's voice sounded gargled, as if he were crying.

"When his baby died, Muhammad was left without an heir. His adopted son Zayd is dead, also. Who else is there but you, the father of his grandsons, to succeed him?"

"Let him name me, then. I will not ask."

"What if he does not name you?" Al-Abbas said in a hissing voice. "What if he names no one? You are young and without power in this community. Others would certainly seize the position for themselves—Abu Bakr, who is not even related to the Prophet, or Umar! You would be left out. The clan of Hashim would fade into ignominy."

"If I don't ask him, and he names no one, the people of the umma might choose me yet," Ali said. "But if I ask him and he names someone else, they will never choose a Hashimite." Al-Abbas started to protest, but Ali cut him off. "No, Uncle. I will not ask."

I opened the door and called out, hoping they'd think I had just arrived. Al-Abbas gave me his ever-generous smile—one that I now knew concealed a calculating soul. "How fortunate the Prophet is to be waited upon by an angel," he said. "When he awakens, I will tell him so."

I pulled my wrapper more tightly over my face. "I hope he wakes up soon," I said, "because I have a few things to tell him, also."

When Muhammad did awaken—the next morning—neither angels nor successors occupied his mind. He thought only of the Friday services.

"I must lead them," he said. "The *umma* depends on me."

He threw off his cover and tried to stand—but his legs shook so badly he couldn't even get to his knees. Ali and al-Abbas rushed to his aid and helped him back into bed.

"May I suggest that you designate someone else to lead the prayer today?" al-Abbas said. His glance flickered to Ali. "Someone you trust?"

Muhammad sighed. "I suppose it is best," he said. "Soon, all my duties will be performed by another." He paused. The room fell as silent as an unasked question. I stared at him, willing him to choose anyone but Ali. To choose Ali was to choose the conniving al-Abbas, who cared only for power.

"Please send for Abu Bakr," Muhammad said.

Al-Abbas's countenance darkened like a snuffed candle. As for me, I smiled behind my wrapper.

"Hearing is obeying," Ali said, his voice tight. Then he followed al-Abbas out the door.

Warrior Bride

Medina, June 632

*O*n that final day Muhammad roused himself, sweating and shaking, to attend the prayer service. He panted with the exertion of sitting up in his bed, but he sighed with pleasure as I bathed him and washed his hair. I dried him all over with a towel and hummed one of the tunes Maryam had sung to him the night before—not even minding when he smiled at the flatness of my tone. I would have made myself foolish one thousand and one times to hear him laugh again.

He was too weak even for laughter. Fever had consumed Muhammad's very soul, leaving only a barely glowing ember. Yet as I dressed him and wound his turban I allowed myself the thinnest sliver of hope. That he wanted to leave his bed was a sign of something, wasn't it? Maybe God had decided to answer my pleas and let Muhammad live.

I helped him stand. He remained still for a long time, panting and lifting a limp hand to daub his pale face. Then, with one hand on my shoulder and the other against the wall, he shuffled like an arthritic *shaykh* to the door that opened into the mosque. He smoothed his clothes, straightened his back, and took a few labored breaths. Then he nodded, and I pushed the door open.

All sound instantly ceased. My father's prayers flew like doves out the window. Light filled the mosque, shining on Muhammad, making him glow. His skin shone.

"*Assalaamu aleikum.*" Muhammad's strong, clear greeting echoed off the walls of the mosque. I covered my smiling cheeks with my hands and thanked al-Lah. He was restored!

"*Wa aleikum assalaam,*" my father answered. Umar echoed with a cry of his own, and then Ali and Uthman, and soon the mosque reverberated with the cheers and good wishes of hundreds of worshippers singing the praises of God's Prophet. Joy flew around my heart in expansive circles, making me feel as light as air. Muhammad was healing, and everyone could see it!

My father stepped down from the tree stump and stretched a hand toward Muhammad. His smile crinkled his face beneath his long beard. "Please, Prophet, come and lead our service."

"I have come to follow today, not to lead," Muhammad said. "But when you have finished the prayers I would like to speak a while."

My father's sermon was eloquence itself. Words of beauty rolled like music from his tongue, quickening my spirit. He spoke of God's love, of how generously He had revealed Himself to us through His Prophet, of how steadfastly He had defended us against our enemies. "He is all-good and all-powerful," my father said. "None of us can compare to Him—no, not even our Prophet. For Muhammad will tell you himself: He is but a man. Men are born, and men die. But al-Lah lives on forever—and *islam* lives on after we are gone."

While he spoke, Muhammad continued to stand. His hands gripped the doorway on either side of him, making the shape of Maryam's ankh. When my father stopped talking, all eyes in the room turned to Muhammad.

"It is time to settle affairs," Muhammad said. For hours he asked questions of the *umma*'s men. Had Muhammad ever taken anything from anyone without compensating them? Had he treated anyone harshly who didn't deserve it? Did anyone want to ask him for a prayer?

Men stood to speak. Disputes broke out. At one point Umar pulled his sword and threatened a man, irritated by his prayer request. Muhammad lifted his hand and, across the room, Umar's sword clattered to the floor.

"*Yaa* Umar, please hold your temper," Muhammad said. "Every man's troubles are important to al-Lah, no matter how small."

At last Muhammad's voice faded. Perspiration matted his hair. His eyelids drooped like wilting petals.

"Help me sit, A'isha," he said hoarsely.

Umar thundered across the mosque, loudly declaring that the service was over. "*Yaa* Prophet, you have overextended yourself, and for what?" he grumbled. "For fools."

"Those 'fools' are the reason why I live," Muhammad said weakly.

Tears stung my eyes as I and Umar helped him to his bed. "He seemed so much improved," I said. "But now he withers like a rose plucked from the bush."

"Yes, he was improving," Umar said. "His face glowed with health, by al-Lah! But as I said, he has overextended himself. Let him rest, and he will recover."

As he turned to leave the apartment, Muhammad uttered his name. Umar walked over to his side and bent low to hear his words.

"Please bring my sword," Muhammad gasped. "It hangs in the mosque. I need it now."

Umar chuckled as he stepped to the mosque door. "Did I speak correctly, A'isha? Our Prophet is preparing for battle. This does not sound like a man on the brink of death."

But when I looked at my husband, I knew the end was near. His eyes had lost their focus. His breathing had become more labored. I moaned and pressed my head to his chest, listening to his heart keep erratic time, wishing it would beat forever.

Muhammad laid a limp hand on my head. "A'isha," he said, "I wish to clean my teeth. I must prepare myself."

Dread pounded my chest like hands on a drum, but I somehow crossed the room, feeling as if I were in a terrible dream, and plucked a stick of the *miswak* tree from the jar of them soaking by my wash basin. I sat beside Muhammad and chewed the stick to fray its ends, tasting the salt of my tears mingle with the astringent flavor of the wood. For eight years, since the day I'd moved in with Muhammad, I had performed this task for him. I'd never know this pleasure again.

I trembled with the urge to fling myself across his chest. I watched greedily as he rubbed the *miswak* over his teeth and gums, wanting to memorize even his most mundane actions, all precious to me now. The proud bearing of his head, even in sickness. The lowering of his left eye-lid, ever so slightly, as he concentrated. The crinkles at his eyes when he noticed how I drank him in. I met his gaze with my own, and something passed between us, like the spark between two hands in a lightning storm. *I am leaving you, but only for a while,* he seemed to say. And with my own brimming eyes I answered him: *Please stay with me, Muhammad. Tarry a few more years so we can enjoy the love we've made.*

Umar entered so quietly the sound of his voice made me jump.

"He cleans his teeth? Praise be to al-Lah, that is the best sign yet," he said. I hid my face, not wanting my grief to dampen his hope.

He laid the sword on the bed and was about to settle himself on a cush-ion, but Muhammad stopped him.

"*Yaa* Umar, please leave us alone for now. I wish to speak with A'isha."

Umar's smile never wavered. "I will return later, when the full moon is shining," he said. "*Yaa* Prophet, you and I will walk into the courtyard to see it."

Muhammad's eyes flickered like candles in a draught when Umar had gone.

"What do I need with the moon when I have my A'isha?" he said. I clasped his hand and squeezed it, willing my strength to pass from my touch to his, but his fingers only twitched.

"A'isha, take the sword," he said. "Pull it from its scabbard."

I frowned at him, bemused. What would he have me do with an unsheathed sword? But he had closed his eyes and seemed to focus all his thoughts on his next breath. I grasped the golden hilt, warm in my hand, and pulled its long blade slowly away from its jeweled cover. Two golden serpents formed the handle, their heads turned to face each other. Both the handle and the case glittered with turquoise and emerald stones—green, Muhammad's battle color, and more brilliant than ever in the sheen of my tears.

"I have named it *al-Ma'thur*," Muhammad said. "'The Legacy.' My father left it to me in his will. It has protected me in many battles, as you know."

"I've always wondered how you could risk damaging such a precious item by fighting with it," I said. "It's a jewel in itself—so valuable."

"A sword is only as worthy as its user," Muhammad said. "That is why I am giving it to you."

"To me?" I held it up to a window and turned it in the day's fading light, admiring the sharpness of its narrow blade, the warm glisten of color. Then I remembered why he was giving me this gift, and I began to cry so hard I almost dropped al-Ma'thur on his chest.

"I don't want it," I said. "I'd rather have you than all the swords in Hijaz."

"You have me, habibati." His eyes filled. "A'isha, I know you have looked with envy at the necklaces I have given my other wives. In truth, I considered having one made for you. But I could never find a jewel precious enough to express the nature of our love. I hope you will forgive me, Little Red."

"There's nothing to forgive," I said, wiping away my tears. "You gave me your precious love. It's all I've ever needed."

He smiled. "What courage you possess. My little child bride. No—my warrior bride. Take this sword and use it well, habibati. It will serve you in the jihad to come."

"Holy war?" I frowned. "Quraysh would not attack us again, even without you here. Our army would crush them instantly."

"It will be as al-Lah wills," he said. "But I speak also of the inner struggle." He jerked as if a flaming torch had touched his skin, making me flinch.

"A'isha," he rasped. "Comfort me."

Shame jabbed me with its bony fingers for being so skittish. Was death a rat with sharp teeth, able to bite anyone in its presence? I moved behind Muhammad and propped him against my breast. More tears stung my eyes but I willed them away. "Warrior bride," Muhammad had called me. I would not fear his death, or the life to come. I had al-Ma'thur and I had Muhammad's love for all eternity. I smoothed his brow with my palm. If only I could take away his pain.

"A'isha, you have received your wish," he said. "With your touch, you have removed my pain."

I sighed with relief. "Praise al-Lah—"

But his body jerked again, as if life surged through his limbs. He lifted his hands toward the ceiling. "There is no God but al-Lah!" he cried. Then he exhaled deeply and sank against me, as heavy as a rock.

"Muhammad!" I screamed. "Muhammad! Oh, al-Lah, why?" I patted his face and shook him, but he lay as limp as a piece of cloth in my arms. I felt death's claw scrape at the back of my neck, raising chills. Suddenly I wanted my father. Although tears blocked my mouth and nose I managed to call out to him.

"Father! *Yaa abi!* Father, hurry!"

The door between my bedroom and the mosque crashed open and my father raced in with wild eyes.

"I cannot awaken him," I said, sobbing, forgetting that I was a warrior now, forgetting everything except that Muhammad was gone.

My *abi's* face seemed to crumble as if it were made of sand when he looked down at Muhammad. He lifted his eyelids, tried to peer into his soul. He held a palm over his nostrils.

"To al-Lah we belong, and to al-Lah we will return," he murmured, his voice ragged. Tears ran down his face and mingled with my own on Muhammad's brow. He kissed the Prophet of God's salt-streaked forehead.

"Alas! for a Prophet." He kissed Muhammad's forehead again.

"Alas! for a man of purity." He kissed Muhammad's brow a third time. His face cupped sorrow in every crease. "Alas! for a bosom friend. The Messenger of God is dead."

◆

We combed Muhammad's curls and washed his face and smoothed his clothes, fumbling through our tears. Then my father left to inform the *umma* while I sat alone with him, wailing and tearing at my hair and skin. Soon my door burst open, and the sister-wives came running in, filling the room with their cries. Hafsa pulled my hands away from my face and held me, but even her love could not fill the hole inside me. Bilal's call knelled from atop the mosque. Fatima slipped in among us, with Ali and al-Abbas close behind, and fell to her knees to kiss her dead father's feet. Ali knelt by his side while a standing al-Abbas held the weeping Maymunah. His was the only impassive face in the room as he surveyed the scene. I felt his gaze on me and looked up to see his narrowed eyes taking in the sword I clutched.

That evening I stepped into the courtyard to see the moon. It dangled like an ornament from the bejeweled sky, dipped in gold and looming so close it beckoned my fingers to reach out and pluck it. Muhammad would have loved this sight.

My father's voice murmured from inside the mosque. I glided across the grass in search of him. I stopped at the entrance, though, when I saw his hands on Umar's heaving shoulders and their foreheads pressed together.

"We will walk with him again in Paradise," *abi* was saying. "As for now, we must consider the *umma*."

A short, stocky man with a mole on his chin as large as a beetle—Abu Ubaydah, Umar's friend—walked into the mosque and seized Umar's beard. "The men of Aws and Khazraj have called a meeting to decide Medina's next leader," he said. "I think you should attend."

"By al-Lah, the Prophet's body has not yet cooled!" Umar growled, sounding like his old self again.

"I agree, the timing is unfortunate," my father said. "But this development was not unexpected. If this meeting proceeds without us, we will lose everything Muhammad fought for."

"His life will not be in vain, or I am not Umar ibn al-Khattab," Umar gruffed. The three of them hurried into the street—with me following. I felt Muhammad's presence with me, covering me like the moonlight he had loved so much.

They stepped into Medina's meeting hall. I slipped into an alcove and peered inside. The room was spacious and square, with a ceiling so high not even the tallest man could touch it if he stood on another man's shoulders. Stone stairs led steeply upward to a closed door. The stench of unwashed bodies hit so strong I had to cover my nose with my wrapper. Oil lamps studded the unpainted stone walls, flickering dim shadows. The crowd of men inside fell silent when my father, Umar, and Abu Ubaydah entered the room.

A flat-nosed man with large ears stepped forward to seize their beards in greeting. "We are honored by your presence, but I must warn you: We aim to choose a leader from among ourselves."

Umar opened his mouth, but my father was the first to speak.

"We respect your desire to govern yourselves," he said. "But perhaps you have forgotten what it was like before Muhammad came to Medina." He turned to address the room, describing their feuds, how the Aws and

Khazraj had fought so viciously some had worried they'd annihilate each other.

"Under Muhammad, you have enjoyed peace between your tribes," *abi* said. "But truly, it was al-Lah who granted you this peace, as a reward for helping His Prophet. Muhammad died today, yes—but al-Lah never dies. Al-Lah would continue to rule if you would allow it. And in exchange, He will make Medina the most prosperous and revered city in the world. Not even Mecca will be able to compare."

"I remember those feuds all too well," an Aws *shaykh* said, pointing a finger at the Khazraj men opposite him. "You killed two of my sons."

"They deserved to die!" the Khazraj man snarled. "They killed my brother and raped his wife."

"Your brother built a house on our property and claimed it as his own." One of the *shaykh's* remaining sons shook his fist at the Khazraj man. "And when we sent our slaves to inform him he was in the wrong, he stole them, too!"

Soon the entire room was in an uproar. Shouts and accusations bounced off the walls. Swords clashed, daggers drew blood, men kicked those who lay wounded at their feet. Amid the turmoil the men of the *umma* stood and watched with somber eyes. At last my father ascended the stairs and commanded an end to the fighting.

"Clearly, this is what you face again if you try to take Medina back from us," he said. "*Yaa* Aws and Khazraj, I invite you to continue the alliance with our *umma* and our God. We are stronger now than we have ever been, but only with you beside us."

"Abu Bakr speaks the truth," the Aws *shaykh* called. "I would support one of the Prophet's men before I would ever follow a Khazraj."

"And I would follow a man of the *umma* into Hell itself before an Aws would lead me anywhere," his enemy spat.

A few moments later nearly every man in the room was roaring his support for my father, and both Umar and Abu Ubaydah were beaming and shouting his name. I slipped away from the scene, wishing I could run back to tell Muhammad. He would be so pleased! My father loved Muhammad even more than he loved himself. He would govern the *umma* exactly as Muhammad would have done.

Grief wrung hot tears from my eyes. How could I live without

Muhammad? I glanced up at the shining moon, as bright as Muhammad's face, and felt my tears subside. I knew he watched over me from his seat in Paradise. He'd seen the night's events unfold. Perhaps he'd played a part by sowing dissension among the *ansari*. Yet I longed to sit by his side in the dark and discuss the meeting, and perhaps feel his presence with me one last time.

But when I arrived at my hut, the door was open. I paused outside and listened, as I had before, to the voices of al-Abbas and Ali, now mingled with clanking, scraping, and thudding sounds.

"This floor is as hard as stone," Ali said. "I still think we should bury him in the cemetery with his son."

"And let Abu Bakr perform the ceremony?" Al-Abbas grunted. "That would seal him once and for all as the Prophet's successor."

"If the people want Abu Bakr, perhaps they should have him," Ali said.

"The people want full stomachs," al-Abbas said. "Beyond that, they know little of their desires. If Abu Bakr positions himself as their leader— if he says the prayer over the Prophet's body—no one will dare to challenge his authority. You are Muhammad's rightful heir. You are the only hope for our clan. You must resist this attempt to steal your inheritance."

Through the narrow opening I eyed al-Ma'thur, my sword, wishing I could somehow will it to fly to my fingers. Without a weapon I didn't dare try to stop this burial. Al-Abbas, I feared, wouldn't hesitate to kill me and throw me into the grave, also.

I cast about for a solution. My father was a world away, reveling in his election. I could awaken my sister-wives, but Ali and al-Abbas would finish the burial while I was gone—and I would miss hearing their plans. I'd need to be able to tell *abi* everything.

Each thud of the pick felt like a punch in my chest. I leaned against the doorway and listened to their digging, heard them grunt as they lifted Muhammad's body off the bed.

"By al-Lah, he is heavier now without his spirit," al-Abbas said. Muhammad was very light-spirited, I could have told them. But I stood silent, pressing my hands to my heart as if to hold it together.

Another grunt, a thud: Muhammad was in his grave. I imagined his body falling into the hole, and I clung to the door lest the weight of my grief pull me down, also.

"May al-Lah bless you, my beloved cousin," Ali choked. "And may you forgive me for this hasty burial, not at all befitting a Prophet."

"But necessary," al-Abbas added. "Surely he knows that. Besides," he said in a heartier voice, "now his jealous child-bride can sleep with him every night, as she has always wanted."

In a few moments I heard the tamping of earth. Muhammad was covered. I sobbed to imagine him lying in the cold ground, hidden from the moon.

"A job well done," al-Abbas said. "Do not forget your sword."

"What sword?" Ali said. "I brought no sword with me."

"That jeweled sword in the corner. Is it not yours? Muhammad bequeathed his weapons to you, did he not?"

My pulse sped, urging me to action. I threw open the door and lunged for the sword. In an instant I'd grasped the handle and yanked it from its case. "The sword is mine," I said. "If either of you wants to take it from me, I invite you to try."

Al-Abbas smiled as if I were the most delightful sight he'd ever seen.

"A woman warrior!" he said. "*Yaa* Ali, you never told me. Forgive me, A'isha. I thought Muhammad's sword had been left here by mistake."

"Someone has made a mistake here tonight, but it wasn't Muhammad." I kicked the freshly turned dirt with my toe.

"It was the Prophet's wish to be buried in the spot where he died," al-Abbas said smoothly.

"Get out of my apartment, you lying thieves." I waved the tip of my sword before al-Abbas' nose. "Unless you wish to be buried here, also."

When they'd slithered out—al-Abbas wishing me peace me as if he'd just paid a social call, Ali hanging his head and scowling—I stood before the window and stared at the place where my husband lay. Sobs wracked my body, and tears gushed from my eyes like floodwaters rushing through a *wadi*, dripping off my face to moisten Muhammad's grave. His sword dangled heavy in my hand. With an arm that shook, I lifted it to replace it in its sheath, and a flash of light caught my eye. I moved the blade this way and that, viewing the moon's reflection in Muhammad's sword.

And then, as I'd hoped, I felt my husband's presence fill my heart, drying my tears like a warm wind, infusing me with courage.

My sword will serve you well in the jihad to come. Now I knew what

Muhammad had meant by an "inner struggle." On the very day of his death, *jihad* had already begun. And I? I would be there with my sword, free at last to fight, to choose my destiny—to honor my name.

"A'isha." The name means "life." May it be so now, and forevermore.

Afterword

♦

reams do come true. Mine did. On May 21, 2007, I realized my dream of forty years by signing a contract with Ballantine, an imprint of Random House, one of the world's largest publishers, for the publication of my first novel, *The Jewel of Medina*, and its sequel.

A year later, on the eve of *Jewel's* launch, that dream came crashing down when a Random House executive called to say that the company had decided to "indefinitely postpone" publication of my books. The reason: fear of terrorist attack by radical Muslims.

I was crushed—and confused. Random House had not received any terrorist threats, yet the company suddenly wanted to distance itself from my books and my name. It was an abrupt turnaround from a company that had professed love for *The Jewel of Medina* and excitement about its sequel.

The Ballantine team's words of enthusiasm had not been hollow. They had already placed my novel on the fast-track to best-sellerdom, producing beautiful advance copies with exquisite covers, selling foreign rights to several countries, landing deals with Book-of-the-Month Club and the Quality Paperback Book Club, and arranging an eight-city U.S. tour for me. And the publicity had only just begun!

Little did I know how much publicity Random House's decision NOT to publish the novel would generate. Eager to bring my books into the world while they are relevant—while they can contribute to an ongoing, worldwide discussion about Islam—I terminated my publishing contract, confident that my books would soon find another home. A few weeks later, former *Wall Street Journal* correspondent Asra Nomani, a Muslim-American who had read a galley of *Jewel* and enjoyed it, wrote about the publishing giant's decision in an opinion piece with the headline, "You Still Can't Write About Muhammad."

Two days later, the story was all over the Internet, on the radio and television, and in newspapers around the world. Bloggers and interviewers wanted to know: How could this happen in the United States, a staunch protector of free speech? Debates grew heated over the definition of censorship, and whether Random House had censored my novels. (While researching these questions, I decided that the publisher had engaged in "self-censorship," silencing *itself* out of fear.) But the real question people seemed to be asking was this: "What about *my* freedom of speech? Will I be silenced next?"

At the same time, other issues emerged. Moderate Muslims such as Ms. Nomani, author Irshad Manji, and journalist Shahed Amanullah spoke out in support of *Jewel's* publication, arguing that extremists (or, in this case, fear of them) should not be allowed to set the agenda for all Muslims. Others challenged the propriety of fictionalizing sacred figures such as the Prophet Muhammad and Jesus Christ. And then there were questions about historical fiction, and what is, and isn't, allowed. How far can an author's imagination reasonably take her away from the historical record?

The buzz lasted several weeks, making for a frantic time for me. In the dozens of interviews I conducted, I always returned to the topic I was most interested in discussing: my books. I talked about my respect for Islam; about what a gentle, wise, and compassionate leader Muhammad really was; Muhammad's respect for women, especially his wives; and women's crucial roles in the formation of the early Islamic community. I was eager to discuss these issues, but I became frustrated, too. A one-way conversation is not a dialogue; it's a monologue. And, as much as I love to talk, I grew tired of hearing my own voice.

But how could anyone else contribute when no one had read the book?

At last, now that *The Jewel of Medina* is in print, that discussion can begin. I hope this book will inspire you to learn more about the remarkable A'isha bint Abi Bakr as well as Islam and its Prophet. I also hope you will read the sequel once it is available. The sequel alternates between the viewpoints of Ali and a more mature, wise, circumspect A'isha. *The Jewel of Medina* is a book about women's empowerment and the origins of Islam; its sequel is a novel of reconciliation and peace, which the world needs right now.

In this explosive political climate, many people are afraid to express viewpoints that they think might be perceived as inflammatory. This fear stifles lively discourse, which can help people from different cultures and backgrounds understand each other better. Shahed Amanullah, Editor-in-Chief of the online newsmagazine altmuslim.com, said " . . . the best response to free speech is simply more speech in return. Anyone should have the right to publish whatever he or she wants about Islam or Muslims—even if their views are offensive—without fear of censorship or retribution. . . . In an ideal world, both parties would open their minds enough to understand the other point of view." Discussion, debate, and, most important, listening, can help us reach that much-needed mutual understanding—the first, crucial step toward peace. Beginning with this book, that task now lies in the hands, minds, and hearts of you, the readers. I am excited to see how you will carry it forward!

Sherry Jones
sherry@jewelofmedinabook.com

Glossary of Arabic Terms

◆

abi: "my father"

afwan: "Excuse me"; pardon

ahlan: "Welcome"; a greeting

Ahlan wa sahlan: "Welcome and as family"

al-Lah: God

Al-Lahu akbar: "God is great"

al-Ma'thur: "The Legacy"; the name of Muhammad's sword

al-zaniya: adulteress

ansari: "Helpers"; the Medina tribes who followed Muhammad

Assalaamu aleikum: "Peace be with you"; a greeting

barid: a unit of distance, about 20 miles

bint: "daughter of"

dinar: a gold coin, unit of currency

dirham: a silver coin, unit of currency

djann: plural of *djinni*

djinni: a mythical spirit inhabiting the Earth, with supernatural powers

durra: "parrot"; the name for the *harim*'s second wife

fahisha: whore

habib: beloved

habibati: my (female) beloved

habibi: my (male) beloved

hajja: a woman who has made the pilgrimage to Medina

hammam: public baths

harim: the inner sanctum where the women of the household reside

hatun: "Great Lady"; the first-wife of the *harim*

hijab: the curtain or veil

Hijaz: the Arabian western coast, bordering the Red Sea, including Mecca and Medina

hijra: the emigration to Medina

houri: a virtuous woman in Paradise with large, luminous eyes

hawdaj: a curtained seat atop a camel

ibn: son of

islam: submission (to al-Lah)

jahiliyya: the time of ignorance before *islam*

Ka'ba: cube; the name for the sacred shrine in Mecca

kahin: pre-Islamic mystics

khatmi: an herbal remedy made from the mallow plant

khuzama: a sweet desert plant

kohl: a black substance used to line the eyes

Labaykh al-Lahumah labaykh: "We answer your call, our al-Lah"

latheeth: delicious

ma' salaama: "with peace"; a farewell

majlis: sitting room

marhaba: a greeting

miswak: a tree with an astringent quality whose sticks are used to clean the teeth

qur'an: recitations; specifically, Muhammad's recitations from al-Lah

raki'a (pl. raka'at): bows in the ritual of Muslim prayer

sahab: friend

samoom: a violent windstorm that darkens the sky with sand

samneh: clarified butter

shaykh: an old man

suq: market

tanbur: a musical instrument, the precursor to the lyre

tharid: a dish of meat and bread, reputed to be Muhammad's favorite

umma: the Muslim community of Believers; also, mother-land

ummi: "my mother"

wa aleikum assalaam: "and with you be peace"; a return greeting

wadi: a (usually dry) riverbed

wars: a yellow dye made from a Yemeni plant resembling sesame

yaa: loose trans. "hey"; a word used before a person's name to address him/her

zauba'ah: "devils"; or pillars of sand formed in a *samoom*

Muhammad's wives and concubines, in order

◆

Khadija (Ka-DEE-zsa)
Sawdah (SAUW-dah)
A'isha (AH-eesha)
Hafsa (HAF-sah)
Zainab (ZAY-nab) bint Khuzainah (Ku-ZAY-nah)
Umm Salama (Oom Sa-LA-ma)
Zaynab bint Jahsh
Juwairryah (Ju-way-ri-yah)
Raihana (Ray-HA-nah)
Saffiya (Saf-FEE-yah)
Ramlah (RAM-Lah)
Maryam (MAHR-yam)
Maymunah (May-MOO-nah)

Works Consulted
for "The Jewel of Medina"

◆

Abbott, Nabia. *Aishah, The Beloved of Mohammad.* Chicago: The University of Chicago, 1942.

Arberry, A.J. *Aspects of Islamic Civilization As Depicted in the Original Texts.* New York: A.S. Barnes and Co., Inc., 1964.

Armstrong, Karen. *Muhammad: A Biography of the Prophet.* New York: Harper Collins, 1992.

Bodley, R.V.C. *The Messenger: The Life of Mohammad.* New York: Doubleday & Co., 1946.

Brooks, Geraldine. *Nine Parts of Desire: The Hidden World of Islamic Women.* New York: Anchor Books, Doubleday, 1995.

Bulandshehri, Maulana Muhammad Ashiq Elahi. *The Wives of the Prophet Muhammad.* New Delhi: Islamic Books Service, 2002.

Burton, Richard F. *The Book of The Thousand Nights and One Night* (footnotes). New York: The Heritage Press, 1934.

Croutier, Alev Lytle. *Harem: The World Behind the Veil.* New York: Abbeville Press, 1989.

Cuddihy, Kathy. *An A to Z of Places and Things Saudi.* London: Stacey International, 2001.

Elkhadem, Saad. *Old Arabic Sayings Similes & Metaphors*. Fredericton, N.B., Canada: York Pres Ltd., 1991.

Gibb, H.A.R. (trans.). *The Travels of Ibn Battuta, Vol. 1, 1325–1354*. London: Cambridge University Press, 1958.

Goodwin, Jan. *Price of Honor: Muslim Women Lift the Veil of Silence on the Islamic World*. New York: Plume, 1995.

Guthrie, Shirley. *Arab Social Life in the Middle Ages: An Illustrated Study*. London: Saqi Books, 1995.

Guthrie, Shirley. *Arab Women in the Middle Ages: Private Lives and Public Roles*. London: Saqi Books, 2001.

Haleem, M.A.S. Abdel (trans.) *The Qur'an*. London: Oxford University Press, 2004.

Ibn Kathir (1313–1384). *The Life of the Prophet Muhammad, Vols. I-IV*. UK: Garnet Publishing Ltd., 2000.

Ibn Sa'd, Muhammad. *The Women of Madina*. London: Ta-Ha Publishers, Ltd., 1997.

Jones, Jameelah. *The Sahabiyat (During the Prophet's Era)*. London: Ta-Ha Publishers, 1994.

Kabbani, Shaykh Muhammad Hisham, and Laleh Bakhtiar. *Encyclopedia of Muhammad's Women Companions and the Traditions They Related*. ABC International Group, 1998.

Levy, Ruben. *The Social Structure of Islam*. London: Cambridge University Press, 1957.

Mernissi, Fatima. *Women and Islam: An Historical and Theological Enquiry*. New Delhi: Women Unlimited, 2004.

Moosa, Matti and D. Nicholas Ranson (trans.). *The Wives of the Prophet by Sh. Muhammad Ashraf*. Pakistan: Ashraf Press, 1971.

Rodinson, Maxime, and Arthur John Arberry, Charles Perry, Claudia Roden. *Medieval Arab Cookery*. UK: Prospect Books, 2001.

Rodinson, Maxime. *Muhammad*. New York: Random House, 1980.

Salahi, M.A. *Muhammad: Man and Prophet: A Complete Study of the Life of the Prophet of Islam*. Shaftesbury, Dorset, UK: Element Books Ltd., 1995.

Q&A with The Jewel of Medina author Sherry Jones

Q: How did you become interested in the subject of women and Islam?
A: In spring of 2002, when the U.S. sent troops into Afghanistan, I began hearing news about the reversals for women there under the Taliban, how girls were no longer allowed to go to school and women were required to wear burqas, how the windows of their homes had to be painted black so they could not be seen from the outdoors, etc. As a feminist, I was disturbed by these reports and I wanted to learn more.

I knew very little about Middle Eastern culture or Islam at the time, so I read a few books about women in the Middle East by American journalists Geraldine Brooks and Jan Goodwin. In these books I discovered that the Prophet Muhammad had multiple wives and concubines. Being unable to find very much information about any of them made me want to tell their stories to the world.

Q: With twelve women to choose from, why did you settle on A'isha as the protagonist?
A: I didn't choose A'isha; she chose me! Both the books I mentioned told a similar tale of a young girl playing outside on the swing or teeter-totter and her mother calling her inside, washing her face, combing her hair, putting her in a new gown, and taking her into the bedroom to marry a man nearly six times her age. That scene played itself in my mind over and

over again until, while working out in the gym one day, I realized that if I couldn't stop thinking about A'isha, I should probably write about her.

Originally I thought about giving each of the wives a segment of the book in which to tell her own story, but ultimately, A'isha pushed the other wives aside with the sheer force of her personality. She was a quick-witted, sharp-tongued, politically astute survivor. And what a love affair she had with her husband!

Q: What qualifies you, a non-Muslim, to tell this tale?
A: I'm not a Muslim but I am a woman, and I know the rivalries and yearnings and heartaches that women experience in the name of love. I'm also a human being, so I know about love and desire and greed and jealousy and fear. I can't really know what it was like to be alive and a woman in seventh-century Saudi Arabia, but I can certainly start, as Hemingway advised, with what I do know. The rest, as for any writer, is imagination. And while I'm not a Muslim, I have a huge respect and regard for the Muslim faith, which I hope is evident in my novel.

Q: What was your motivation for writing this book?
A: At first, I just wanted to honor these women by telling their stories. Then, during my research, I discovered things about Muhammad and Islam that excited me, and I began to hope that, in writing this book, I could help increase inter-cultural empathy and understanding and that I could empower women, especially Muslim women, by showing that Islam is, at its source, an egalitarian religion. I think Islam gets a bad rap in that regard, whereas the oppression of women really comes from male insecurity more than anything Muhammad ever advocated. From what I've read, he was actually fairly egalitarian in his attitudes toward women.

Q: In your book, Muhammad, the Prophet of God, is a man of great physical passion and also a man who becomes seduced by power. Ali, revered by Shi'ites, is depicted as an impulsive, hostile, somewhat immature young man. Muhammad's daughter, Fatima, also revered by Shi'ites, comes off as jealous and possessive of her father, and unpleasant. Are you concerned that Muslims will be offended by your depictions of certain characters and events?

A: Remember, this story is A'isha's, told from her point of view. She was jealous of Muhammad's other wives, and must have felt critical of his decision to marry again and again. She also had a very antagonistic relationship with Ali as well as with Fatima. Eventually, A'isha and Ali clashed in the first Islamic civil war which began the Sunni-Shi'ite split. So of course these characters are not portrayed in a flattering light!

The sequel to *The Jewel of Medina*, which is nearing completion, continues the tale of Islam's development through alternating points of view, both A'isha's and Ali's. So readers will get much better-rounded, sympathetic portraits of Ali as well as Fatima, whom Ali married.

Q: Did you take literary license with any of the facts in writing this book?
A: Yes! I've never read anything about A'isha wielding a sword, but I wanted to demonstrate that some women did fight in early Islamic battles under Muhammad. It wasn't common, but it did happen. Plus, the sword represents A'isha's strength, and the fact that later in life she did lead troops in the Battle of the Camel against Ali.

Also, A'isha was not engaged to Safwan at birth, but to the son of one of her father's friends. And her struggle to become *hatun*, or the Great Lady of the harem, is fabricated. The *hatun* was a concept I picked up from reading about Turkish harems of later times. But I know A'isha was very competitive with her sister-wives, so I felt comfortable inventing this particular contest to illustrate the problems she grappled with as Muhammad's youngest wife and also as a woman who loved her husband very much and suffered from his polygamy.

Most of the license I've taken has to do with the wives, since I could not find many details about most of them. The stories that have come down mostly concern what they did, not why they did those things. I had to invent motives, which, as a fiction writer, I appreciated being able to do.

Q: How can you say Muhammad helped women when he had such a large harem? Wasn't that disrespectful to his wives?
A: Many scholars and Muslims contend that Muhammad married for political, not personal, reasons. Of course, nearly all his wives and concubines were supposedly very beautiful, which tells me he might have had personal reasons for these marriages, too.

I believe these practices that are so unfamiliar — and unacceptable — to us today should be considered in the context of the time period and culture in which they occurred. The most powerful men — chieftains, kings — had many wives as a sign of their power. Muhammad may have been trying to establish himself as a powerful man, too — for survival in a warrior culture, for spreading Islam and thereby saving souls, or for political power.

For the wives who loved Muhammad, such as A'isha, these marriages must have been painful. Historical accounts are full of anecdotes illustrating her competitiveness with her other wives, not all of which I was able to use in my book. One that I loved was the story of the "honey trick." Muhammad was spending an inordinate amount of time with one of his wives — some accounts say Hafsa, others say Zaynab. Usually he was very conscientious about dividing his time equally among his wives, so A'isha knew there was some extenuating circumstance. She discovered that this other wife had a jar of honey — very rare and precious, and one of the few indulgences that Muhammad allowed himself.

A'isha, knowing that Muhammad was extremely fastidious in his personal hygiene, pretended on his next visit that his breath smelled horrible. "What have you been eating?" she said. She got a couple of her sister-wives, including Sawdah, to do the same. Mortified, Muhammad refused that honey in the future, and stopped spending so much time with the wife who had it. But Sawdah felt guilty and confessed, and A'isha got in trouble. This was when A'isha was a young girl, but supposedly she used other, more sophisticated, tactics later to dissuade Muhammad's interest in other women.

Q: What do you hope readers will take away from the book?
A: I hope the readers of The Jewel of Medina will be entertained and uplifted, inspired to take control of their own destinies and empathetic to this other culture that we in the West know so little about but that we tend to demonize because we are at war in the Middle East. Muslim, Christian, Jew, atheist, Buddhist — we are all human beings with needs, desires, and fears, all "created from the same soul." The sooner we as a species can embrace the concept of unity, the closer we will be to achieving Paradise right here on Earth. Because Paradise means living continually in the presence of God, and, as the Bible says, "God is love."